Torchship

Karl K. Gallagher

Published by Kelt Haven Press, Saginaw, TX.

Cover art and design by Stephanie G. Folse (www.scarlettebooks.com).
Editing by Laura Gallagher.
Audio Recording by Laura Gallagher.

First edition.

To Laura:

Friend, Lover, Wife, Muse

FIVES FULL
CROSS-SECTION

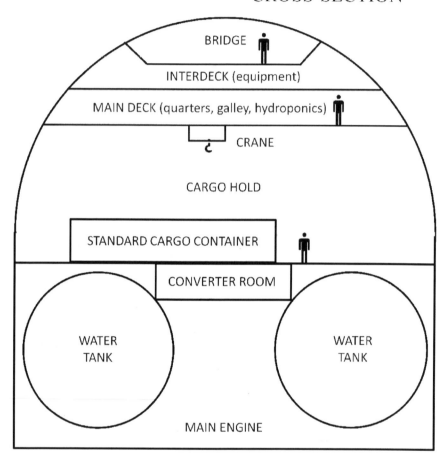

BRIDGE

INTERDECK (equipment)

MAIN DECK (quarters, galley, hydroponics)

CRANE

CARGO HOLD

STANDARD CARGO CONTAINER

CONVERTER ROOM

WATER
TANK

WATER
TANK

MAIN ENGINE

Fives Full Cross Section

Part One: Tourists

Planet Lapis. Gravity 10.2 m/s^2

Mitchie cursed as the "Don't Walk" sign switched to a wanted poster. "Have you seen this man?" hovered over a rotating image of a dark-haired, bearded man's head. Smaller text at the bottom explained that he was an illegal artificial intelligence researcher and, of course, threat to public safety. *Dammit*, she thought, *I promised I'd keep him safe.* If security was already escalating the search it might be a hard promise to keep.

The target of the poster indignantly burst out, "I wasn't trying to—ow!" Wrapping her arm cozily around his waist let Mitchie jab a thumb into the man's ribs without being too obvious about it.

"Shut up," she muttered up at him. "Don't say any keywords. We only have another half-klick to get to the spaceport, don't blow it now." She'd given him a shave and bleached his hair to keep any casual passers-by from recognizing him. Serious observers would be reviewing the surveillance imagery from this intersection within the day. They were looking for a lone man. Mitchie was the best camouflage against them for her cargo. She tugged his arm onto her shoulder. "Hold me. Gently. I'm your girlfriend, we're going for a walk. It's a nice day to watch the rockets take off." She sighed. "Pretend that you've held a woman like this before."

The sign changed to "Walk." They strolled down the street between warehouses. "Okay," said Mitchie, "we're safe for five minutes. Vent now, then shut up when we get to the port."

"I wasn't researching artificial intelligence!" complained the scientist. "It's just simple optimization. Okay, complex optimization, but it had no danger of going rogue. This is completely unreasonable."

"Pete, your planet has lots more unreasonable stuff than how they define AI research. But do you think a jury is going to care about your distinction? Or those guys?" Some waldo operators across the street watched a news report and bragged to each other what they'd do if they caught "that world-melter."

"Well, if I'd had a chance to do a practical demonstration people would slow down enough to think about it. I wasn't ready. I don't know why they're bothering me. I didn't do anything to set off any alarms."

Which was true. The alarms had probably been triggered by the datatrawling Mitchie had done from his system. Once the code police had realized what Pete was developing they'd lost all interest in why he'd been prying and focused on containing it—and him. But she didn't feel any need to enlighten him. If he'd been staying inside the law they wouldn't have bothered him.

"Well, they're looking for you now," she said. "Do you want to take your chances with a trial? Gotta make up your mind now. I'm not asking my friends to stick out their necks if you're going to jump ship before they lift."

Pete let out a deep breath. "I'm going. No sense staying here. Even if I'm acquitted of illegal research they'll never let me code again. If I emigrate I'll be able to finish my work someday. And anything beats getting executed."

"No stipend," Mitchie pointed out. "You'll have to buy your own computing gear."

"I know. I watch frontier vids, you know, we all do."

The Disconnected Worlds native bit her tongue. She'd seen some of those vids and hated to think that he was basing decisions on them. "Okay, time for you to shush again until we're on the ship." Mitchie pulled out her comm. "Agum, it's time."

"Will do. You're going to owe me for this, Mitchie," answered the spacer on the ship they hoped to reach.

"I'm good for it," she insisted.

"Going." The comm went silent.

"Now we stroll some more," she said, looking up at Pete with a bright smile. She tightened her arm around him again.

Pete had never seen a bigger open space than the spaceport in his whole urbanized life. He gawked like a tourist. Mitchie snuggled into him, relieved that she didn't have to play acting coach again.

The security post had the usual two guards. Agum strolled toward them on the far side. By the time Mitchie and Pete got to the post the argument was in full progress. "This is a perfectly legal device!" protested Agum. "It's a dedicated reading unit, in full compliance with Fusion of Inhabited Worlds regulations." He added some extra sarcasm over the Fusion's belief it represented all inhabited worlds.

"Sir, that is an unmonitored processor capable of general-purpose computation," declared the guard. "All such hardware is forbidden from import and must be destroyed on entry."

"I'm not letting anyone pry my reader apart for parts! And I'm not letting you petty thugs harass me into giving up my gear just because you're bored and hate Diskers!" Agum actually turned a dark red, impressive given his tropical ancestry. Mitchie decided she'd have to figure out something extra for him.

"Um, ma'am?" Mitchie distracted the female guard from the confrontation. "We've been invited on board the *MS Barito*. Uh . . . do we need to come back later?"

"No, no, this won't take long." The guard kept looking back at her partner, making sure Agum hadn't gotten physical. He and the first guard were now quoting regulations at each other by the paragraph. The female guard briefed them. "As visitors to an unsecure area you must avoid all possible data contamination. Read/writable devices must be restored from the network on exit. Any device you don't want erased must be left in secure storage at the guard post. Do you have any questions on these restrictions?"

"No, that's fine," said Mitchie. Pete stared at a descending freightliner. The guard didn't press him for an answer.

Agum was now accusing the other guard of making up the regulations he quoted. Pete moved along to Mitchie's prodding.

The *Barito's* crew gave a warm welcome to Mitchie, and a wary one to Pete. "Who's he?" asked the captain bluntly.

"Pete. New immigrant. Willing to work hard. He's got some friends on Akiak who'll cover his passage."

A crewman laughed. "A Fusion boy working hard? This I got to see. I'm Hatta. You ever use a mop, Pete?"

Pete accepted the handshake from Hatta. "No, I haven't. What's that stand for?" That got all the Disconnected Worlds natives laughing.

"Doesn't stand for anything Pete, it's what we use in the Disconnect instead of floorbots. I'll show you." Hatta led Pete below decks.

"Friends?" asked the captain.

"Yes, someone will come aboard and pay his fare at Akiak," promised Mitchie. "And pick up these." She laid some data crystals on the console. The captain swept them into a drawer.

"All right, I trust you. And Hatta may get a passage's worth of work out of him anyway. What about you? Working or riding with us?"

"Neither. I'm not going back to the Disconnect any time soon. Time to find a new job. Can I get a favor from Otto?"

"Of course. But you be careful, little girl," said the captain.

Mitchie blew the captain a kiss and headed downbelow.

"Otto!" called Mitchie as she came through the converter room hatch.

"Little Michigan!" replied *MS Barito's* mechanic. He wrapped her in a hug. "So what's the favor?"

"Hey, that's not fair. I'm not always hitting you up for favors."

"True, true, but favor is the way to bet. What is it?"

She felt herself blush a little, and hated that her fair skin made her so easy to read. "I need a data crystal destroyed." She held out a cloth holding some shards.

"It'd take some work to reconstruct that. But if you want it obliterated I'll put it through the pipes."

"Thank you." She pulled on his collar and stood tip-toe to kiss Otto's cheek.

"Are you riding with us?"

"No, not this trip. Can't go back to the Disconnect yet."

"Best get this done and you off. We're lifting soon." The mechanic levered open an inspection port on the start tank pipe. Water spilled out. Mitchie dumped the glittering shards into it, scraping the cloth back and forth to make sure they all went in. He closed the port. "All right, no one's going to read that again," said Otto. "Go on, I'll see you next time."

"Thanks, Otto!" She scampered up the ladder. At the end of the ship's ramp she turned right toward the shuttle to the orbital highport. She didn't want to cross the security line again. Somebody might have recognized Pete in one of those videos with her. The spacer hall had a wing by the shuttles. That gave her a place to stay and check for ships that were hiring. If nobody was she'd just have to talk her way onto one headed inward.

***

The shards sat on the bottom of the water tank until the *Barito* cleared atmosphere. They ignored the chatter as orbit control granted permission to fire the torch. The start tank warmed a bit as the converter started turning iridium into energy and iron. Then the valves opened and the water swept the shards through the heating coils. Data storage matrices separated as the plastic holding them evaporated. The water flashed into steam.

The pressure split them among dozens of pipes. A high-voltage current ran through the steam, superheating it into plasma, water molecules breaking up and electrons popping off the hydrogen. The silicon/gallium data matrices shattered, going from complex crystals to handfuls of atoms.

Rippling magnetic fields accelerated the plasma out the magnetoplasmadynamic nozzles. The remnants of the data crystal flew off at half a percent of lightspeed. The captain had kept the thrust low while maneuvering in crowded low orbit.

When the last few molecules hit Lapis' atmosphere they broke apart. No two atoms of the data crystal were still bonded to each other. No one else would read Michigan Long's instructions.

Jason Station (Lapis Highport). Centrifugal Acceleration 5 m/s^2

The *Fives Full* was at dock 37A. It was a pleasant walk from the station's shuttle bays empty handed. Carrying her duffle that far tired Mitchie enough to wish she'd spent a half-key to rent a cart. No one was on watch in the accessway but the airlock stood invitingly open. She went in and grounded her duffle out of the way.

She was in the cargo hold. This ship just had the one circular hold, a hollow middle between the fuel tanks below and crew quarters above. It was barely wide enough to fit a couple of standard containers end to end. A crane on the ceiling stood ready to move cargo.

"Hi there." A middle-aged Han woman sat on one crate while doing accounts on a datasheet balanced on another.

"Hello. I'm Michigan Long. I'm applying for the pilot berth." She spoke in her thickest Akiak accent.

"Captain's expecting you. He's on the bridge." She waved at a ladder on the forward bulkhead of the cargo hold.

"Thank you." The datasheet—one of the starport loaners—was the only non-Disconnected Worlds product in sight. The few containers in the hold were against the starboard bulkhead. Mitchie guessed the ship was preparing to receive an oversized item.

She climbed up the ladder into a long corridor, then headed to the ladder at the midpoint. The ship didn't exactly match the plans she'd looked up. A couple of the portside crew compartments had been converted to expand the galley. She went a few rungs up the bridge ladder and rapped on the edge of the open hatch. "Hello?"

"Enter!"

As she stepped onto the bridge Mitchie saw the captain standing straight and glaring at her. She snapped to a matching attention. "Michigan Long, applying for pilot position, sir."

The captain wore a faded blue jumpsuit with SCHWARTZENBERGER written on the right chest and no sign of his rank. After studying her a moment he asked, "Where'd you learn to fly, Long?"

"Akiak. Surface-to-surface shuttle runs to the mining towns."

"Any electronics on your birds?"

"Not much, sir. Commo and a locator for when I was within sight of the highport."

"Your note said you did mechanic work."

"If the shuttle broke on a run I'd have to fix it up enough to get back to the port. The delivery service couldn't afford a hauler, it'd be three month's profit to rent one. I've kept up on shuttle maintenance since then but haven't done any for a ship."

"They're not that different. On this ship when there's a problem everyone turns to." She nodded. "So how'd you get into the black?" asked the captain.

"*Elephant's Tail* fired her co-pilot when she landed at Akiak. I'd had the advanced course on analog navigation so they took me. Signed on as co-, I worked up to navigator, then lead pilot when Chauncey transferred."

"Quick work in five years. Why'd you wind up dirtside?"

Mitchie reddened and looked away. "When the *Tail* went into overhaul the crew had a choice between half-pay until it finished or a separation bonus. This boy convinced me to give life in the Fusion a try. So I took the money. Didn't take me long to decide that was a mistake. I've been looking for a berth for over a month now." Did his stern look have a flicker of a smile at that? She wasn't sure.

"You had the class on analog navigation," said Captain Schwartzenberger. "Some analog ships calculate their courses on the port computers and just follow them when they leave the network. Or try to sneak a computer on board and hope the Fusion won't seize them for having an unsupervised processor. How much actual analog plotting have you done?"

"Lots, sir. *Elephant's Tail's* master insisted on doing courses ourselves."

"All right." He pointed at the plotting table. "Give me a course for Yulin, leaving at 1800."

"Yes, sir." The Almanac for the system rested on the table. She looked up the vectors for Yulin, Lapis, and Jason (the station they were docked to above Lapis). "Least time course?" she asked.

The captain snorted. "Fuel costs money. Five day transit. Orbit at 400 klicks, standard inc."

Mitchie pulled out the slide rule labeled "*Fives Full* torch." The steel rods slid easily under her fingers. Clean, not over oiled, no sticky spots.

The captain took good care of his tools. She aligned a vector stick from Lapis to Yulin. A lunar disk—multiple circles stacked together—went on top of the Lapis marker. Mitchie adjusted the outermost to show the station's vector. With the velocity vectors identified she started doing time and distance calculations on a pad of butcher paper.

Captain Schwartzenberger stood silently behind her as the page filled up. At last she wrote out a summary—boost lengths, transit times, fuel usage—for a direct transfer with an aerobrake at the destination. She felt the captain lean in to look over her shoulder at the totals. He made a satisfied grunt. *Must be pretty close to what he got for the problem*, she thought.

Mitchie flipped to a blank page and got out another lunar disk. Setting that for Yulin's moons required three different consults of the Almanac. A slightly-dusty sliderule came out to calculate the vector change from a fly-by of the outer moon. The calculations took two pages this time. Inserting into orbit around Yulin now took four burns instead of two, but the aerobraking was gentler and total fuel usage lower by 7%. She summed up the course in a few crisp sentences.

"That's from book learning on Akiak?" the captain asked.

"More from practice, sir. *Elephant's Tail's* master had everyone nav-qualified calculate maneuvers. It was a contest. Who could finish first, use least fuel, shortest flight time, whatever. So we learned a lot of tricks. I think I could save more fuel with a three-cushion shot but we'd have to wait a week or so for the moons to line up right."

Schwartzenberger traced through the calculations. The flyby hadn't just slowed the ship relative to the planet, it had also done part of the plane change from the ecliptic to the parking orbit inclination. "Okay, you're an analog nav. I'll get us some time on the station simulators and you can show me how you can fly her."

***

Captain Schwartzenberger led Mitchie into the galley. "Everyone, I'd like you to meet our new—probationary—pilot. Michigan Long, from Akiak."

She looked over the rest of the crew. *You'd think in a half-Chinese crew I wouldn't be the shortest.*

The middle-aged woman from the cargo hold turned away from the oven and offered her hand. "Hi, Michigan. I'm Shi Bingrong, the first mate." She turned to the two younger men. "This is Guo Kwan, our mechanic, and Billy the deckhand." Mitchie shook hands with them in turn.

"Pleased to meet you. Call me Mitchie." The captain took his seat at the head of the table. Mitchie hopped up to sit on a counter where she could have a view of the cooking. "That smells great." Someone had painted a flowering vine along the top of the wall. She traced it past the stove, behind the cabinets set along the outside of the hull, and along the other wall, ending up—she twisted her neck—in a swirl of flowers behind her head.

The mechanic worked a wok. "Food's always better in port," he said. "Nothing like having fresh ingredients."

The captain snorted. "You turn your nose up at the fresh option when we've been cruising for a few weeks."

Guo laughed. "No matter what spices you use there's not much you can do to make algae tasty." He sprinkled a bit from a bottle into the wok. The mate opened the oven and took out some rolls, filling the air with a scent that made Mitchie ravenous. Billy started setting the table.

In a few minutes Mitchie sat next to the mate—"Bing"—with the boys across from them. The foot of the table and a couple of chairs flanking it were empty. Clearly the ship had room for more crew than Schwartzenberger had hired. The captain said a brief prayer and they dove in. Conversation revolved around the food until everyone had their first servings down.

Bing asked, "So how did you get to Lapis from Akiak?"

"Oh, I've been to a lot of systems," answered Mitchie. "I was pilot on *Elephant's Tail*. But when she went in for overhaul I took the chance to play tourist here for a couple of months. Finally got tired of having dirt on my feet so I asked the captain to take me back into space." A few more questions from Bing led to a paean to skin diving, something inconceivable on Mitchie's cold homeworld. "So how much card playing do y'all do of nights?"

Guo shook his head in warning.

"None," growled the captain. "Poker's a silly game."

"Um, when I saw the ship name . . ." backpedaled Mitchie.

"Oh, the previous owner won her in a poker game. The crest over the airlock is the exact hand he won her with. Then he had this ridiculous idea to set her up as a flying gambling palace but found out the rich people wouldn't play with him any more after he took so much of their money. So I picked her up cheap at the bankruptcy auction. Good thing, too. She's a good ship. I'd hate to think what condition she'd be in if the fool had been flying her about."

"So why didn't you change the name?"

"I'll be damned if I'll spend money redoing perfectly good paperwork."

Guo rescued Mitchie from the downward trend. "So now you know the Secret History of the *Fives Full*. In a few more years we'll probably add a ghost haunting the cargo hold and leaving poker chips everywhere." Billy joined in with banter about cleaning up after ghosts and midnight FOD checks.

Bing turned the conversation back to Mitchie. "So when did you last see Akiak?"

"It's been . . . over two years now. Had a week there when *Elephant* dropped off some cargo. We were working some long trading chains. Is *Fives Full* going back to the Disconnect soon?"

Billy replied, "We're heading all the way through the Fusion this time. Have some oversized cargo bound for Demeter. A reactor core shell."

Captain Schwartzenberger added, "None of the freightliners wanted to deal with it. They just do containers. So we're getting a nice bonus. The risk is whether we can get a full hold to work our way back toward the Disconnect." He stood and cleared his place. "Good night, all."

As the mechanic and deckhand finished their meals Bing turned to discussing the nuts and bolts of working on *Fives Full*. "Shifts" weren't an option with so few crew. Work hours depended on the ship's take-off and landing schedule. More tasks, from power system maintenance to washing dishes, were on a rotating schedule posted in the galley. "But we'll hold off a couple of days putting you on the schedule so you settle in." Mitchie caught Billy's sigh at that, and Guo elbowing him in the ribs for it. "Let's go look at the open cabins. You can pick out whichever you like as your bunk."

Danu System. Acceleration 10 m/s^2

A week later Mitchie had a turn on galley duty. She rinsed the last spoon and put it in the drying rack. Being lead pilot on the *Tail* had got her out of galley duty for a year. Only the captain avoided chores on this ship. Or possibly they were avoiding his cooking, from the mate's jokes. A man came into the galley as she wiped down the counter. She glanced over as he took some crackers from the cupboard. It was Billy, the handsome deckhand. He said, "Hi," with a bright smile.

"Evenin'," she replied, pulling out a towel. The plates in the rack could wait until morning to be put away but drying them gave her something to do with her hands.

"How are you liking the ship?"

She kept facing the counter. "It's cozy. Feels like a family. Is your big cargo behaving?"

He chuckled. "Completely. It's so strapped down it didn't budge through any of your maneuvers." Mitchie kept drying dishes. Billy continued, "There's enough empty room in the hold for a dance floor. I got some new music at the station so I can practice the latest dances. I'd love to practice them with you."

Mitchie dropped the towel on the counter and turned around. "Do you give dance lessons to the whole crew?"

"I've offered. They're not interested. But a beautiful woman like you would make a great impression at a club."

"Did you ever hear how I got my job on the *Elephant's Tail?*"

"Um, no."

"The captain had the port authorities arrest the pilot for murder."

"Damn!"

"Yep. Pilot was married to the supercargo. Well, about three weeks before they arrived at Akiak he catches her with the mechanic using some cargo crates as a mattress. Slapped both of them around. Didn't end there, pilot and mechanic kept brawling whenever they saw each other. Wife screaming at the pilot the rest of the time. So a week out from planetfall the airlock cycled on night shift. Supercargo's gone. There's a suicide note from her typed up in the hold. Mechanic says pilot faked the note and murdered her, goes for him with a wrench. Crew get them separated and locked up. Captain ditched the pilot at Akiak, hired me, then dropped the mechanic at the next port. And put out a real strict rule about crew dating."

"Wow. Yeah, guess that's a good rule." Billy swallowed a cracker. "Well, good night."

"Good night," said Mitchie as he left.

Planet Demeter. Gravity 7.5 m/s²

Bing served lunch outside. *Fives Full* had a half-klick wide landing pad all to herself so they didn't have to worry about anyone interrupting them (Demeter didn't trust analog ships to make precision landings). The crew had an awning hanging from the cargo hatch against the sun. A few crates were set up as tables to hold the picnic.

Captain Schwartzenberger came up on a scooter and dismounted. He took a seat and tossed his hat on the table.

"Any luck, sir?" asked Bing as she handed him a sandwich.

"Not really," said the captain. "We could take some containers to cover fuel and chow. I was hoping to find another irregular like that generator to make a profit. Struck out, so I'm looking at some goods we could take out to the Disconnect for spec sale. Hate to risk the cash though." He dove into the sandwich.

Billy and Guo started debating which Fusion products best fit through the hoops of profitable and export-legal. Bing chimed in occasionally to shoot down Billy's wildest ideas. Precision machine parts were winning the argument when a purple speed-flyer landed nearby.

The short man getting out of the flyer wore a matching purple suit. "Nice threads," said Billy. The man responded to their attention with a smile and wave as he strolled over.

"Good day. I'm looking for the captain of the *Fives Full*," he said.

"I'm Captain Schwartzenberger."

"Malachi Jones, pleased to meet you, sir."

"Have a seat, Mr. Jones," said the captain.

"I understand you haven't set a departure date."

"We're looking at a couple of offers but haven't committed to a contract yet." The crew tried to make their eavesdropping look discreet.

"Well, if the negotiations have a bit longer to go, would you be willing to undertake a short-term charter? About a week, returning here."

"I'll certainly consider it. You are aware that we're a Disconnected Worlds ship, yes?"

"Oh, certainly. That's essential to the deal." Malachi pulled a crumpled datasheet out of his pocket. It flattened itself and projected an image of a blue gas giant with green and yellow rings. "Kronos, sixth planet of our system. Beautiful sight, there's pictures of it all over. I think there's real money in taking tourists to get a close look at it. No Fusion ship will go out that far. They'd lose connection with the datanet and shut down. A Disconnect ship can do the trip." He paused to let the captain think it through.

"We can certainly go out there," said Schwartzenberger. "We have a few passenger berths. But the only big windows are on the bridge and I can't let a bunch of untrained people bounce around in there." He glanced around. Mitchie scribbled on her loaner datasheet. The rest looked away.

Malachi wasn't discouraged. "I expected some modification would be needed for your ship to do this venture. I see it as a proof of concept and advertising for future regular trips. Some beacons to extend the datanet will be the expensive end of those. So there's no need for the tourist fees to cover your shipyard bills, I'll cover that out of my capital."

Schwartzenberger mentally added a zero to how much Jones might pay for that little trip. "We can look at how quick we can put a big viewport in and have the shipyard give you an estimate."

"Great! Once you get started on the viewport I'll send out some advertisements with the date for the trip. Won't get very many for the first time but they should give me good word of mouth. I can judge the response and decide whether to invest in some datanet beacons."

"You wouldn't use a Disconnect ship for a regular run?" asked the captain, not that he wanted to permanently port on a Fusion world.

"Telling people they'll be off-net for a day cuts out 90% of my customers. These people want to tell their friends about things as they're doing it."

"Huh. Well, it's your customers." The captain picked up the contact card Malachi had laid on the table. "We'll get you that estimate as quick as we can."

"Good. I'm looking forward to hearing from you." He stood and shook hands with the captain. "Good to meet you, sir. Ladies, gentlemen."

Everyone waited until the purple flyer went out of sight before starting to chatter. Schwartzenberger fielded Billy's "Is this for real?" first.

"Yes, I think it's real. There's a lot of bored rich people on this ball, and a lot of them got rich by finding a way to get bored people excited. So our new friend may pull in a lot of money by the time the fad runs its course. Now, the opportunity being real doesn't mean Jones is real. Bing, do some research on the guy, let's see if he really has the money. Guo, think about where we can have a window that can go back to structure after our little trip. Mitchie, figure out a course to Kronos that gives a few different views of the rings. Give me some time versus fuel options."

"Working it, Skipper." Mitchie held up her datasheet. Kronos' rings turned slowly as an overlay tracked the ship's position.

"Good. Let's get to work."

                              ***

Billy whistled cheerfully as he entered through the open airlock. He stopped when he saw the hold. "Shit! What are all the frigging lights on for? It's the middle of the night!"

Guo shouted back "I'm working here!"

"Okay, okay, just leave the lights on quietly." Billy walked carefully over. "You're not working, you're staring."

"I'm trying to figure out how big a viewport we can put in the main cargo hatch. It's the thinnest big structural panel. Just have to avoid the wires and supports."

Billy looked over the sketch in the mechanic's hand. "Wiggly. How are you going to get it in?"

"Welding," said Guo. "Cut out the panels, weld in some transparent aluminum, then reverse. That way we can do most of it ourselves and not have to pay shipyard rates."

"Oh, God." Billy flashed back to his last time sweating for hours in a welding mask. Unlike Guo, he wasn't going to have more important things to do. "Isn't there an easier way to do it?"

"How? The only weaker spots in the hull are too small for a decent viewport. We have to use the hatch."

Billy looked at the cargo hatch. A quarter of the hold's circumference opened out as two doors. "Yeah... but why cut holes in it?" he asked. *Cause that would suck.* "Just yank out the whole hatch."

"The whole thing?" Guo pivoted to look over the entire hatch.

"Sure. We're not loading any cargo until we get back. Just tackweld a panel over the hole and we're good."

Guo paused to absorb this. "Tackwelds wouldn't hold the pressure. We'd need to put a reinforcing ring over the edge and weld both edges. But that'd work, yeah. Just get the yard to bend some TAl to the right shape and we can put it on."

"Okay, I'm going to go sleep off this head before I do any welding. G'night."

"Good night." Guo shook his head as Billy wandered to the ladder.

***

Bing entered the captain's cabin without knocking. "He's for real, Alois. He spots fads, popularizes them, then sells out at the peak. Or goes bankrupt. Done each about half a dozen times. Last one was a bust. Probably has a silent partner putting in the money for this one."

"I don't care if he makes a profit as long as we do." He put his book down gently and picked up a datasheet. He re-read his proposed letter carefully. A tap sent it off to Malachi Jones. His mind cleared, he let Bing start going over the ship's inventory with him.

They were only a quarter into it when the sheet chimed with a call from Malachi. "Hello, Captain! Thank you for the quick turnaround. I've deposited the funds for the modification and the half down for the trip in your account."

Schwartzenberger's poker face almost slipped. "You're welcome, sir, and thank you."

"Those animations should help too, thank you for sending them. Well, I have to round up some customers. Please keep me posted on how the mods go, Captain."

"Of course, sir. Good day." The sheet went dark again. Schwartzenberger leaned against the wall. "Holy shit. He didn't haggle at all."

Bing smirked. "How much did you soak him for?"

"Enough to charter a luxury liner for that long."

"Well … hazard pay. We'll be off-net. Fuzies get all rabbitty when there's no rescuebot standing by to pull them out of the fire."

"Maybe." The captain laughed. "He paid it! Even if he stiffs us on the second half, we're a couple months ahead now."

"Instead of three months behind?"

"One behind. Hauling that tokamak shell here was a nice run. We just started to lose ground with not finding a run back out to the Disconnect."

"Oh, what were the animations?" asked Bing.

"Mitchie did some tourist's eye views of Kronos. Something to catch their eye. Her idea. Sharp kid. She's a lucky find, almost as lucky as this tourist job."

"Yeah, she's sharp. But I'm still not easy about the job. It's just too good."

"We're not getting asked to smuggle anything. I don't care if they're money laundering. If they're hiding from cops they're only getting a week of it. So I don't care what the catch is."

"You admit there's a catch then."

"There always is. But the money's good."

***

Guo pivoted the chair toward Mitchie. She grabbed its leg and butted it up against one of the pop-up handholds in the cargo hold floor. A bit of wire held it firmly in place. Guo finished with his end and gave the whole thing a firm shake. "That'll hold. I guess it's safe enough. I'm just amazed we can get away with it."

Mitchie laughed. "Disconnect ships are death traps, Guo. The Fusion thinks anyone setting foot on one deserves to be out of the gene pool." She hushed as they heard voices from the personnel lock. "Skipper, they're here."

The captain wiped his hands on his polishing cloth. He tossed it to Billy. The deckhand gathered up the cleaning supplies. He headed for the storage cabinet, thankful the synchronized wiping game was over. The captain put on his best smile to welcome his guests.

Bing and Malachi led a gaggle of groundhogs into the hold. "Hello, I'm Captain Alois Schwartzenberger, master of the *Fives Full*. Welcome aboard. I hope your time here will be entertaining and educational. You've met my first mate, Shi Bingrong. Here's the rest of our crew. Guo Kwan, mechanic. Michigan Long, pilot. And William Lee, deckhand." Billy welcomed them with a blinding smile. Or possibly that was just for the three teenage girls. "For your safety you'll need to stay in this room for the trip. When we're maneuvering you'll have to belt yourselves in to your seats." He waved toward the patio furniture Malachi had delivered that morning. "We have a variety of drinks and snacks available for the trip. Bing will stay with you here, please ask her for anything you need. Thank you for coming with us. We'll be ready for lift-off in about twenty minutes. Crew, to your stations." Mitchie and Guo headed for opposite ladders.

Schwartzenberger detoured to grab Billy's shoulder. He whispered, "They're underage. Touch them and it's the airlock." The smile went away.

Bing shepherded her charges into the seats. They promptly split into groups. An expensively-dressed teenage girl named Bobbie was celebrating her birthday. A couple of friends and a relative made it a party. An astronomy professor dragged three graduate students with him. One tourist wasn't in either group, an accountant named Mussa.

The birthday girl claimed the seat closest to the center of the viewport. Her two friends took the flanking seats. Her uncle hung back, waving the other tourists ahead of him. Billy found himself drafted to help secure the professor's recording gear to the deck. A brief argument led to Bing ruling in favor of giving humans a better view than machines. The professor settled his grad students to the left. The birthday party's chaperoning uncle played "After-you-sir-no-after-you" with the remaining tourist until he took the front row seat and the uncle got the back row one "away from the giggles."

With everyone seated Billy began the safety lecture. Bing faded to the back of the hold and pulled out her comm. "Mitchie, we're ready to go."

"Good," replied the pilot. "We're ten minutes into our launch window." The private chat clicked off as Mitchie came on the PA. "All hands, lift-off in three minutes." The aeroturbines started whining as they spun up. Several of the passengers clapped their hands to their ears. Bing added earplugs to her list of things for next time.

"All hands, brace for lift-off." Bing reached out to the wall to steady herself but needn't have bothered. The pilot wasted fuel to give them a slow, gentle ascent. Billy walked among the passengers to check their comfort. The seats' fabric had stretched a little, but no one looked alarmed. As *Fives Full* cleared the spaceport the pre-dawn city came into view. Familiar landmarks distracted the tourists. *Easy money*, thought Bing. *As long as there's no catch for us.*

Demeter System, En Route to Kronos. Acceleration 10 m/s²

Fives Full boosted at ten gravs, close to what humans had felt on ancestral Earth. The tourists had all grown up on gentle Demeter and felt a third heavier than they were used to. The crew used that to encourage them to stay put. Billy served lunches to their seats. Bing chatted a bit with each, answering all the usual groundhog questions.

Six hours into flight Bing commed the captain. "Sir, they're stable enough to handle free fall when you want to do the cool-down."

"Guo says we're good for 80 minutes before we hit the limit," answered Schwartzenberger. "I'll make sure you get plenty of warning."

"Thanks."

In a bit Mitchie activated the PA. "All hands, stand by for free-falling in thirty minutes. Free falling in three zero minutes."

Bing stepped in front of the passengers as the announcement ended. "To keep our torch operating at peak efficiency we have to let it cool off periodically. We'll be deploying the cooling wings, don't worry if you hear a rattling sound. You won't be able to see them from this window, which is a shame because they're gorgeous. We'll be coasting until the torch is ready to fire again. This gives you all a chance to practice zero-gee maneuvering before we get to Kronos. We're going to start off simple. Billy is rigging a net in front of the window. When we're free-falling I'd like each of you to go end to end a few times. But first let's take a chance to make bio stops while we still have acceleration." The younger people all leapt up. Uncle John trailed after his charges.

The professor went to check on his equipment. "How did you get all this high-tech gear on board?" asked the ninth tourist. "All they let me have was a dumb-reader." Bing turned away to hide a resentful expression. The uneditable library he waved around would fetch real money on a Disconnected World.

"Oh, it's licensed for off-world use," said Professor Tsugawa. "The Astronomy department developed it for unmanned observation missions. It has separate processors for self-monitoring. If any code goes corrupt it detonates a self-destruct charge." His interlocutor turned pale. "Well, this is a prototype, so it just has an alarm to tell us to disassemble it."

"Oh. I guess that's more trouble than I'd want to take. I just hate to miss out on a whole week of work."

Professor Tsugawa shrugged. "I'm not getting much work in either. I wanted to bring a datasheet for organizing the data we collect but they're all net-bound."

"Well, that must be for the best. Don't want to risk their software going corrupt."

"Of course." Tsugawa turned back to the gear. The other joined the line for the refreshers.

Near Planet Kronos. Acceleration 10 m/s^2

Bing checked the time again. Seventy minutes until they finished this boost. After three days of near-constant acceleration they'd coast over Kronos' north pole and see the whole ring system. While the tourists pressed their noses to the window she intended to go get a nap. Keeping them entertained had been more work than she expected even with Billy organizing the free-fall soccer and other games. For now the groundhogs still slept in their tents. She hoped Malachi would let them keep those tents–space rated ones were valuable in the Disconnect. Overkill for this job but the captain had squeezed Jones for every key he could get.

She walked over to the one family-size tent. After the first morning she'd decided to let the teenagers have first turn at the facilities while the others slept. The chaperone stuck his head out of his tent as she approached. "Wake up call," Bing reassured him. He nodded but kept watching her. The girls woke more cheerfully today. Bobbie was as eager as she must have been for Christmas mornings.

Once the girls were mostly through their routines Bing crossed the hold to wake the next. Mr. Mussa had fallen asleep holding his dumb-reader again. The accountant had been more or less adopted by the university group as another student. "Good morning, everyone! We'll be arriving at Kronos within the hour. Billy is cooking breakfast so get ready fast." Mussa got up. The rest stirred and grumbled. Astronomy departments didn't attract morning people.

The captain came down the forward ladder. Billy passed him baskets of food and dishes. Soon the tourists were all eating, cabin fever dispelled by bacon and eggs. "That worked well," the captain said to Bing.

"Thanks. Nothing like saving the best meal for when they're crankiest."

Mitchie's voice came over the PA. "All hands, end acceleration in five minutes. Secure for free falling." The officers pitched in to help Billy gather up the dishes. The passengers belted themselves into their usual seats.

"All hands, free falling in ten seconds. Five seconds. End acceleration. Stand by for maneuver." The window had been facing away from Kronos on the last boost. Now Mitchie flipped the ship. The window filled with the shining rings. Gasps came from the tourists. Even the crew were transfixed by the sight. "All hands, secure for free falling."

Chatter started up again. Professor Tsugawa hung over his students' shoulders as they collected data. Billy joined the officers in the back. "They look happy," he said.

"Mostly," said Bing as she stifled a yawn.

"Why don't you go get that nap," said the captain. "I can keep an eye on them for this shift."

"Okay. Make sure you keep an eye on 'Uncle John.' There's something wrong about him."

"Oh, not this again," groaned Billy. "He's fine. Hasn't done anything wrong. He's been the least trouble of any of them."

"He's not her uncle. He doesn't look a thing like her."

"So he's an in-law. This is exactly the kind of thing you'd stick an unemployed son-in-law with."

"Keep it down," muttered the captain.

"He doesn't act unemployed," said Bing. "Too alert. Look at him now. He's not staring at the rings. He's looking all around."

"Including at us. So don't stare at him." Schwartzenberger shifted to put his back to the tourists.

Billy turned away as well. "I think you're just being paranoid. The guy hasn't been any trouble at all."

WHANG WHANG WHANG WHANG WHANG. Everyone started as the hull rang with impacts. "A bit of space junk, folks," announced Captain Schwartzenberger. "Happens all the time. That's why the hull's so thick. Nothing to worry about." He kept an ear cocked for the whistle of escaping air–nothing. He was still uneasy. The impacts had been regularly spaced, not the usual random distribution. He wasn't sure where they'd been hit but it felt like the impacts were on the lee side. His comm chirped. "Yes?" Bing and Billy leaned in to hear.

Mitchie reported, "Sir, I've got a ship on local comm. He says those were his cannon rounds. He said if we don't give Bobbie Smith to him he's going to switch to armor-piercing."

Billy said, "Well, maybe she brought a bodyguard along."

***

Schwartzenberger climbed up the ladder into the bridge and bolted the hatch after him. The radio buzzed with another threat. Mitchie answered in a high-pitched, panicked voice, "I'm just the pilot! I can't promise anything! The captain will be here in a minute!" She closed the mike and turned to the captain. "I spotted him, sir," she said in her normal tone. "It looks like a Bolt-class interceptor."

Schwartzenberger followed her finger to a gleam paralleling the ship's path. He nodded and strapped into the co-pilot seat.

"This is Captain Alois Schwartzenberger of the *Fives Full*. Who am I talking to?"

"Call me the Kronos Taxi Service, Captain." The voice was cold, calm, male, with a Demeter accent. "I'm here to give one of your passengers a lift."

"I'm sorry, they've all bought round-trip tickets."

"You won't need to give her a refund. We'll even compensate you for your trouble."

"My passengers are not for sale, pirate!"

"Look—I'm taking the girl. I've got armor-piercing loads for the cannon and a few missiles. You can hand her over and be half a million keys richer ... or I can shred your ship and you freeze out here with your crew and passengers."

"Half a million bullshit. It's easy to make promises when you're going to kill us anyway."

"The money's real. We can even deposit it in advance. And I won't hurt anyone if you cooperate."

"Double bullshit. You can't afford to have witnesses to a kidnapping." Mitchie handed him a note. He read *Sent tightbeam distress call to Kerberos Base* and gave her a thumbs-up.

"My orders are to have as many witnesses as possible. Seems that makes it more likely the ransom will be paid. Doesn't say much for her family, does it?"

"So... you actually have a half mill in cash in your little boat there?"

"Better," answered the stranger. "I say the word and it drops into your trading account on Demeter. Then you can just float the girl across to me in an emergency pod. Nobody gets hurt. Not even her."

Schwartzenberger sighed into the mike. "Okay. Make the deposit. We'll get her ready." He turned the mike off.

"Nice to work with a sensible man."

The captain felt Mitchie's stare on him. "We'll keep stalling for time. I'll get an empty pod set up to go over. Your job will be to watch for when they go to pick it up. When they're closest pivot and give them a blast with the torch. With luck we can cause enough damage to break contact until the Navy gets out here." A sharper tone, "Don't look so damn relieved. Buying time is our priority here."

"Sorry, sir," said Mitchie. "Um… if you want to break contact I might be able to do that now."

"Seriously?"

Mitchie pointed at the rings. "That's pretty dense for a spaceship to fly though. I've flown through Akiak mountains in thunderstorms. A bunch of ice doesn't scare me. That guy–" pointing at the interceptor "– probably does all his flying by telling the autopilot where to go. First time he tries to go within fifty klicks of an unplotted rock it'll execute an automatic anticollision maneuver. A couple of those and we should be out of sight. Plenty of places to hide in the rings."

"A torchship isn't much like flying a winged shuttle, girl. You think you can get through there without smacking some ice?"

"I've flown sims like that." She gave him a hard look. "Captain, I *promise* I can take us through there safely."

"Well. I can't argue with an Akiak promise. We'll do it. They're probably still dealing with the money. Best time." The captain activated the PA. "ALL HANDS, ALL HANDS. STRAP IN. STRAP IN FOR ACCELERATION AND MANEUVER. ACCELERATION AND MANEUVER IN THIRTY SECONDS. STRAP IN. THIS MEANS YOU, GUO. THIRTY SECONDS."

Mitchie grabbed a pair of sliders for a quick calculation on the pilot station's mini-plotting board. She ignored Bing's voice coming from the captain's comm. He barked back, "Just tell them it's pirates."

The thirty seconds were up. Mitchie fired the torch. *Fives Full* leapt forward at ten gravs. *Hopefully everyone's strapped in*, she thought. She fired the pitch thrusters to bring the nose down. A second firing stopped the ship pointed straight at the rings. She pressed the converter room intercom button. "Guo, can I get forty gravs for a few minutes?"

The mechanic wasn't fazed by the request, but his tone made it clear he wondered what the sudden emergency was. "Maybe a few seconds. We barely started cooling off from the last leg. Run too hard and we'll bust the thermal limits."

"Okay, I want a few minutes of high accel, as much as you can give me, then probably a couple hours of running at ten gravs."

"Damn. What—okay. You can have four minutes of twenty-five gravs."

The captain entered the conversation. "Mr. Kwan. Ignore the yellow limits. We are going to red-line all parameters until further notice."

The intercom stayed silent long enough for a few syllables to go by. Then Guo Kwan answered. "Aye, aye, sir. Stand by." They heard a slide rule clicking. "You can have thirty-two gravs for six minutes."

"Perfect! I'll try to not use it all," Mitchie promised. That made turnover time easy enough to do in her head.

"They noticed," said the captain calmly. The kidnappers' ship was close to out of sight now, until it lit off its torch with a bright blue glare.

The ship-to-ship radio sounded. "*Fives*, where the fuck do you think you're going? We have three times your accel and twice your delta-V." Schwartzenberger contemplated the transmit button and decided to let them wonder.

Mitchie left the torch on as she flipped the ship end for end. Every bit of in-plane velocity would help. Once the maneuver finished she took the ship to Guo's limit. She sank back into her cushions. The couch was fully reclined. She focused on the chronometer, trying to ignore the ship growing in the cockpit window.

"You're right," said the captain. "He's autopiloting. Missed your turnover. He went to max accel to compensate, then went ballistic. Over a hundred gravs must've hurt enough to make him hit the emergency switch. Now he's at forty-five gravs but still going to overshoot."

"Let's see how many more mistakes he makes, sir." Mitchie grinned. She'd never gotten to red-line a ship before. Might never get to again.

The end of the 32-grav burn zeroed their southward velocity as they entered the densest part of the middle ring. *Fives Full* now paralleled the chunks of ice in their orbits—but at ten times their speed. Mitchie aligned the ship to the right of the velocity vector. Enough yaw would keep them in the ring even at ten gravs acceleration.

Both eyeball and radar confirmed the gap she'd aimed for was empty. Mitchie looked ahead and nudged the ship north to pass close over the rock in her path. She kept switching between looking at the radar scope and the window. The echoes displayed by the primitive radar depended more on the shape and composition of objects than their size. Not that her eyes were foolproof. They were on the sunward side of Kronos. If the chase lasted until they went into the planet's shadow she'd have to leave the ring. Best if they solved this before then. She yawed thirty degrees to the left then forty to the right to weave among the next few rocks.

"He's back," said the captain. "In plane with us. Not in gun range yet." Mitchie kept maneuvering. Pitch down, yaw right, pitch up. "Ha!" Schwartzenberger burst out. "He's still on autopilot. He set it to follow. It's matching us turn for turn."

"Good," answered the pilot. She stopped looking along her present course. Swiveling her head to scan the whole sky she spotted her goal. A quick radar pulse confirmed it. Mitchie yawed the ship eighty degrees left and more than doubled the torch thrust. *Fives Full* slid sideways through the sky. The pursuer shifted course to follow her rapidly changing velocity vector.

Schwartzenberger lifted himself in his seat. Turning his head unsupported hurt in the high acceleration. He pushed to see over the edge of the bridge window. The target was obvious as soon as he saw it. Three snowballs, each about fifty klicks across, in a neat triangle. The captain lay quietly back. Too late to pass it by. Best not to distract her.

"Guo, how long can we keep up this accel?" asked the pilot.

"I can't reach my damn slide rule," complained the mechanic. His voice was strained by the acceleration. "Twenty or thirty minutes. I'll inform you before we hit the limit."

"That should be plenty," said Mitchie calmly.

***

Conditions in the hold were starting to improve. Billy had been low-crawling on the deck to collect the used spacesick bags and towels. With those stuffed into the trash locker the air recycling started to clear out the smell. The groundhogs had mostly emptied their stomachs. Bing was impressed that a couple had kept their rich breakfast down. The panicked chatter had been silenced by the latest boost.

Bobbie was the first to notice the snowballs. Her "Ooh, pretty," made her friends look up. They were too panicked to appreciate the beauty of them.

As they visibly grew in the window everyone wound up staring at them. Professor Tsugawa shifted in his straps to glare at Bing. He labored to yell, "Is. Your. Pilot. Insane?" at her.

Bing didn't reply. All she could think to say was "I hope not." That didn't seem helpful.

Some of the passengers closed their eyes as the ship closed on the snowballs. The grad students traded speculation on their composition in gallows-humor tones. Bobbie was the only one enjoying the sight. Her eyes shone. But even she flinched as they swept through the center of the triangle.

***

Mitchie eased the thrust back down to ten gravs. *Fives Full* headed toward the outer edge of the rings. She brought the nose gently back around and studied the radar to pick a path back to the center. "Sir, is he still following us?"

The captain tracked the other ship on the landing cameras. "So far. Not to the gap yet." They waited tensely. The interceptor was certainly agile enough to go anywhere they could. If the pilot was good enough to use it fully–"There he goes! Max-accel avoidance burn. That had to hurt."

"Which way?"

"Plus-zee."

"Thanks." Mitchie shifted course to the south side of the ring. The more ice between them and the hunter the harder they'd be to spot again. "Should be smooth flying until he comes back."

"Okay. Holler if you have to maneuver." The captain left the bridge. She wondered where he was going but couldn't come up with a polite way to ask before the hatch dogged shut.

Maybe he wants to give the passengers some hand-holding, she thought. A check of the cameras showed the interceptor staying ballistic. She set a straight course through empty space below the ring. It was a chance to relax, unkink some muscles, and look around. *This really is a beautiful place. Piloting a regular tourist run through here would be a lovely job.* Not one for her, of course.

Captain Schwartzenberger undogged the hatch and came up the ladder dragging a pile of gear. "Here." Mitchie helped pull it up. Spread out it became two spacesuits and a thruster pack. "We scraped through some gravel while going through the dense patches. Don't think it did any more than scratch the paint. But best to be safe."

Mitchie looked up at the bridge window, a clear dome covering the top of the ship. It wouldn't take a big chunk of ice to punch a hole in it at these speeds. She could get into an emergency pod quickly enough but it would be a lonely way to wait for the out of control ship to have a fatal crash. "Good thinking." She put her purple suit next to the control couch. The captain did the same with his red one.

Schwartzenberger touched his earpiece. "Ah, he's awake." He'd taken the ship-to-ship off speakers earlier. He could monitor the stream of threats and profanities without letting it be a distraction. "Moving. Staying above the ring, not coming toward us." He studied the screen. Was this stalling or had their enemy come up with an idea? "By the way, Pilot Long. Your skill is far greater than I'd believed. I apologize for doubting you."

She gave his stiff nod, almost a bow, a smile in return. "Thank you, sir, but don't apologize. Just remember it when it's time to write that recommendation letter." She steered the ship around a small iceberg as they approached the dense core of the ring.

"I'm more likely to recommend you to the Space Guard than a merchant ship. They can use that kind of flying."

"Guard doesn't let pilots put cushions under their butts, Skipper."

"I'll tell them to make an exception. When did you check out the Guard?"

"When I was a shuttle pilot. They threw me out of the recruiting office."

"Good thing for our passengers that they did. The SOB is ahead of us now. Still over a thousand klicks above the ring. I'm not getting a good look at him."

"Might just be waiting for us to overshoot. We can't keep this up until the Navy gets here," said Mitchie.

"Longer than you think. We've got water and converter metal for days. If we push the redline too hard I can always make Guo suit up and we dump reaction mass in the converter room for active cooling."

"Whoa. Yeah, that solves cooling. Won't we have corrosion problems?"

"Eventually. Fixing that will be one item on an enormous bill I'm going to hand to somebody." Clearly the captain thought all this was about more than one teenaged astronomy fan. "Here he comes. Maneuvering minus-zee. Going to reach the ring ahead of us. Shit. Launched a missile."

"What's the angle?"

"It's—no. Ignore it. He's bluffing. He needs her alive."

"Aye-aye." Mitchie concentrated on keeping the densest part of the ring between them and the missile. She could see it now, flickering between the chunks of ice. The missile itself was invisibly small but the rocket plume shone bright blue. It moved across their path until it was directly ahead of them. The plume closed on a medium-small snowball and vanished in a bright flash.

"Conversion bomb!" shouted the captain.

Mitchie aimed the ship south and cranked up the acceleration. The expanding cloud of snow and gas hid part of the ring already. She had to get them clear enough to safely fly blind before they got caught in the cloud. As it reached up to catch them she turned the ship to put the thrust plate to the blast wave and cut thrust.

The debris from the missile explosion was too finely divided to penetrate the hull. It hissed against the ship with a sound like snow on a tin roof. Mitchie felt a sudden chill of nostalgia for Akiak. Visibility behind the wave wasn't much better. She left them ballistic.

"Here he comes," said the captain. The interceptor approached from planetward, below the rings. "Looks like he's trying for a close pass. Rip up our tanks so we can't run anymore."

Mitchie turned the ship to face the brittle window away from the enemy and started boosting back to the ring. Her fingers sweated as she gripped the throttle control. The other hand pressed the intercom button for the converter room. "How's the weather down there?"

"Tropical," laughed Guo. "Send down some ice if you get a break. We're halfway to red. Not straining things yet."

"Good. I'm going to have to do some evasive here in a moment."

"I'll hold her together for you. Hot jets, pilot."

"Approaching cannon range," reported Schwartzenberger.

The pilot put a gentle curve on their course. Something that would take a human a moment to notice. The interceptor followed instantly. "Think that autopilot has a gunnery routine, sir?"

"They haven't skimped on anything else."

"Uh-huh." The other ship started to flicker with muzzle blasts. She pushed the throttle in and triggered the plus-pitch jets. *Don't have a pattern.* Minus-yaw, lower thrust, plus yaw. Minus pitch. Max thrust. Pull thrust back to 20 gravs. Plus yaw and minus pitch together. *Don't have a pattern.* Minus yaw. More minus yaw. Max thrust. Plus pitch around that iceberg. Lower thrust. WHANG. Plus yaw and three-quarter thrust. *Don't have a pattern.* Minus pitch. Minus yaw. Cut thrust. WHANG. Half-thrust. Plus pitch and plus yaw together. Max thrust for two seconds then cut thrust for three. Plus pitch.

"Okay, he's out of range. He's stopped firing," Captain Schwartzenberger reported. "Guo, what's the damage?"

"No pressure lost anywhere, sir," said the mechanic. "Felt like they just glanced off. We'll have some holes in the reentry protection."

"Thank you." He switched the intercom off. "Nicely done, Mitchie. I think he only got that lucky because he gave up on trying for direct hits and just shot area patterns."

She let out a sigh. "Yeah. But he can keep doing that–firing patterns on high-speed passes–and he only needs to get lucky once."

"He only has so much ammo and so much time. If he runs out of either he's done. For now we're winning."

Navigating through the ring was almost easy now. "Winning but scared as hell."

The captain burst out laughing. "You're scared? You ever think about what kind of people that guy works for? And what they do to people who fail them? The bottom of his pressure suit has to be full of bricks by now."

He actually got a chuckle out of her. "Yeah, we've got him sweating. And probably a nosebleed from those anti-collision maneuvers."

"Yep." The captain had spotted the interceptor again. "There he goes. Passing sunward of us, well clear of the ice."

"Setting up for another pass," said Mitchie. The fatigue made her speech rougher, the backwoods accent creeping out.

"Eventually. He'll want to wait until he has a good spot." He was being more honest than reassuring. For once Mitchie wouldn't have minded a boss going the other way. She stuck to the north side of the ring. The interceptor had gone out of sight again so they didn't know which way to jump. Just stay close to cover and keep their speed up so they wouldn't be a sitting duck.

Mitchie spotted him first this time. She'd come out into a gap in the ring and saw the torch plume on the other side. "Dead ahead. Matched our course." Both sides of the gap were too far away to help. She picked planetside and headed for it at full acceleration.

Schwartzenberger studied the radar returns. "Better sensors. He can track us from outside visual. Reciprocal of our course gives his shells a better hit zone. He can fire a pattern at extreme range and we can't get outside it." More data came in. "His course is paralleling ours, only a few klicks off. Probably as close as he could program it."

"Shit! Point blank shots."

"I see him firing. A few patterns already on the way to us. He's scared enough to risk killing Bobbie now." There was no way to safely aim at the fuel tanks coming in at that angle.

"As close as he could–damn!" Mitchie pivoted back toward their attacker. The throttle was already at max. Intercom time. "Hey! More thrust! All you got!"

Guo's voice was already strained by acceleration. "We're redlined!"

"Gimme the real redline! Two minutes!"

"We'll melt!"

The captain slapped his intercom switch, flinching as his hand came down hard on it. "Do it." He couldn't have forced out a longer speech.

Guo didn't reply. *Fives Full* pushed a few gravs harder, a loud CRACK and scream of air announced a cannon shot penetrating the bridge window. Mitchie felt a splinter land on her face before the escaping air blew it away.

The captain gasped "Cut ac! Patch!" She grimaced and pulled the throttle back to 10 gravs.

Nine seconds later he yelled "GO!" in the sudden relative quiet and she pushed the knob to the end again. An audible thump told her the captain hadn't laid down in his control couch before he gave the word.

"One patch hole?" she asked.

"Yep." He sounded amused "Poor. Bing. Got. Bunk." The shot had put a hole in the bridge deck and gone into Bing's cabin.

The ship's acceleration dropped. Guo had taken back some of the extra thrust. Mitchie thought *It must be hot as a volcano down there.* She kept steering for the interceptor. A cannon shell flashing past the window made her flinch but not change course. She ignored the blood trickling down her face too.

The interceptor autopilot matched the *Fives Full's* straight line acceleration and extrapolated as it was taught to. When that vector reached the same time and place of its own, it took the proper action—120 gravs of acceleration for five seconds.

Mitchie yelled "Ha! Computers can't play chicken!" as the plume in front of her turned ninety degrees and brightened. She shifted her course to follow. Less than half a minute later she'd forced it into another maneuver. She grinned wolfishly as she shifted after it again. With thoroughly predictable results. "It's like kicking a can down the road!"

Captain Schwartzenberger let her have two more kicks before stopping her. "Enough, Michigan. We've won. He's gotta be out cold."

"Yeah, but if I let up he'll recover."

"Not soon. And we can't take much more of this. The ship's not designed for this kind of maneuvering. The passengers haven't had the health checks we've had. We've got to stop."

She cut their thrust. The captain luxuriated in taking full breaths of air. With the torch stilled they could hear a whistle around the ill-fitting patch. "Now what?" Mitchie asked.

"Now we go to ground. Hide. Find an iceberg with a crack we can fit into. Wait for the Navy to come." He thought a minute. "We've probably got a few hours. That's a damn rough ride you gave him."

"Okay." She got the mechanic on the line. "Hey. We're safe for a bit. What thrust can I use to get us to a hiding spot?"

Guo sounded tired too. "Safe. I like that word. If we stay ballistic for twenty minutes and then go at six gravs I can have everything back in the yellow." He coughed harshly. Probably needed a drink.

"Works." She unbelted and went to the plotting table. The hardest part of this maneuver would be slowing down to the speed of the rings.

Schwartzenberger switched on the PA. "All hands. We have broken contact with pirate vessel. We will be moving to a safe place to await assistance. Once we've done so I will give you a full briefing. Captain out."

***

The captain left the hatch open as he climbed back into the bridge. He poked at the sealant he'd put around the window patch to make sure it had cured properly. Mitchie thought he looked calm considering how frustrating his talk with Bobbie and her "uncle" was. She'd used the corridor intercom to eavesdrop. Other than admitting John was a professional bodyguard they hadn't given up a single bit of solid information. "My father is rich and well connected" had to be true for anyone worth kidnapping.

Schwartzenberger pulled out another patch and started sealing the hole in the deck. "I'll take the con for a bit. Go get yourself a sandwich or something."

"All right." Mitchie unstrapped and started down the ladder.

"Oh, do me a favor?"

"Yes, sir?"

"Break the news to Bing about her bunk."

There wasn't any way to get out of it. "Yes, sir."

***

Someone had taken the lunch fixings out of the galley already. Lacking another excuse to procrastinate she went down to the hold. The coolers were right by the upper deck ladder. She snagged a sandwich and ate as she dawdled her way to the other side of the deck.

Bing had Guo sitting up by the lower deck hatch. One of his hands held an iced drink. The other arm had an IV in it. He still looked flushed. "You look done medium rare," said Mitchie.

The mechanic chuckled. "About. It's still pretty warm down there if you wanted to get some baking done." He pointed at a bulge in the overhead. "What do I need to fix from that?"

"Um. The captain put some pressure patches in. The rest is up to Bing."

Bing looked up from the rehydration drink she was mixing. "Oh?"

There had to be some gentle way to say it, but Mitchie couldn't think of one. "The cannon shot hit your cabin."

"How bad?" Bing looked up at the dent. "Must be pretty bad."

"We couldn't see much through the hole. Looked like it hit your bunk."

"But it probably threw junk all over." Bing looked like she'd be doing some serious cussing if she'd ever learned the habit. "Hell. My goods are all trash now."

"Sentimental stuff?" asked Mitchie.

"No, trade goods. I've been doing some personal trading to build up my savings. Had a bunch of porcelain crated so it could survive sixty gravs. But it's probably all trash now."

"It's insured." Bobbie had wandered over during this discussion.

Bing gave her a disbelieving look.

"The tourism corporation had standard insurance," continued Bobbie. John tried to shush her but she waved him off. "We checked it when we signed up. None of you have to worry about financial loss from this . . . crime."

The spacers quietly absorbed this. "Thank you, that's good to know," said Mitchie.

With a muttered "Fine, you've said your piece," John sheparded Bobbie back to her friends.

When they'd gotten halfway across the hold Bing whispered, "If there's insurance that covers damage to personal possessions from third party criminal behavior it has to cost more than we were paid for this job."

"She sounded pretty certain," said Guo.

"Certain that we'd be paid," said Mitchie. "She's not caring much about the insurance policy. I'd bet we're covered some other way."

"At least rich girl is noticing that she's not the only one suffering here," said Bing.

***

A dense cluster of icebergs looked like the best hiding spot. *Fives Full* drifted through the middle of it. One chunk had a half-klick deep chasm in it, as if it was starting to split in half. "Can you fit us in there?" asked Captain Schwartzenberger.

"Yes, sir," replied Mitchie. He nodded. She fired the maneuvering thrusters to back them into the gap. The torch was shut down. Guo trickled water out the nozzles to cool the system down. The builders rated the base plate to handle a water landing at max temperature. Putting a hot base into space-cold ice might crack it.

As the ship entered the chasm snow began flying past the bridge windows, blasted loose by the thruster exhaust. As the snow cloud cast a shadow on them Mitchie hastily turned on the running lights. The reflections were startlingly bright on the ice. Mitchie cautiously guided them down. The captain breathed calmly, not reacting even when she needed multiple jets to fix an overcorrection. His hands were folded out of her sight.

350 meters in she started looking for a safe parking place. She'd maneuvered around some outcrops that would have held the whole ship. This stretch had smaller lumps on the chasm walls. Trying to edge past one the base caught on it, tipping the ship toward the other side. Her counter burn was too weak to overcome the momentum. The starboard side leaned into the ice with a hiss as it melted the crystals in contact. More snow flew up from the base melting into its foothold. A few coughs from the thrusters broke them free of the melt. The ship floated free and still. This close to the center of the iceberg it had no noticeable gravity.

Schwartzenberger burst out laughing and instantly apologized. "I'm sorry. No complaints about the landing. That was tougher than any I've done in my whole career. It's a great landing. It's just—we're not going to walk away from it."

Mitchie giggled. She wouldn't want to take a vacuum suit across those crystals either. She turned off the running lights. "What now, sir?"

"Now we wait. Get some rest." She nodded and partially unstrapped. With just the hip belt on she curled up and fell asleep. Schwartzenberger went below.

The captain's briefing to the passengers had no new information other than, "Wrap up, it's going to get cold." They still seemed reassured by his hold on the situation and confidence that the Navy would arrive soon. When he finished his first mate insisted he take time for a sandwich. The passengers returned to their positions. Bobbie and her friends stared at the sliver of sky still visible. John watched everyone from a perch behind her. Everyone else clustered around the observation device, pretending they were attracted to it instead of repelled by John's glare.

"How's Guo doing?" the captain asked between bites.

Bing answered, "Fine. I gave him an IV to get his fluids back up. He fairly well cooked in there. Didn't complain but he flunked a pinch test. His color's a lot better now."

"Good. And Billy?"

"Just some bruises from crawling around during the high accel. Some of the maneuvers rolled him around. I sent him and Guo down below for a nap."

He nodded and chewed. He relaxed a bit as the food replaced some of the energy he'd burned off in stress. He could actually believe they were safe for the moment.

"Captain, could I have a word?"

"Certainly, Professor . . . Tsugawa?"

"We were studying the composition of this object as we descended. I've never had the chance to examine a ring component so closely before. It's really an excellent opportunity to research the origins of the ring system."

"Well, I'm glad this side trip had a silver lining for you." Schwartzenberger hoped he'd managed to keep most of the sarcasm out of his voice. This was still a paying customer.

"I'm wondering if you'd be willing to do us a favor as long as we're going to be here for a while."

"Oh?" The captain diplomatically suppressed several variations on *Get to the point.*

"Would it be possible for you to obtain some samples from the object for us? Doing a chemical analysis of their composition could provide an immense amount of insight for us."

"Huh. Maybe. I don't know if we have anything we could store that in."

Bing offered, "We've got three days' worth of empty food coolers. Wouldn't be hard to make them airtight. You'd still have slush when you got home though."

The professor smiled. "Slush is fine. Thank you."

"Don't thank us yet," said the captain. "We'll have to see if we can do it safely. I'll talk to my crew when they're back on duty." He suppressed the urge to charge him for the extra services.

"Of course, sir. Thanks for your consideration."

When Billy woke he was eager to do the vacuum work. The captain and mate were unsurprised. The deckhand was always up for anything he might be able to impress girls with. Bing had stacked half a dozen coolers and a roll of vacctape in the airlock. To Billy's dismay the captain insisted on both a safety tether and a maneuvering pack.

"The girls won't think any less of you for it," whispered Schwartzenberger as he checked the straps and seals of Billy's suit.

"I'm not—hmpf." Billy put his helmet on and locked it in place. "Comm check, do you read?" His voice came from the comm the professor held. "Comm check." Bing nudged Tsugawa.

"Oh! Yes, I hear you clearly."

"I hear you. Getting in the lock now."

The bodyguard took the captain aside. "Wait—you're broadcasting? How is that hiding?"

Schwartzenberger put on his tolerant face. "Suit radios are very low power, Mr. Smith. If they're close enough to pick that up our thermal signature will be as strong as a flare to them. It's not adding any danger."

"So you're sure we're still safe here?"

"No. I think if that pirate goes iceberg by iceberg looking for the warm one the odds are good he'll still be at it when the Navy gets here. Even if that takes a week."

"All right." John seemed a bit abashed. "It's my job to worry about her."

"Fine. You worry about the people. Let me worry about the ship. That's my job."

They turned back to the window. It framed Billy in the center, filling a cooler with a scoop Guo had welded up. He cut a few lengths of vacctape to seal it and hooked it back onto his tether. Tsugawa started talking him to the next target. "Warmer-cooler" had proved to work better than trying to agree on a common left and right in micrograv.

The grad students pressed against the window, debating which odd-colored chunk should be sampled next. Mussa had drifted behind their gadget to stay out of the way. The teenagers were unusually quiet as they watched the show.

Billy took full advantage of his freedom to show off. Instead of carefully crawling over the ice to the next target he kicked off it to the ship and bounced back. He picked grace over precision. An extra couple of leaps was a chance to do more flips. Schwartzenberger frowned at the wasted time. The professor kept a deliberately cheerful tone as he persuaded Billy toward the next intriguing bit of ice.

Eventually all the coolers were full. Billy placed them just inside the hold before unsuiting. Bing herded the grad students as they took their samples to the freezer. The captain met Billy at the suit locker. "Hydroponics maintenance."

The deckhand's face fell. "Isn't it Mitchie's turn today?"

"She's sleeping. We're going to let her sleep as long as we can. We need her rested."

For once the captain didn't get any more argument. "Aye, aye, sir."

***

Mitchie's dreams were visited by icebergs and cannon shells but none woke her. Eventually her bladder forced her out of the pilot couch. The pull-out was private enough with no one else on the bridge. She spared a paranoid look at the stars but nothing moved.

A brief chat with Bing established that most aboard were asleep. Mitchie was too slept out to take her suggestion to nap some more. She busied herself putting away the navigation aids she'd strewn about while finding this hiding place. The emergency radio channel was quiet. No Navy yet.

She moved to the full spectrum scanner. Maybe there was another ship out there. The scanner showed nothing on the voice channels except Kronos' background radiation. A high frequency channel showed a strong signal. Mitchie frowned and tuned the speakers to it. White noise. Something out there was transmitting a lot of data.

She studied the sky. The chasm they were hiding in was narrow but long. She opened up the communications console and switched the scanner's cable from the omnidirectional to a parabolic antenna. Rotating that would show what direction the signal came from. If a research ship was out there she might be able to hit it with a tightbeam distress signal. Two ships cooperating might be able to keep the pirate out of cannon range if it found them again.

The crank for the parabolic was set into the deck. Mitchie braced herself against the console and started turning it. Every thirty degrees or so she peeked up to see if the scanner display had changed. It had started with the signal at high intensity which should mean the antenna pointed straight at it. After 180 degrees the signal stayed strong, only showing minor fluctuations. She turned it through another full circle before accepting the bad news. Mitchie pressed the intercom button for Bing's handcomm. "Hey. Um. We're transmitting something."

"What?" The first mate didn't want to believe it either.

"There's a high-frequency data transmission coming from our ship."

Bing cursed. She'd been napping in the hold to keep an eye on the passengers, and because she didn't have a bunk any more. Now she unhooked her tether and bounded over to where the astronomers slept. Once she had a firm foothold she grabbed the nearest grad student by the ankle and shook him hard. "Is that thing on?" she barked.

"Gah! What?" protested the hapless academic.

"Your camera! Is it on?"

"Of course it is, it's collecting data continuously."

"Is it transmitting anything?"

"What? No! That'd get us all killed!"

"Check it." She flung him at the gadget. He didn't land gracefully, just wrapped himself around the observatory and held on enough to not bounce. One look at First Mate Bingrong was enough to make him swallow all complaints. He turned to align himself with the controls and started typing.

The commotion had woken up most of the passengers. When the grad student shrieked, "Holy shit!" even Billy woke up. A frantic flurry of keystrokes ended with a report of, "Okay, it's off now. Someone turned on the real-time imagery broadcast."

Bing had already taken a headcount. "Where's Mr. Mussa?" she called. Uncle John launched himself at the portable refreshers. He yanked open both doors. Empty. The astronomers all began babbling their denials of responsibility for the disaster. Her handcomm added to the noise with Mitchie's confirmation that the transmitter was off. "Everybody shut up! Who saw Mussa last?"

Bing's victim said, "He was in his tent, next to mine, when I went to sleep."

"Anyone else see him go anywhere?" demanded Bing. Headshakes all over the hold. As she scanned the faces a drifting object caught her eye. Mussa's dumb-reader, its back panel open, revealing an empty compartment where a library's worth of read-only datacrystals should be. "Billy! Go below and look for him. Be careful." The deckhand gave her a vague wave and headed for the hatch. Bing pulled out her handcomm. "Guo, what's your status?" No answer. "Guo, report!"

The answer was Mussa's voice. "He's fine, Mate Bingrong. Just going to sleep a bit longer than he planned is all."

Bing switched channels. "Captain! It's in the impeller!"

"On my way."

She switched back to Guo's channel. Mussa was saying, "—so don't bother trying to get at me. And I've taken a few key pieces off the converter so we're all staying here for a while."

Billy gave up wrestling with the hatch. "It's jammed good. I can suit up and go in the lower airlock."

Bing shook her head. She spoke into the handcomm. "You realize you've locked yourself into a ship with a lot of people who don't like you very much now, right? But if you come back to our side now we'll be nice instead of making you learn how to breathe vacuum."

Mussa laughed. "I think I'm safer on this side. And much better paid. I suggest you find a way to hand the girl over that doesn't leave you all in a vacuum."

Captain Schwartzenberger arrived in the hold. The passengers gathered around him and Bing as she briefed him. "When did the broadcast start?" he asked. One of the grad students went back to the observatory to check. Five hours ago during Billy's sample collecting. "Billy, disconnect the lower deck air feed." One of the teenagers gasped in shock. The captain grinned in a not reassuring way. "They'll still have air. But it'll get stale in a while. We'll see if that makes him flexible."

"Could you cut open that hatch?" asked a passenger.

"We could, if we didn't keep the welding gear in the converter room." Several less-practical suggestions were tossed at the captain. He dealt with them calmly. Billy's request to try the airlock met a gentle reminder that the airlock hatches were as easy to jam as the deck ones. When acrimony broke out among the astronomers over who should have been protecting the gadget from Mussa the captain let his mate handle calming it. He took Bobbie and John aside for another discreet chat. "I hope it doesn't come to this but I have a firearm. I can lend it to you if you're a better shot."

John answered for them. "Thank you, but we're equipped."

"Offnet capable?"

"Yes." John was too professional to take offense at the accusation he could be that naïve.

"Good. You're welcome to shift to my cabin. Left-hand door at the end of the corridor. Access combo one-two-three."

"Thanks again. We'll do that if we need to. For now I'd rather be where we can see what's coming."

"Your business. Let me know if there's anything else I can do." Schwartzenberger went back up to the bridge, stopping at his quarters on the way. He filled Mitchie in. She took it more calmly than he'd expected. A quick test confirmed that Mussa had taken the converter out of action.

"I could run the maneuvering thrusters off the auxiliary. But we'd get less than a grav out of them," Mitchie said.

"Don't bother," the captain replied. "At this point we're just hoping the Navy gets here in time. Well—if you see a boarder coming do that. We can try to run his jetpack dry."

"I'll keep an eye out. But this place is going to be in full dark in a couple of hours." The chasm was lit only by sunlight reflecting off one rim already. "It'll be seven hours until sunrise then." Schwartzenberger grunted. "But I'll watch for any torch plumes," she promised. A loud buzzing started up. "What the hell is that?"

"A reaction mass pump running with no load," growled the captain. "Mussa's figured out how to cover the noise of us getting boarded."

"That must be really loud in the hold."

"Probably. I'll go help Bing hold down the panic." By the time Schwartzenberger reached the hold everyone was calm if tense. The tension kept going up as they waited.

The first one to snap under the strain was the pump. The steady buzz became a rhythmic beat. "Great. Now we're going to have to completely replace that," groused the captain to Bing. She reassured him that it would be covered by Bobbie's insurance. He replied, "*If* we get her home."

The sought after passenger used the beat to sing along to. She and her friends were veterans of the same camping program. The campfire songs were close enough for the pump to count as accompaniment. One of the grad students offered a boy's version of a song. Soon most of the passengers were singing non-parentally-approved verses.

Only John noticed when the deck hatch popped open and a grenade flew out. "Eyes!" he yelled, covering his own.

The grenade's flash was bright enough to briefly blind anyone looking that direction. Even the reflection off the walls was enough to leave victims looking at green afterimages. The deafening shockwave spread out too much in the huge hold to stun anyone. The viewing window held. Two meter long cracks appeared at each corner.

John fired into the hatchway before the spacesuited boarder came through. A few bullets hit the boarder but no blood appeared. John leapt for Bobbie. The intruder returned fire at John. Heavy bullets left a line of stars in the window. He stopped firing when John got close to Bobbie. John grabbed her away from her clutching friends, scattering them, threw her toward the upper hatch, and kicked off to follow her. More bullets followed him. The last couple hit the wall instead of the window.

The intruder had magnetic boots. He began walking after Bobbie. Bing looked at the window and yelled, "Air leak! Everyone into survival bubbles!" She hastily zipped her own closed.

Over a dozen shots had hit the transparent aluminum viewport. Cracks in its crystalline structure spread as Billy watched. He looked around the hold. Most of the passengers had gotten to the ladder or rescue bubbles. Bobbie's two friends had been knocked off their grips in the scuffle and were drifting through the air. He leapt for the nearest, grabbed her by the waist, and threw her toward the girls' sleeping tent. A quick rebound off the deck let him grab the other girl. Their momentum took them toward the professor's observation gear. He kicked off it to get them to the tent. In a moment all three were in it as he turned to seal the entrance. *Thank God for vacuum-proof zippers,* he thought.

He had it closed just as the window gave way in a roar of escaping air. The tent's air pressure pulled its walls tight. A sharp whistle came from the entry. "Fuck." A quick inspection showed Billy some bent teeth were letting air through the zipper. He slapped his palm on the leak. The whistle stopped. No sound except the girls crying in fear. "Only one leak, that's easy. Got any water?"

One held up an empty bottle.

"Crap." The suction on his hand hurt. He pulled his hand off and yanked his fly open. A stream of urine splashed messily around the leak. Some was on target. Most bubbled away. Enough froze to seal the leak with an irregular block of ice. Quiet fell again. "Um, sorry," Billy said over his shoulder as he refastened. "Only idea I came up with."

The brown-haired girl muttered, "I thought boys thinking with it was an *expression.*"

***

The cabins by the hatch to the hold were both empty. Captain Schwartzenberger waited in the starboard one, feet and shoulders braced in a corner. He aimed his pistol at the latch side of the cabin hatch. He heard the deck hatch unbolt. A great whoosh as corridor air escaped into the hold. Then the hatch rebolting. A few magnetic footsteps. A creak as the other cabin's hatch opened.

The captain pulled his hatch open and braced himself on the rim. The intruder held a mirror to peer around the hatch into the right-hand cabin. Schwartzenberger fired half a dozen shots into the back of his head. The lead bullets blasted the dark grey paint off the gleaming armor of the helmet. The intruder back-kicked the captain off his perch, sending him spinning into the middle of the cabin.

A marksmanship instructor's mocking voice echoed in his head. "*Always* aim for the center of mass." Schwartzenberger tried a couple of shots as he spun. Neither came close. He landed well on the far wall but the intruder had followed too closely for him to get a shot off. The captain blocked a punch to his face but an arm bone broke under the suited fist. A kick to the knee was even more painful. The intruder dodged a left-hand punch then slammed his hand into the side of Schwartzenberger's head.

Blackness.

***

Bobbie and John waited in the captain's cabin, feet braced on his bed. She was amazed at how cheerful she felt. It must be the familiarity of it. John ran her through a hide and ambush drill at least twice a month. If she could hit the pop-up target before he put three holes in it there'd be ice cream. Lately he'd been threatening to change it to two holes.

She almost fired as the hatch opened. Nothing was visible in the gap. Then some fingers grabbed the edge, a mirror mounted to their back. Bobbie's shot missed. John missed the fingers but shattered the mirror. They vanished, then flicked back into view as they threw something into the cabin.

Bobbie couldn't see what it was, just John's back as he sprang to intercept. He grabbed, cocked his arm to throw, the grenade went off. His body went limply across the cabin. The concussion shook Bobbie but she had drilled in far worse condition than this.

The intruder came through the hatch, still using the magnetic boots to maneuver. John had trained her to aim for the least armored part of her target. The first bullet into the faceplate sent cracks from top to bottom. She emptied the magazine before the intruder could reach her.

The faceplate was almost pure white in the center, spider webs of cracks going to the edge.

Bobbie kicked away, reloading as she soared across the cabin. The intruder turned slowly, looking for her out the corners of the faceplate. She grabbed a shelf and steadied herself. This time she aimed for the heart. She saw the bullets make holes in the suit. The intruder jumped for her. Bobbie leapt, not fast enough. A hand grabbed her ankle painfully hard. It swung her through the air. Her head struck the deck. The gun flew out of her hand. "That hurt, bitch." The intruder swung her again. This time she went limp.

The intruder released her and took a tube from a belt pouch. A dollop of goo went into each bullet hole on his chest. Then he began a search of Bobbie's body. Once a magazine, knife and lipstick were removed he stuffed her into a heavy-duty bubble.

***

Mitchie followed the battle by sound. Gunshots and hatches slamming were audible. The grenade rattled the bridge. When the shots stopped and more hatches slammed she assumed the worst. Bing had reported she and Billy were trapped in the hold. Captain Schwartzenberger had ditched his handcomm before setting up his ambush. Clearly he hadn't succeeded. That left her.

By the time the hatch to the hold closed Mitchie had her suit on and the bridge almost depressurized. One window panel had its edges painted red. She carefully armed the explosive bolts and yanked the emergency release. The panel flew point-first into the ice and stuck. She took a deep breath and listened for leaks in her suit. Not a single whistle or squeak. She pushed the maneuvering pack out the hole and followed after.

Her goal was to zip past the kidnapper and cut his suit open. Right now she was on the step of the plan before that: "Don't let him see you and shoot you." The chasm was only starlit so she should be safe as long as she clung to the ice. She crept around the hull to where she could just peek at the shattered cargo hold window.

The red emergency lights shone out through the window. The remaining shards of transparent aluminum refracted the light in bright beams across the ice. One shadow moved. A little study resolved it as a spacesuit holding a rescue bubble under one arm. He shuffled across the floor on magboots. Every dozen or so steps he would stop and turn back and forth in place.

Mitchie crept slowly over the ice sticking to the deepest shadows. More of the hold came into view. The tents and a few emergency bubbles still held pressure. Hopefully all the passengers had survived. She froze as the intruder approached the window. He faced her in clear line of sight. He turned back and forth in place then moved a few meters along the window.

This time as he turned around a light shone clear on his faceplate. *Blind!* thought Mitchie. The intruder needed to turn to see out the edges of the cracked faceplate. He couldn't see where he was going. Mitchie sheathed her utility blade. A new plan was bubbling up.

The intruder had found the biggest gap in the window. He broke his boots loose from the deck with a hop then gave a puff of maneuvering jets to float through the gap. Once clear of the ship he started twisting about, trying to get a good look at the chasm walls. Mitchie didn't bother firing her maneuvering pack. *Bobbie first.* She leapt hard, slamming into the intruder, and knocking the bubble out of his grasp. The bubble floated up toward the stars.

The intruder wrapped arms and legs around Mitchie painfully hard. She fired her thrusters on full.

Transparent aluminum achieved its optical properties by forming a single huge crystal. Instead of a fog bank, bouncing light among the droplets, it was an aquarium tank letting photons go straight through. When fractured it split along the planes of the crystal. The edges produced were single lines of aluminum atoms. TAl instruments were widely used in surgery.

The intruder groped for a hold on Mitchie's arm while she steered him onto one of the window shards. The arms flung wide as the tip pierced the propellant tank on his back. Mitchie kept her thrusters on until the tip came through the intruder's chest and punctured her suit.

She stopped thrust and kicked away from the ship. A red circle appeared on the crazed-white faceplate. Another overlapped it a few seconds later.

Mitchie looked down at her belt pouch. Her hands shook too much to get it open. She pushed her left hand onto her chest, quieting but not eliminating the hiss of escaping air. The other finally got the pouch open. She bounced off the chasm wall. Her right hand pulled the sealant tube out. Trying to take the cap off without releasing the pressure on the leak sent the tube spinning off. Catching it took both hands. She panted frantically trying to fill her lungs from the thinning air. First glob of sealant bounced off the suit. Second was in place. She smeared it flat. Blessed silence. Another squeeze of sealant to thicken it. Air still felt thin. She twisted the oxygen valve. A cold breeze blew on her cheek. Mitchie took deep breaths, feeling her pulse slow.

The intruder's faceplate was solid red. His limbs swayed limply. Mitchie looked away, scanning the chasm for Bobbie's bubble. She headed up the wall, waving her flashlight about in hopes of seeing a reflection.

***

The hold was calm now. Bing had used a pair of magnets to roll her bubble over to the suit locker. She could pop her bubble, open the locker, grab out her suit, slide it on, and seal it up in . . . about sixty seconds. Which is about how long it would take to pass out from hypoxia. And assuming that a full body case of vacbite wouldn't slow her down. So she just waited, rehearsing how to do it without any missed steps, hoping someone else would come along in a suit before her bubble's air ran low.

Professor Tsugawa was in his pressure tent. He also had a bubble with him so he had plenty of air available. He kept worrying about his data. The observatory was vacuum-rated but he had no idea how well it stood up to the explosion. One of those gunshots would have completely destroyed it. He couldn't see it from the window of his tent. Without that data this whole trip would have been a waste. Part of him felt guilty that he wasn't worried about the lives at risk from the violence. But he was just an innocent bystander and no one else was going to worry about the data.

Billy's improvised leak seal still held tight. Other things in the big tent were less stable. "I know that, and you know that, but the captain said you're underage, so the age on this ship is higher than that! Stay at your damn end of the tent."

Bing had twisted her bubble around until she could look over the rest of the hold. The intruder looked very dead on that spike. She wondered how that'd happened. Two tents were occupied and a couple of rescue bubbles floated loose in the hold. She'd seen all three grad students donning bubbles when the blow-out happened. Hopefully the third was safe in the chasm. She suppressed a vision of a bubble drifting against a window shard and being blown about by air escaping from the cut.

"Mitchie to *Fives Full*. Anyone there?"

Bing grasped her handcomm. "Bing here. How are you? Where are you?"

"I'm outside. No injuries." *If you don't count some vacbite to the chest.* "I have Bobbie, she's unconscious."

"Good. Someone took out the intruder. I don't know what's up with Mussa."

Guo broke in. "I took Musha out. Lower deck is shafe now."

"You're alive!" cried Bing. "You sound like hell."

"Jusht woozy," answered Guo. "It'sh wearing off."

"Is the lower airlock working?" asked Mitchie.

"Yesh."

"Anybody else around?" broadcast Bing.

"I'm here, fine, with two uninjured passengers," reported Billy.

"Good. Captain, are you out there?" asked Bing. No reply.

Guo waited in the corridor as the inner airlock door opened. Mitchie handed him the bubble before taking off her helmet. She studied him for a moment. His face had a huge red blotch on one cheek surrounding a small scab. "What'd the guy do to you?"

The mechanic shrugged. "Had a dart pistol. Got me in the face as I told him he wasn't allowed down here. So I woke up strapped down in my acc couch. Idiot had no idea there were extra release buttons. I waited until he was distracted, popped the straps, and let him have it with a wrench."

When they reached the converter room Mitchie saw Mussa tied up in a corner. The wrench had clearly been a 5cm crow's foot. The dent in the thug's skull was so large she was surprised he was still breathing.

"Let's see what she needs." Guo unzipped the bubble. Bobbie was limp but had strong breathing and pulse. "Pupils aren't bad. Mild concussion at most." He took a drugpatch from the first aid kit and applied it to her neck.

"Did you give Mussa anything?" asked Mitchie.

"Fuck no."

"Well, we don't want him dying before he confesses. The other guy isn't talking." She grabbed another patch out of the kit and applied to it Mussa.

"Hey, he could've waited until we had a headcount. We don't know how many other injured we've got." Mitchie ignored Guo while checking Mussa's restraints. The mechanic had used fuel wire on the wrists and ankles. Looked like he'd cut circulation off to the hands. That didn't bother her.

Bobbie started coughing. Guo handed her a waterbulb. She sucked it dry before trying to talk. "Is John okay? Have you seen him? He was hurt bad in the fight."

"No, I'm sorry, we haven't had time to look for him. We just got you back," answered Mitchie.

"Please look for him! It was bad. He might not have much longer if he doesn't get help." The girl teared up.

"Well, you're stable here, I'll see what I can do," said Mitchie.

Guo strapped the first aid kit onto her suit as she put her helmet back on. He followed her to the airlock.

"Take care of her, okay? She's just a kid."

Guo smiled. "Don't worry. I'll keep an eye on her. You be careful."

Mitchie's first stop was the hold. She got Bing's suit out of the locker and put it and the first mate's bubble in the hold airlock. Then she went outside again to enter through the upper airlock. No evidence of the struggle was visible in the corridor. She checked the captain's cabin first.

John's body spun as it drifted. There was no need to check for signs of life. The stun grenade had visibly crushed his ribcage. He must have died instantly. She braced herself against the hatch and gave the body a parade ground salute.

There was no sign of the captain in his cabin. Bing's across the hall was also empty of life. She looked in the unused cabins by the hatch to the hold next. Schwartzenberger was unconscious but breathing strongly. Mitchie applied a drug patch to him and strapped him down in the bed. She reported in to Bing.

The mate had finished a headcount of the passengers—all fine except for missing one student. "I'll come take care of Alois. Leave the kit there. You get to the bridge and see if we've got any more visitors coming."

"Aye-aye." Mitchie headed back out the airlock. The window panel she'd blasted free from the bridge had stuck in the chasm wall. Some fiddling and scraping got her and it both on the inside of the bridge. She put it against the window frame and started liberally applying sealant goo. With her own tube and the one Captain Schwartzenberger had opened to deal with the cannon shot holes she had barely enough. The surviving tube went into her pouch. She gave the stuff ten minutes to harden then started up the air vents. She felt her suit relax around her as the pressure went up.

Once there was a full atmosphere in place it only took her a few moments to work up the nerve to take the helmet off. Her improvised seal held. Not that she'd want to take it through an atmosphere. Or put more than a few gravs on it. She turned to the comm console and activated the guard channel. "Any ships, any ships, this is *Fives Full* requesting assistance. Repeat, *Fives Full* is requesting assistance. Mayday, mayday, mayday."

A Demeter-accented voice answered immediately. "*Fives Full*, this FNS *Assaye*, here in response to your distress call. Please relay your coordinates."

"Navy, we are on an uncharted rock. Approximate coordinates . . ." she reeled off the numbers from the plotting table. "We require medical and engineering assistance. Also we're missing a rescue bubble, please watch for a beacon. Um, there may be a hostile ship out there as well."

"Roger, *Fives*. How many casualties do you have?"

"Two dead, five injured." She used her handcomm to let the rest of the crew know help was on the way.

"*Fives*, we've been asked to check on the status of your special passenger."

No mystery who that was. "Injured, stable, receiving care, in safe place."

"Thank you, *Fives Full*. We expect to rendezvous in two hours."

"Looking forward to seeing you, *Assaye*."

***

"Sorry, folks, he needs a few more minutes," apologized the corpsman second class. His comment that the captain was "almost ready to unbox" had brought the whole crew over to the autodoc.

Mitchie eased back from the huddle to look around the cargo hold. The Navy had been overjoyed at a chance to put its damage control training to work. A pressure tent had been put up over the shattered window. Welders were slicing off the shards of transparent aluminum. The observatory was gone. Tsugawa had talked his way onto a cruiser detailed to search the area for any possible accomplice ships.

"Here he comes!" called the corpsman.

The top of the autodoc folded open. Schwartzenberger woke up. A glance took in his waiting crew. "I guess the good guys won," he croaked.

Bing offered a squeeze bottle of water and quickly brought him up to speed on events.

Bobbie shyly picked her way along the deck as she approached the crew. An older Navy man followed her. The captain saw her coming. "Hello, Bobbie. Good to see you looking so well." That was a relative 'well.' Bobbie's eyes were red from crying. Guo had broken the news as gently as he could but she still took John's death hard.

She flushed. "Thank you, captain. I'm glad you're feeling better. And thank you—and your crew—for everything you did for me."

"Just doing our duty."

The Navy man broke in. "Sir, I'm Lieutenant Commander Trevayne, master of the *Assaye*. We're truly impressed with how you stood up to that pirate. Absolutely outstanding work. Nothing left for us to do except clean up." He gestured at the welding team. "We're trying to do what we can for you."

"I appreciate that, Commander. It's been a rough day." Schwartzenberger started questioning Guo about the state of repairs. The mechanic was confident they could be on their way in less than a day. The Navy officer chimed in with more offers of help.

A rating came in through the airlock and bounded over to the captain's group. "Sir, secure message came in." He held out a blank sheet to his commander.

"Thank you, Moxley." Trevayne moved off to read it. His thumbprint produced a single line of text. "Huh. Miss Smith? This is actually a message for you."

Bobbie floated over and took the sheet. Her thumb filled the sheet with text. She turned to read it privately. As she reached the end she snarled, "Stupid romantic bastard." She looked up and blushed as she realized how many stares her outburst had drawn. "Sorry. I was surprised. John listed me as his next of kin." A blink sent a tear out into the hold. "Can we bury him here?"

"I think the investigation might require—" began Lt. Cdr. Trevayne.

"Yes," said Captain Schwartzenberger. "Guo, we'll need a shovel." The mechanic nodded.

Mitchie offered, "My suit should stretch enough to fit Bobbie."

"Good. She should be there." A wave sent pilot and passenger to the suit locker.

Forty minutes later Mitchie watched the burial party from the bridge. Billy and Guo had carved a notch in the side of the chasm. Trevayne had brought a squad of marines from his ship. Schwartzenberger and Bingrong carried John's corpse, wrapped in a thermal blanket. Bobbie followed them. The pilot spent the wait shelving. The captain had gone through all his reference books without finding an appropriate prayer.

The mourners tucked the body gently into the hole. Schwartzenberger floated by the head. The rest formed flanking lines. He began, "Let us pray. We brought nothing into this world and it is certain we will take nothing out. We have gathered to commit our brother John to the sky. Let us remember his sacrifice as we prepare to join with him in the resurrection of all. The Lord giveth and the Lord taketh away. Blessed be the name of the Lord. Amen." When the captain finished the marine sergeant gestured sharply to his squad. The laser rifles blasted puffs of steam off the opposite wall. Then twice more.

When the steam dissipated Guo and Billy began shoving ice in the grave. When it was as full as they could make it the marines applied some low-power shots to melt it all together. After a respectful pause the Navy contingent headed back to their ship. The captain led the gravediggers back to theirs.

Bobbie had anchored herself next to the grave. She sat facing it, hands clasped together. Bing floated behind her, waiting. Finally the first mate moved up to touch helmets. Mitchie wished Bing had used the suit radios instead. Not that hearing their conversation would be of much use to her. When they started back to the ship Mitchie left the bridge. Bobbie would need help getting out of the suit.

By the time *Fives Full* was ready to fly Bobbie was the only passenger left on board. Tsugawa was on the survey cruiser with his observatory and two grad students. The third student had been found after fourteen hours in empty space, sedated, and returned to Demeter aboard a Navy courier. The courier also carried Bobbie's friends, whose parents wanted them home immediately. The courier had apparently been arranged by "friends of Daddy" but Bobbie declined a ride on it.

Lt. Cdr. Trevayne had objected. "Miss, I think it would be best if you returned home on an armed vessel for your security."

"Really?" answered Bobbie. "You think putting me on one of your ships would be the safest thing for me?"

"Of course," said the naval officer. "You'd have armed personnel with full background checks around you."

"No offense, Commander, but the crew of this ship passed a better check than anything the Navy can do. For all I know half your crew is just waiting for an opportunity to mutiny and grab me. I can trust Captain Schwartzenberger and his crew. I don't know your crew."

Trevayne's jaw tightened. He took a few deep breaths before speaking again. "Miss Smith, I really must insist that you . . ." He was speaking to empty air. Bobbie had bounced across the hold. Trevayne turned to Schwartzenberger, who'd been listening intently. "Can't you make her see reason?"

A merchant 'Captain' didn't outrank a Navy officer, but Schwartzenberger addressed Trevayne as if he was a midshipman. "No. She's reasoning clearer than you are. She has the right to make her own decisions. And I have an obligation to take her home." He shifted to a friendlier tone. "Thank you very much for all your help getting us ready to steam again. Is there anything I can do for you before you return to your ship?"

"No," said Trevayne. "We're all good. I will escort your ship on the return to Demeter."

"We'll be happy to have the company." Captain Schwartzenberger accompanied him to the airlock.

Demeter System. Acceleration 10 m/s^2

The captain put Bobbie in one of the unused cabins after a little fixing up. Bing took another—hers would need a shipyard to be livable again. Bobbie seemed willing to spend the whole trip holed up in her room. Billy delivered breakfast and lunch to the bridge, converter room, and Bobbie's cabin. Twelve hours into the trip Captain Schwartzenberger declared the ship stable enough to cruise unsupervised again. Dinner would be an all-hands event.

Bobbie was last to arrive, escorted by Bing. By the look on the first mate's face no physical force had been needed to pry the girl out of her room, just lots of browbeating. The passenger was seated at the end of the table, opposite the captain. All the food waited on the counter. A bottle of whiskey sat in the middle of the table. Mitchie filled the shot glasses in front of the late arrivals. Bobbie said, "I can't drink that, I'm too young."

The captain smiled. "On Demeter, you're too young. On this ship, I set the rules, and you're old enough." He stood and raised his glass. "Ladies and gentlemen, I give you John Smith."

"John Smith," echoed the crew. They drank. Bobbie managed to not spill any.

"I didn't know John Smith well," began Schwartzenberger. "In most ways I didn't know him at all. What I do know is his devotion to duty, and to the young woman he'd sworn to protect." The bottle went around the table again. "In all my dealings with him he was focused on that duty. Which is admirable. But many men do that well. What distinguishes John is that he was faced with more than doing his duty. When that moment came, he did not flinch, he did not beg, he did not freeze, he did not hesitate, he just did what he needed to do." He paused, swallowed. "Greater love hath no man. I pray that such a cup never be brought before any of us. And I pray that if such a one does come to me, that I should have even half the strength he did." He raised his glass again. "John Smith." They drank.

The captain sat. Bobbie took a deep breath to gather herself and stood up. "I knew John about as well as anyone. Which wasn't much. He wouldn't talk about his past. Said people who knew too much about him kept dying and he wasn't having any more of that. But he spent more time with me than anyone since . . . since I was—for years. He tried to teach me to survive, and to be a grown-up. And if I'd learned he'd still be alive."

Bing reached out and put a hand on Bobbie's arm. "Honey, you can't blame yourself." Bobbie shook her off.

"Patterns. That was John's biggest lesson on defense. Never make patterns. We'd always go and leave at different times. Take a different route each way even if it meant going an hour out of our way. Practice different drills. But I didn't learn the lesson and I killed him."

Mitchie passed her a cloth.

Bobbie wiped her eyes. "Three years ago I made Daddy rent out a planetarium for me and my friends. Next year it was a visiting astronomy professor—one of Tsugawa's colleagues, actually. Last year he built an orrery in the garden. So this year, Daddy's asking himself what to get the astronomy nut who has everything. And there's a giftwrapped answer, a tour. Security investigated you, and the company, and you're all clean. Because you weren't the trap." She waved the flimsy she'd gotten yesterday. "Malachi's disappeared so we can't ask him where the tourism idea came from. We just know it was set to catch me because I had that pattern." She looked up. "I'm sorry, John. I won't have a pattern again. And I won't look at the sky except to look at your grave. Good-bye, John." She snatched up her refilled glass and drank.

"John Smith," chorused the crew as they drank. The captain gave a nod to Billy. He and Guo stood and began filling plates. Bobbie fell into her seat and cried into her hands. Billy served her first. Chicken, gravy, and biscuits, chosen as comfort food. She'd never had it before. After a few bites taken out of good manners she found it comforting enough to finish.

***

Mitchie was pleased with her docking at the orbital shipyard. *Fives Full* was down a few thrusters but she'd still matched the coupling as gentle as a kiss. Captain Schwartzenberger wanted to get repairs dirtside to save money, but with two turbines out on the same side (one crushed in the chasm, the other cored out by a cannon shot they hadn't even noticed at the time) they couldn't even try to land.

Waiting for them were a squad of marines and several tough-looking civilians. After Bobbie went off with them a couple of shipyard staff emerged. The account director took Captain Schwartzenberger to his office to discuss the repairs. A clerk passed Bing a stack of loaner datasheets and asked if any supplies were needed. She declined and went back to the ship to do some research.

The captain returned a few hours later. The crew were gathered in the galley. Mitchie read letters from home. Billy listened to the latest music (on earphones, at Bing's insistence). Guo caught up on the news. Schwartzenberger greeted Bing first. "So who was our guest?"

"No idea," she answered. "Turns out the fashionable thing for the rich folk here is to hire gossip writers to tell lies about them. That's according to the gossips who deny being on the take. But they all accuse each other of taking money under the table. So there's so much BS out there I can't figure out who little Bobbie is."

"I guess I should have expected that. Gotta love the Fusion. You can get a chemical analysis of your neighbor every time he takes a piss but anybody you really want to know about is obscured."

"That's the Fusion," answered Bing. "So, can we afford to get fixed?"

"Repairs won't cost us a key. Seems they get a subsidy to do work for the Navy . . . but the Navy isn't using this month's slot so we can have their repair slip for free. There's a converter they had in storage too long, an MC897, so they're replacing ours with it so they don't get hit with inventory tax. They have no Disconnect compatible turbines in stock so we're getting ones taken off a Navy ship booked as scrap. And so on."

"So why are you so unhappy?" asked the mate.

"It's . . . creepy. There's no one in the system authorizing it. They all just appear as if it's perfectly obvious and no one had to make a decision. We tried tracing back some of the decision trees but the director got cold feet. Said he didn't want to know any more if it was all that anonymous." Bing gave him a patient look. "And, dammit, it's all in-kind so I can't squeeze a copper out of them." A chuckle ran around the table. "Anyway. Guo, check out the specs on that 897 before I let them install it."

"Don't have to, Skipper," replied the mechanic. "That's been at the top of my wish list since I came on board. It's a huge jump in efficiency. Much stabler waste products. Heck, we could start buying iridium for power fuel."

"Seriously?" asked Bing. "I thought you still wanted kids."

"An 897 will eat iridium and just give out direct current and some stable isotopes of iron. None of this short-halflife crap our current converter puts out if we don't feed it just right."

"Okay, we'll take it," said the captain. "Huh. What's the odds they'd have something that sweet sitting around?"

"Well . . . it's Disconnect-compatible gear. Fusion ships would buy the version with lots of readouts and integrated controls. 897s just have some analog dials and manual controls." Guo wasn't convincing himself with that.

"Wouldn't cost much to refit. I'll just chalk it up to our fairy godmother." He made sure he had everyone's attention "We'll have shore leave while the repairs are being done. I'll have a couple of crew meetings planetside, you'll get advance notice, but stay on twelve-hour recall. Oh, and the Navy wants each of us to go to their hospital for a check-up after that unpleasantness. That's free so be sure to ask about any coughs or moles you've noticed."

***

Mitchie didn't want to deal with the Navy any more than she had to. After a second reminder showed up on her sheet she decided it would be less suspicious to go. Demeter had a more efficient military than most. In a few hours she was in an examining room watching a doctor fiddle with 3-D displays of her insides. "No physical trauma. Good health overall." He paused. "How old are you?"

"Twenty-five," answered Mitchie.

"Huh."

"I grew up on Akiak, in a rural area," she explained. "It's a rough place to live."

"Ah. Well, there's nothing that needs repair. So we can talk upgrades. There's a lot that's covered by the citizen stipend. I can give you an immuno-monitor or basic comm implant."

"I'm a Disconnected Worlds citizen."

"Oh, I'm sorry. When I saw the coverage I assumed you'd been granted residency." The doctor went through the list again. "There's an upgrade we give to Marines, bone reinforcements. It's purely structural so it wouldn't matter that you're living outside the network."

"I don't think I'd get much benefit from that," said Mitchie. Which was also what she felt about the doctor. She still had to suffer through some diet and exercise recommendations before she could escape.

FIVES FULL
BRIDGE DECK

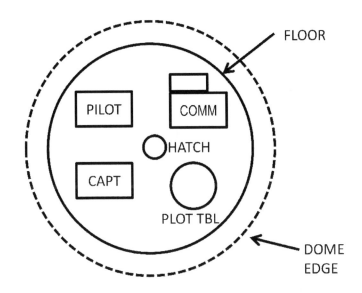

Fives Full Bridge Deck

Interlude One

MS *Barito*, Near Akiak, acceleration 0 m/s²

Pete floated through the hatch without bumping the rim. A month ago he hadn't thought he'd ever be that graceful in free fall. Now he'd mastered it just in time to be grounded again.

"Take a look," said Agum from the pilot's couch. "Your new home." Akiak filled the bridge windows, its daylight side dazzlingly bright.

"Wow," said Pete. "It looks like someone painted an Easter egg and didn't let go of the ends." The planet's equatorial belt was a band of green and blue between the massive icecaps.

Agum laughed. "The story is two terraforming ships arrived here at once. They argued whether it could actually be terraformed. First ship bet a ton of antimatter it could do it. Second one left and came back thirty years later. It looked over Akiak, gave the first ship half a ton, and left without a word."

"Ha! Yeah, it's on the edge. I'm surprised they have room for more immigrants."

"The ice shrinks a little each year."

MS *Barito*, Akiak, gravity 10.3 m/s²

"Pete!" yelled Hatta. "You're clear to off-board."

"Finally." Pete started gathering up the cleaning brushes and bucket.

"Leave that, I'll have to finish the job later."

"Sorry,"

"Nah, you've done good. I don't think the ship was this clean when she came from the builders. Grab your bag and meet the captain at the mid airlock."

"Aye-aye." Pete had already packed his duffle in a fit of optimism this morning. He shouldered it and headed for the ladder. Hatta followed.

A stranger in a dark suit stood with the captain. The rest of the crew spread out through the corridor. "Mr. Smith," said the captain, stepping forward to shake Pete's hand. "We'll be leaving you here. I want to thank

you for all your hard work. You've been good company on this trip."
The rest of the crew gathered around offering handshakes, backslaps, and
a mighty hug from Otto the mechanic.

Agum stepped forward, holding a small bag. "We don't want you
starving your first week there so we all chipped in our pocket change."
Pete stammered thanks as he took the heavy bag. Agum leaned in to
whisper, "Cap'n put in gold."

After some more farewells the suit led Pete off the ship. "Party's
over," said the captain. "Rig for cargo handling."

"Already?" said Hatta.

"Michigan's friend has some ore he needs moved."

Primary Starport, Akiak, gravity 10.3 m/s^2

The suit had confined his conversation to making sure Pete
understood the difference between the different coins in his bag.
Apparently the frontier vids got that one right. When they arrived in the
Immigrant Lobby the suit pointed him at the receptionist and walked off
without a word.

"Hi! Are you immigrating?" said the young woman at the left-hand
desk. The room had ten desks along one wall and more than two
hundred seats in back-to-back rows. Wordy posters covered the walls.
The two of them were the only people there.

"Yes. Yes I am," said Pete. He sat down in the chair by her desk.

"What's your name?"

"Peter Smith."

"You can take all the time you need to think of one, no need to make
a snap decision."

"No, that's my real name."

"Oh. Well, this is Akiak. You can pick whatever you want for your
name. We don't care what you went by elsewhere."

"Um. I'll stick with it. Peter Smith."

The receptionist gave a tiny shrug and typed it in. Pete realized the
keyboard had to be physical. He didn't have a display to see a shared
virtual overlay with.

"Date of birth?" She extracted all the information a triage nurse would want. There weren't any questions about his non-medical history. Soon she handed him a small card. "This gives you basic access to the public library network. Don't use your password on that for any private system. Welcome to Akiak, Probationary Citizen Smith."

"That's it?"

"Yes, you're done. I recommend taking some time to read the posters before you go. They're written by recent immigrants so there's a lot of practical advice."

"Thank you." He started with the one titled 'NEVER BREAK A PROMISE.'

***

The starport's main entrance had benches outside. Pete sat as the culture shock slammed into him. He'd expected the naked feeling of not having a HUD to explain things to him. But the differences were obvious to the naked eye.

Pedestrians kept almost bumping into each on the sidewalk. One pair did collide, elbow brushing purse. They kept walking, muttering "excuse me" over their shoulders. No sign of an Anti-Social Contact Warning lighting up on their HUDs.

Some people didn't bother with HUDs. Pete saw a man put a HUD on, check something, then put it back in his pocket. The voluntary isolation shocked him.

The street traffic looked as chaotic as the sidewalk but they didn't hit each other. He kept watching until he picked out which occupants operated their vehicles on manual and which left the vehicle in control. The ones on manual pushed the limits of the autocars to squeeze ahead but gave each other plenty of room.

So much dangerous behavior and no arrests being made. His head hurt.

His stomach hurt too. Hunger finally pried Pete off the bench. He'd taken six copper coins out of the bag before stashing it in his duffle (per the "Avoid Petty Crime" poster). It was time to find out how much food they'd buy.

A thick sandwich and mug of beer only cost four of them. Pete ate slowly, appreciating the taste of the beef. *Barito's* crew had fed him well but all he could taste was the spices.

His table had a small display reading "Dine-Net. Free to customers. No login required." Job listings were a top level menu item. Pete typed in the name of his favorite programming language. A dozen listings came up. All were Fusion immigrants offering to work for free to prove themselves.

He chewed another bit of his sandwich. He'd kept telling himself not to count on getting professional work but it still hurt to feel the hope die. Fortunately he had another skill.

Typing in "Cleaning" brought up pages of listings. The first one was titled "SILVER IN YOUR HAND FIRST DAY." *Well, it might take a long time to save up for a programming rig, but I won't starve.*

FIVES FULL
MAIN DECK

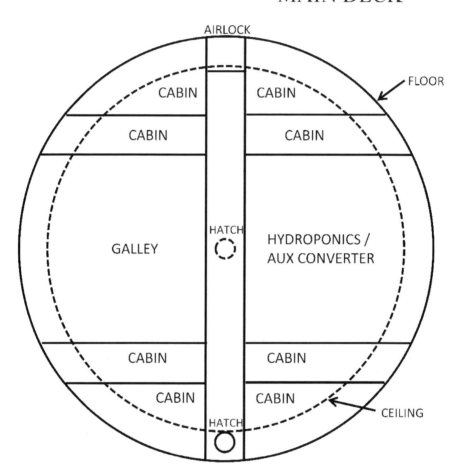

Fives Full Main Deck

Part Two: Kitty Chow

Planet Demeter. Gravity 7.5 m/s^2

In three months on Lapis Mitchie had never explored the dance clubs. She'd decided to correct that on Demeter. Billy had promised to play tour guide. An autocab had picked him up just outside the spaceport with the message "A young lady wishes to see you." Mitchie couldn't hold it against him but she still missed him as she entered the chaos of the club.

Getting a drink and a table with a good view was easy. Figuring out the dynamics of the club wasn't. Billy had mentioned people researching each other on the dance floor. The concept was so opposed to Disconnected Worlds life that he'd dropped it with "it makes more sense when you see it." She could spot the virtual activity by its effects. Two strangers got up, met on the dance floor, then left together.

Mitchie decided to give the local style a try. A bland-looking man danced by himself at the edge of the dance floor. The datasheet identified him as Jaime Sienta, 33 years old. He lived a few klicks away. Worked as a "data integrity consultant," whatever that meant. No criminal record, just a typical set of traffic and privacy violation offenses. Clean finances. No current legal partner. Looking into his social and reputation networks showed no current romantic partner. He'd had a dozen of various degrees of seriousness over the years. The last had dumped him eight months back. Investigating that found a quote from the ex describing him as "sweet, but boring." She'd quickly acquired a new partner. He'd taken it less well, lying low for a couple of months, then taking a high workload assignment. He'd just started having an active social life again in the past month.

"Hello, mysterious lady." Mitchie looked up to see her research subject standing in front of her. He placed another daiquiri next to her almost empty one.

Oh, crap, she thought. *He got a ping from my searches.* She put on a friendly smile.

"What's a Disconnect spacer doing here?" Sienta asked.

"Just checking out the exotic native customs," she answered.

"Was that your answer for Demeter or just the club?"

"The club. But Demeter's pretty exotic too. It's so *crowded.*"

"Why did you come to our crowded planet then?"

"A job. Somebody needed some big cargo hauled here and we needed to get paid."

"Why did a little ship like yours get a big cargo? I'd think that would go on one of those huge freightliners."

Realizing this stranger had already looked up the *Fives Full* set Mitchie even more on edge. It took work to maintain a cheerful tone as she explained how the liners insisted on standard container sizes to let them make their turnaround times, leaving oddball cargo to the tramp ships like hers.

"How long a turnaround are you—" Sienta cut himself off. Mitchie saw his glasses flicker with something new being displayed. "Shucks. My client just called me in. Lousy timing. That's the price of being a free-lancer." He presented her with his contact info and dashed off to "piss on the fire."

Mitchie sipped the drink he'd bought her—certified as the same contents as before by the bar tracking system—and tried to wrap her head around what had happened. She couldn't remember the last time she'd had so little control over a conversation. An alert popped up on her datasheet. She opened it, expecting an order from her captain.

TO ASSOCIATES OF JAIME SIENTA, it began. BE ADVISED HE HAS BEEN EXPOSED TO VIRUS WHB05749. MONITOR YOURSELF FOR SYMPTOMS. SEEK MEDICAL ATTENTION IF YOU MAY BE INFECTED. Mitchie burst out laughing. Sienta's work emergency was just a feeble excuse to cover for having gotten his disease warning. Curious what venereal diseases were a problem in the Fusion, Mitchie researched the virus and how Sienta was exposed. It turned out to be one of the few surviving strains of the common cold. *They sent out a disease vector warning because the poor guy got sneezed on? Fuzies are so paranoid.*

That tipped the balance. Mitchie left the club and started walking back to the hostel. She wanted a guide the next time she went dancing.

***

Guo arrived a little early for the crew meeting. The purpose wasn't specified. Once he saw the address was for a firing range he stopped wondering. Mitchie was already there. She waved him over. "Is this a normal thing for this ship?" she asked.

"No, new on me. But the captain always prepares for disasters. You should see the fire suppression gear in the hold."

"There was a fire on the ship?"

"Not this one, his last one. Bad cargo. He got all the crew off but couldn't save the ship. Hit him hard—it was a big ship, four times the size of *Fives Full*, and he was half-owner. If you ever see him in shorts he's got burn scars on—" Guo cut off as the captain and mate came into the lobby. They made small talk for a few minutes. The mechanic touted the Demeter Opera's new show to everyone. Bing let them know how the repairs were progressing. Finally Billy arrived, sporting a black eye and some cheek abrasions.

"Oh, no! Did someone set you up with that car ride?" exclaimed Mitchie.

"Nope, that was exactly was I thought it was," said Billy with a grin. "The wear and tear are from when her parents caught up with us." He clearly had no regrets over it.

Schwartzenberger decided to ignore his deckhand's misadventure. "I don't think we'll ever face a situation like that boarder again. But there's other hazards out there. Ships have been hijacked or had their cargos stolen. So I've decided we're going to be better prepared the next time someone attacks us." A salesman had come up holding several cases. "We'll have weapons for each of us and armor-piercing ammunition." The salesman started a demo on how to use mechanical sights and unpowered ammo. Apparently some locals liked to try out such exotic and tightly-restricted items. The *Fives Full's* crew was all Disconnect-bred so the captain hurried the salesman past the theory and got everyone into the firing range. The rangemaster handed them each a pistol. An instructor ushered the salesman out and took over making sure everyone knew the basics. The employees ignored Mitchie—she'd arrived an hour early and they'd already learned she didn't need any help.

Once Schwartzenberger had gotten a feel for his new weapon—larger than the one that had failed him against the boarder—he switched to the armor-piercing ammo. Twenty rounds later he was content that the ammo wouldn't behave differently than the practice rounds. He looked over the rest of the crew. Billy had some holes in the bullseye, others outside the rings completely. Bing was being tutored by the instructor. Guo plugged away with a slow rate of fire. Mitchie—"Where'd you get that gun?"

"I picked it out earlier. I can afford it, I've got some savings."

"You don't need to buy your own, we're getting weapons for the crew." Mitchie put down the one she'd been firing, picked up the pistol the captain had picked, and pivoted her body away from the firing line so he could see her hold on it. About a third of the grip stuck out below the edge of her hand. "Right. Well, is that one working well for you? Never mind." The target for her lane had a tight cluster of marks in the center. The hologram had blue and green spots indicating where two or three bullets had gone through the same place. "I'll add that one to the ship buy. Unless you really want it out of pocket?"

Mitchie chuckled. "You're not paying me that much, sir. It can be issue gear." She went back to firing the small pistol. Schwartzenberger went off to find the salesman and argue him into applying the group discount to the non-overstock gun.

Guo leaned over from his lane. "Were you a sniper or something?" he asked her.

"It's called real shooting, city boy. Rabbits don't have those three and four rings around them so you can say 'I got close.' You have to actually hit them."

"Arsenic Creek is not a 'city.'" He put another round into the four ring.

"If you see three houses at once my family calls it a city." She watched Guo's next two shots. "Mind your breathing."

"I know how to control my breathing."

"Yeah, but you're not doing it. You need to get the sights and focus and breathing and trigger control all together. You're only doing two at a time." The mechanic grunted. Mitchie coached him through a few more shots until he regularly put them in the center ring. "Okay, now make sure you have the sights absolutely straight on." That shot went to the bottom edge of the four ring. "See, you can't just concentrate on one and forget the rest. Have to do them all together. That's how you keep those damn rabbits from stealing your veggies."

Guo laughed. "Right. I guess I'll be coming back here a few times."

The captain called his crew meeting to an end. The weapons were paid for but wouldn't be delivered until the ship was out of yard hands. The salesman explained how incredibly illegal it was to carry such primitive weapons on the streets of Demeter and promised to have guards escort the delivery. As the meeting broke up Guo said to Mitchie, "I'm fine with the slow delivery. Having the guns here makes it easier for me to get more practice."

"Go for it. The instructor's pretty good, he can work with you to get your form down."

Before Guo could answer Billy butted in. "Hey, Mitchie, you still want that tour of the club scene?"

"Sure! I'll get back to the hall and change. Meet you there." She scampered out.

Billy turned to Guo. "You up for any dancing tonight?"

"No," answered the mechanic, looking out the door, "I'm going to a show."

"Have fun then."

***

Billy's favorite dance club was an easy walk from the spacers' hall. Ahead of them some commotion disrupted the flow of pedestrians. Mitchie hopped up on the back of a bench to get a look. "Looks like a couple of cops arresting someone. Must be a big deal, there's some more following with evidence."

"Damn. They're going to tie up this block for an hour. Let's double back and take Magnolia there," said Billy.

"We're in no rush. I'm curious. Never seen Fusion cops in action before." Mitchie didn't stay to argue her point. She had already wormed her way into the gathering crowd. Billy muttered and trudged after her. By the time he caught up she had a front-row view. The cops had cleared out a twenty-meter circle around their arrestee. He looked nothing like the Disconnect's thug class to Mitchie. This guy was well fed and huddled into himself. The cops stacked a telepresence rig next to him. Probably was a serious virtual reality gamer if he spent his whole citizen stipend on that.

A senior cop walked up to Billy. "Sir, you are requested to serve as a trial juror."

"Um, sorry, sir, I'm a non-resident." Billy held out his spaceport pass. The cop nodded and turned to Mitchie. She pulled out her pass. He moved on around the perimeter, eventually ushering a dozen locals into a group near the edge of the circle. Flyers dropped off officials and their gear.

"Hey, that's a judge!" said Mitchie, pointing at a black-robed woman who'd just arrived.

"Can't have a speedy trial without one," replied Billy.

"Well, yeah, I'd read it, but I'm just used to everyone coming to the courtroom."

"HEY, GEETER, GEETER, THIS IS YOUR FAULT!" The arrestee's shout was followed by his lawyer's call to the cops. "Officer, I'm subpoenaing that man as a witness!" An on-looker was escorted into the circle.

The judge called the boss cop over for a chat, to Mitchie's joy close enough for her to overhear. "What are we waiting on?"

"Just the parents, your honor. Should arrive in another seven minutes."

"That's fine. We'll give them ten minutes with him."

A quarter-hour until the start of the trial sounded like more reason to leave to Billy, but he wasn't bored enough to ditch his shipmate yet. Mitchie was fascinated. She'd sweet-talked a local into identifying some of the players. "That one's a network security analyst. Probably third trial for him this year. Prosecutor always uses him."

Once the trial started it went by too fast for Mitchie to follow even with her new friend's help. Apparently the young man had added unlicensed processors to his computer to win at a team game. He'd blamed Geeter for suggesting it but the jury accepted the witness's claim he'd intended "You'll only be on top with a breaker rig" as a joke. To avoid being forced out of the game for cheating he'd diddled the network monitoring of his system, which was the real crime.

Witnesses went back and forth. The defendant's lawyer talked more than his witnesses did. Heavy emphasis on youth and lack of actual harm. The prosecutor pulled up a school transcript proving the guy'd passed a test on the applicable law. That provoked enough mutters from the crowd for the judge to warn them she'd set up a sound barrier if it kept up. The jury kept its debate short before returning a unanimous guilty.

The judge had the defendant brought before her. "Jerome Bessem, you have been found guilty of endangering our society. By your knowing actions you have provided a garden that a random weed could sprout in. Such weeds ruined the home of our race. We must all stand watch and make sure that no places are left for such, because, as probes falling from the sky or corruption in our own software, they seek places they can grow. And growing, they will ruin our world and our lives as they ruined Earth and the lives of all who lived there. We must watch to be safe. You hid a safe place for an AI from our watching. You endangered our entire world. You must now pay the penalty for your crime, that by your example others will know to not follow your path. I grant you ten minutes for your farewells."

The bailiffs parted to let the young man's parents embrace him. The brief conversation seemed to consist of variations on "sorry" from both sides. Another team of bailiffs set up a contraption with a short white pillar in the center. When the time was up two large bailiffs took him by the arms and set him on the pillar. Clear panels rose up to surround him in a soundproof cylinder. He slumped against the side. Then a brief hum came from the machine as his body liquefied and drained into the tank below him. His mother fainted.

"Shit!" exclaimed Mitchie.

"What were you expecting?" asked Billy.

"For a first offense? A little mercy. He'd never been in trouble before."

"This is Demeter. They get hit with AI probes two-three times a year. They don't leave any slack on that."

"Goddamn straight," injected the explaining stranger. "Miracle we've lasted as long as we have." He walked off.

Mitchie kept watching as the bailiffs packed up the apparatus of the court and flew off. "Um, Billy, I don't think I'm in the mood for dancing any more."

"Nah. Neither is anybody else probably. Everybody at the club is just going to babbling about this all night instead of going out on the floor." Billy sighed. "I'll walk you back."

***

The next night Billy finally came through on his promise to explain Fusion-world socializing. Indirect searches could reveal a lot about someone without triggering a notice that they were being observed. The true key to social success, according to Billy, was to get other people to do searches on you. The notices let you know who was interested. You'd do a bit of indirect to see which ones you wanted to follow up with. Then real searches to send a notice to the ones you had some mutual interest with. After that you saw who had the nerve to make the first real contact.

Mitchie hadn't decided if he believed all that or had just made it up as an elaborate way to get her out on the dance floor with him. She had a good time either way. Billy took full advantage of her size to not just twirl her around but toss her over his head. Working with him in free fall and varying accelerations let her relax and trust him now. It's not like there was a chance of him slipping and dropping her in Demeter's lighter gravity. He moved perfectly to the music. She only had to follow his lead or flow into his tosses.

Eventually she needed a break. When the music switched to a slower song she mimed drinking at Billy. He nodded, set her down, and led off the dance floor. She'd been too caught up in the movement to pay attention to the other dancers before. Now she was surrounded by smiles and inaudible clapping hands. Mitchie smiled and waved back. As they moved off the dance floor onto the carpeting the music volume dropped to background levels. The buzzing in her chest went away. The conversations around them were still muffled. Her ears would need a bit to recover.

Billy seated her at an empty table and leaned in to talk to her. "I told you you'd be a great dancer. Can you imagine the attention we'd be getting if we'd rehearsed that?"

His exultant grin hit Mitchie like a punch to the belly. She was actually starting to feel tempted. *No more dancing with Billy tonight*, she decided.

They pulled out their datasheets and ordered drinks. Both sheets were covered with search notifications. Billy began scrolling through his. Mitchie ignored hers. She surveyed the crowd.

A group of leather-jacketed men had come in. They shoved a couple of tables together. Mitchie saw one's back and burst out laughing. She elbowed Billy. "That's great!"

He looked puzzled. "What's that on their jackets? Looks like housefly wings."

"Yep, exactly," she said. "They're fighter pilots on the anti-AI patrols."

"What's that got to do with bugs?"

Mitchie rolled her eyes. "Old joke. Little boys pull the wings off flies for the fun of it. Scientists dissect flies for data. But it's all the same to the flies."

"Oh," said Billy. "So it's an AI motivation joke? I never got into those arguments. The whole point is humans can't understand them, so why bother?"

"It's not about that. It's the pilots being the flies." She gave up trying to explain it to him. "I'm going to say hi to them." Mitchie hopped down and crossed over to the pilots. They were loudly debating the beer choices. No one noticed her walking up. Her head didn't clear their shoulders. Inserting herself into the argument would take a loud shout. Instead she punched the tallest under the short ribs.

"Hey!" The pilot looked for someone to punch back, glancing left and right before looking down. His glare softened as he saw Mitchie's face.

"What's with the bug wings?" she asked.

Billy saw her get seated as the pilots settled down. A lithe woman then distracted him from his crewmate by demanding to know which Old Earth traditions he'd drawn on for his dance moves. He ordered drinks and leaned in to explain. "I'm drawing on two different traditions. My father was Bantu. He met my mother at a dance competition. She was with a Tamil troupe. I grew up learning both."

Explanations turned into demonstrations on the dance floor, then more drinks. Eventually Billy accepted her suggestion to go elsewhere. As they headed out they passed Mitchie drinking with the fighter pilots. "So you just sit there waiting for them to pop out and zap you? I should embroider a duck on your jackets. A fluffy, yellow, sitting, baby duck."

"We're not sitting," protested a pilot. "We run an ever-changing—" Billy shook his head and moved on. Pilots were crazy. He could think of much better things to talk about with a girl than work.

***

Mitchie leaned against the wall of the nightclub. She watched the other dancers while catching her breath. A couple of them glanced her way, possibly hoping she'd come back to the pattern. She looked at her data sheet. The usual number of search notifications. Including, finally, one from the man she'd been curious about. She'd done some indirect searching, finding out all she could about him without triggering a notification.

Now she initiated a prepared search. Half a dozen queries at once would only give him one notice. She skimmed through the results. Her guesses had been right. She wanted to meet Chetty Meena. Another notice popped up on her sheet. He had done more research on her. *They sure know how to flirt in the Fusion.* Some men would keep an exchange of searches going for hours. Mitchie didn't have the patience for that. She walked over to Chetty's table. "Hi. Don't bother searching more. I'm an offworlder. Not in the database."

Chetty blushed a bit—probably just shy—and said, "Hello, Michigan. There's more than you might think. The Navy said your flying saved the ship from that pirate."

Her turn to blush. "The newsies exaggerate. I just ran away to buy time for the Navy to show up." She'd been impressed by how few details of the incident had gotten out. "Do you read up on pilots a lot, Chetty?"

"No. I wondered why you had such a presence on the dance floor. Does flying make you a better dancer?"

"They're not directly related. I have a good kinesthetic sense which helps with both." She shifted the conversation to his dancing ability, or lack thereof. 'Chet' was competent at strictly choreographed dances but had no talent for the free-form dancing popular in the clubs. Analyzing the hows and whys of that took up most of dinner at a nearby seafood place. With a detour into describing the hazards of fishing on Akiak (mostly hypothermia).

Angel Creek Park was one block over. A stroll to settle dinner was so obvious neither needed to suggest it. They went hand-in-hand into the park. A couple of klicks upstream they stopped to admire a waterfall. Chet led her off the path for a better view. Then he lost interest in nature and began kissing her, even more competently than she'd hoped. Mitchie held him tight as he explored her neck. "Um, wait. What's that?" She pointed to her left.

Chet glanced that way. "Oh, just an observation bot." He leaned in to kiss her lips. She closed her eyes and opened to the kiss. A few pleasant minutes later she peeked.

"Chet, it's still watching us."

He straightened up. "Well, they're attracted to heat and movement. We're the only interesting thing around."

"I don't like being watched."

"Nobody's watching. It just records. If nobody makes a complaint the images get overwritten in 24 hours. Nobody's going to see that record."

"Okay, I guess that's all right." Mitchie pulled him to her. A few more minutes went by before she stepped back. The plastic sphere still hovered a dozen meters away. "I'm sorry. I can't ignore it. It's a Disconnect thing, we're too used to privacy. Can we find some place to be alone? Your place?"

"We can go to my place, but I've got a roommate so no alone time there."

"I'm staying in a coffin at the spacer hostel. I don't think we'd both *fit* in it."

Chet had popped his HUD glasses back on. "I know there's some nice hotels in the area. Let me see if there's any rooms open. . . . Ack."

"No rooms?"

"The price depends on how far in advance you make your reservation. The 'now' price is steep. Um. I can afford to get a room for tomorrow night."

Mitchie slid her hands under his shirt. "Chet, all night I've been waiting for my sheet to beep with my captain saying, 'Got a cargo, get back to the ship and plot a course.' I don't know if I'll be here tomorrow night."

"Um. Right. Sorry. Well. Um. My office has soft carpet?"

She kissed him. "Sounds great."

The floater ride to the Operational Analysis Institute had more chatting than kissing. Naturally his work there came up. If Chet had hoped to impress her it backfired.

"You play games."

"They're not games, they're simulations," he said defensively.

"You don't want to be one of the guys just drawing his stipend and spending it on games. So you're getting a salary to play them *and* getting the Navy to buy your games for you. I'm impressed. You looked like such an honest guy. What a con." She was pretty sure a junior analyst's salary was lower than the stipend though.

"It's serious work. The Navy bases important decisions on our results. Lives are at stake." He paused to deal with the building's security codes.

"I'm a 'research associate'?" Mitchie giggled.

"Yes. You described how piloting worked in variable acceleration. That's useful for me."

"Oh, good. I'd hate to think I've been wasting your time." That got her a kiss instead of an argument.

Chet was still irked enough by the games crack that he fired up his console when they got to his office. His current project was a simulation of an AI attack on Demeter. Attack drones engaged the Navy defenders at the gate while data probes skittered past toward the planet. Mitchie avoided connecting the vanishing dots to the pilots she'd been drinking with. Chet lectured on how the Navy's deployment needed to be changed to handle multiple-intensity attacks.

Mitchie stood behind his chair and rubbed her breasts on the back of his head. Chet shut up. "Sweetie, you're right, that's brilliant and important and I'm impressed. But it's not what I came here for."

He swiveled in the chair, grabbed her, and laid her down on the carpet. They made love by the light of clashing fleets in the holographic display.

***

Afterwards Chet lay beside her, an arm and leg wrapped around her, as he drifted toward sleep. Mitchie whispered affectionate words at him as his breathing slowed. She reached out for her discarded clothing and pulled it to her. The pocket of her jacket held a sampler pack she'd gotten from the nightclub vending machine. The Fusion's paranoia about data technology didn't overflow into pharmaceuticals. Adults could alter their brain chemistry any way they wanted. She popped out the sedative capsule from the pack. Timing it for an inhalation she crushed it under Chet's nose. He sucked in a puff of green mist. His breathing started to deepen. The empty capsule went back in her pocket. When he was soundly asleep she stood up.

Her dress went on the seat of Chet's chair. She donned her jacket and took a write-once data crystal out of her pocket. She could access the files without needing to interrupt the simulation. The OAI network had a "Naval Systems Reports" directory. Under that were a set of directories by topic: "Human vs. AI Probe," "Human vs. AI Sortie," "Human vs. AI Assault," "Human vs. AI Offensive," and "Human vs. Human." The last was immediately copied onto her write-once. Mitchie went back up the list copying files over until the crystal was full.

She carefully put the console back to how Chet had left it. She stripped and cuddled up to Chet again. She laid her clothes over her Chet-free side for warmth. It'd be a few hours until he woke up. She might as well be comfortable.

***

Alois Schwartzenberger dealt with insurance paperwork over a restaurant dinner. Bing had dumped her damage claim onto him the moment the company disputed something. He took the chance to squeeze them for all the keys he hadn't been able to get out of the shipyard. The adjustor hadn't let him get away with double-billing anything the shipyard would fix. His best leverage was Bing's marketing plan. She'd invested her retirement savings in an estate sale. The porcelain would have gone for 5-10 times that when delivered to Corcyra. The insurance company had offered to reimburse the original purchase price. Schwartzenberger was still holding out for in-kind replacement with equivalent sale value. The adjustor sounded a bit frayed in the last message. Possibly there was pressure coming from Bobbie's end of things. If they broke down and issued a cash payment for the expected sale value Bing wouldn't complain.

A slim woman walked up to his table. "You are the master of the merchant ship *Fives Full?*"

Schwartzenberger bit back on a cold reply when he recognized her uniform. He'd identified it instantly, it had just taken a moment to adjust to seeing one in person. "Yes, I am. How may I assist you?" She sat down. "I, uh, was surprised to see you. I thought the terraforming ship had left this system." The news had been full of relieved stories celebrating the departure.

"Yes, *Gaia's Heart* has continued on its mission. I have been detached for a specific task. I need a ship capable of delivering cargo to an off-network location. This is in support of an on-going terraforming effort." A waiter obsequiously inquired as to her desires. "I'll have what Captain Schwartzenberger is having."

"I hope you like spicy food," he commented. The goulash here was fierce. He used the food distraction to identify her with his datasheet. Yukio 23 of the Terraforming Service, followed by the usual long paragraph about giving them whatever they want and not doing anything to upset them.

"Yours has a novel smell," was her answer. The waiter returned quickly with a steaming plate. Another patron must have lost his meal to the VIP. Yukio dug in. Her pleased expression brought sighs of relief from Schwartzenberger, the waiter, and a suited man at the bar who'd followed her in.

"So what's your cargo?" asked the captain. "And where will I be picking it up?"

Yukio put down her spoon. "Animal carcasses. Five hundred tons of them. You'll handle the logistics of procuring them."

"What kind of animals? Cows? Dogs?"

"Herbivores. Preferably ones bred for consumption." The goulash disappeared rapidly. Schwartzenberger concluded terraforming ships didn't carry paprika. Odd for something that could supposedly synthesize *anything.*

"Why not use vatmeat? You'd get more nutrition for the same mass."

Yukio shook her head. "We tried that. My kitties turned their noses up at it. They'll eat it if we crate them but if they're loose they'll keep hunting prey instead. It's interfering with our plan to grow a self-sustaining prey population. Real flesh will keep the predators content enough to reduce the pressure on the prey. Or so the theory says. We'll have to see how it works in practice."

"I see. Is frozen meat acceptable?" Schwartzenberger said a brief, silent prayer to be saved from carrying live cattle.

"Oh, yes. They've had thawed meat before. Well, the previous generation did."

Thank you, God. "Where will we be delivering it? Somewhere in the Disconnect I presume."

"No, we're going to Savannah. You'd know it by the old name, Tsing Yi."

Schwartzenberger's hands clenched hard on the table. He took several moments to compose himself. He spoke quite calmly. "I thought the Betrayal destroyed Tsing Yi."

The goulash had totally occupied Yukio's attention during the pause. She seemed almost startled that the conversation continued. "The human colony was destroyed, yes. The human counter-attack destroyed the Hostile AI outpost. The ecosystem survived. There were breeding populations left of all flora and fauna. Radioactivity has decayed to normal background levels over most of the planet. That's what makes it a perfect candidate for this terraforming project."

"I'm surprised no Hostile AI took it over."

Yukio shrugged. "With no infosystem in place it's just dirt to an AI. The Hostiles have plenty of that in their current systems. We have set up some automated defenses as a precaution."

Using automated systems to guard against AIs struck Schwartzenberger as oxymoronic but he wasn't going to argue with a terraformer. "Will we need an escort through the defenses?"

She scraped the last of the sauce out of the bowl. "I'll be on board to give the passwords. What is this dish called?"

"Goulash. It's an Old Earth recipe."

"Goulash. I'll have to share that with my shipmates."

"When will you be ready to leave for Savannah?"

"I'm ready now. Just let me know when you have the cargo ready. The sooner we get it there the faster the prey population will recover." Yukio passed him her secure contact information and left. Terraformers weren't much for small talk apparently.

The suit from the bar slid into her still-warm seat. "Carstairs. Liaison Office."

"You're not very subtle," said the captain.

"We're not trying for subtle. The point is to make it obvious she's under protection."

"Shouldn't you be following her?"

"My partner is. I need to make sure you understand your role. Have you worked with TFS before?"

"No. But I know the drill. Give them whatever they want and bill local government for it. I take it that's you guys?"

Carstairs nodded. "Including your dinner here." A message popped up on Schwartzenberger's datasheet. "There's the info for the logistics office. Just make the arrangements and send the bill to them."

"Including my own bill?"

"We won't be stingy. Making sure you stay nice to the TFS is more important than trying to save a few keyneses. We've got a nice planet. We don't want them deciding to edit it."

"I'm from a nice planet. I think they're smart enough to figure out where I'm from if they get mad at me. I don't want Bonaventure getting edited either."

The government agent gave that a firm nod and left. The waiter came by. "Want dessert? The tab's still open."

"Maybe. Give me a whiskey. Get yourself one if you want."

***

Mitchie was the first to arrive for the crew meeting the next morning. Schwartzenberger sat at a table in the shade of the ship. With the repairs complete he'd moved the ship to a cheap groundside landing pad. "Morning, Skipper. You found us a cargo?"

The captain shrugged. "Not exactly."

Mitchie looked to her right. A pair of refrigerated containers sat at the edge of the pad, waiting to be put aboard. She pointed at the reefers.

"It's complicated. Wait for the rest to arrive so I only have to explain it once."

"Okay, sir." She pulled out her datasheet. Schwartzenberger went back to studying his. They only had a few minutes wait before the rest arrived in a shared floater. Once the amenities were over the captain launched into his briefing.

"This isn't going to be a regular cargo run. *Fives Full* has been requisitioned by the Terraforming Service." He explained the mission to an uninhabited star system, concluding with a warning that Yukio would be traveling with them. "So we'll be walking on eggshells the whole time on our own ship." He paused for questions but they were all still trying to assimilate the news. "Now, TFS can requisition the ship but no matter what the Fusion government says you are all free citizens. So you can't be forced to do this. I can't blame you if you want to avoid terraformers or not go off the edge of the map. But if you're willing to come along I'd very much appreciate it. This could be rough enough without me breaking in some raw crew."

Billy broke the silence. "I'm in. Ought to get a good story or two out of it." The hazards of uninhabited space meant nothing to him next to a better chance at picking up girls.

Mitchie said, "Me, too," hoping none of the crew had noticed how intensely curious the mention of terraformers had made her. Bing and Guo just nodded.

"Thank you, all of you," said the captain. "Shore leave's over. We'll have a few days of just working one shift until we have all the cargo and our employer on board."

***

Getting that much animal flesh actually took five days. Vatmeat dominated the market so animal breeders only had enough for the luxury trade. Two containers were filled by convincing zoos to cull some of their overpopulated exhibits.

Schwartzenberger had rented a cable camera to inspect the containers. When a new one arrived he'd thread it through the whole volume. One container came during lunchtime, giving Mitchie a chance to ask Guo about it. "Is he that worried about someone slipping in some vatmeat?"

Guo shook his head. "He always checks cargo like that. That fire on his last ship was started by some discount reactors someone tried to smuggle in a container. Bribed a customs inspector to give them a clean manifest. One of them broke down and started a fire. Spread to the rest of the cargo. He got the whole crew off but lost the ship. He's still paying for it."

"Wow. How'd he get a new ship with that hanging over him?"

"*Fives* technically isn't his ship. When he pays off the *Jefferson Harbor* he can start buying into *Fives* but for now he's just a hired hand."

The captain's frantic money-squeezing suddenly made more sense to Mitchie. "Still, I don't think someone's going to slip some exploding meat into our cargo."

"Don't be so sure. A lot of people don't like terraformers."

"That's so ridiculous. They've never done anything to an inhabited planet." Though Mitchie had seen her share of disaster vids featuring a terraformer taking revenge for some slight.

"Not that. They're friends with AIs and that creeps out people in the Fusion."

"Seriously? None of the terraforming ship AIs have gone bad. They're pure Golden Age tech."

Guo shrugged. "Go talk to someone here on Demeter. They think an AI is an AI, and they're all ready to use us as spare atoms."

"Idiots."

"The idiots don't worry me. It's the ones smart enough to try something like offing one lone terraformer by blowing up her ship."

Mitchie made a face. "Yuck. Think the captain could use some help with it?"

"He has Bing helping out and they're training Billy."

"Too much fun for me. I'll go back to plotting courses." Any error in passing through the gate would be magnified to tens of millions of kilometers in the next system. She was building a set of trajectories to cover all the likely possibilities.

***

"Mail call!" cried Billy as he entered the cargo hold. The crew made double takes as they took in his burden. In addition to the usual handful of data crystals he had a heavy package nearly as tall as he was.

"What's that?" asked the captain.

"Dunno, but it's for me." He leaned the box against the bulkhead while handing out messages. Everyone pocketed their crystals. Billy opened the shipping note on the box. "Oh, it's from, um, a friend of mine."

"The friend whose father blacked your eye?" asked Guo.

"He didn't do it, he hired it out." The package peeled open to reveal a hunting rifle. "Oh, wow. This looks top of the line. That's a fancy scope, too." He checked that it was unloaded and put it to his shoulder. "Real comfortable fit. Scope can do visual or IR. When I get home next the deer won't know what hit them."

Schwartzenberger had backed out of the group. He closed the airlock door. The rifle's sweetly synthesized voice announced, "Network connectivity lost. Initiating emergency shutdown." Billy cursed as the eyepiece went black.

"Welcome to the Fusion, Billy," said the captain. "You can have any gun you want as long as it continually uploads the sight picture and the prints of whoever's holding the grips."

The deckhand pulled on the trigger. With the gun shut down it wouldn't even budge. "Crap."

"Cheer up, lover-boy. She meant well," said Bing.

Demeter System. Acceleration 10 m/s^2

The gate to the Savannah system was a four day cruise from Demeter. They'd lifted shortly after noon ship time so the first meal on board was a formal dinner to welcome their employer. Schwartzenberger had swiped a few pounds of beef out of a container. Bing turned it into a savory stroganoff. The scent had everyone on board at the table early.

Conversation started out slowly. Yukio was too entranced by her food to say anything. The rest were too scared of offending her to open any interesting topic. The captain tried to get people talking but wound up receiving a series of status reports.

Mitchie's turn was last. "We're in the groove for a normal approach to the gate. I've finished plotting a set of courses for Savannah. Wherever the gate dumps us we can start boosting immediately. There's about a twenty percent chance we'll wind up close enough to one of the gas giants to get a fuel savings."

Yukio looked up from her second helping. "Why aren't you exiting toward the gas giant if it's so helpful?"

The question didn't make sense to Mitchie. "We're aiming for the star. We just have a probable error sphere with a sixty million kilometer radius, which might drop us usefully close to one of the giants."

"Oh, no. We retuned that gate when *Gaia's Heart* returned from Savannah. There won't be nearly that much error. And an off-normal transit can put you wherever you like this side of the star."

"Or we'll never be seen again!" Mitchie shot back indignantly.

"It's perfectly safe if you have a current transition angles matrix. I delivered the new one to the Demeter Observatory Office myself." The terraformer was taken aback by Mitchie's hostility.

"I'm certain you did," soothed the captain. "But they undoubtedly declared it classified data and won't give it to civilians."

"Well, what good is it if nobody sees it?" asked Yukio.

Nobody wanted to tackle explaining Fusion paranoia to their employer. Guo shifted to the technical side. "Why a matrix? Couldn't you give us a set of equations to model it? Then we wouldn't have to worry about it going out of date."

Yukio shrugged. "We don't have a human-understandable theory of gates yet. We're getting closer. Our genetic improvement program has increased our average intelligence over five percent in each generation of terraformers. *Heart* estimates we're less than two hundred years from producing a human who can grasp gate theory."

"That really drives home how far behind we are from the Golden Age AIs," commented Guo.

"It's not all that complex," said Yukio. "There's a physicist on *Rite of Spring* who's working on matter converters. He thinks we're less than fifty years from a comprehensive theory of direct matter to energy conversion."

"That would be a tremendous breakthrough," said the mechanic. Much of his work dealt with the failure of converters to live up to their manufacturers' promises.

"How reliable is that physicist?" asked Bing.

"His theories have survived replicated experiments. He's too young to have any track record as a prophet yet."

Bing wasn't comforted. "I mean, how trustworthy is he as a person. Experimenting with converters puts a lot of destructive power in the hands of someone who might not be . . . stable."

"Making people completely stable destroys their creativity," said Yukio. "*That* dead end was explored by genetic engineers before the first terraforming ship was built."

"That's not the level of instability that worries me." Bing ignored the captain's warning cough. "Or rather a different kind of stability—the stable state where your gengineered geniuses start thinking they're a different species."

Yukio delayed answering while she refilled her plate with more stroganoff. "Our children are still the same species as us. Am I human?"

Whatever answer Bing had was overridden by Billy. "Yes. You're perfectly human."

Schwartzenberger tried a less dangerous topic. "It's hard for us to imagine dealing with a superhuman intelligence. We've never met one. What's it like living with an AI on your ship?"

"Well—*Heart* is a person. She's like having a smart relative always available to give advice. As if your grandmother didn't get tired, didn't get cranky, never slept. You could call her whenever you got stuck."

"Does the AI ever start conversations with you? Or break into one you're having with someone else?" Schwartzenberger felt calling the AI "it" would be rude, but couldn't bring himself to use "she" for a computer.

"Just about terraforming operations, and only if there's a real need. She has a rule about not meddling unnecessarily."

"So what kind of advice do you ask for? Solving technical problems or finding who'd make a good match for the breeding program?" asked Billy.

"Oh, technical," replied Yukio. "*Heart* would never play matchmaker. She has a hard constraint against acting on humans that way. We think that's part of what kept the terraforming AIs safe during the Betrayal."

The silence after that last word went long. Mitchie finished buttering a roll and decided it was her turn. "What's *Heart's* personality like? Is she different from the other AIs?"

"*Heart* is cheerful, determined, sometimes impatient. There's so much waiting you have to do in terraforming that she doesn't want to waste any time when we can do something. I've heard *Rite of Spring* is finicky, almost afraid of making mistakes. I've never actually met another AI."

"You haven't visited any of the other TFS ships?" asked Mitchie.

"No, terraforming ships don't rendezvous often. There's really no task that takes two of them. The last time *Gaia's Heart* met another was when my mother came on board. The breeding program had declared several families unsuitable for reproduction and part of another ship's crew transferred over to expand the gene pool."

"That's not very romantic," said Billy.

Yukio gave him a long look. He met her eyes firmly. "Are you sexually attracted to me?" she asked.

Mitchie had caught Billy sneaking enough peeks at the terraformer to consider it a stupid question. *Maybe it's a cultural thing to want open confirmation.* The table was silent, all the silverware was still.

Billy went for the direct answer. "Yes. You're very beautiful," with his best smile.

"Come to my quarters two hours after the meal ends," said the terraformer. Mitchie surveyed the table. Bing looked worried. Guo tried to conceal his amusement. The captain . . . seemed to be restraining himself from kicking Billy's ankle hard enough to break it.

"So! Who's ready for a cupcake?" said Bing.

***

Captain Schwartzenberger insisted on a daily inspection of the cargo to make sure no container had shifted position under acceleration or maneuver. Bing accompanied him on the second day's visit to the hold.

Normally Billy would be waiting at the ladder for them to report on any changes he'd need to make to the strap-downs. Tracking some snores led them to the top of a container. Apparently he'd finished tightening a strap then laid his head down on the Cargo Handler's Manual. "That looks pretty damn uncomfortable," said the captain.

"Yep," replied the first mate. After a long silence she mentioned, "You made some pretty elaborate threats about what you were going to do the next time you caught him asleep during duty hours."

He pondered his reply a bit. "Let's log him as working the night shift. He looks like he needs the sleep."

***

That night's dinner had Billy seated next to Yukio. He drew out the story of how she'd broken an arm in a zero-g playground when she was eight. The rest of the meal was an exchange of childhood injuries and other hijinks. Guo won with three bones broken while exploring a played-out mine. The captain began to hope they'd survive the trip without infuriating their employer after all.

***

An hour after dinner Guo passed the galley and saw Mitchie working on dishes. "Isn't it Billy's turn for clean-up?"

She chuckled. "We traded. Apparently the terraformer is fascinated by our low tech hydroponics set-up so he's doing all the maintenance for now. Not what I'd pick for a date but if it works for him, great."

He picked up a towel and started drying one of the pots in the rack. "Better him than me."

"What, you don't think she's pretty?"

"No, she's pretty, their gengineers are keeping her in spec. It's more . . . remember that show when we were kids, *Eddore's Quest*?"

"Half-elf boy kicked out of his human home for being strange, elves won't let him in because he's not good enough, so he saves the world to impress them both?"

"Right. My problem with it was the elves looked so strange I couldn't imagine anyone getting intimate enough with one to have a kid. Terraformers are that strange too."

"Oh, god, I'm working with an elf-hater." Mitchie chuckled. "How do you feel about dwarves?"

Guo smiled down at her. "They're growing on me."

She started scrubbing some gunk off a frying pan. "How do you like your fancy new converter?"

"Happy with it so far. It's a direct copy of a Golden Age design. It's giving cleaner waste products, more stable isotopes. Haven't gotten to see how it performs at max output yet."

"Yeah. Let's hope we can get through this job without redlining the thing."

"That's a prayer."

***

The bang was too drawn out to be a gunshot. The scream could have been Billy or Guo, neither had come to lunch. Mitchie leapt up from the table and dashed to the cargo hold hatch. Halfway down the ladder the voice was clearly Billy cursing a streak. She slowed, not wanting to break an ankle at the bottom. The captain and mate followed her without excitement.

"Since we've got everyone here, I want it on the record. I told you so." Guo didn't let his statement interfere with applying quick-heal cream to Billy's hand.

"Told him what?" asked Bing.

Billy answered, "I thought I could bypass the network module in my rifle. Instead it blew up." The rifle lay on the deck, its wood veneer burnt off and the scope cracked. A full face visor was next to it, charred in several spots.

"I told you it had to have anti-tamper circuits," said Guo.

"How's his hand?"

"Just surface burns. This stuff'll have him back to work tomorrow." Guo wrapped a thick bandage over the cream. Billy lifted his other hand.

Guo slapped it. "Don't scratch. Leave it alone until the new skin's grown."

"Crap. It's junk now, isn't it?" mourned Billy.

"Oh, the hardware's good," said the mechanic. "I could rig a mechanical link easily enough for the trigger. Put some iron sights on. You'd burn through all your ammo calibrating them though."

"Don't be working on that until everything else is done," said the captain. "And Billy, those first aid supplies are coming out of your pay. Everybody else get back to work." They dispersed. "Not you, Billy. You're confined to quarters until that's healed. And don't scratch."

***

Mitchie cut the thrust to zero an hour out from the gate. *Fives Full* was exactly on track, or at least as exact as her instruments could measure. The first off-normal approach Yukio proposed had far too narrow a corridor for an analog ship to stay in. Searching through the matrix found one that had a degree and a half of safety margin on all sides, if they kept their speed fixed. That was easier to calculate against the warning buoys around the gate than their precise approach angle.

Checks every five minutes showed they were coming in a little slow. Some puffs on the maneuvering thrusters brought them to optimum speed. For the last thirty minutes the ship just coasted. The captain and Mitchie alternated rechecking their vector against the buoys and taking positions from star and planet sightings. Yukio sat at the communications console and occasionally muttered comments about the dark ages.

The terraformer did have to do some work on the approach. Schwartzenberger tasked her with explaining to the Navy patrol squadron that, yes, they really did have a good reason to be out there and didn't need a rescue and tow from their accidental dangerous course. Eventually their chain of command checked with the Liaison Office and they shut up.

The gate was almost visible as they approached. The loop of cosmic string blurred stars as it occulted them. Mitchie could trace the outline of the circle by the flickering. Once she had a feel for it she could pick a star on the outside and take a sighting on it as it passed behind the gate. A few readings verified that they were at the proper angle relative to the gate. Not that there was much chance of the buoys being misaligned at this gate but it was a good habit. Captain Schwartzenberger liked to encourage paranoid habits.

As always she kept her eyes open as they passed through. She'd never seen anything dramatic, just the flicker of the buoys vanishing and a new sun appearing in front of them. They were almost a billion kilometers out from it. Savannah was on the far side. She sighted on the innermost gas giant to verify they were close to where Yukio had promised and started them toward it at ten gravs.

Savannah System. Acceleration 0 m/s^2

Yukio was pretty scarce during the transit. She did show up for the approach to Savannah holding a head-sized box. "Oh, this is the password for the defenses." The captain raised an eyebrow but didn't reply. She'd been evasive when asked about the planet's security before.

"On course to land at your base's coordinates," said Mitchie. "We can aerobrake down to the landing point. Won't need to fire anything until we need the turbines for landing."

"Good," said the captain. "Wait until 300 klicks to flip us for entry. I'm enjoying the view."

"Aye-aye." Mitchie pivoted the ship to put the planet directly above. Savannah was a lovely example of the terraformer's art. Smaller ice caps than most worlds, but Mitchie had gotten enough ice at home. Patches of green showed where the biosphere expanded out from the initial plantings. She started a timer to warn her when she'd have to swing the ship around for reentry.

The pilot rotated through her instruments, pausing on the radar screen. "Sir, I'm picking up a number of objects orbiting the planet. Can't get a good fix on them."

"Oh, that's the defense satellites," said Yukio. "Don't worry about them."

"I'm trying to make sure I don't run into one. Hard to do when they fuzz their radar returns."

"Once we've passed the security check they'll maneuver clear of us." Neither spacer was reassured by Yukio's statement. They covered their eyes as a bright green light illuminated the cockpit. When it faded Mitchie noticed the box emitting a series of multi-colored flashes. "There's the first one," chirped the terraformer. "Only two more."

"Can you warn us?" demanded the pilot.

"Sorry, the satellites pick the challenge time stochastically, it's part of the password system." The other two covered their eyes again. The next two flashes were closer together. "Done now. We're clear to land."

Mitchie ran a radar sweep on their path. The one she'd been worried about had maneuvered clear of them. Even more satellites were detectable now as the ship came close enough to see through their stealthing. Apparently the Terraforming Service was serious about no person or AI messing with their private project world. "Okay. Permission to take us down, sir?"

"Granted," said the captain.

Mitchie activated the intercom. "All hands, rotating for re-entry. Brace for rotation and aerobraking. We'll be on the ground in . . . thirty-five minutes."

Planet Savannah. Gravity 9.6 m/s^2

The research base was a twenty meter dome standing in an utterly flat stretch of grassland. Mitchie placed *Fives Full* due west of it, on a previous ship's landing marks. Yukio radioed it again. "Savannah Research, this is Yukio, I'm here with the kitty chow." Again, no response. She looked at the dome from the bridge windows. "A couple of the floaters are out. I guess they're running a survey." She kept staring out with a puzzled expression.

"Well, let's go get a truck. We can start unloading before they get back," said the captain. By the time everyone gathered in the cargo hold Billy had the hatch open and the elevator platform rigged to the crane. They were only fifteen meters off the ground but still had a wide view.

"Oh, how beautiful," murmured Bing. The late-spring grass rippled like ocean waves in the wind. The air smelled shockingly alive, a thousand scents blowing the smell of hydroponic algae and lubricants out of their noses. Mitchie pointed out a herd of antelope grazing a couple of klicks away. Yukio beamed with proprietary pride.

The ten minute walk to the dome left them dripping with sweat. Billy joked, "Did it ever get this hot on Old Earth?"

Yukio snapped back, "We matched the local climate to the original biome. This is the most Earth-like part of the whole planet."

An oversized hovercraft was in a fenced area next to the dome. There was enough room for several more in there. "Okay, they're doing a survey," said Yukio. "I'll put an autorepeat on the dome radio asking them to call in. Still a bit funny that nobody stayed here." She typed a code into the doorpad. The crew followed her into the blessedly cool shade.

The room took up a quarter of the ground floor. All the cabinets hung open. Abandoned gear covered the floor. Billy said, "I thought terraformers would be neater than this."

"We are! Nobody would ever leave a compartment like this. It's unsafe!"

Schwartzenberger rested his hand on the pistol in his belt. He'd handed the weapons out in case of wildlife attacks. Now it felt comforting. "Guo, go around the outside, check for any signs of trouble. Rest of you go through the building. See if it's all like this." He stayed with their employer.

Yukio poked through the piles. "Samplers are still here. And cameras. Looks like just the survival gear is gone. I'm going to try the radio again." The captain followed her upstairs to a communications room. He studied the displays of weather patterns and solar activity while she pleaded for an answer. After a few attempts she put it on autorepeat. "Damn." Schwartzenberger looked over to see her studying a map display. "All the floaters have tracking beacons. But I'm only picking up the one here. There should be two more on the display."

Guo came slowly up the stairs. "Sir, ma'am . . . I found something you ought to see." He led them out to the north side of the dome. Two graves had been filled in there. The dirt hadn't been smoothed by wind or rain. A jumble of tools had been dropped on top of each one to discourage scavengers.

Yukio, stone-faced, turned and walked back into the dome. She came back holding a scanner. When placed between the graves it formed a hologram. The terraformer muttered as she studied the image. "Two bodies. Less than two weeks dead. Larger one is definitely Junde. Smaller . . . can't tell."

"Did an animal attack them?" asked Schwartzenberger.

"No—we have good repellants. And there's no pieces missing. Junde has a chunk of skull shattered so it wasn't disease."

"Those look like they could take off a chunk of skull." Guo faced the ship. He'd grabbed his pistol but hadn't drawn it. A pride of lions had gathered in the shade of *Five Full's* hull. The cubs ran in circles around the adults. A second lion limped into the group and flopped on his side. Two cubs started wrestling over the right to climb on him.

"You're perfectly safe as long as you wear your repellant bracelet." Yukio held up her left arm to display a thick copper bracelet. "Oh. I should get you these." She headed back into the dome without looking back at the graves.

The rest of the crew were back in the first room. Nothing interesting had turned up on their search. Schwartzenberger briefed them while Yukio searched through cabinets. Billy promptly opened the door to get a look at the lions. Bing leaned around him. "When she said 'kitties' I kept visualizing bobcats or maybe leopards."

Billy laughed. "That guy looks like he could eat a container of meat all by himself."

"Ha!" Yukio pulled a box of bracelets off a top shelf. "Everybody put on one of these. If a kitty gets too close squeeze it with your other hand and it'll induce a fear reaction. Don't use it on the wildebeests. Just stay away from them."

"How close is too close?" asked Guo. He'd snapped it onto his left wrist.

"It's effective for at least ten meters. Most of them have learned to stay away from humans by now. It's just the cubs you need it for." The crew all took the gadgets. No one looked reassured.

Yukio had clipped a small radio to her belt. It had been turned down to whisper-level as it repeated her emergency call. Now a new voice came on. "Are you there?"

She grabbed it off her belt. "Yes! Jisi, where are you?"

"I'm safe. You're in danger. Turn that repeater off. Is that ship by the dome yours?"

"Yes. What's hap—?"

The other terraformer cut her off. "We'll meet you at the ship. Stop transmitting before they hear you. Out."

"Jisi? Jisi!" No answer. Yukio lowered her radio. "I guess I'll turn the transmitter off."

***

The crew clustered behind Yukio as they walked back to the ship. The cubs were fascinated by the approaching creatures and tried to bounce out to investigate. The youngest lioness cuffed them back into the shade. The other adults stared at the humans without getting up.

"I feel like I'm on a platter," muttered Mitchie.

"Oh, they're just being lazy," replied Yukio. "When we get close enough they'll leave."

Sure enough, once the people were close enough there was no pretending they might turn and go someplace else the pride stood and began to saunter off. The cubs kept dashing back and forth until they all activated their bracelets.

"Poor things," said Bing. The cubs whimpered as they scurried away. "What's wrong with that one?" One lion lagged behind the pride, favoring a foreleg.

Yukio pulled a 'scope from the survival harness she'd donned in the dome. "Obviously injured. Bleeding's stopped. A lot of blood stained fur. Can't make out the wound itself, must be small."

"Bullet hole?" asked the captain.

The terraformer looked puzzled. "It could be. But your people are the only ones with guns here. We only have dart-throwers and some stunners."

"Damn strange then," said Schwartzenberger.

Mitchie called, "Company coming." A pair of hovercraft approached from the south.

Yukio lifted her 'scope again. "It's Jisi and . . . Roark." She drooped. "So that's Wang in the other grave." The terraformer stared at the ground for a few moments then shook herself. When her face came up she wore a cool professional expression again. "They better be able to explain what the hell's been going on around here."

Bing took the captain aside. "Do we want to be out in the open like this? If those two murdered the others they might not want to leave witnesses."

Schwartzenberger contemplated a vision of violence among the famously rational terraformers. "Murder over what? Who gets to gene-tweak the cheetahs?"

"They're probably just as crazy about sex as anybody."

"Maybe. But Yukio knows these people. She's not worried. And we're probably better-armed than them." Bing still looked worried. "Hide behind a landing leg if you want."

"Hmph." The first mate picked a leg on the shady side of the ship. She leaned on it as if she was tired but kept peeking around it at the oncoming floaters.

Mitchie was surprised by how quiet the hovercraft were. The TFS put a lot of work into muffling the sound of the airjets—or their AI did. Maybe they were afraid of disturbing their pets? The air cushion was unusually wide, reducing the pressure on the ground. "They don't want to leave footprints," said the pilot.

Guo was the only one who heard her. "It's a work of art for them. Don't want to scuff it up." Mitchie nodded.

The floaters killed their motors just short of the ship. The drivers hopped across the collapsed skirts. Yukio met them with a joint hug. The three terraformers stood clasped together for a long moment.

Mitchie studied the new arrivals. The living quarters in the dome had been prissily neat. These two were a mess. Jumpsuits muddy, hair unwashed for more than a week, the man unshaven for at least that long.

Yukio broke the embrace to make introductions. "This is the crew of the *Fives Full*. They're hauling a load of kitty chow for us." After listing the crew she introduced Jisi (Asian, female, exhausted) and Roark (blond, male, wary).

"Great, a ship," said Roark. "Let's get on it and get out of here before that maniac kills us." The crew turned to survey the horizon. Some grazing antelope. Annoyed lions sharing a lone tree's inadequate shade. No maniacs any closer than the hills to the north.

Yukio gently asked, "What maniac, Roark?" The blond terraformer cursed and looked around, afraid his enemy might be sneaking up.

Jisi answered the question. "He's a hunter. He's here to kill the animals. When Junde and Wang tried to stop him he killed them. Shot them with his rifle. So we buried them and ran." She sat on the ground, exhausted by her little speech.

Yukio sat next to her. "Where did he come from?"

"A ship landed in those hills." Jisi pointed north. "We saw him the next day on a four-wheeler, skinning a lion. Well, one of his flunkies skinned it. He's got a bunch for the dirty work."

"How did they try to stop him?"

"Junde confronted him. Said he wasn't allowed here and the animals were protected. Hunter just laughed at him. So Junde waited for him the next day and tried to tranq him. Missed. The hunter shot him. And Wang too. Just left them there." Bing handed her a handkerchief. The terraformer wiped her tears away. "We came and got the bodies. Buried them by the dome. Then we went south to hide. We were afraid he'd kill us next. We saw your ship come down but it wasn't TFS so we thought it was more hunters. But it's you and we can escape now." Jisi broke down in sobs. Yukio wrapped her arms tightly around her.

Roark was still trying to look in all directions at once. The captain asked him gently, "So where's this hunter's base?"

"Don't know," he answered. "Probably near where their ship landed." Roark pointed to a dip in the line of northern hills. "He has a couple of ATVs he uses to roam the savannah. That's the only times we've seen him."

"Let's go get him, then!" said Billy. He was eager to pitch in on his girlfriend's side.

The captain gave him a weary look. "Billy, do you have any idea how much a good hunting rifle outranges our little popguns?"

"Um . . . three times the range?"

"Try ten times. More if he has modern ammo and sights." Illegal off-network on Fusion worlds, but military surplus did get out. Billy frowned, then brightened up. "And he might have a night scope, which we don't," said Schwartzenberger. Frown again.

"The hunter had a long gun. He had a couple of bodyguards with different guns," added Roark. Schwartzenberger drew out some more details, enough to convince him the bodyguards carried automatic weapons.

"Not anything we want to tangle with," he explained to Billy.

"Sir," asked Mitchie, "what exactly does our contract require us to do for the TFS?"

Schwartzenberger drew his crew aside. "Well, we don't have a contract as such. The Fusion's rule is what the TFS wants, the TFS gets, and planetary government picks up the tab. So they can ask for anything. I'm going to say no to anything suicidal. That said, I don't want to let a murderer get away with it if we can do something about it." Disconnected Worlds law enforcers relied on volunteers to back them up against dangerous criminals. None of the crew batted an eye at the prospect of being deputized.

Yukio stood up. "I want to talk to this hunter."

"He'll shoot you!" shouted Roark.

"I doubt it. He didn't bother the dome. He didn't go look for you two. And he hasn't bothered us since we landed. Junde was never good at inter-personal communications. Obviously that confrontation went badly. It doesn't mean there's no rational agreement possible. I'm going to talk to him."

Yukio overruled their protests and ordered Jisi and Roark to steer their floaters north. Yukio sat up front in Jisi's, Billy and the captain sitting behind her. The rest of the crew rode with Roark. Schwartzenberger had vetoed the idea of leaving someone to watch the ship. Bringing the crane remote kept her safe from anyone without a ten-meter ladder.

A bit of casting about found a clearing at the edge of the hills cut through with multiple tire tracks. The terraformers complained that their vehicles were unsafe on the slopes. Schwartzenberger, fearing an ambush, supported them. Yukio led the search east. No other trails were found by the time Mitchie spoke up. "There's some dust behind us. Might be a vehicle."

"Turn around, let's go look," directed Yukio.

"We don't want the sun in our eyes while we talk to them," advised the captain. "Swing around and approach them from the south." Yukio agreed. The floaters went back out on the savannah.

The dust came from a pair of open-topped wheeled vehicles. When they spotted the floaters they turned south and halted. "Bring me close enough to talk, then kill the engine," ordered Yukio.

"Yes'm," said Jisi nervously.

Like the floaters, the cars were four-seaters with a cargo platform on the back. The floaters carried camping gear. The cars had dead animals—a hyena on the lead one, a pair of gazelles on the other. The lead car's front passenger seat was occupied by the hunter. He wore a tailored khaki safari suit with gleaming gold buttons, sported a hat with a snakeskin band, and rested his right hand on his rifle case. He stood and called out, "Hello! Are you our new neighbors or the old neighbors?" The two thugs seated behind him studied the floaters intently. His driver hunched down as if he hoped no one would notice him.

Yukio stood to reply. "I'm Yukio 23, Director of the Savannah Biome Project. Why are you trespassing on TFS property?"

"This is an uninhabited planet, no one's property until some settlers make improvements. I'm not claiming it either. I'm just visiting. How about you? Whose ship is that?"

Captain Schwartzenberger stood. "I'm Alois Schwartzenberger, master of the merchant vessel *Fives Full*. We're under charter to the

Terraforming Service. Who are you?" He sat. The thugs exchanged whispers.

"And here I was hoping you were tinkers coming to sell us everything we'd forgotten to pack for our camping trip. Oh, well. I'm Max. The rest of this merry band work for me."

"Well, Max, you need to take your merry men and get off this planet. You're disrupting crucial scientific research," said Yukio.

"Research? These species were analyzed down to their atoms before the first gate was deployed. That's the only way you'd be able to do this." He waved an arm at the savannah. "It's a hobby project for you people. Wasting resources on animals when you should be making places for people to live like you're supposed to."

"We're supposed to spread life. All of Earth's life, not just humans." Yukio's tone had become defensive. "I'm not going to let you destroy this creation."

Max gave a theatrical shrug. "You're not re-creating Earth here. All these species went extinct when the AIs became hostile. They should stay extinct. This lovely plain will be farms someday. I'm just clearing the way for the settlers."

"Don't worry about future settlers. Think about the settlers on your own world. A single terraforming ship could edit one of Demeter's continents to restart the Savannah Project there. We'll do that if you destroy these animals. Think about it. Millions of your relatives, friends, neighbors, all killed or driven from their homes. Leave this planet now if you want to keep them safe."

Schwartzenberger studied the reactions to her threat. The thugs were poker-faced. The driver and the flunkies in the second car all looked terrified. Max was still cheerful as he replied, "Bullshit. The ships have the power but the TFS has never intentionally taken a human life. You people never will. It's just too big a conflict with your 'ethos of life.' Does make for some great fiction, though. I love those shows." The thugs burst out laughing—not at their boss's speech but at Yukio's shocked expression. The captain could see her jaw hanging down from where he sat.

For the first time in his life Alois Schwartzenberger regretted not hosting poker games on his ship.

Max went on. "If any of you decide to emulate your late colleagues, keep in mind that injecting me with a tranquillizer dose sized for an adult male lion is a lethal attack. I'll respond appropriately. And I'm better at it than you are. Stay out of my way and play with your pets. While they last." He cuffed his driver on the head. The cars drove off.

Yukio closed her mouth.

***

Yukio gathered everyone between the floaters. "We need to find something we can offer him, some compromise that will make him go away happy."

"We can offer him some bullets if Guo fixes my rifle," said Billy.

"Yeah!" Roark was thrilled at the prospect of revenge.

Bing cut him off. "If we're going to do anything with him we should go get a terraforming ship so we've got enough force to control the situation."

"Yes, let's take off and get help," added Jisi.

"We don't have the time," said Yukio. "By the time a terraformer, or even a cruiser, got here we may have lost whole species."

"Calm down, people," soothed Captain Schwartzenberger. "We've got time to consider our options. Let's do some brainstorming. Max isn't afraid of the TFS going after Demeter, can we threaten him with the TFS coming here?"

The attempt to focus them on his employer's preferred strategy went nowhere. Guo got drawn into a side discussion on how the dome's equipment could be used to put a scope on the rifle. Jisi and Bing kept looking for any excuse to get off the planet. Some of Roark's threats were inventive but there was no way this group could back them up. Yukio's suggestions got torn apart by one side or the other.

Mitchie drifted out of the group unnoticed. They'd mostly been talking over her head anyway. She took a canteen from the back of one of the floaters and started emptying out her pockets. Everything she wasn't sure she'd need went into the pile, including her pistol. A few items were tucked carefully back in. Her handcomm was tweaked to mute the speaker before going back on her belt. She grabbed a half-empty ration box and carried it over between Billy and Roark.

She stood on it and yelled, "This is a waste of time!" The parade-ground bellow silenced them all. She continued more quietly, "We've all got different guesses about what Max has for resources. We're basing plans on those guesses. But we're not going to agree on anything until we have some actual data to go on. The sun's setting. I'm short and sneaky. So I'm going to look at their camp and tell you what they've got. Then we can make a plan."

Mitchie hopped off the box and started trotting north. The captain walked after her, pushing Billy aside. "Hang on, Mitchie, I don't think that's a good idea," he said.

"Don't worry, sir, I know what I'm doing," she replied over her shoulder.

"Wait, we should have someone go with you as back-up." That got a headshake. "Pilot Long, get back here! That's an order!"

"Trust me, Skipper!" Mitchie half-turned to wave at him then picked up her pace. The captain glared after her. Once he had his face under control he rejoined the group. No one dared say anything to him.

***

Mitchie's voice sounded from the crew's handcomms. "I'm paralleling their vehicle track. It's going to the east of those three hills. No sign of sentries."

Jisi dug a mapboard out of her floater. Guo had a directional antenna for his handcomm. He quickly confirmed which hills she meant. Bing pulled out her notebook.

***

Mitchie found the hunter's camp in a bowl about a hundred meters higher than the savannah. Most of the space was taken up by their ship, a high-performance belly-lander. Some tarps hung off the left wing to make a shelter. A dozen tents clustered next to it. Max's tent was obvious from both its size and the respectful distance the other tents kept from it.

She'd described the lay-out from up on the hill. The staff had turned in early. Only Max's tent had lights on. A pair of goons walked the perimeter of the camp. Between snack breaks, piss breaks, and rest breaks their schedule was hard to predict but after two laps she was sure there was just the one pair. Their path stuck to easy terrain, sometimes wandering ten to twenty meters from the actual camp. When they passed under her hill on the next lap she started moving as soon as their backs were to her.

Between the dark blue utilities and the mud on her face and hands Mitchie didn't think she'd be noticed but movement does catch the eye. She moved slowly to not disturb anything that might noisily roll downhill. Once across the patrol path she tucked under some thorn bushes and waited for the thugs to go by again.

***

Schwartzenberger was chewing on a thumbnail as he listened to Mitchie's reports.

"Tent seven, two males."

We know that. We could hear them talking, thought the captain. The radio was at maximum volume so they could make out Mitchie's whispers. Her footsteps were audible, sometimes louder than the voices of the people she was sneaking among. The captain was dreading a shout of "Hey, someone's out there!" He'd considered sending a couple of boys after her to back her up. Instead he was hoping she actually was as sneaky as she said she was.

So far she'd turned out right. And wasn't that going to lead to discipline problems down the line.

"Tents eight and nine, one male each." Bing and Jisi made quick notes. Schwartzenberger studied the sketch of the camp. Those were two of the bigger tents. Maybe the thugs got private quarters, unlike the servants?

"Tents ten and eleven, empty."

Those would belong to the two walking perimeter then. That was all the tents. *I hope she isn't crazy enough to sneak onto their damn ship.*

***

Leaving would be the hard part. Random noises were normal enough in camp. She'd already hid from a guy going for a midnight piss. The perimeter was supposed to be quiet. This side of camp didn't have much brush between the tents and the patrol path. The rain had dug a mini-gully through there, which the path avoided. She picked a steep sided spot and waited for the patrol to go out of sight again.

A crouching walk took her to the gully in a minute. The spot she'd picked had a smooth layer of sand on the bottom. She stretched out, thankful for the lack of rocks. The patrollers were coming round again. She could hear them bickering. The younger one wanted another break. Mitchie tucked her nose into her elbow. Covering the eyes was the hard part of hiding. She always wanted to peek out.

Over her waist a black nose poked out of the dirt. The critter chittered softly. Mitchie shifted away. It pulled back into its burrow then popped out again. It growled loud enough to drown out the thugs. *Crap. That's going to attract attention.* She squeezed her animal repellant bracelet.

The critter disappeared into its hole with an ear-splitting squeal. *Shit.* More squeals followed. She turned off the bracelet but the animal kept complaining.

"What the fuck is that?"

"It's just a damn animal."

"No shit. What's making it act like that? Spread out, dammit. Go around that side."

Bullshitting time. Mitchie put her hands on the edge and pulled herself partly up. "Hey, I'm sorry. I was waiting for morning. Didn't want to wake y'all up." She put on an awkward, nervous smile. Easy to do with a submachine gun pointed at her face.

"What the fuck are you doing here? Get out of there!" The older goon waggled his weapon toward a flat patch of ground.

Mitchie obediently climbed out and stood there, hands at her shoulders, palms out. "See, those terraformers are crazy. I was scared to stay there. So I figured what the hell, everybody needs a cook, I'd see if you guys were hiring. Snuck out as soon as they were asleep."

The SMG was still pointed at her. The younger goon had his weapon slung, though. He looked much less hostile. "If you didn't want to talk to us until morning why are you hiding here? You could've been anywhere," demanded the older one.

"Jeez, boss, have you seen the animals running around here? I'd be two bites for some of them. I wanted to get close enough to your camp to be safe. Without, you know, bothering anyone with guns. Sorry to bother you." The SMG was lowered, safed, and slung. "So do you need a cook? If you've got one I can be assistant. Or I can clean. I'm a really neat person." Mitchie gave the younger one a smile. She only needed to convince one of them to get into the camp.

The fist landed squarely on her cheek. For a moment all she felt was her teeth shifting in their sockets. She was on her side in the dirt. Some stars were visible over the hillside. She picked a bright star to focus on so she could hold onto consciousness. The star wiggled, danced, and went out.

***

Bing turned the volume down before the squealing animal ruined the speakers. The thugs' voices were muffled at first. Mitchie's story came across clearly. Then a thump.

Tenor-voiced goon: "What the hell did you do that for?"

Gravel voice: "Probably should've shot her. But we ought to ask a few questions before we finish her."

"C'mon, she's harmless. Look at her."

"Ain't nobody harmless since guns were invented. Search her." Guo emptied out his pockets. "Check her for guns, you pervert."

"Guo, what are you doing?" asked Captain Schwartzenberger.

"Going after her," answered the mechanic.

"Running off solo like that is what got her in this mess," said the captain. Guo racked his pistol to put a round in the chamber. Then he ejected the magazine, added one more cartridge, and slid it back in. "We'll put a plan together and all go rescue her."

"She might not have that long." Guo started jogging north, left hand on the head of his hammer to keep it from banging his leg.

"Okay, this is an order, get back here!"

"I ain't on your ship, Captain." The mechanic headed out of sight in the moonlight.

Schwartzenberger ground his teeth with rage. He turned to Billy and snapped, "Well? Aren't you going to join the mutiny?"

The deckhand held up his hands placatingly. "Skipper, if I ever tell you to piss up a rope, it'll be on a planet I like more than this one."

***

"Fine. I'll shoot her and then you can fuck her."

"I like them warm, you sick piece of shit."

"Oh, she'll be warm for a few hours."

That was the third time Mitchie had heard them cycle through that stage of the argument. She'd revived enough to eavesdrop after being dropped on the floor of this tent. By the size it was the one overlooking their vehicle trail. The inside was bare. Likely just a place for the on-duty sentries to snack.

"Look, you can't just kill someone on your own say-so. We work for Max. He makes all the big decisions."

"He's the boss here but he's not paying the bills. So our job is to keep him safe. Which includes not letting him get his throat cut by sneaky terraformers."

"Sheesh. You are so ridiculously paranoid. We just leave her tied up."

"It'd serve you right if I did leave you alone with her. Three minutes later you'd be asleep and she'd be strangling you."

Mitchie decided she liked the second part of that. The rest was bad for her either way. Hopefully they'd keep arguing until someone sane woke up and put a stop to it. Assuming there was someone sane in this camp. Her favorite fictional hero would be interjecting comments to egg them on. She didn't have anything witty to contribute. If she did say something it would likely just get her a boot in the ribs or worse. Probably worse. Mitchie focused on lying still and being uninteresting.

Besides, these guys would probably go until dawn without help. The argument had circled around to personal failings again. "If you had the sense to say please and thank you sometimes you might get some without paying for it. Or committing a felony."

"What's a felony? There's no law here. We caught her, we can do what we want."

"Actions have consequences, you fucking idiot."

The younger goon stood with his head pressed against the tent roof, trying to compose a rebuttal. Then Mitchie heard a WHACK. She twisted around in time to see him drop to his knees, then plant his face on the floor. A small splotch of blood marked where his head had been. The other one unslung his weapon and ducked out the tent flap. He hadn't gotten all the way through when more whacks sounded and his limp body was shoved back in.

Guo came in waving a bloody hammer. His intent expression changed to relief when he met Mitchie's eyes. She twisted onto her belly to hold up her bound hands. Instead of cutting her loose he grabbed the ankle ties and hauled her out of the tent. A quick glance around revealed no watchers. He flung her over his shoulder and started moving.

Mitchie clamped her jaw tightly shut. Vomiting on her rescuer was a poor way to thank him. Between his shoulder pressing into her belly and her aching head being shaken about it might happen anyway. When they passed around the curve of the hill she looked up to check for movement. "No one's following us. Please, can we stop? Stop!"

Guo staggered to a halt. He paused to steady himself before lowering Mitchie down. "'Kay. How bad are you hurt?"

"Head's sore. Hands and feet are going numb. Can you cut the ties? I'm scared I'm going to lose them if I don't get circulation back soon."

"Okay." He checked his tool belt. "Um, if I put them against a rock I can probably break it with the hammer."

"You don't have a knife?"

"No."

"You went on a *combat mission* and didn't bring a *knife?*"

"The hammer *worked.*"

Mitchie sighed. "Check my left sleeve."

He poked at the sheath. "Empty."

"Right boot."

"Nope."

"Crap." She rolled onto her back. "Okay, there's a small knife in my underwear. I'm pretty sure it's still there."

"Um . . ."

"Don't waste time." Guo tentatively pulled her shirt out and poked into her waistband. "Ow! Unzip them first, dammit."

"Sorry."

"Try to not enjoy this too much."

"I'm just enjoying it the appropriate—ouch! Shit. You could've warned me."

"I said *knife.*" She bit back more comments as he sucked on the cut. Fortunately for her temper he didn't take too long before cutting the tie between her wrists. Her shoulders screamed as blood flowed back into muscles which had been squeezed tight for hours. When she stopped waving her arms around Guo grabbed one and cut the tie off her wrist. Circulation in her hand came back painfully. She stifled whimpers as he sawed at the other wrist.

By the time he had her feet freed the pain had subsided. Her workboots had saved her feet so she could actually stand on her own. Well, stand leaning on a tree. She fumbled with the fastenings but finally managed to get her pants closed back up again.

"Right, let's go." Guo grabbed Mitchie's hand and headed south. Once they got down on the flat she'd recovered enough to run without his help. Only one of the floaters was still there. Captain Schwartzenberger leaned against it as he waited for them.

"Nice to see you two again. Pilot, are you going to be fit for duty?"

"Uh, yessir. Could use a day off, sir," she answered. Guo confined his greetings to a nod.

"So your radio got quiet suddenly. Can I assume that's when you arrived, Guo?" Another nod. "Did you kill those evil thugs or just knock them out?"

"I, uh, didn't check, sir."

"Really. In a big hurry, were you?"

"Didn't know when someone else would come along."

Schwartzenberger turned his gaze to Mitchie. She'd gotten a good look at the head injuries while being dragged over the bodies. "They, they probably won't live long," she reported.

"Well, I won't miss them," said the captain. "Max probably will since he hired them. Though I think Max will most care that someone waltzed into his camp, killed two of his men, and left without a message. Which makes the two dead bodies the message."

He paused to see if either crewman wanted to say something. They stayed silent.

"You two arrogant, impulsive idiots just declared war on a group that outnumbers us, outguns us, and, oh yes, has a leader who's killed people before. There's no Navy here to bail us out this time. We've got to work together if any of us are going to have a chance to survive this. So try to not fuck the rest of us over any worse than you already have." The captain let silence stretch out after that for a painfully long time. Neither said anything. "Get in the floater." Schwartzenberger climbed in beside Jisi and they headed back to the dome.

***

The terraformers' dome wasn't a bad place for a siege. The thick earthen shell was meant to keep out the stifling heat but would stand up to most bullets. The supplies and water recycling were good for at least a couple of months. The doors and windows were small enough to block easily. With good enough weapons and training a garrison could hold out indefinitely.

The actual arsenal was five pistols, a broken hunting rifle, and three dart guns. Schwartzenberger contemplated the available military experience—Bing's three year tour as a medic—and decided to just improvise. He sent Guo to join Billy and Roark on the rifle project. The rest were working on blocking the doors.

Yukio objected to gluing a workbench against one door. "We're going to need a chisel to get this open again."

"Beats being dead," replied Schwartzenberger.

Roark yelled, "We're testing the gun!" down the stairs. Mitchie slapped her hands over her ears. The rest followed her example. Three shots rang out. Not that bad downstairs. Mitchie thought the guys working on the rifle were probably deafened. A couple of minutes later they heard more shots.

"I wonder how much of our ammo they'll need to get it calibrated," muttered the captain.

A dozen shots later the three came downstairs to show off their results. The scope was a hastily-modified spotting telescope. The trigger linkage looked likely to break the moment it bumped into something. "It's not perfect," said Billy, "but all I need is one good hit."

"It'll do," said Schwartzenberger. "Set up a couple of firing positions at each of the upstairs windows. Keep as far back as you can. Everybody else, let's finish getting this place sealed up."

Once the downstairs windows were sealed the captain sent the more tired troops for a nap. Mitchie found herself in the room of one of the dead terraformers. She was too exhausted to even look at what was on the shelves. The luxury of a private shower did keep her awake for a few minutes. She collapsed into the bed still wet.

***

Mitchie leapt out of bed and stood straight up on the rug, not even knowing what woke her. Then a few more gunshots sounded. She grabbed her clothes out of the cleaning bin. *Got to get into the action.* By the time she had her shirt on this became *Got to get some more pain meds from Bing.* The pain was worst on her cheekbone but she hurt all over. Even her calves complained about the running she'd been doing after all that time on the pilot couch.

Billy was in the genetics lab. He flashed an excited grin as she came in. "Missed Max, winged the driver instead. Should've seen him take off running." The room was hazy with dust. The windows had craters scattered around them, places where an SMG bullet hitting the dome had spalled off material from the inside. Asking for Bing got a thumb pointed clockwise before Billy scooted to his next firing position.

Another lab had been turned into Bing's first aid ward. Jisi was lying in the corner. Her belly had a bloody bandage on it. When Mitchie came in Bing snapped, "I'm saying this to everyone. Stay away from the damn windows." Then she chuckled.

"What's so funny?" asked the pilot.

"Girl, wrap a towel around your head if you're going to bed with your hair wet."

"We're getting shot at and you're worrying about hair?"

"Just taking my laughs where I can get them. Here." The mate handed over a pair of pain relievers. Mitchie swallowed them dry. "This bag has your next dose. The blue ones are stimulants. Take them at least an hour apart and not unless you really need them."

"Thanks."

"Stay low."

"I always do." Mitchie went to find the captain. He was covered in brown dust. Max had given up on finding targets in the windows. When Billy fired at him the return shot was aimed for where someone would go for cover. The custom rifle and its high-tech ammo could pierce the dome and a couple of interior walls. So far the wall material had caused more discomfort than the bullets.

Schwartzenberger put Mitchie on patrolling the lower floor. "They sent a few guys in on foot. They might try to break in."

Yukio was already downstairs. She held Billy's pistol in a nervous grip. "Hi, Mi—uh?" She broke off her greeting as Mitchie grabbed her arm.

"Just point it at the bad guys, okay?"

"Oh, right. Sorry." The terraformer self-consciously pointed the pistol straight down.

"Let's circle opposite directions. We'll get better coverage that way."
And I can duck when I see you coming.

"All right," said Yukio. They moved off.

The windows and doors looked undisturbed. Mitchie tried to follow the progress of the battle by the sound of shots. Max's thugs had plenty of ammo. Bursts of automatic fire followed each of Billy's shots. Probably just trying to keep everyone away from the windows. The deeper sound of a rifle bullet smashing through the wall stood out. Max focused on Billy, taking two or three shots each time the deckhand revealed his position.

In one lab she caught a reflection of herself in a glass cabinet. *Bing's right. Looks like a peacock.* She resolved to shower again as soon as the battle was over.

She smelled the attack before she saw anything. She forced her sore legs into a jog to find the source. The fourth window she checked had a corner of the cover forced open and a tube pouring out some fluid. She aimed a handwidth above it and fired as fast as she could. A yell and string of curses came from outside as the tube disappeared. Mitchie dropped flat as SMG bullets zipped past her head. She started to crawl behind a workbench. Something stung her in the back. She heard shouts from outside.

"Light it!"

"Fuck you!"

"Light it or I'll finish you myself!"

More curses. Then a burning branch poked through the hole in the window. Mitchie fired a couple of wild shots. The branch fell. Flames leapt up from the puddle of fuel. She crawled toward the door, making it just as the ceiling began spraying foam.

Yukio ran up. "What happened?"

Mitchie rolled away from her gun muzzle. "Bastards tried to burn us out."

"You're bleeding!"

"Crap. Keep patrolling while I go see Bing." Mitchie took a deep breath. No need to cough. So it hadn't penetrated her lung at least. She went upstairs. Captain Schwartzenberger was checking on the wounded.

Jisi hadn't moved. Billy had taken a bullet in the leg. The captain had a bandage on his head but clearly didn't consider himself a patient.

"What do you need?" asked Bing.

"Yukio says I'm bleeding," answered Mitchie as she turned around.

"Yep, you are. Not much though."

"Ow!"

"And it didn't even crack the rib. Ricochet. Maybe a two-cushion shot even." She started applying antiseptic and bandage.

"How'd you get that?" asked Schwartzenberger.

Mitchie gave him a crisp report ending with "I hope I winged the arsonist. Might've just scared him."

"No, you got him. We saw a couple of guys running out. One had a bloody shirt."

"Good. How's the leg, Billy?"

"Could be better. But, hey, chicks dig scars, right?" The deckhand still had his grin.

"Some do. Want me back on patrol, sir?"

"Yes. But upstairs this time. Take some shots if you get the chance. We need to discourage them more."

"Aye-aye." Taking pistol shots from the windows sounded like a good way to get killed but she didn't want to argue.

Mitchie found a shady spot in a lab to observe from. Max's position was one car being used as cover with a few dead animals piled up to provide more shelter. Some scattered dirt showed someone had tried to dig a foxhole and given up.

They were a couple of hundred meters away. Mitchie's pistol could throw bullets much farther than that. She'd never tried to hit a target at even a quarter of that distance before. *This is just for drawing their fire.* She fired a shot, dropped flat, and crawled out of the room. Bits of debris fell on her as bullets chewed up the interior walls. *It's working.* She froze as a rifle bullet passed over her head, trailing a cloud of dirt.

Mitchie forced herself to crawl a few more meters, then jumped up and ran to another room. After shooting and running twice more she noticed a change. Max fired at a steady pace, seemingly picking targets at random.

She passed Guo and Roark in the hall again. They were taking turns firing Billy's rifle. Neither had his deer-hunting experience, "But we just need one lucky shot," said Guo.

A bit later the captain stopped her in the hall. "Drink this." Mitchie intended to just take a few swallows but finished the bottle before she realized it. "Eat." He handed her a ration bar.

"Thanks." When the first bite hit her stomach she realized how hungry she'd gotten. Before taking another she asked, "Think he'll give up soon?"

"Not from what he said." At her puzzled look Schwartzenberger explained, "Right, you slept through his speech. He rolled up, turned on a loudspeaker, and ranted for fifteen minutes about how we were treacherous dogs, there was no law here to turn to, and he'd never sleep well again until we were all dead. Then the shooting started."

"Great. I'd better get back to work."

A scream sounded. "Bing," said the captain. He turned and raced down the corridor.

Roark had gotten there first. He applied a bandage to a divot in Bing's arm. A rifle bullet had come through the wall and ripped through her triceps. The bandage was high-tech stuff from a TFS first aid kit. It snugged up to the wound so smoothly Mitchie could see the curve of the exposed bone under it. The bandage sprouted lines as it reconnected blood vessels by forming channels along its surface.

"Never seen one like that before," said the captain.

"TFS gear," said Mitchie. "The Disconnect can't afford it and the Fusion is afraid it'll outsmart them."

Roark gave Bing three injections. "She should be okay if we get her some rest," he said. A rifle bullet smashed through the room to their left.

"God, I hate this," said Schwartzenberger. "I want to have the law on him. But there's no law here." His eyes went distant. "No law. Not any law. No laws at all." He stepped into the corridor. "Guo! Stop shooting! Find some good cover!" A muffled acknowledgement came back. He went down the corridor until he found an intercom panel. Mitchie followed curiously.

The captain fiddled with the intercom until it displayed "EXTERNAL PA ON." He said, "Okay, Max, you win." Another rifle shot hit the dome. "I said you win. We give up."

The shooting stopped. An amplified voice came through the broken windows. "Fine. Come on out. We'll make it quick and easy on you."

"No, it's not going to be that easy. We're going to all get on our ship and fly away. You get the whole planet to yourself. Including all the TFS toys in here. They've got some doozies."

"You people killed two of my men," growled Max. "I want blood."

"You've gotten blood. You already killed two terraformers. Most of the people in here are wounded. One may die. But we're still up for fighting if you want more blood. We could get lucky. It only takes one bullet to kill you. Here's the deal. You and your whole crew go back to the hills. Once you're there we'll go to the ship. Then we'll take off and you'll never see us again."

Yukio panted up the stairwell. "What are you doing? We can't leave! He'll slaughter everything!"

Schwartzenberger glared at Mitchie. "Shut her up."

Michigan had already shifted to Yukio's left side to stay clear of the wildly swinging gun. The terraformer didn't see the tackle coming. Yukio fell through the door marked "Atmosphere Lab." The gun bounced off the doorframe. Mitchie kicked it down the corridor.

Yukio got to her hands and knees. Mitchie kicked her in the shoulder hard enough to put the taller woman on her side. A roll of vacctape sat on a counter. She waved it in the terraformer's face. "If you don't behave I'm going to tape your mouth shut. And this stuff will rip your lips off when you remove it."

"I won't disarm the defense system," Yukio threatened.

"That'd scare me more if Max hadn't gotten through it. Now are you going to be quiet or do I tape you?" Yukio clenched her jaw and nodded.

Captain Schwartzenberger bellowed, "We're leaving in fifteen minutes! Stay clear of the windows! Guo, get the west door open! Everyone else get to work on stretchers!"

***

Billy's leg had started bleeding again. "Told you crutches were a bad idea," carped Roark.

"I'm fine," said Billy as he swung along. "That's nothing."

"Enough," said the captain. It's not like they had enough hands to carry a third stretcher anyway. "We're almost there."

Fives Full waited for them, unmolested by Max's goons. Billy pulled the crane remote out of his pocket and sent the elevator down. Schwartzenberger and Guo carried Bing into it. Billy sent them up. At the shout of "Clear" he brought it down for Jisi. The other terraformers carried her on and were sent up. Some muffled shouting drifted from the cargo hatch. After a few minutes another shout of "clear" came.

"Stop using that leg," muttered Mitchie as they stepped in. "You're making it worse. Lean on the crutches."

"My armpits are hurting."

"Fine. Use the crutches until your armpits bleed, then stop."

Billy busied himself with retracting the elevator into the hold. Mitchie ran ahead of him to unhook it from the crane and secure it to its brackets beside the hatch.

"Hook that back up," ordered Schwartzenberger.

"Sir?" she asked.

"I want the stretcher cases strapped into bunks. Getting to the hatch will be a lot easier with the crane than the ladder. Billy, you supervise that. You two, come with me." Mitchie and Guo followed the captain over to the lower deck hatch, across the deck from the ladder going up.

He glared at them a moment before speaking. They shifted uncomfortably, wondering if he intended to bring up last night's expedition again. His first question caught her off guard. "Long, have you done many airless landings?"

"Um, some, sir. I'm not very efficient," she stammered.

"Not worried about that. Kwan, can we reverse the turbines while running the torch?"

That wasn't something Guo had ever thought about before. "There's a set of interlocks to prevent that. I can remove them. Wouldn't take long."

"Good. Help him out with that, Long. I want to lift as soon as we can."

The pilot and mechanic looked at each other. They were equally confused. Mitchie was more curious. "Sir, why do you want the interlocks out?"

Schwartzenberger looked across the hold. Roark was forcing more bandages onto Billy. No one over there paid any attention to the trio. "We're going to hover over Max's camp. Burn it out. Reversing the turbines lets us run the torch at higher thrust. I want to blast it as hard as we can."

"That's—that's—sir, you can't do that!" burst out Guo.

"We'd never be allowed to land on an inhabited world again," agreed Mitchie.

"Oh?"

She went on, "Every world has strict laws forbidding—"

The captain cut her off. "This world has no laws. There's nothing to keep us from doing whatever we want. Our employer wants Max smacked down. So we're going to do it. Hard."

Guo nodded. Mitchie kept arguing. "If word of this gets out we'll be banned from every port."

"Then we won't tell them. We can keep our mouths shut. The terraformers want to stay here. And Max's people are going nowhere."

The pilot wasn't convinced. But she looked at the determined look on his face and the gun on his hip and decided to stop arguing. "Aye-aye."

Schwartzenberger waved them into the hatch. Billy tried to coach Yukio and Roark through getting Jisi's stretcher through the hatch. They weren't doing well. The captain climbed the ladder to them. "This won't work. Let's unstrap her, I'll carry her through, and we'll put her back on the stretcher."

***

Mitchie stopped off in the galley to wash some of the grease off her hands. Being there to hand tools and parts to Guo had sped up the task.

At least it had once she'd memorized where he wanted everything to go. He'd tried to not complain much but the set of his jaw made it clear when she'd put a tool in the wrong place. As she rinsed the last of the soap off she decided she was fine with the guy maintaining her life support system being a detail-obsessed control freak.

After drying her hands she pulled one of Bing's blue pills out of her pocket. This would need her to be at her best. She swallowed it dry.

Captain Schwartzenberger was already on the bridge when she arrived. "Interlocks disabled, sir."

"Good. The wounded and passengers are strapped in. Lift when you're ready." He climbed into the co-pilot couch and fastened the harness tightly.

"Aye-aye." Mitchie secured herself, checked Guo's readiness, and started the turbines. The two of them had gone through the operations and maintenance manual for the ship earlier. Apparently the manufacturer had never imagined anyone intentionally setting the torch and turbines to work against each other. They'd agreed to get some elbow room around the ship before trying it.

She flipped on the PA—"Up ship!"—and throttled up the turbines to lift off. "We'll light the torch at twenty klicks, sir."

"Very well," said the captain.

She let the ship slow to a hover at that altitude. The turbines were still working hard to produce enough thrust from the thin air. She left the converter room intercom locked on. If the ship started to get out of control she might not have time to hit an extra button. "Ready for cold start."

"Initiating cold," answered Guo. A trickle of water began dripping from each of the sixty-four nozzles ringing the flat base of the ship.

"Heat it up," directed Mitchie.

"Heat aye." The converter began heating the water, first to supercritical steam then plasma. The nozzle plumes merged into one big flame pressing against the base of the ship. As she felt the torch thrust come up Mitchie backed off the turbines to keep them at a hover. She couldn't help thinking that the rocket exhaust had to be visible from Max's camp.

When the turbines went to idle she called, "Hold thrust steady. Shutting down turbines."

Guo echoed, "Steady aye. Shutdown, aye."

Mitchie powered down the turbines and confirmed that the blades had stopped spinning. "Turbines shut down. Ready for reverse thrust."

"Okay, reversing turbines. Stand by."

After two minutes went by Captain Schwartzenberger asked, "How long is this going to take?" He'd never reversed *Fives Full's* turbines before. The main use for the capability was adding delta-V to aerobraking plane changes, an aggressive maneuver he considered gambling.

"At least ten minutes. Maybe twice that. He has to crawl into the accessway for each turbine and switch a valve manually."

"All right." The captain lay back with a patient expression on his face. After five minutes with no word from Guo he started drumming his fingers on the edge of his couch.

Mitchie enjoyed the delay. It was her last few minutes of not committing a capital crime.

Guo finally reported, "Turbines set for reverse. I'm strapped in."

"Reversing aye." Mitchie fired them up at low thrust. *Fives Full* began to descend. She increased the torch thrust to bring them back to a hover. Repeating that moved the ship down a few klicks. The turbines pushed slightly harder in the denser air. "Guo, I've got a calibration mismatch. The turbines aren't producing the thrust they should."

The intercom stayed silent a few moments as the mechanic checked his gauges. "Yeah, we're not getting full voltage in the power lines. The distributor can't handle serving both at once." The captain cursed quietly.

"Can you give me an offset I can work with?"

"No. Looks to be a non-linear effect. Just handle it by feel."

Mitchie thought to herself *Doing it by feel is not how I want to handle hovering ten meters up* but said only, "Acknowledged." She turned to the captain. "Ready to buzz them, sir."

"Do it," said Schwartzenberger.

Savannah's atmosphere had been engineered to standard pressure at sea level. Sucking in that dense air let the turbines push down on the ship almost three times as a hard as gravity did. Mitchie set the torch to not much more than that, letting the ship fall on the camp like a burning meteor. Hopefully Max would be caught by surprise, or at least too shocked to get away in time. She watched the ground altitude radar report their descent and boosted thrust to bring them to a halt just above the camp.

She saw the blue sky above the bridge canopy replaced with a gray cloud—steam from the reflected torch plume, smoke as everything burnable ignited below them, and dust and other debris kicked up by their exhaust. The ship suddenly pivoted off vertical. Mitchie pushed the torch to maximum thrust and cut the turbine on the top side. They were six klicks east of their target by the time she had the ship under control again.

Mitchie yelled, "What the hell was that?" into the intercom.

"I think we just fodded the hell out of number three turbine," answered Guo.

"Can we get it back?"

"Shut it down and restart it in idle. Let's see if that'll clear out whatever junk it sucked in."

"Okay." The turbine was already shut down. Starting it up meant blowing in a gentle puff of supercritical steam. The normal start-up sequence didn't work, but a stronger jolt did get it turning again. The ship rocked back and forth as Mitchie adjusted the opposite turbine to compensate.

"It's running at 83%. I think that's as good as we're getting," said Guo.

"Then let's finish the job," ordered Captain Schwartzenberger.

"Aye, aye, sir," said Mitchie. She put *Fives Full* into a gentle arc back to the camp. Since surprise was no longer an issue she made it a slow descent. Hopefully this would let the site be blown clean before they were close enough to get hit by flying debris again.

It seemed to work. The ship was unsteady when she brought it to a hover, but that seemed to be the irregular ground causing an asymmetrical ground effect. Mitchie wondered how much blasting the camp the captain would consider *enough* when a *wheet* sound rang through the bridge.

"Ha! Bastard did get out in time," said the captain as he unbuckled. He'd raised his voice over the sound of the torch coming through two holes in the canopy. The noise grew worse as another bullet slammed into the comm console. "He's on top of the hill to the west!" he shouted over the noise. He had his nose to the canopy, staring at his enemy.

The turbines reacted faster than the torch. Mitchie cut their thrust to bounce *Fives Full* above the hill. A bullet hit the hull without penetrating, striking a crisp bell note. Another hit was quieter—Max must have given up on hitting the bridge and aimed lower on the hull.

"Hover over the hill," ordered the captain.

Mitchie protested, "That's going to—"

"Do it!" yelled Schwartzenberger.

She cursed and drifted the ship west. It wobbled as the plume struck the side of the hill. The slope compressed one side of the plasma cloud, exerting higher pressure on the base plate than the side open to air. Mitchie frantically tweaked the turbine controls to keep *Fives Full* upright. The irregular hill sent changing pressure waves across the base as the ship moved closer to the peak. Schwartzenberger's grip on the canopy frame didn't keep him from being thrown to the deck and rolled back and forth. Mitchie's straps were secure but her stomach tried to escape.

Once she fought the ship to the peak the ship was steady. Not stable, the turbines were running hard to keep it balanced in place, but calm enough for Schwartzenberger to crawl back into the co-pilot couch.

As his straps clicked into place Mitchie reported, "That's a full minute, sir. Enough?"

"Yes."

She cut the turbines and took them ten klicks higher to hover on just the torch again. "Sir, can you take the con while Guo gets the turbines switched back?"

He ran through some finger exercises before answering. "All right."

"Good. I need to go pee." And put on some dry clothes. "Your ship, sir."

"My ship, Pilot Long."

***

Mitchie volunteered to show Guo the repairs needed on the bridge. Her plan failed. When they went down to the hold Yukio was still ranting. The open cargo hold hatch framed the hills nicely. The trees had mostly burnt out. A grassfire spread to the east. No live herds were visible.

"And it's not just that the microorganisms were killed! That much heat will have baked the inorganic components of the soil to rock! We won't even be able to restore the soil. We'll have to bring in new top soil or wait a century for it to erode into something that will support a root system again!" The terraformer went on to detail how much this would disrupt the TFS plans for expanding their megafauna habitat.

Captain Schwartzenberger listened nonapologetically to his employer's complaints. When she ran down he said, "Max and his thugs are dead. We're alive. That's how I wanted it to be. Now we've got some work to do. You and Roark need to get in the floaters and find any survivors. Guo will help you with that."

"I can help, too, Cap'n," said Billy. When the officer lifted an eyebrow he continued, "I can drive a floater. It only needs one foot for the controls."

"All right," said the captain, turning back to Yukio. "You can have both of them. Get going. Some of them are going to need medical help. I'll be trying to come up with a report that will explain all the damage without incriminating us. Long, you'll be helping with that."

She nodded. Mitchie had to admit she probably was the best bullshit artist on the crew. She just didn't like anyone realizing it.

***

Bing had recovered enough to come join the report writers. Schwartzenberger hadn't allowed her to take notes. That left her with nothing to do but chortle at the brainstorms.

"No, this'll tie it all together," said Mitchie. "When we got to the planet Max's ship was already wrecked in orbit by the defense system. We sent out Bing and Billy on an EVA to check for survivors. That was when a cloud of debris in a crossing orbit hit. So all the damage and injuries are a single incident." Schwartzenberger scribbled it down.

Billy and Guo came in and sat at the galley table with them. Billy was only limping now. The TFS meds had almost finished regenerating the damaged muscles.

"Well?" asked the captain.

"About half of them survived," reported Guo. "Minus a couple some hyenas got. The rest are at the dome now, getting burn cream."

"They know they can't go home, right?"

"Yukio's been very clear with them. Spend the rest of their lives working for TFS, or try your luck with the kitties." Some grim chuckles went around the table. "Biggest news is they told us who Max was." Guo took a long drink of water.

"Out with it," said Bing.

"Maximilian Murtaza . . . the Fourth."

"Oh, shit," said Mitchie and Schwartzenberger together.

"Yep. We just killed the son of Demeter's Planetary Coordinator. Which explains how he got this." He produced a cube, twin to the one Yukio had used on their bridge.

Billy took up the story. "Yukio says they'd left one with the Demeter government in case of emergencies. We found it when we checked their ship for salvageable parts."

"Find anything sellable?" asked Bing.

"Lots," said Guo. "But I tossed them when we found out who Max was."

"Good," said the captain. "We're in enough trouble."

"Dammit, we're not going to get any good stories out of this trip, are we?" complained Billy.

"You'd damn well better not be talking about this stuff or we'll all be fertilizer," snarled Schwartzenberger.

"You can talk about the lion cubs playing under the ship," said Mitchie. "Girls love stuff like that."

Billy brightened up. "Oh, good. So it's not a total loss."

Schwartzenberger shook his head. "Let's get started unloading. As soon as all the containers are off I want to lift."

Savannah System. Acceleration 10 m/s²

Yukio had given them directions for using the password cube. Schwartzenberger had promised to send it to a Terraforming Service ship when they had the opportunity. He'd had a paranoid fear that she would betray them to keep the secret of what had happened, but the defense satellites moved out of their way without fuss.

The captain spent most of his time on the return trip fussing over Bing's recovery and trying to edit Mitchie's "death in orbit" scenario into a report that would sound convincing to the Space Safety Office on Demeter.

***

"Seriously, man, she owes you. You need to collect."

"Billy, I didn't do it to get a reward. She's part of the crew. Just like you. If I saved your life would you be writing me a blank check?" Guo had gone beyond polite brush-off and was now openly annoyed by the deckhand's smarmy urgings.

"Well, sure, I'd feel obligated. Not saying I'd enjoy it but I'd deliver. But you can't tell me you'd rather collect from me than—oh, um, er, hi, Michigan." At the far end of the galley table Bing lifted up the form she was editing to hide her smirk. She needn't have bothered. The boys weren't paying her any attention as Mitchie entered the galley.

The pilot hopped up and perched on the table next to Guo. She looked sideways at him—hiding the bruised side of her face—and asked, "So, sir knight, how may this fair maiden reward you?"

He gave it a few seconds' thought. "Make me a sandwich."

"Okay." She jumped down and opened the fridge.

"Seriously?" Billy was actually shocked.

"What?" replied Guo.

Mitchie put the tuna salad and mayo on the counter.

"You're asking for a sandwich?"

"We have a cooling cycle in an hour. I have to babysit the radiator wings for deployment and retraction so I'm missing lunch break."

"A sandwich," repeated Billy.

Mitchie took a couple of slices of rye out of the bread box.

"I need something I can eat in free fall." Guo bit back a laugh as Billy stalked out of the galley, muttering under his breath.

Mitchie added a few cookies to the sandwich bag. She offered it to Guo with the best approximation of a curtsey she could manage in a jumpsuit.

"Thank you, my lady," said Guo. He headed below decks.

Mitchie cleaned up the counter. Bing smirked openly. "What?" asked the pilot. "We were just messing with Billy."

"Oh, I know," said the first mate.

"Then what's so funny?"

"You didn't ask what kind of sandwich he wanted."

Mitchie looked at the chronometer on the bulkhead. "I, uh, need to take a position sighting." She headed for the bridge.

Interlude Two

Akiak, gravity 10.3 m/s^2

"I really appreciate this, Pete," said Connie.

"Happy to help," he answered. "It's no trouble." He'd invested in the open-top four wheeler to carry cleaning tools, but it was the perfect size to take a friend with luggage to the shuttleport.

"You should be coming too. I'd love to hear your take on the AI tracks." The conference attracted researchers in all fields discouraged by the Fusion, not just the artificial intelligence problems it focused on.

"I'll go to the next one. But I won't stick to AI. I'll want to hear your paper." Connie had emigrated from the Fusion to study the history of Earth's last human century.

"Oh, I'm in the main AI track."

"Why? You're talking about anti-AI." She'd collected all surviving data on the Vetoers, people who'd had laws passed to keep AIs from affecting them.

"The chair scheduled me for before lunch. I get to break up the tired old arguments and give them something new to talk about while they're eating. Not the slot I wanted, but it's an audience."

Pete chuckled. He parked the four wheeler and picked up her bag.

"You don't have to carry that," said Connie.

He pulled it out of her reach. "I don't mind." They walked to the terminal. "Besides, this is pretty heavy for you. What all are you carrying?"

"Um—food and water, mostly. They gave me a free membership and paid for the shuttle and room. But I can't afford resort restaurant prices." Connie did enough odd jobs to keep from starving in her garret but she begrudged all time away from her research.

"Sensible." Pete was saving up for real programming gear. He wanted to attend the next AI technology conference as a participant, not a wanna-be.

"There's my shuttle." She wrested the wheeled bag from him. "I'll tell you all about it when I get back." Connie gave him a quick hug and kiss. "Thank you so much."

Pete sternly ordered himself to not get his hopes too high. The PA blared, "All passengers for Noisy Water should board Shuttle Five. Last call for Noisy Water." Connie waved from the shuttle hatch. He waved back.

From the shuttleport Pete went to Zoltan's Diner. They'd shut down after one of their cooks quit the day before and posted nasty comments about the kitchen hygiene. Zoltan hired Stacey's Sweepers to scrub it out. Stace had promised Pete double pay to do the stoves.

Eleven hours later he staggered into his apartment and collapsed on the bed. Disassembling, degreasing, sterilizing, and reassembling three industrial stoves had strained every back muscle. He'd gotten a bonus, which would cover the day off he'd take to recover.

A chirp woke him from a dream of fitting pipes together. He'd tagged Connie's messages with a birdcall. He pulled the datasheet from under his pillow.

"Dearest Pete," her message began.

"My presentation was a complete success. Hardly anyone had heard about the Vetoers before. I kept getting questions through lunch and they added a follow-up session in the morning.

"I couldn't answer most of the questions, of course. There's so little data from before the Betrayal. They did come up with one I'm hoping you can help me with."

Pete let out a soft "Ah." He hadn't expected to hear from Connie until he picked her up at the shuttleport tomorrow.

"Jordan Hammerstein fascinated them. He was the last living Vetoer. They want to know if he lived to see the Betrayal. The possibility of him yelling 'I told you so!' as he got dissolved got a huge laugh.

"If you have a couple hours to spare could you go by my place? I have the record of Hammerstein's last medical exam. That should be enough for you to get an estimate of his lifespan. Hopefully it'll settle some of the arguments here.

"I have so much to tell you about, Pete. You really should have come. The discussions here are amazing. You can feel decades-old problems getting solved right in the hallway. Gotta run!" It ended with a kiss-sound.

The worst part was now Pete wanted to know if the old crank had seen the Betrayal. He levered himself out of bed and staggered to his medicine cabinet.

By the time he got to Connie's apartment he felt almost normal again. He had copies of the physical keys and passwords for both door and computer. Her perfectly indexed files gave up Hammerstein's data. Finding a medical simulation willing to make a forecast was harder.

Pete finally had to hire a human doctor to convince a sim that Hammerstein had no access to medical care. Under protest it disgorged a time versus probability series. Pete plugged in the date of the Betrayal.

"44%" glowed on the datasheet.

Pete thought about that. The Vetoer probably died before the Betrayal. Unless he had some medicine stashed away to improve his odds, which was possible. So quite possibly Hammerstein was disassembled in the first wave of the Betrayal. Or if the veto code held while the rest of the AI safeguards broke down he could have sat in his bubble of San Francisco while outside his 500 meter radius the rest of the world was reduced to gray goo.

Pete sent the report off to Connie then lay down in her bed for a nap.

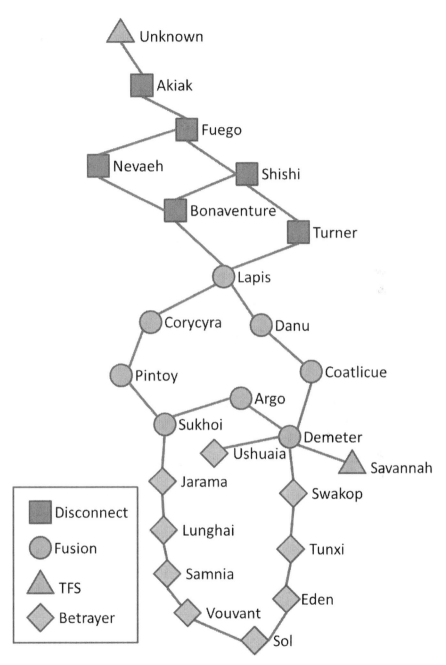

Starmap (not all connections shown)

Part Three: Old Home

Planet Argo. Gravity 9 m/s^2

They were going to be late to the opera. It was Billy's fault, of course. Guo had gotten everybody out of the ship on time but the pass he'd secured for the deckhand hadn't been enough for the port guards. They'd insisted on every member of the crew making statements accepting responsibility for any misbehavior on Billy's part. Talking Bing and Mitchie into just considering it a formality went nowhere. Finally Billy pledged to go directly from the opera back to the ship and consume no alcohol. With the statements recorded the guards let them through into Argopolis.

Guo paid extra for an express vanbot. Its arrival interrupted Billy complaining about the unfairness of it all.

"Be glad they let you on the planet at all," said the captain.

"That brawl was started by the locals!"

"I don't care. And neither did the judge. Be grateful." The stare that went with that finally got through to him.

"Um, right," said Billy. "Guo, thank you for treating us to this show, and for getting me a visiting pass. And thank you everyone for vouching for me."

Cool nods all around. The silence extended. Billy seemed done for the moment.

Mitchie studied the rest of the crew. Bing's silver dress was a nice complement to the captain's dark grey suit. Both were creased from storage. Billy's black suit looked like it had been at the bottom of a trunk. The heavily embroidered wide-sleeved robe fit Guo as if he wore it all the time. Which, given that he was enough of an opera junkie to drag the whole crew to one, he probably did. *Does clean up nice.* She was glad she'd gotten the silk jacket. Her dress was too clubby for a formal event by itself.

She turned back to Billy. "What did you get that suit for?"

"A funeral," answered the deckhand. "The mechanic on the *Angels Ten* went dutchman trying to do an EVA repair. That's where I met the captain."

"We gave him a good send-off," said Schwartzenberger. "Spacers have to be family for each other. Also a lot of us wanted to steal all the crew we could from Meng before he got anyone else killed on that deathtrap."

"Worked. He didn't have the hands to lift so he just sold it for scrap." Billy almost chuckled. "It was strange though. Having a funeral with no body. Can you imagine how weird that was?" he asked.

"Don't need to," retorted Mitchie. "My fiancé's funeral was one of those." *Crap.* Blurting out that bit of history had everyone's attention. She resorted to the truth. "It was another EVA death. He was a rating on the *BDS Brave*. Akiak's Space Guard had loaned him to the Bonaventure Defense Force."

"We've always had more hulls than hands," said Schwartzenberger.

"Yeah, half his boot class went exchange. They had him doing maintenance on the hull when, when a Fusion ship plumed them." Her listeners flinched. A ship hull would be slightly eroded by even the fringes of another ship's torch. A spacesuit would fail in seconds.

"Bastards," snarled Billy.

"I'm surprised the Guard told you what happened," said Schwartzenberger. The Disconnected Worlds governments usually hushed up the Fusion's efforts to keep them in their place. They were afraid of escalation.

"They didn't. Officially it was a training accident. I, uh, had to ask around a bunch."

That raised the captain's eyebrows. "You must have annoyed some people."

Mitchie shrugged. "I do that sometimes, sir." And the consequences of annoying them still kept her busy.

The vanbot sighed to a stop. "They're still doing announcements," said Guo, waving his datasheet. "We haven't missed any of the show yet." He led them into the Argo Opera House at a trot.

Mitchie counted an amazing total of six real people working in the lobby. It took two to collect a thumbprint and admit that Guo really had reserved five seats. A third said, "Welcome to *Three Wars In Five Generations*," as she led them toward the door.

RAT-A-TAT-TAT, RAT-A-TAT-TAT.

"Oh, sorry," said Guo to his cringing shipmates. "That's the percussion section of the overture."

Mitchie popped up from behind a chair. "Automatic weapons fire is the overture?"

"Well, it starts during a civil war." The gunfire sounds repeated with strings and woodwinds matching the rhythm. The guide shushed them and got everyone into their seats.

Mitchie had pocketed her datasheet. Ten minutes of singing forced her to admit her Cantonese vocabulary had gaps she hadn't noticed when talking to Orbit Control. The sheet had a running translation with links to explanations of the historical references. She resisted diving into the articles and soon was caught up in the family's lament for their two sons being conscripted by the local warlord. As the sergeant led them offstage a young woman ran out of the villager chorus and kissed one on the cheek. Mitchie flinched.

In Act Two the surviving son had grown to be the village scholar, sharing the Master's teachings with the community. Naturally that made him a target in the War on Culture. By now Billy had completely lost the thread. He leaned over Mitchie to ask Guo, "What's the government got against books?"

"The government wants everyone to live by their new religion. The books teach the old traditions."

Billy went back to watching the show. The commissar's song threatening to take the scholar's daughter if he didn't reveal his library's hiding place had him questioning Guo again. "Why not just give them up and replace them later?"

"This is industrial times. They can't back up books. If the last copy is destroyed it's gone forever."

"But still, that's his daughter . . ." Guo tried to explain the dilemma of conflicting duties to Billy until even with the sound baffles around their seats other members of the audience glared at them.

Mitchie cut the argument short. "It's his job to be father to the books, so he can't give them up. Now shut up." Bing and Schwartzenberger exchanged quick smiles.

Their attention returned to the stage as the scholar produced a knife and plunged it into his heart. The villagers hustled the daughter offstage then sang praises to the scholar's wisdom by the light of his burning house.

"Over a book?" complained Billy.

"Shhh!" hissed Mitchie.

***

Billy joined in the standing ovation at the end. "At least it had a happy ending."

"Close enough," said Captain Schwartzenberger. "The next happy ending is for you three kids to make it back to the ship before Mr. Lee turns into a pumpkin."

"Can I at least get some dinner first?" asked the gourd-to-be.

"You can pick up something to eat on the ship," said the captain. The trio left.

"And what's keeping us from taking our troublemaker home?" asked Bing.

"Reconnaissance."

"Of what?"

"Of the bar in this place. May I buy you a drink, Shi?"

"Certainly, Alois." She went down to the bar on his arm.

The selection was as impressive as their prices. Schwartzenberger decided they were on vacation. He brought the drinks back to Bing at their table. "To a successful night out."

She clinked glasses with him. "To crew morale."

"Guo looks to have potential as a morale officer."

"If he's properly motivated. I don't know how much good it did for Billy. Hopefully it cheered Michigan up. She had a sad start it sounds like."

"It did sound like it. If we can believe it." Bing cocked her head to encourage him to continue. Schwartzenberger sighed. "I had a turn on the committee that tracked reparations over the Brave Incident. It was ten years ago. Add a bit for her young man to get trained and to his ship. Little Michigan was engaged at fourteen years old or less. Even for Akiak that's damn young. If it happened as she said. I don't think the numbers add up."

"I hadn't realized." She sipped her drink. "So what are you going to do about it?"

He shrugged. "She's a superb pilot."

***

Captain Schwartzenberger had grabbed the first cargo that would get them off Demeter. They'd taken a slight loss on the run to Argo but he accepted that to get away before their report received any serious study. For the next trip he wanted a solid profit.

Fortunately for Billy an urgent load of fresh fruit came on the market before he went completely stir-crazy. The deckhand actually cheered when the captain announced they were headed for Sukhoi. Bing echoed the cheer.

"What do you have against Argo?" Mitchie asked her.

"Nothing. But I've got friends on Sukhoi. I've just had mail from them for a couple of years now. It'll be nice to see them in person."

"Not that you do see them in person," muttered Schwartzenberger.

"Well, to have a real-time conversation."

Planet Sukhoi. Gravity 12 m/s^2

A medical safety inspection was the only hitch on the job. All the ripe fruit had to be unloaded, rolled past the scanners, and reloaded for delivery. It was sweet work for the crew, who'd peel an orange whenever they needed a break. The captain muttered a bible verse and billed the missing weight to "lost or damaged during inspection."

Once offloading was done Bing cried, "Shore leave!" and left the ship.

The captain glared at the rest of the crew. "Don't get any ideas. She spent a lot of time working in port while y'all played. Now it's her turn for some time off while we work. It's time for external fitting inspections."

Bing returned for dinner. The captain had ordered pizza delivered from one of the places around the port. Everyone was too tired from crawling over the hull to cook. She cheerfully carried the conversation as they ate. Her friends were a group of virtual reality gamers scattered all over Sukhoi. She'd been catching up with them from a VR parlor, or, from their point of view, in their new stronghold. "It's gorgeous—a castle on a thunderhead. They can throw lightning at anyone assaulting it. The clouds trailing behind it form a maze. We wandered in there for hours. That's where they hide all their trophies to keep them safe."

"That sounds very . . . grey," said Mitchie.

"No, it's beautiful," said Bing. "The walls of the castle are crystal. They break the sunlight into rainbows, shifting and merging as you walk. The central tower shines with a three-sixty rainbow at noon. And the labyrinth walls are covered with bas-relief. Static while you look at them. Turn around and it's changed to a new scene. I could wander in there for days."

Schwartzenberger dropped a crust on his plate and took another slice. "How'd they like your stories?"

"Oh, I'm a hit again. Being so exotic and all. They're jealous as hell that I got to meet a real terraformer. Creating with matter is the ultimate goal to these artists."

"I'd think Sukhoi's citizen stipend would be enough to let them do hands-on art," said Guo.

"Sure. Most of them have two or three rooms filled with sculptures or paintings. But they can't get anyone to look at them except in VR. It's worst for Yanglo. He creates landscapes but every square meter of this planet is sewn up. It's a shame. He has some lovely gardens in game."

"He should emigrate," said Guo. "We've got plenty of dirt in the Disconnect."

"Yanglo was sounding me out about that, actually. He's been researching it. He'd have to work his passage, though. Just has his stipend." Bing glanced at the captain as she said that.

Schwartzenberger shrugged. "Plenty of room, plenty of work. Usual rule—if he doesn't produce he gets dropped at the next port."

"I'll tell him that."

"How did he sound you out?" asked Mitchie.

"Asking what it's like in the Disconnect, how hard it is to get land there."

"Did he ever ask about that before?"

"No, he said he'd been too shy to ask about it." Bing smiled. "Afraid I'd think he had an ulterior motive. But hearing about our adventures made him brave."

Or they triggered some orders he already had, thought Mitchie.

Bing pushed away her plate with her second slice half-eaten. "I'm going to sleep this off and head out early tomorrow. Good night, all."

Everyone focused on their food until they heard her hatch close. "She seems very, um, caught up in that," said Guo.

"Our agreement is she has to sleep on ship and have one meal a day with us. As long as she does that she can virt out to her heart's content."

"I've never seen her go into VR before."

"She had a long layover here once. Made friends with some of the artists and they talked her into that stuff. She's kept in touch since."

"Sounds kinda strange, that guy just deciding to emigrate," said Mitchie.

"Some people get tired of lotus eating," said the captain.

"Or everybody knowing their business," added Billy.

The last slices were soon eaten. Schwartzenberger made some noises about "early start." They all headed for bed.

***

The Planetary Trade Center was refreshingly low-tech for a Fusion world. The brokers had elaborate data support tools but the security arms race had circled back around to "nothing is as unforgeable as a handshake." After a long morning of pitching the unique virtues of his ship to every agent and broker he could catch Alois Schwartzenberger was in the mood for a quiet lunch alone. He still put on his professional smile when a stranger came up to his table.

"I'm sorry to intrude, Captain, but may I beg a moment of your time?" His suit had the subtle texturing that showed it had been made by humans, not machines. He didn't have the forceful extroversion of the brokers. Schwartzenberger read him as an executive or senior analyst.

He swallowed his pastrami and waved to a chair. "Certainly."

"Thank you. I'm Burton Reed, coordinator of the Origin Set. We'd like to charter your vessel for an extended voyage."

"We have some cargo delivery obligations, but after those are complete we could certainly schedule your trip. Are you planning to go to the Disconnect?" If these guys *needed* a non-networked ship he could jack the rates up.

"No, we're a pilgrimage group. We want you to take us to Old Earth."

"No."

"We're successful professionals and have accumulated over ten million keyneses to—"

"Go away."

"You'd be paid millions on top of all expenses—"

"Shut up."

"The *Fives Full* is uniquely qualified to—"

"May I help you, sir?" Schwartzenberger's wave had brought the waiter scurrying over.

"This man is harassing me." The captain picked up his sandwich and took a bite.

The waiter turned to Reed. "Sir, I must ask you to leave."

"If the captain would just give me two minutes . . ."

"We will make a public announcement that you've been banned from this establishment if you don't leave immediately." Planetary infamy was enough of a threat to make Reed walk out. The waiter followed him to the door than returned to apologize.

Schwartzenberger waved it off. "Don't worry about it. I thought he was a businessman until he started talking."

"What was he?"

"A suicidal psychotic."

"Should I notify Safety about him?"

"No." Schwartzenberger drained his beer. "He's fine as long as no one's stupid enough to take him off the planet."

***

Mitchie followed the sound of grumbling down the corridor. She saw Billy emerge from one unused stateroom holding a box and cross into another. When he emerged empty-handed she asked, "What's up?"

The deckhand shrugged. "Bing wants a room cleared for the working passage guy. So I'm moving the storage over."

"Has anyone really met him yet? Like seen him in person?"

"Don't think so. Bing just talks to him in that game."

"It feels creepy, letting someone onto the ship without knowing who he really is."

"Yeah—but it ain't our call."

"Maybe we should look him up, just say hi, see what he's like."

"Who's *we*? I don't have time for that."

Mitchie looked over the stacks of spare parts and preserved food. "How about I help you move all that and you come with me on the visit?"

Billy grinned. "Deal."

***

Locating their future shipmate was easy. His name, the game he played, and (unmentioned to Billy) Bing's message logs sent them to a gamer hostel a few hundred klicks from the spaceport. Mitchie had a line of patter ready for the receptionist but there wasn't one. The hostel door only kept out weather.

"Don't they want some security?" she complained.

"Everything's recorded. Nobody here is worth going to therapy for. Who's going to bother them?"

"Us."

"I'm not going to do anything to him. Are you?"

Depends on his real reason for wanting on our ship. "No, of course not."

The ground floor of the hostel was VR bubbles, most of them occupied by people going through vigorous gyrations. Upstairs had coffin beds and hygiene facilities. Yanglo's bubble was near the center—and empty. His bed was also vacant. Interrogating someone emerging from another room seemed futile—the name meant nothing to him—but their victim decoded the decorations on Yanglo's bunk. "Oh, he's a Struggle for Shaping guy. They're all having a rally at Denisovitch Park."

Mitchie pulled out her datasheet. There was a newsfeed showing tens of thousands of players standing about in the sunlight. Another autocab ride had them there.

"What a mob," said Billy.

"Healthier than I expected," said Mitchie.

"The games make them work hard. It's the law."

"Hah! This way." They were close enough to search directly for Yanglo without triggering stalker alerts. In a few minutes the datasheet highlighted a middle-aged man standing under a tree. "Hi, Yanglo," said Mitchie.

"Hi! Um . . . hi." His HUD glasses didn't give him any useful info on the spacers.

"We're friends of Bing. Wanted to meet you before you came on the ship. I'm Mitchie and this is Billy."

"Pleased to meet—oh, the Stakeholder's talking." A smooth voice replaced the music drifting over the park.

"My fellow citizens! Effective at noon on the fourteenth of this month, the Council of Stakeholders has approved release of the continent of Y'Laqxi!" The crowd erupted in cheers.

"Isn't it exciting?" yelled Yanglo as he applauded.

"Where is . . . Ill-whatever?" asked Billy.

"It's the new area for our game world. We'll have a landrush as soon as it's open." The speaker continued on, alternating praise for the game developers and testers with complaints about the paranoia and sloth of Stakeholders for worlds less-enlightened than Sukhoi. "Should've had it a year ago, but other planets kept holding it up as a bargaining chip."

"If you're so happy about the landrush why do you want to leave?" asked Mitchie.

"Well, um, the expansion's more *fun*, but I want to do something more *real*. If I go to the Disconnect I can get some land to do art on."

Billy chuckled. "It'll take you a while to earn some good land as unskilled labor."

"I'm not unskilled. I'm an *artist!*" Two sophisticated men would have followed that with a discussion about the Disconnected Worlds' lack of economic surplus for supporting aesthetics and the value of a VR portfolio for demonstrating talent. Billy and Yanglo wound up name-calling. Mitchie was amazed how fast it degenerated.

"Shut up, you fucker!" The gamer swung a fist at Billy.

The spacer side-stepped and slapped Yanglo on the shoulder as he stumbled past. Arms flailing, he fell toward some prickly bushes. Stopping himself short left Yanglo wrist-deep in the surrounding compost. "Ugh!" He rolled onto his back and frantically wiped his hands on his clothes.

Mitchie blushed. Her paranoid fantasy of a Fusion intelligence operative trying to infiltrate their ship vanished like a soap bubble.

"Those VR guys think they can fight, but they spend all their time in spheres. It's amazing they can walk on flat ground without falling down." Billy's gloat trailed off as he realized how upset Yanglo was. "Dude, it's just dirt."

"It's got germs and bugs and I don't know what all else!"

"Let's get you cleaned up." Billy pulled the gamer to his feet. Mitchie led them to the nearest necessaries room. "You know gardening means handling dirt, don't you?"

"That's what bots are for."

Billy sighed. "We don't have gardenbots in the Disconnect. They cost too much."

"Oh." Yanglo was silent until they dropped him off at the necessary. "Thanks. Bye."

The spacers waved and headed back to the park gate. The Stakeholder droned on with praise for the new software's resistance to AI probes. "Well, I owe you an apology, Michigan," said Billy.

"Oh?"

"Yeah. I thought this was a waste of time but you probably saved that guy's life. In the Disconnect he'd've starved inside twelve months trying to be an artist. Hell, with that temper he'd get killed inside six months. You made a good call."

Mitchie said, "Thanks," and stayed silent the whole way back to the ship.

Planet Pintoy. Gravity 9.4 m/s^2

Hauling three thousand decorative fish to Pintoy sounded like a vacation to the crew. After they rigged extra lighting in the hold they expected to just watch the show the rest of the trip. Then Captain Schwartzenberger explained "daily cleaning" meant cleaning the *inside* of the tanks. By arrival they were ready to blow their share of the profit on perfume and incense.

Guo had volunteered to run over to Port Services to pick up loaner datasheets and downloads of the latest news. When he came into the galley it was clear he'd checked the headlines and didn't like them. "Mitchie? Do you know anyone in Noisy Water?"

She looked up from her soup bowl. "Yeah, it was a stop on my shuttle run. Really just knew the field boss, Mbenga. I'd stay at his house if I had to overnight there. Why?" Guo held out a datasheet. "Akiak made the news? What happened?"

"It's—it's gone. Noisy Water was destroyed."

Even Billy grabbed one of the datasheets. The top headline was "FLEET SMASHES WORLD-MELTER NEST ON OUTER WORLD." Curses went around the table as they dug into the story. A

Fusion Navy ship with a Demeter crew had gone into orbit on a "port call" then fired a modest nuke at the town.

"No survivors in the whole valley," said Bing.

"Hah! The defense network took the bastards out," exulted Billy.

Guo had found the motive for the attack. "There was a conference of AI researchers there. Guys trying to recreate the Friendly AIs from the Golden Age. Just theorists it sounds like."

"Theories like that can be dangerous," replied Bing. "Anybody can try to implement them."

"Akiak is banning Fusion military vessels from their space and calling for the committee of Disconnected Worlds governments to craft a joint response," said the captain. "I expect Bonaventure will support that."

Mitchie stared at a pre-attack image of Noisy Water, a small town below a rapids flowing through a grassy valley. "It was a beautiful place. I always liked landing there." She wiped her eyes. "I took a lot of tourists there. After the mine played out they built a hotel. Said they made more money from skiers than tantalum."

"Is there going to be a war?" blurted Billy.

Bing shuddered. Schwartzenberger answered, "Only if the Disconnect's being suicidal. Or like you. Demeter has to be freelancing on this. The rest of the Fusion will lean on them to pay reparations."

"I hate to put a price on killing our citizens," said Guo. Arsenic Creek was on the other side of planet from the attack. He'd never heard of Noisy Water before the news. It was just luck that kept the researchers from having their conference somewhere near his relatives.

"The Fusion's too big for us to have a vendetta with it." Guo nodded. Private justice wasn't uncommon in the Disconnected Worlds but it kept to areas too poor to support organized law enforcement.

Bing gave Mitchie a hug. "Are you going to be okay, honey?"

"Yeah." She leaned into the hug. "It's just a shock." A moment went by. "I'll be fine."

Bing looked up at the captain. "What are we going to do?"

"About this? Nothing," said Schwartzenberger. "It's not our job, and the people whose job it is are working on it. If Bonaventure signs on to an embargo, or"—he glanced at Billy—"calls for enlistments, we'll head home. Until then we'll do our job. Starting by getting those fish unloaded."

***

Guo and Mitchie hurried into the ship. They'd shared an autocab to the port when the captain called a crew meeting. They weren't the last to arrive. Billy's chair in the galley was still empty.

"Did you see Billy coming?" asked the captain.

"No," answered Guo. "Can we start without him?" New cargo briefings usually covered navigation decisions the deckhand had no input on.

"He asked for the meeting."

Mitchie gave Guo an inquiring look. He shook his head—that had never happened before.

It was only ten minutes before Billy showed up. He'd brought along a tall stranger in a suit that had been elegant five years ago. "Sir, I'd like to present my friend Alexi Frankovitch. He has a proposition I think we should consider." He briefly introduced the crew then took his seat, leaving Alexi the floor.

"None of you have heard of me before," began Alexi. "But you've heard of my great-grandfather, Maxim Frankovitch. Yes, the same one who founded the Eden colony. At one point the richest human alive." He held out his arms, showing worn patches on his suit. "You can see we didn't keep the money."

"Eden was one of the first worlds lost after Earth," said Captain Schwartzenberger.

"Yes. My family was on the last ship out, including my father as a boy. We brought out a bit but it was all spent fighting the Betrayal. We all work for a living now." His audience paid polite attention. "But we left a lot of wealth behind. Now, obviously everything on the planet is lost. It's probably all reduced to atoms and made into something else by now. But the best of it was taken off-planet. They couldn't take it with them—it massed too much—but they hid it in interplanetary space. The heart of our fortune. Art from Old Earth centuries old. Some statues over two thousand years old. Tons of heavy metals. A back-up of the planetary archive. And whatever else my grandfather grabbed on his way out the door."

"If that's been in free space, or in a container floating free, it's all probably ruined now from solar heating," said the captain.

"Yes, sir, it would be. But Grandpa put it in vacuum-rated containers and then buried them on a comet."

"You have the coordinates of this comet?" asked Schwartzenberger. Alexi nodded. "Who else does?"

"No one else. My grandfather and his brother were the only ones on the bridge for the drop-off. Vanya died in the Betrayal. Grandpa only told my father. And he only told me."

"But other people know about the treasure?"

"A dozen men helped bury the containers. There's rumors. But nobody knows for sure what's in them or where the comet is except me."

"What's your proposition?"

"I join your crew. We go to Eden System. Once we're there I give you the coordinates. When we get back to civilization I get a quarter of the price of each piece as it's sold off. All expenses come out of the other three quarters. I don't care how you divvy it up."

"That's pretty trusting of you," said the captain.

Alexi shrugged. "If you'll fight to keep a passenger alive I'll trust you to do right by a partner."

"Can you front some of the expenses?"

"No. I'd put some money together, trying to make enough to charter a ship, and lost it. I'm living paycheck to paycheck."

Bing spoke up. "Why not just sell the coordinates to some rich outfit?"

"Because that's mine, my family's, I'm not going to give it away. And nobody in the Fusion has the guts for an expedition like this anyway. They'd just file it away."

"How much stuff is there exactly?" asked Guo.

"Three classical sculptures. About twenty from the Renaissance. Dozens from more recent periods. Fifteen kilograms of stable artificial metals, atomic numbers between 130 and 180." Guo gasped. Creating stable synthetic atoms was a lost art for humans. Even the terraforming AIs couldn't do it. "Other valuables, jewelry, and such. It's two standard thirteen-meter containers, fully loaded."

Schwartzenberger swallowed saliva. "Okay, we'll consider your proposal. But we'll have to sleep on it. I'll contact you tomorrow. Billy, please see your friend off."

"Yessir." The deckhand led his new friend out.

Guo reached for his datasheet. Mitchie grabbed it away from him. "Don't. We don't want to search anything he's told us from here. We have to keep our research as secure as we can."

"Agreed," said the captain. "Starting by finding out what Billy already knows about him."

***

Putting Alexi in an autocab didn't take long. Billy returned to find the galley free of datasheets. Schwartzenberger didn't wait for him to sit down. "How'd you meet him?"

"At a dance parlor." Billy stood easily. He'd been expecting an interrogation. "I'm pretty sure he was looking for me. He wasn't a regular there. We chatted a while. He was feeling me out before talking about the treasure."

"Did you check up on him at all?"

"I did the usual checks at the parlor—identity verification, health and criminal background. He's who he says he is. Historians interview him about his family. There's even rumors about the treasure. Most them pretty far off from what he told us."

"Good work," said the captain. Billy stood straighter.

"This could be dangerous," said Bing. "Ships going into non-human space mostly don't come back."

"About half of them do," said Schwartzenberger. "Not counting the ones with Pilgrim crews."

"I'd hate for my atoms to wind up in some incomprehensible art project," said Guo.

"We could minimize the risk," countered Mitchie. "Take wide routes. Stay clear of planets and bases, just go to the gate."

"That'd be a long cruise. We'd need a hold full of supplies. And extra water tankage," said Bing.

Guo said, "Water's not a worry. We can bring an ice refiner and top the tanks off at a comet. Getting enough fuel metal for the whole trip would be expensive."

"Probably not the most expensive part of the trip," said Captain Schwartzenberger. "Getting enough up-front cash is going to be one of the risks for this."

"What are all the risks for it?" asked Bing.

Mitchie found some paper and a pen on the counter. She sat down at the table and started a list. "Getting supplies to start. Getting through the hostile AI systems. Finding the treasure comet. Whether it's still there. Can we carry it back. Will anyone take it from us. Can we sell it for a reasonable price. Anybody have something I missed?"

"I think that's plenty," said Guo.

"There's one more," said Billy. They all turned to look at him. "We'll regret it forever if we don't give it a try."

Captain Schwartzenberger looked around the table. No one looked regretful. "I won't order anyone onto a treasure hunt. The only way we'll do this is if we all agree. And I won't have anyone hassled for wanting out. So we'll do a secret ballot. Billy, get us some more pens." The captain pulled a deck of cards out of the morale cabinet and dealt one to everyone. "Mark a circle if you want to do this. An X if you don't. One X means we drop the whole thing."

Bing held her card below the table to mark it. The rest followed her example. Schwartzenberger picked up the pile of cards from the middle and shuffled them. He flipped them onto the table one at a time.

O. Schwartzenberger dreamed of owning his ship free and clear.

O. Bing could not say no to something Alois truly wanted.

O. Billy's blood was on fire for money and adventure.

O. Mitchie wanted to see the lost star systems for herself.

O. Guo also couldn't say no to Mitchie.

"Well, that settles it then," said the captain.

Mitchie picked up her list. "Let's see if we can knock any of these off. Billy, are there any rumors of the loot being found already?"

"Not a one. I checked."

"That's strange. I'd think some good art forgers could make up some Old Earth artifacts and claim they were from Eden."

"One get-rich-quick scheme at a time," said the captain.

"Okay, it's probably still there. How can we keep it from being taken from us?"

"If we leave human-controlled space people are going to wonder why," said Guo. "Could get us some thorough searches when we come back."

"What we need is some other reason to go to Eden," said Mitchie. "An explanation everyone will buy."

Captain Schwartzenberger looked sour. "I don't know about Eden. But I can find an excuse to go to Earth."

"A good excuse?" asked Bing.

"A Pilgrim group. They approached me on Sukhoi wanting a ride. I turned them down."

"Rudely?"

"I didn't throw a drink in his face."

"But you were rude." Bing didn't have any question in it.

"Some. It won't matter. It's not like Pilgrims can be fussy about their rides."

"Did they have money?" asked Billy.

"Millions of keys. So he claimed. I didn't check."

"That solves two problems," said Mitchie as she crossed them out. "Maybe three. If we're secure it'll be easier to sell it."

"One we haven't tackled yet," said Bing. "Can Alexi actually find the comet?"

"He's an astrogator," answered Billy. "Used to have an MSS ticket as a third-class but let it lapse. I think he's smart enough to keep the coords memorized."

"I expect so," said the captain. "That leaves us one risk. Getting past the Betrayers."

"Shouldn't be hard to stay out of their way." Mitchie sketched a solar system on another sheet. "Dog-leg courses. Go above or below the ecliptic. Coasting when close to a world to be less visible." She drew a few arcs around the edge.

"The gate is the danger point," said Guo. "There's only one way to get to the next system."

Mitchie drew a circle at the top of the page, then a straight line through it to the arcs. "We'll have time to watch and see if there's any danger at the gate. If there's something there we can toss it in or take a gate to a different system to try another route."

"There's been Pilgrim ships. How did they make it through?" asked Billy.

People glanced at each other around the table.

"We could research it," said Mitchie. "See if any of them said how they did it. Try to interview any of the crews we can find. If we're hauling pilgrims we should do that anyway."

The captain nodded. "Okay, we're ready to get to work now. Mitchie, plot us a course from Sukhoi to Earth returning via Eden. Guo, figure out what gear we'll need to keep going without port stops. Bing, consumables, round trip for us, one way for the pilgrims. Billy—research. Find out all the pilgrim ships that have ever returned." He took a breath. "I'm going to find some excuse to be back on Sukhoi desperate enough to hire out to pilgrims."

People started getting to their feet. Billy asked, "How are we going to divvy up the loot?" He met the captain's eyes firmly.

"We agreed to give Alexi a quarter off the top. The rest needs to cover expenses. Whatever we need to front for supplies, repairs, medical expenses, bribes, what-have-you. The remainder we share out equally. One share for each of us, and a share for the ship. For upgrades and overhauls and the mortgage."

A fancy way of saying two shares for the captain, thought Mitchie. She stayed silent when Schwartzenberger asked for discussion. So did Billy.

"That's good for everyone then?" Nods around the room. "Let's get to work."

Sukhoi System. Acceleration 10 m/s²

Fives Full jumped in only a few million klicks from one of Sukhoi's network relay buoys. Analog ships, of course, couldn't carry the digital gear to communicate with it. Schwartzenberger glared at it as they went by.

"Traffic!" called Mitchie as another ship appeared between them and the relay. After pinging it with the radar she said, "Oh. It's the heartbeat ship that was in line behind us. Must've hit the gate going fast to emerge ahead of us."

"Don't know what his hurry is," said the captain. "He's going to head back in an hour." The other ship was pivoting to face the buoy. It would transmit the mail and Pintoy's network status then head for the gate. The mail was free-riding. The heartbeat ship's job was to convince Sukhoi that Pintoy had not fallen to corruption or subversion since the last hourly update. *The Fusion wastes so much money on its paranoia*, thought Schwartzenberger.

Planet Sukhoi. Gravity 12 m/s²

On landing Guo fetched a new set of datasheets from the port office (Akiak had sent a second round of complaints to the Council of Stakeholders). The captain snatched one and did a search for Burton Reed. The top result was an advertisement trying to charter a crewed spaceship, followed by posts warning other captains that this was a pilgrim run. Schwartzenberger sighed, tossed the datasheet onto the table, and refilled his coffee cup.

A few sips later Alexi asked, "You're not going to call him?"

"Nope." Sip. "He'll see the search. He'll follow up with us. Once he finds out how little we made on this load of garbage he'll show up waving money."

"Hey, that stuff's pretty," said Billy.

"It's pretty, but it's no better than what the stipend kids make here. We're hauling this load of art just to get the artists out of some poor gallery owner's hair. That's why it's so cheap."

The bridge light lit up on the galley intercom. "Trucks are here," reported Bing.

The captain finished off his coffee. "Let's get that pretty stuff off-loaded." Billy and Alexi followed him to the hold.

***

The Sukhoi Exchange didn't have better opportunities than last time. Schwartzenberger chatted up some of the brokers who'd been friendly. The most sympathetic one asked why he'd taken a cargo back here instead of holding out for something headed for the Disconnected Worlds. "Just figured we'd be better off getting some pay than sitting on our tails," he answered. The broker visibly contemplated giving a lecture on opportunity costs, then decided Schwartzenberger was too dumb to appreciate it. *I guess looking like an idiot is the price of a good cover story.*

Reed didn't turn up at the Exchange. The captain returned to the ship for dinner with Bing. The rest had been given shore leave. By the pie they were arguing over what the best and worst meals they'd ever shared were. "Senator Awaki's reception," said Bing. "With the caviar and poached jellyfish."

"Okay, that beats pressed hydroponics algae."

"I'm still amazed you ate it, Alois."

"I was working. Paid off, we got his vote. Aha!" His datasheet had chirped. "Letter from Reed. Apologies for being rude, hopes I'll consider his offer, thanks for my time, nine point three million keys, and more apologies." He tossed it back on the table. "Nicely phrased, too. Must've spent all day working on it. Good. He's hungry. Probably afraid his rich guys will run off to some other cult if he doesn't get a ride soon."

"Going to let him stew?"

"Yep. If they've got that much he can probably shake the tree for some more when he's got a ride lined up."

"Mmmm." Bing kept her eyes on her plate.

"Still not liking it?"

"Gambling isn't like you, Alois."

Schwartzenberger sighed. "I want those bloodsuckers off my back. Just one roll of the dice and I'll be free. If it gets too hairy I'll pull the plug and we'll go back to honest work."

"All right." Bing opened a normally locked cabinet and took out a bottle. "I think having the pilgrim dancing to your tune is worth celebrating." She put two glasses in front of them.

He hesitated. "I don't know."

"None of the kids are coming back tonight. They've all got rooms at the spacers' hall. I checked."

***

Schwartzenberger replied from the Exchange. Reed scurried over to meet face-to-face. The captain had borrowed a meeting room. Lists of supplies and gear scrolling down the wall greeted the pilgrim. After a few pleasantries Schwartzenberger began interrogating Reed about his plan for reaching Old Earth. It didn't take long to discover he had no idea of the logistics involved.

"No, it's not a *standard* trip. We'll be covering billions of klicks. More, because we can't take straight paths. We have to detour to keep to empty space. Then slow down and line up for the next gate. Five times. Six or eight times if we have to by-pass an inaccessible gate. This will take *months.*"

"I'm sorry, you're right, I should have made plans." Reed looked to the display. "It looks like you have."

"Not me. Fortunately for you my crew includes some young, adventurous souls. They did the work and convinced me to talk to you."

"Thank you."

"Thank them. I'm not sure you actually have enough to make the trip worth our while. Unlike my deckhand, I can't afford to take a few months off for a vacation. And we'll need to be compensated for the risk we're taking."

"Of course. Um, how much . . . ?"

Schwartzenberger took him through the lists. Reed balked at the requirement for a landing craft of some sort. "Can't your ship land on Earth? When I researched you the records said *Fives Full* could land without navigational support."

"If you think my ship is going to touch an AI-controlled world we're just wasting time here. We're not landing. We're not even going to enter any world's atmosphere." Mitchie claimed that rule had added two weeks to the journey.

"I see. I'll have to find a ship broker then. What else?"

A non-networked, vacuum-rated ice converter was the next item. After that came additional life support gear, enough power metal for the round trip, and accommodations for the pilgrims. Food and other consumables were minor costs in comparison.

The last item was the charter fee and risk bonus. Schwartzenberger led Reed through the detailed calculations, including the percentage of pilgrim ships that actually returned.

"I, um, I'm not sure I can find that much."

"Try. I'm due for a vacation. I'll rest for three days. If I don't hear from you I'll start looking for another job."

***

Reed walked out of the exchange and stood under a tree. The Pilgrim board was quiet. His HUD showed a few ongoing discussions branching as the full-timers argued back and forth about obscure points. He started a new topic with the attention-getting headline "WE HAVE A SHIP." All the participants switched to reading him as he spilled out the details. Threads branched off with complaints about the captain's demands for more money and refusal to land on Earth. Reed ignored them until he finished the whole announcement.

More Pilgrims joined in as they received the announcement ping. A few updated their pledges. It only added a hundred thousand keys all told. The landing craft thread had spawned some actual research. It turned out there were an amazing number of small spacecraft on the market. The number meeting their needs of cheap, seating forty, fitting in the ship, and having a non-networked autopilot was zero. The technically inclined—a group having high overlap with the pledgers—discussed how to upgrade one.

Reed turned to the money thread. After a minute he suppressed all the demands that he bargain down the captain to what they already had. Most of the posts faded out. A later branch stood out. One of the new members had suggested asking one of the religious pilgrim groups to join if they could bring enough cash. The newbie had been savaged enough to leave the board, hopefully not permanently. He sighed. Status in the Origin Set went to those most eloquent in defending their philosophy of transcendence. Normally he encouraged that to keep his members from joining other groups. Now it was in the way of actually achieving their goal. He promoted the suggestion to top level, sent a notification to the author, and created a new post.

"WE NEED MORE MONEY." Here he put more details on the costs and suggestions for raising funds. The stipend kids were prohibited from having savings but most had accumulated salable property. Reed added some hints on asking relatives for money (there were a few members he'd pay money to get rid of). The post had a sizable cloud of complaints attached before he even finished writing it. He suppressed them and added a follow-up. "If we can't fund this from our own resources I WILL bring in other groups starting with the religious. If we can't pay them the ship will leave and we'll lose our chance."

Before the complaints could start again he yanked off his HUD. Burton sat on the grass, back against the tree. He pressed a finger to his wrist, amazed at the speed of his pulse. *We're finally going to do this.*

***

Printouts covered the galley table. The crew looked up from their reading to wave at the captain as he came in. "What's all this?" he asked.

"Research," said Billy. He pointed out his trophies—interviews with survivors of trips into non-human space, articles about past pilgrims, and big as the rest put together, a captain's book describing his journey to Old Earth a decade ago.

"Why the hardcopies?"

"Well, um . . ."

Mitchie jumped in. "This lets us dig through it without anyone knowing what we're reading. The good stuff we can bring on the trip with us."

"Find anything good yet?"

"Confirmation of what we thought. There's no records from anyone taking a least-time course. They all took roundabout ones. Some reports of weird stuff, AIs observing them or provoking them. A few chases." Billy nodded along with Mitchie's report. He'd found the data but had only read half as much as she had.

"Good work. See anything we want to add to the shopping list?"

"Nothing the Fusion lets civilian ships carry."

***

Burton usually slept through notifications of Pilgrim board activity. It was the only way to get any sleep. It took a continuous howl of posts, complaints, personal messages, and griefing accusations to jolt him awake.

All the discussions going on when he turned in had been overrun by a new controversy. In less than two hours this had escalated to using the words "coup," "betrayal," "rupture," and other signifiers of imminent intragroup violence. He called in a sociology consultant to find the patterns while he searched for the start point.

The ignition source seemed mild enough. The landing craft committee had announced their success. An emergency landing barge off a scrapped passenger liner would be rebuilt. The shipyard had demanded cash up front and been paid two million keys out of the committee members' pockets (counted as part of their pledges, naturally).

This had been promptly denounced by the highest-status members of the community in widely-diverging but always furious tones. Reed was slightly irked himself—he would have appreciated being consulted on that big an expense—but it was their money.

His consulting sociologist produced a report. The denunciations had responded directly to the original post but only after a subpost had been made. There'd been few direct responses to that one but after it the attitude toward the top post had changed.

Burton read the catalyst. It pointed out that the barge only had twenty-four seats and made a few suggestions for how the occupants could be selected. One was taking the members with the highest "insight" scores on the board. The resident curmudgeon had pointed out that this standard would exclude the members who paid for the barge— and since it was their property they could allocate seats as they pleased. Which ended that thread, and started the nastiness.

He went back to the sociology report. The conclusion was stark: "The basis of group status has shifted from success in advocating group ideals (verbal fluency, participation time) to being able to provide resources for the group project. High-status members are trying to maintain their positions by attacking providers and setting rules for implementing the project. Middle-ranking members are considering new alliances." The good news was that both factions considered Reed their leader. The report detoured into an analogy to medieval Japan before laying out several scenarios for the future of the group.

Reed shot the consultant a question. "What's my best option for maximizing project resources?"

"Endorse providing as a high-status activity. Attack members Brightlight, Unlimited, and Cirrus for not helping with the project." He flinched at the target list—all old friends who'd made his parties sparkle, recruited followers, and honed Reed's thoughts into a doctrine that stood against all comers. *I didn't create this movement to make friends.*

He made a top-priority post, "CONGRATULATIONS TO THE LANDER COMMITTEE." He included the opponents by name, saying he was "disappointed that for all the thought you've apparently put into our goals you've never been willing to consider the key issues of resource constraints and priorities." *Well, if the schism is bad enough I won't have more people than seats.*

***

Schwartzenberger popped open the inspection hatch on the barge's engine compartment. No frayed wires. Tight fittings on the pipes. No sign of leaks or sparking. "Seems to be in good shape."

Reed let out a sigh behind him. If the captain rejected the barge he couldn't afford a replacement. "Do you want to inspect the autopilot programming?"

"That's your worry. I just want to make sure you don't blow up my ship. I'll drop you off by Old Earth. You can make it to the ground however you want." He stood in the doorway looking at the close-packed seats. "You'd said you wanted to bring forty or so people on this trip?"

"We couldn't afford a bigger lander. So I resorted to auctioning off the seats." Schwartzenberger laughed. "It worked," said Reed defensively. "Pilgrims from several groups have contributed. We may even have something left for extra above your fee."

"Good. Might want to get some extra supplies in case the trip runs long."

"I already promised the excess to the stay-behinders. There's some hard feelings." The captain shrugged.

***

The ship's landing gear was hidden behind the stacks of containers. Alexi had hooked one up to the crane, only to have Billy disconnect the cables and return the container to its stack. Now they were arguing over a layout diagram. Schwartzenberger had been watching from up in the hold. He considered the several hundred keys a day he was paying for the idle cargo lifter and decided it was time for an indirect intervention.

Guo walked up to the bickering deckhands. "How's it going?"

"This lazy idiot won't let me get any work done," said Alexi.

Billy waved his diagram of where the containers were supposed to go. "The recycler unit has to go in first. It needs access to the high voltage couplings. If we put anything else in before it gets here we'll just have to pull it out again."

Guo took the datasheet. "You've got the recycler in the bottom layer?"

"Yeah. That's where the couplings are."

"I have some extenders. They're long enough to let you put it in the upper layer."

"Huh." Billy took his datasheet back. "I can switch the recycler with the storage unit I was going to put on top of it . . . Alexi, get Food 3 on the lifter and in position."

With a muttered "Finally" the Edenite climbed into the lifter's cab.

"How's he working out?" asked Guo.

"Tolerably. Knows the work. Kinda rusty. Hates being low man on the totem pole."

"Whereas you always know your place."

"I never tell people how to do stuff they've already been doing. Alexi loves his Fusion standardization manuals too much." A hauler towing an open-top container turned off the ring road onto *Fives Full's* hard pad. "This might be the recycler now, solving our whole problem."

The new container distinctly lacked air vents and plumbing attachments. A man in a dark suit climbed out of the truck cab as the driver started unloading the container. Billy glanced at Guo. He didn't recognize the suit either. "Captain, we have a visitor with a container we didn't order," said Billy into his handcomm.

"On my way." A rope ladder had been rigged from the hold. Schwartzenberger descended cautiously—Sukhoi's gravity wasn't that much higher than what he was used to but the pad would make for a hard landing.

The suit waited with Billy and Guo. They'd given up trying to make small talk with him. "Are you Captain Alois Schwartzenberger?"

"I am."

"I'm Arto Lee of the Sukhoi Liaison Office. You have been tasked to transport this material for the Terraforming Service. The instructions are sealed for your eyes only." He held out a blank sheet.

Schwartzenberger took it with a nod and stepped back. His thumbprint revealed the message.

Dear Captain Schwartzenberger,

The TFS truly appreciates the extraordinary service you provided. Unfortunately we have not been able to express that without drawing undesirable attention to the incident.

On hearing of your current venture we resolved to assist. The equipment delivered is for your use. We hope that you will complete your journey safely.

Pandion 7, Coordinator

A file was embedded at the end. Schwartzenberger opened it. It was a naval manual, titled "Operating Manual: A47Q Semi-Autonomous Target Drone." He walked over to the container and looked in. Eighteen missiles and a console for programming them to fly fixed courses.

"I accept this task, Mr. Lee." The relieved Liaison Office bureaucrat made Schwartzenberger thumbprint ten times as many forms as his Demeter counterpart had. Once he'd driven off the captain tossed the letter to Guo. "You and Long need to read through this. We'll have to put some thought into how best to use them. But I think our odds just went up. Billy, this one gets the slot closest to the airlock."

***

Guo was curious about their new passengers, but not curious enough to help welcome them aboard. He'd put off finishing the connections between the recycler and the hygiene unit. That put him on top of the containers as they came in.

The passengers stuck tightly to members of their own groups. Reed had the biggest contingent. They had their hands full guiding friends with bandaged eyes or unsteady walks. Even some of the helpers had bandages or scars from recent surgery. Another group all wore white robes and refused to speak to anyone else. The rest were typical Fuzies. Maybe longer beards than usual.

Bickering began over the bunks. Two containers were set up as dorms, with movable curtains for subdividing them. The white robes claimed the end of one. Reed's group tried to have the other to themselves. A couple of men emerged from the free-for-all and persuaded their way into Reed's. Mitchie and Bing had to intervene to calm things down. A couple of extra curtains came out of a supply hatch.

Guo was tightening the fittings on the grey water lines when his handcomm sounded. "Can you put some extra doors in the dorm?" asked Bing.

"Sure."

"Can you get that done before lift?"

"Not if you want it to stay airtight."

"Stand by." He started on the clean water return. "Okay, we're going to give up on that one as a shelter for now. I'll mark where we need the doors."

"Seriously?"

"Yes. I'm trying to keep people from strangling each other here."

"I'll go get the rig."

Guo considered welding with an electrical arc instead of lasers the worst part of working on an analog ship. It wasn't too bad if he could do the work in free-fall. Hauling the gear up from the converter room . . . he was delighted when Mitchie reached through the hatch to help guide them up the ladder.

"Thanks." She grunted a reply that would have been "you're welcome" in lower gravity.

Bing had gathered the passengers by the main hatch for a combination welcome speech and safety briefing. Guo looked at the crowd. "Where's the rest?"

"In bed," answered Mitchie. "Half the Origin Set waited to the last minute to have their implants removed. They're still feeling the anesthetic."

"That's one way to deal with lift stress." He made a small cut on the oval Bing had marked on the container wall. "Go inside and see if I just burnt something important."

Journey Day 0. Sukhoi System. Acceleration: 0 m/s²

Fives Full was in the groove for the gate. She coasted at 10% over the minimum transition speed, aimed straight at the center of the circle.

This time they didn't have the Terraforming Service authorizing their trip. The local naval flotilla felt obligated to talk them out of passing through the gate.

"Thank you for your concern, SUKGATCOM," said Captain Schwartzenberger. "We appreciate you taking the time to talk with us. This is *Fives Full*, en route to Old Earth, returning Demeter." The commodore on the radio demanded an explanation of why they weren't coming back to Sukhoi. "We're not retracing our path through any system. If anything tries something on the way we don't want to give it a second chance. I don't want them learning from their mistakes on the second try." This triggered a new speech focusing on a captain's duty to the safety of passengers.

Schwartzenberger turned the speaker volume down. "Any of 'em actually in our way?"

"No, sir," said Mitchie. "A couple of fighters hanging around. Not close enough to get plumed."

He went back to giving soothing answers to the Navy. Mitchie took new sightings to verify they were still on course. The commodore went abruptly silent as they passed through. Jarama's sun appeared in the center of the cockpit dome.

Mitchie laughed. "A new system! We must be the first humans to see this in years."

"Well, the Navy sends scouts through every few months."

"Oh."

"Next system we'll be the first in five years. Longer if that Pilgrim ship didn't make it through here."

"That'll be exciting. Hah! Spotted a gas giant." She secured the telescope and took the sextant out of its case. "I should have our position and a rough course in an hour."

"Good. I'll go let the passengers know we've started on the way."

The gate had dropped them into a nicely empty part of the system. An above the ecliptic dogleg let them stay twenty million klicks from any planet. The only one with any noticeable radio traffic was Jarama, grave of 180 million people.

Mitchie alternated between studying Jarama through the telescope and watching the full spectrum scanner as they coasted by it. Continuous boost would have cost too much fuel so half their time in the system was spent in a ballistic trajectory.

"Whoa! Captain, look at this." The radio spectrum display had gone off the scale. She turned up the resistance.

"Looks like we've been noticed."

Mitchie triggered the radar. Nothing was closer than the planet. The scanner showed the signal marching up and down the spectrum with varying patterns.

"Is it trying to communicate with us?" she asked.

"No," said Schwartzenberger. "With the ship. It's a data attack, trying to subvert our computers." He patted the window frame. "*Fives* is just too dumb for that to work."

"Guess the AI isn't too smart if it can't realize that won't work on us."

"It's smart enough. This isn't costing it anything. And it has no way to know we're an analog ship from our thermal signs."

"I'm tempted to send 'give up' in Morse."

"Let's not encourage it."

The transmissions stopped shortly after they began the deceleration burn for the gate.

Journey Day 17. Jarama System. Acceleration: 10 m/s²

Billy escorted the guests to the galley. "Welcome," said Captain Schwartzenberger. "Thank you for joining us for Sunday dinner. We've never had enough passengers to make a tradition of this on this ship, but I think this will be a long enough voyage for us to start one."

"You're quite welcome, Captain," said Burton Reed. The leader of the pilgrims had brought three of his members along. "May I introduce the senior members of our fellowship? Rene Figallo, Poseci Waradi, and John Bertelsen." The middle-aged men nodded in turn. Mitchie was certain they all had spent their days wrestling computers into submission.

The galley table fit nine reasonably well. The passengers were mixed in with the crew except for Burton, who got the end seat opposite the captain. It was just as well Alexi was on bridge watch. Guo maneuvered for a seat in the middle where he could talk to all of them. Bing handled introductions going the other way. A few minutes went by explaining what a "deckhand" actually did. Rene compared it to his work keeping Sukhoi's water systems running. Burton said, "That's important work, mind you. It pays an enormous amount, which is how we've been able to pay for this trip."

"I hope the planet won't suffer from you being gone," said Bing. She passed bowls with the last salad down the table.

"No, I trained my assistant well," replied Rene. "They'll be fine."

"So why did you want to leave?" asked Guo.

"To Transcend," Rene answered.

None of the crew had a reply to that. Poseci jumped in. "The AIs and human population on Earth have merged into a higher being, transcending our physical existence. We want to be part of that, to be recorded and uploaded. We'll have a permanent life, able to explore concepts we can't even conceive of now."

"How can you be sure you'll be—recorded?" asked Guo.

"There's no reason for them not to. It's a trivial amount of effort for an AI of that level, instantaneous."

"But why would they bother?"

"Why wouldn't they? There's data to be had, so they'd collect it. Lack of curiosity is an organic flaw."

"Just because they observe your data doesn't mean they're going to save it," said Guo.

"Or another AI might wipe out the one that recorded you with its data," added Mitchie.

"Ludicrous. They'd never be so inefficient as to destroy data," countered John.

"AI disputes have always reached a Pareto optimum within a very short period. It's illogical to think any could be continuing on Earth after this much time," said Rene.

Bing lost interest in her salad. "AIs fought each other during the Betrayal. Gave a lot of people a chance to escape."

"Transitions are always difficult," said Burton, unhappy with the tone of the discussion. "It's unfortunate that so much harm took place. I wish people could have recognized it was coming and cooperated. It would have been easier on everyone."

"Cooperated how?" demanded Bing. "Just laid down and died when the AIs wanted to use them as raw materials? Billions died in the Betrayal! Most of the humans who ever lived died then!" She cut herself off as Schwartzenberger laid a hand on her wrist.

"Uploading isn't killing," said Rene.

"How can you tell?" asked Guo. "Seriously, when you go down to Earth, how do you know you won't be killed?"

"AIs collect all the data they can. They'll record us in exact detail, including our memories and personality to add to their databases."

"And your current bodies?"

"Are just unnecessary raw material once we've been uploaded."

"You're assuming your personalities will still be active afterwards. You could be erased, or archived in passive storage. That's a permanent death."

"That's scarcity-driven thinking. AI worlds have an abundance of processing power. With all matter and energy devoted to meeting needs even the lowest priority demand can be met."

"You're making a profession of faith."

"No, this is a clear extrapolation from existing data."

"Then why have we never gotten real communications from the uploaded?" Guo looked smug as he delivered this thrust.

"An uploaded mind has new and greater concerns than what those left behind are thinking."

Billy paused in passing out plates of meatloaf to say, "Sounds like what my pastor said when I asked why Grandma couldn't send me Christmas presents from heaven."

Rene didn't appreciate the wisecrack. "Superstition is irrelevant to this discussion."

Guo did. "Theology seems very relevant. Your logic has led you to the same place as revelation, needing to explain a key issue in life after death. So uploading is equivalent to death."

"It's not *death*. It's just a more efficient way of holding us. Our bodies are just a recording medium for the data that forms our mind. An inefficient one."

"More efficient is better?"

"Always."

"I disagree," said Guo. "Take our pilot's hand." He turned to Mitchie beside him and reached toward her hand with an inquiring lift of his brows. She set her fork on the plate and placed her hand in his. "For flying the ship, replacing it with a servomotor would be more efficient and accurate. But her hand can do more than control engines. It can be a weapon," curling it into a fist, "or a communications device," to Schwartzenberger's relief he shaped a 'thumbs-up,' "or a sensor," he stroked the inside of her forearm, "sensitive enough to tell if I'm using one finger or two."

The tingle up her spine had been equally strong both times. Mitchie withdrew her hand. "Efficiency means giving up many capabilities," Guo concluded.

"Those aren't mental capabilities, but physical ones. If an uploaded mind needs some fingers it can just desire them and the AI can create them in an instant."

"If the AI desires to help the upload. And if the uploaded mind hasn't had its ability to desire fingers edited away."

"There's no motive for an AI to edit the mind. It's too powerful to need to."

"Then why haven't any of those billions of uploaded minds sent messages to the people they loved?"

"Something other than 'come join us,'" said Bing.

"I'll ask them when I'm on Earth," said Rene.

"Do that. Then send me a message with their answer," said Guo.

"Why should I bother?"

"That's how you'll win this argument."

"I think I'll have better things to do with all of infinity to explore."

"Guo. Your food's getting cold," said Captain Schwartzenberger. The mechanic nodded, took a forkful of meatloaf, and let the passenger have the last word.

Journey Day 29. Lunghai System. Acceleration: 0 m/s^2

After a week the captain had given permission for individual watches. Mitchie liked having the bridge to herself. Not working a sixteen hour day was even better. The downside was boredom. Lunghai displayed even less interest in them than Jarama had.

She'd taken up astrography as a hobby. The almanacs for AI-controlled systems were just extrapolations from when humans had lived there. She filled the ship's log with sightings she'd taken and the calculated errors from the almanac. She was down to finding the larger asteroids when something flashed across the telescope.

She flipped on the radar. A blip appeared, shockingly close. Nothing showed in that direction to her bare eye. The second sweep of the radar showed it closing. A quick scan with the telescope found nothing. The radar pinged it a third time—closer, and closing damn fast. The telescope went back in its case.

Mitchie pulled herself into the pilot couch and buckled the hip strap. The rest could wait. She flipped on the PA. "All hands! All hands! Secure for acceleration and maneuver! Secure for acceleration and maneuver! This is no drill!" Fortunately the radiators had been retracted once they'd cooled down from the last burn so she didn't have to wait for them to reel back in.

It was Billy's turn to watch the passengers. She switched to his handcomm. "How soon can I light up?"

"They're moving," answered Billy. "But they're shit at free-fall. Give us a few gravs for a couple minutes and we can get them in bunks faster." She could hear Reed in the background shouting about forming a line.

"Will do." She switched back to PA. "Three gravs acceleration starting in ten seconds. Secure for high acceleration and maneuver. Five seconds." Her fingers twitched on the throttle until she shoved it one notch forward. As she settled into the couch she fastened the rest of the straps. A glance in the object's direction showed a small but bright torch plume.

"Shit." Back to Billy's channel. "We need to boost. What's your status?"

"Settling the last of them. Okay, I'm in a spare bunk. Go!"

PA again. "All hands, high acceleration and maneuver now." A quick pivot to put *Fives Full* perpendicular to the object's approach. Then she slammed the torch to thirty gravs. Switching her screen to the port camera showed the plume brightening. Back to the radar display. The blip drew nearer. Mitchie pivoted the ship again, pointing the torch exhaust straight at the stranger. Now it was hidden in their blind spot.

When it didn't reappear she called the captain and briefed him. He replied, "Good work. Keep me posted."

"Aye-aye." Still no sign of the stranger. The radar readings had the object accelerating at more than forty gravs. So it could catch them—but it would have to turn or burn up in the plume. If she kept pivoting the ship to track it she could burn it up or at least force it to use more fuel to evade. She watched the radar, waiting for a blip to emerge from the blind spot.

What came out was a blur, a plume extending past *Five Full's* nose, the stranger decelerating at nearly a hundred gravs as it shot through the ship's plume and braked to a halt alongside. Then as Mitchie triggered the maneuvering thrusters it vanished. No plume, no radar blip, nothing visible to her eyes. She switched through the cameras. Nothing.

High-pitched scratching sounded in the bridge. Mitchie looked to port. Something bug-like was on the dome, tunneling its way in. She cut thrust to three gravs and turned on the PA. "All hands, prepare to repel boarders." *That's not very useful.* "Boarders are small robots, thumb-sized, spider shaped." It emerged into the bridge with no whistle of escaping air, pausing to polish the window surface flat.

Mitchie pulled her steel sliderule from its bracket and started undoing her harness. The intruder jumped for her. She batted it away. It bounced off the deck and came for her again. She flipped out of the pilot couch and let it sail by.

The bridge had a mini-toolbox for emergencies. She swapped the sliderule for a heftier crescent wrench. The enemy had changed tactics, crawling instead of leaping. She turned to face the tick-tick-tick-tick noise.

It had gone behind the comm console. As it came over the edge Mitchie swung the wrench. The robot bounced off the dome twice then landed in the captain's couch. She followed but couldn't spot it in the cushions.

As she poked them with the wrench the robot sprang onto her left wrist. "Ow!" She scraped it off with the wrench. The robot landed on the deck and skittered toward the hatch. A drop of blood clung to her wrist, nothing needing urgent attention.

Mitchie flung herself flat on the deck swinging her weapon. The robot dodged as it came down then launched itself through the hatch. She followed more slowly on the ladder.

The robot and three more like it scurried for the cargo hold hatch. Mitchie ran after, wanting to smash them all.

The hold was in chaos, passengers running out of the dorms waving improvised clubs and hammers. Guo chased after a robot with a crowbar. Several dozen robots had merged into a ball halfway up the hull. Captain Schwartzenberger braced himself on the ladder and fired a shot into the ball. Bullet fragments ricocheted off the hull but the ball was unaffected. With a shrill buzzing the ball pressed itself flat against the hull.

Then there was just a polished circle on the hull and the sound of a panicked crowd. A "whoosh" sounded, as if a plume impinged on the hull, then faded.

"Quiet!" yelled Bing. "Anybody hurt?" Lots of yeses. "Anybody have worse than a bug bite?" Two passengers exhibited broken fingers from the sudden acceleration. "Anybody get worse than one bite from the bugs?" Silence.

"I guess they just wanted some samples," said Reed.

"Or to inject us with something," said another passenger.

Bing had been looking at the bite marks. "No sign of anything injected. Looks like they just took a little divot out of the skin."

"Could have deposited some nanobots . . ." the passengers started arguing the possibilities.

Schwartzenberger waved his crew over. "We don't have the gear to check for infections before they spread so let's not worry about that."

Bing corrected him. "There's a microscope in the pharmacist kit. I can check some blood samples for anything unusual."

"Fine, do that. Billy, bandage anyone who wants it. Guo, Alexi, inspect the hull, make sure we don't have any weak spots from those . . . things. Mitchie, see if there's any other visitors around then get us back on ballistic." They got to work. The captain returned to his cabin. He knelt by his bed and whispered a prayer of thanks that his ship had lived, and pled for further mercy.

Journey Day 37. Lunghai System. Acceleration: 10 m/s^2

The next "Sunday dinner" was held on Tuesday after they started decelerating toward the gate. Dining in free fall didn't have the formal feel the captain wanted. Alexi volunteered for bridge watch again.

Mitchie wondered if the guests had been chosen by beard length. Bing handled introductions. "Rabbi Uri Orbakh, Rabbi Hyman Wortzman, Imam Majead Torkan, his wife Malak, and son Abdul." Abdul had a few wisps on his chin and lip. His father looked like he'd never touched a razor. The rabbis had trimmed theirs to heart-high.

"So why do you want to go to Earth?" asked Guo. Billy passed out bowls of vegetable soup.

"Duty," answered Majead. "One of the pillars of the Muslim faith is the Hajj, the pilgrimage to Mecca, a shrine on Earth. Few can do so in these times but when the opportunity appeared it would be sinful for me to decline."

"It's similar for us," said Orbakh. "Each year we say 'next year in Jerusalem,' which is a city not far from Mecca. We decided we wanted to change it from a prayer to a promise."

"Retroactively," said Wortzman.

"Well, yes."

"Which one are you landing at?" asked Mitchie.

"Neither," said Majead.

"We're splitting the difference. We'll land at the exact spot between them," said Orbakh.

"How'd you talk Reed into that?" asked the captain.

"We didn't," said Wortzman. "As soon as the argument over where to land started he put the right to pick the site up for auction."

"We bid against each other, then the damned Crystallites jumped in," said Majead.

"They wanted to land at coordinate zero-zero. Amusingly the Origin Set didn't care where they went," said Wortzman.

"Idiots would have drowned us all," growled Majead.

"So we pooled our money and outbid them for a compromise site," finished Orbakh.

"Efficient way to settle the issue," said Schwartzenberger.

"You always love auctions," said Bing. Orbakh's inquiring look made her explain, "The Captain's from Bonaventure."

"Oh, the plutocracy planet," said Wortzman.

"It's not a plutocracy, dammit," said Schwartzenberger. "Anyone can win office." The other passengers had blank looks. "We auction off seats in the legislature. Top ten bids are councilors who propose laws, next hundred are the senators who can amend them, and then a thousand assemblers who vote yes or no on them. That's over half our tax revenue right there."

Majead pulled on his beard. "Sounds like your politicians are very corrupt."

"Y'all put a couple of Stakeholders in jail every year for taking bribes or steering contracts. Money and politicians are like water and downhill. The Fusion builds a dam. We put in a waterwheel and get some work out of them. No losses to the middlemen."

Rabbi Orbakh laughed. "I had no idea the Disconnected Worlds were such a fount of political experimentation."

"Hey, don't paint all of us with that," said Mitchie. "Akiak has perfectly normal elections. 'Cause we're so poor auctioning them off wouldn't get a quorum."

"We are unconventional by Fusion standards," countered Guo. "One house is geographic, the other proportional representation. Gives two cuts at what the electorate is really thinking."

"My word," said Wortzman. "Doesn't it get gridlocked? How does your government get anything done?"

"It doesn't," answered Mitchie. "We like it that way."

Billy replaced empty soup bowls with plates of lasagna and hoped no one would ask him how Shishi was run.

"Bonaventure does have a significant accomplishment," said Wortzman. "Though I don't know if it's due to your system of government. The higher an emigrant's intelligence rating, the more likely he is to choose Bonaventure as a destination."

"I'm happy for the compliment," said Schwartzenberger, "but there's some geniuses I'd rather went elsewhere."

"You don't like having smart workers?"

"Smarter than average, sure. I'll take them. It's the supersmart ones I have trouble with. It's like putting treads instead of wheels on your groundcar. You can go more places, but when you finally do get stuck no one can get there to help you out. These smart guys get wrapped up in some idea and shoot down any arguments against it. So no matter how badly it works in the real world they're stuck."

Orbakh burst out laughing. Wortzman smiled tightly. Orbakh slapped his friend's shoulder. "Oh, come on, Hymie. Doesn't that sound just like those leveler academics you always feuded with?"

"I suppose."

"Geniuses getting themselves stuck is nothing," said Majead. "It's when they come up with ways to kill us all that I get angry."

"What do you mean by that?" snapped Wortzman.

"That smart people like you created the machines that killed most of the human race and drove my people from their sacred lands!"

"Creating AIs gave us the Golden Age, the greatest prosperity, progress, and peace humanity has ever known. If it hadn't been for stupid, greedy fools tampering with things they couldn't understand we'd still be in that paradise."

"So now you're blaming us, you—" Majead spewed obscenities at the top of his lungs. Wortzman replied with equal venom and volume.

Schwartzenberger bellowed, "Gentlemen, be quiet!" to no effect.

Orbakh protested, "Hyman, don't make trouble." Majead's wife pulled on his arm. The two started around the table as they kept yelling.

Billy and Guo put themselves between the older men. The fighters shoved the crewmen back to back as they tried to get at each other. Punches hit the crewmen as often as their targets. Majead shoved his wife away. Abdul caught her as she fell.

Then the rest of the crew got to them. The other rabbi helped pull Wortzman away. After a minute both stopped struggling.

"Gentlemen, can I expect civil behavior from you?" asked the captain.

"I will not tolerate this," said Majead. He walked out of the galley. When he snapped his fingers his wife and son followed.

The galley suddenly only had the sound of men trying to catch their breath. Orbakh kicked his friend's ankle. "Captain, I apologize for my behavior," said Rabbi Wortzman. "Gentlemen, I apologize for any injury I may have caused you. Ladies, I apologize for my language. I'm sorry."

"Well, let's not let the food get cold," said Bing. They all sat and applied themselves to the lasagna. Billy poked through it wondering where the meat was hiding. Some garlic bread came out of the oven and swiftly vanished.

Rabbi Orbakh decided to revisit a safer topic. "Captain, you objected to your world being called a plutocracy. But doesn't buying legislative seats restrict them to the rich?"

Schwartzenberger swallowed his bread. "If legislators had to bid with their own money, yes. We get a few of those every term but if they keep it up they stop being rich quickly. Most legislators are funded by supporters or represent an organization."

"Corporations?"

"No," said Schwartzenberger. "Stockholders figured out a long time ago that senators are a bad investment in an auctionocracy. Mostly issue-oriented non-profits. What on other worlds would be political parties or lobbying groups."

"Still, anyone holding such an office would make connections, the sort of thing that leads to personal profits."

Bing laughed. "Rabbi, I should warn you that you're discussing this with a former senator." Mitchie and Billy were as surprised as the guests.

"Not that it's relevant," Schwartzenberger muttered, taking a chance to eat some of his seconds.

"Actually, I think the story would be fascinating," said Wortzman. The rest of the table endorsed this.

The captain sighed. "There's really not that much to tell. I was on the beach receiving medical treatment." His face tightened in memory. "The Free Traders' Guild usually fields a legislator. We want to make sure the ports are maintained, inspections are reasonable, and so on. Some groups hire a professional lobbyist to warm the seat but that doesn't work for us. They don't know the issues well enough. So we find a spacer willing to take the job. Someone just retired, or a female wanting some kid time, or an oddball like me.

"Our current senator wanted to move on. I was available. It was something I could do while finishing my physical therapy. I had a decent reputation in the Guild." Bing snorted. "So they offered me the job and I took it. Didn't really have anything else to do at the time."

"So how did you get from there to here?"

"After four years my legs were fine, my feet were itchy, and I was fed up with being polite to idiots who wanted my vote. So I found someone else to drop the job on—Sparrow still has it, she's sharp—and swung a deal to captain this ship." Bing passed out cupcakes.

"Did the 'deal' use your contacts from being senator?" asked Orbakh.

"No, it counted against me. I had to retake my master's exam to prove I hadn't forgotten how to run a ship while going to all those cocktail parties. I found *Fives Full* going up for sale and arranged a loan to put her back in service."

"I'm glad you did, Captain. Otherwise we'd still be on Sukhoi trying to find a way to keep another Passover Seder interesting."

"Don't thank me until after you land. But I thank you gentlemen for joining us for a most memorable dinner."

***

The next dinner with passengers was on Sunday. The ship was still boosting up to coast speed in the Samnia system. The meal was free of rude outbursts until after the four white-robed members of the Crystalline Order bowed and left.

"Let me see if I have this straight," said Billy. "Their plan is to get uploaded, have the AIs read their grand idea, and then because the idea is so obviously perfect the AIs put all their resources into totally remaking the galaxy to comply with it."

"Yes," said Guo.

"That's . . . I don't have words for how nuts that is."

"Infinitely?" offered Mitchie.

"Yeah, that's good."

"We're not their pastors or therapists," said Captain Schwartzenberger. "Just transportation. Their money's good so we're hauling them. That's it."

"I should have taken bridge watch."

"And missed meeting three girls?" teased Mitchie.

"Listening to them recite their doctrine in unison is not 'meeting,'" said Billy.

Journey Day 46. Samnia System. Acceleration: 10 m/s^2

Captain Schwartzenberger had come early for shift change. This was normal. He liked to review the log, take a position sighting, and otherwise assure himself that no unreported disasters had happened while he was off-watch. This shift called for some extra sightings. They were about to cease thrusting to conserve fuel. The ballistic trajectory would take them through (well, around) the system to the gate. Any error would be more expensive to correct the closer they were to the gate.

After four days they'd learned the system well enough to take sextant sights without needing to use the telescope to identify their targets. Sighting on two planets and the star, with half a page of calculations, gave them an exact location. Checking a third planet told them how big their measurement errors were. Schwartzenberger picked a fourth and measured its angles to all the others. Mitchie started to wonder if they'd have enough paper for the journey. He tore off a sheet of equations and handed it to her. "Check me."

She went through the rows of figures. She'd caught him in a few mistakes in her time on board. One may have been accidental. She was certain the rest were just to see if she was paying attention. But being in non-human space had cured the captain of those games. "I check you, sir."

"We're in the groove, then." He secured the sextant in its case. Schwartzenberger stood and gazed out at the stars, trying to relax in their beauty. His eye drifted back to Samnia. Their course had been driven by his desire to stay at least five million klicks from the former human colony.

The blue-white planet suddenly changed to a brighter shade of blue. Schwartzenberger grabbed the telescope. A perfect blue circle, darker at the edges, with a black dot in the center. "It's coming straight at us," he said.

"What is, sir?" asked Mitchie.

"A ship. From Samnia. High thrust."

She activated the radar. "There it is."

"Log the reading. Then get us away from Samnia."

"Aye-aye." PA switch. "All hands, brace for maneuver. Grab something now!" She counted off five seconds then fired the thrusters to point the ship directly away from the planet. Schwartzenberger didn't bother with his couch, just bracing himself with a hand on the comm console.

The AI ship was now hidden behind their exhaust. The captain lifted his mike and switched on the PA. "All hands, this is the captain speaking. We've spotted another torchship in this system. We're going to plot its course. If it's coming toward us we'll maneuver to evade it. We'll need to maneuver at short notice. Everyone please secure themselves in their bunks until further notice. I'll make further announcements as there's news." Then he strapped himself in.

At the ten minute mark the captain said, "Let's take a peek."

Mitchie pivoted the ship to let them look around the plume at Samnia. They studied the radar. "Heading straight for us," she said. She pulled her acceleration sliderule out of its holster. "If it was stationary the first time we ranged it, it's accelerating at about fifty gravs. So the real accel is closer to forty."

"Which is more than our passengers can handle. Take us up to thirty and turn away from it. We've got a head start, let's use it."

"Aye-aye." They sank deeper into their cushions as the thrust built up.

Schwartzenberger noted the time and forced himself to wait a whole hour before taking another look at their pursuer. Mitchie worked her sliderule and announced, "About forty-three gravs. On average. Don't know if they're taking any cool-down breaks."

"I doubt they'll need to."

"Sir, permission to go to ten gravs for a minute? I want to check something."

"Granted."

When the weight let up Mitchie grabbed the telescope and a reference book. A look at the AI vessel and the system primary sent her to a lookup table of stellar magnitudes, then another in the same book. "The brightness of its plume gives us a rough thrust estimate. If their drive is as efficient as ours then that ship is about ten times our mass."

"So whatever they want with us, they want it bad. Resume course and full thrust."

"Aye-aye."

Schwartzenberger switched to the converter room intercom. "Guo, if we're still being chased an hour from now we'll try a discourager on it."

"Will do, sir."

"Mitchie, get him angles for Samnia."

"On it." That gave his subordinates something useful to focus on. Schwartzenberger spent the next hour brooding. The peek at the pursuer was a relief, even knowing the ship was still coming at them.

"Do it," he ordered.

Mitchie cut thrust to ten gravs. Guo and Alexi scrambled from the converter room to the hold. The mechanic went to the target drone programmer and tapped in the direction to Samnia in the ship's current reference frame. It spit out a card which he inserted in the drone's "brain." The inertial tracking unit booted up. Alexi handled getting the drone into the airlock while Guo suited up.

Fitting himself into the airlock with the drone was a tight squeeze. When the door could finally be closed he transmitted, "Cut thrust." When the ship was in free fall he pushed the drone out. Careful to keep from putting any spin on it he pressed the start button and shoved it away from the ship hard. Then it was just a matter of getting back in the airlock and closing the door before the delay ran out.

He had fifteen seconds to spare. As Guo opened the inner door the drone's torch exhaust slapped the hull like a crack of thunder. It was off to Samnia—and, not incidentally, their pursuer—at a hundred gravs. *Fives Full* went back to ten gravs without any announcement.

Mitchie had been watching their enemy with the port camera. It was a perfect bright circle. The drone obscured the screen for several minutes before it was far enough away to see around. The ship's plume had changed to a streak, round on one end. The perfect image of a torchship thrusting perpendicular to the observer.

She laughed out loud. "They bought it! They're running."

"For now," said Schwartzenberger. "Until it notices our missile isn't reacting to their maneuvers."

"But that buys us some time."

"That it does."

The intercom sounded. "Converter room strapped in," said Guo.

"Roger, converter room," said Mitchie as she sent the ship back to fleeing.

The next few hourly peeks showed the other ship evading, then ignoring, and finally closing with and destroying the drone. "Just as well," said the captain. "We shouldn't make craters in worlds unless we know exactly what we're blowing up." The crew spent some time on the intercom discussing the option of sending a dozen drones to the planet on divergent courses. Bing ended it by pointing out that whatever the ship's current motive for chasing them was, "wipe out the genocidal maniacs" was not an improvement.

At twelve hours they spent fifteen minutes at ten gravs to let everyone have a potty break. Bing and Billy volunteered for shift changes. The control freaks on duty declined.

The prolonged high acceleration wore on Mitchie. Her neck ached. Her arms were exhausted. The most trivial tasks felt like climbing a cliff. She didn't complain. It had to be worse for the others.

Guo was the first to complain. Technically he spoke for the equipment. "Sir, it's getting pretty hot in here. Do you think we might be able to coast for a bit?"

"Not an option," said the captain into the intercom. "It's still closing. How bad is it down there?"

"I sent Alexi to his quarters. Converter efficiency is down 18%. I have gauges too warped for me to get an accurate reading. And the mechanic's out of spec too." Mitchie chuckled at Guo's phrasing. Still, he had to be in bad shape if he admitted to it.

"I see. You'll have to soak it."

"Sir, I can't guarantee we won't lose something critical if I do that."

"Not asking you to, Mr. Kwan. It's just the least bad option."

"Okay. I'll need some ten grav time to prep."

"Right." At the captain's nod Mitchie cut thrust.

Guo started securing everything that could be water damaged. Manuals, tools, sliderules all came out of their handy niches by the acceleration couch and into vacuum-tight cabinets. Once the fragile items were secure he donned his pressure suit. With his air supply safe he sealed all the hatches and ventilation ducts.

The converter room was walled with pipes connecting the water tanks with each other and the converter. Inspection ports, relief valves, drain spigots—plenty of options for dumping water on the floor. Guo started with inspection valves, spraying water up to the ceiling. If he could cool the instruments gently they might get through this without fractures. He started a drain valve streaming onto the floor. Steam poured off the converter. An ammeter's cover shattered.

Mitchie's voice sounded on his helmet radio. "How are you doing down there?"

"Switching from baked to boiled. There's a few spots on the floor bubbling. The converter's cooling down though."

"How's your temp?"

He glanced at the gauge by his chin. "A bit high. I'd better vent the room." One pipe went to vacuum. He waded over and twisted the valve open—one hand on the valve, the other on the safety release. Steam blew past him into it. A hammer disabled the safety. He tied on two ropes to handle opening and closing it, using a nearby pipe as a pulley. Another rope toggled a drain valve by his couch.

"I'll be ready for full thrust again in a moment," he reported. The ropes were tied to the acceleration couch. Guo sloshed around turning off the other valves. The vent had some ice forming on it from vacuum freezing. He knocked the crystals off then climbed into the couch. "Ready for boost." His weight tripled.

The captain came on the radio. "Eleven minutes. Good work, Mr. Kwan."

"Thank you, sir."

"We're going to stay at this accel for a while."

"Yes, sir."

On the bridge they could see when Guo vented. Puffs of steam were visible at the edge of the dome.

Mitchie had finally tired enough to sleep at thirty gravs. It wasn't a restful nap, just a break from feeling her body squeezed flat. The captain woke her up for the next peek at the pursuer.

The bogey was noticeably brighter. "Crap," said the captain. "We'll have to double thrust. That'll kill some of the passengers. What's its accel up to?"

Mitchie worked her sliderule, plugging in the latest range number from the radar. "It's . . . this doesn't make sense. Its overtake is down. Should be closer if it had kept on its old boost."

Schwartzenberger looked at the camera image again. "Jesus, Mary, and Joseph. It's flipped. Gave up on trying to catch us." It was a solid blue circle, no dot in the middle.

Mitchie calculated an answer that fit all the data. "They turned over four hours ago and kept the same accel."

The captain crossed himself. "Straighten her out. We'll boost another three hours then peek again. If they're still decelerating we'll go ballistic then."

"Aye-aye." Mitchie paused. "Do you think they just hit their limit?"

"Maybe. Or all that steam venting makes them think we'd blow up before they could board us. You take the watch, I'm going to nap. Don't tell anyone until we confirm it next peek."

"Aye, sir."

Unlike his supposed naps earlier, the captain did fall asleep this time. Or so Mitchie inferred from his snores. She decided to let him sleep until she'd confirmed the enemy ship's new trajectory, but he woke as the ship pivoted. One pulse from the radar proved it was on the course she'd calculated for it. "It's been thrusting away from us the whole time, sir."

"Good. Cut thrust." The ship went into free fall. Schwartzenberger flipped on the PA. "All hands. The pursuing ship has turned back. We're going to take at least a twelve hour rest before resuming our original course. Resume normal cruise activities. Captain out." Flipping to the crew intercom. "Mr. Kwan, shut down the converter. First Mate, take bridge watch and deploy the radiators. Billy and Alexi, suit up and get the converter room dried out. Everyone else, get ten hours of sleep."

"Done, sir," said Guo.

Journey Day 48. Samnia System. Acceleration: 0 m/s^2

Mitchie drew a circle around the coordinates with a flourish. Her position sighting matched the acceleration log as accurately as they could measure. She turned to plotting out a new course to the gate. Staying at least a hundred million klicks from any world with radio activity wasn't going to be hard at this point. They were headed out of the system at over a percent of lightspeed. By the time they worked off that velocity they'd be well clear of everything. The dogleg to get on-vector for the gate would be expensive. She set a start time two hours in the future and got to work.

Guo's voice came over the intercom. "Converter room to bridge."

"Captain here," answered Schwartzenberger.

"Sir, I'm going to need some time to get ready to boost again."

"What's the problem?"

"Converter didn't like the fast shutdown. I've got some clogged pipes I need to clear."

"I thought that fancy MC978 put up with everything better than the old one." It had certainly let them boost continuously much longer than the original had.

"I'm still discovering what it's finicky about."

"All right. How long do you need?"

"Not sure yet. I'm going to have to open up the sump plumbing."

"Want me to send Billy down to give you a hand?"

"No, I don't—this is going to be too complicated for that."

Mitchie made sure her mike was off before asking, "I thought Billy was apprenticing as mechanic?"

Schwartzenberger switched his off. "That would be working better if Guo had more patience with fools."

She turned her mike back on. "Can I give you a hand down there?"

"Sure. You probably fit better into the access than I do."

"Sir?"

The captain waved toward the hatch. "Granted. I have the con."

The converter room had always reminded Mitchie of an ancient temple: a big open area surrounding the statue of the god with a ring of columns on the outside. The converter still held the center but the pipes and tanks on the outside were covered with panels. Guo had dismantled most of the firedeck making up the room's floor. The exposed plumbing looked like a bramble bush with thicker vines. A pair of legs and some low curses emerged from a gap near the base of the converter.

"How's it going?" she asked.

Guo pushed himself out and caught himself on one of the wire feeds. "Badly. All the sludge pipes are clogged. They're going to have to come out to get cleared. Let's get some safety gear on you." His gear was limited. All she could see was gloves and, as he turned to face her, a codpiece inside his jumpsuit. Only worried about radiation hazards then. He tossed her a wide leadweave belt which she wrapped around her hips.

"What's the dosage?"

He pointed at the Geiger counter on top of the converter. "A bit above background. I'm mostly worried about something nastier coming out of the pipes when we unmount them. Thanks for coming down. Alexi wimped out when he found out we had to deal with sludge."

"Fuzies like to pretend everything's safe. This where you're starting?" She looked into where Guo had been working.

"I was trying. Couldn't get in far enough to apply the wrench."

She took the gloves and wrench and started floating in. "What happened?"

"I screwed up."

"That's just making me more curious."

"The emergency shutdown on the old GNX converter pushed water through to clean it out and cool everything down. Then I'd get to spend a day drying it out and dealing with corrosion. The, the, um, 978 has separate cooling pipes."

She wondered why he fumbled his words, then remembered she'd changed after her sleep shift. This jumpsuit had always been a bit too snug in the hips. She wiggled her hips back and forth to push herself between the pipes.

"It also has an air pressure, um, system for forcing out the sludge. I, ah, hit, um, triggered both at once. Should've given the air a minute to force it clean first. Instead, uh, it, uh, froze the sludge in place and the air couldn't budge it."

Behave, girl, she told herself. *Fix the ship first, tease the mechanic later.* She pulled herself the rest of the way in with her hands. "So the sludge pipes are full?"

"Probably. Nastier than usual, too. The overheating was trashing converter efficiency so it wasn't going down to stable isotopes. That's why I've got the counter out. If we clean out the pipes then I can chip out the residue in the converter and get started again."

"This is going to take a while." She got the wrench on the first bolt and started turning. "Okay, I'm disconnecting the converter end first."

"Wait a minute between bolts, in case there's some mercury or other liquid in there."

"Right." She started on the second one. "You realize we're headed away from the gate really fast, right?"

"So we don't have time to clean up any liquid short-half-life sludge."

"Right." She shone her flashlight on the pipe flange. Nothing seeping out. She went back to turning the bolts.

The pipe didn't leak anything after she unbolted it. The sludge was solid enough it took running a cable around it with both of them pulling to break it free. The Geiger counter didn't complain so the isotopes were stable enough to not make them put on any more gear. Guo made them both drink some water before starting on the next pipe.

When all six pipes were dismounted Guo told her to take a break while he went in with a chisel and hammer. The sludge was brittle so it only took a few swings to get a hole through the residue at each port. Then he held a suction bag to the inspection port on the converter's side to gather up the fragments.

"Not going to clear the sludge tank ports?" asked Mitchie.

Guo shook his head. "Not until we're remounting the pipes. I don't have a good way to collect the chips." He grinned. "Now it's time for the pretty part." She went off to get her pressure suit. The next step they'd do out on the hull.

Mitchie had to admit watching molten metal drops fly past her faceplate was pretty. They glowed different colors depending on the element. But it was not her favorite thing to do in vacuum. Cleaning out the pipes was a two-spacer job. One spun the pipe, angling it so neither end pointed toward the ship. The other held the welding torch to the center of spin. As the pipe heated the sludge melted and drops came out the end. Very pretty, if you could stop worrying about one melting a hole in your suit.

Journey Day 49. Samnia System. Acceleration: 10 m/s²

The captain had started them on ten gravs acceleration as soon as Guo reported the converter repaired. Mitchie stopped by her cabin for a shower before reporting to the bridge. After six hours in a spacesuit she was marinated in her own sweat.

Schwartzenberger held a stack of calculation sheets. He handed her the top one as soon as she came through the hatch. "Course for the gate. Check me."

"Yes, sir." It was the same one she'd been looking at before, modified for an extra day of coasting. "Looks good."

"Now look at these." He handed over the rest of the stack. She flipped through them quickly before starting to check his math. He'd updated their courses for the rest of the systems through Earth and back to the Fusion. She went through it line by line. When she put the last one down the captain asked, "How do those look?"

"Terrible. I kept hoping I'd find a math error."

"So did I. But we burned a lot of metal getting away from that thing. That means shorter boosts and longer ballistics for the rest of the trip. Even more so if we hold back a reserve for another chase like that. Which means more travel time."

Mitchie flipped through the stack again. "This isn't leaving much of a reserve."

"No. I figure we need to take it slower than I've got there."

"I hate algae crackers."

"You haven't started hating them yet. Which reminds me." He connected the intercom to Billy's handcomm. "What strain are you using for hydroponics algae?"

"Maximum oxygen production, why? That's what we've always been using," replied the deckhand.

"Switch to the calorie production strains."

"Oh, no. Captain, are you going to make us eat crackers?"

"No. You can just sit there and look at them all you want."

"Yes, sir. I'll start the switch on the maintenance cycle this afternoon."

"Thank you." Schwartzenberger turned the intercom off. "This is not going to go over well with the passengers."

***

Reed had gathered the passengers in the hold. Schwartzenberger looked them over. The cliques were obvious. People left empty spaces between them, hanging back from the speaker rather than brush up against a rival. "Thank you all for coming. It's obvious we're not having this meeting to discuss some good news." He summarized the escape from the AI ship, and how much that would delay their reaching the next gate. "The amount of fuel metal we used to escape was as much as we'd normally use to cross an entire star system. That's destroyed most of the reserve of fuel we had loaded. So we're going to have to take slower routes to conserve fuel. We're also going to stay farther from AI-controlled worlds to avoid attacks like that, which is also going to slow down our journey. Taken together our arrival at Old Earth will be delayed by at least a month, probably closer to two months."

He gestured to Reed, who stepped forward and explained how food servings would be reduced to stretch out the available supply over the longer trip. "Now, we have a recycler that will ensure we have unlimited air and water available. So it's only food we have to worry about. The crew will also be shifting their hydroponics production to produce some supplemental food, bad tasting, but better than starving."

Billy whispered "Barely" behind them. Bing shushed him.

The passengers had begun chatting among themselves. No one had panicked. "Are there any questions?" said Reed.

The leader of the white-robes stepped forward. Schwartzenberger tried to remember his name. It was on the manifest, but he kept wanting to be called "Crystal One" on the ship. "The success of our mission requires some of us to reach Earth. It does not require all of us to do so. The hazards of the journey may cause additional delays and we should prepare for this."

"There's a limit to how much we can stretch out the food before deficiency diseases start to be a problem," said Reed.

"Of course. We will have to use additional food supplies," said Crystal One.

"We're already doing that. The crew will be providing us algae crackers from the hydroponics," answered Reed. Schwartzenberger rested his hand on the butt of his pistol, hidden in his pants pocket. He'd ordered the crew to attend the meeting armed in case a passenger proposed seizing their food for the trip home.

"Limited, and lacking essential nutrients. We have to embrace the reality that we are all part of the energy cycle. Each of us is a substantial food source. We need to donate a few so that the rest may complete the mission." A few passengers gasped as they grasped his intent. "This should be shared equally among the factions of our company. As a gesture of good faith, the Crystalline Order will sponsor the first volunteer." He turned to the cluster of white-robes behind him. "Crystal Six?"

A young woman stepped forward, bowed, and returned to the group. Angry mutters came from the passengers. Rabbi Orbakh shouted, "Treyf!"

Billy said, "No point, she'd only dress out at fifteen kilo—Ow! I was just—Ow!" Schwartzenberger looked back to see Bing holding up her elbow as Billy rubbed his ribs.

Reed tried to calm the crowd. "Crystal One, this is clearly premature. We are not facing such an emergency."

The white-robe held his ground. "There is every reason to make that decision promptly. The available food supplies will go farther divided among fewer people. And our individual food value is at a maximum that will only decline as we are fed more poorly."

The crowd got louder. Schwartzenberger stepped in front of Reed. "There will be no homicides on this ship, voluntary or not. This subject is tabled. Crystal One, do not raise it again."

The cult leader bowed. "Of course, sir. I'm sure once it's too late many others will be willing to suggest it." He moved back to his group.

"This concludes this meeting," said the captain. "Please return to your quarters." The passengers dispersed. They gave the Crystalline Order a wide berth as they moved toward their entrance to the dorm container. The crew drifted back to the ladder.

"That could have gone worse," said Bing.

"How?" asked Billy.

"They could've wanted to eat us."

Journey Day 78. Vouvant System. Acceleration: 0 m/s^2

Bing floated through the bridge hatch. "How's the work going?" she asked.

"Good," said Mitchie. She pointed at the comet *Fives Full* snuggled up to. "Billy found a water-rich patch so they're ahead of schedule." He was visible through the haze of ammonia ice and other material being spat out by the mass processor as he shoveled ice into the intake. Alexi, managing the hose to the reaction mass tanks, was completely hidden.

"That's good news." Bing took up a handhold next to Mitchie's couch. "What are you working on?" A stack of well-covered scratch paper was in the pilot's lap.

"Astrography. Checking sightings against the almanac. They've all been pretty close."

"You don't sound happy about it," said the mate.

"It's this thing." Mitchie pulled out a rough-bound book. The cover read *A Captain's Tale of a Journey To Old Earth and a Safe Return.*

"I thought we'd gotten some useful tips out of that."

"We did. Until Samnia. The astrography's off. This system's even worse. It's like he took the Vouvant almanac and just added some random offsets."

"Is it just the observations that are off?"

"No. I went back through the food logs. Starting in Samnia the consumption becomes constant. Some of the incidents don't ring true either."

"So what do you think really happened?"

"They jumped into Samnia, got scared, and ran back to the prior system. But nobody would buy a book called *We Went Halfway to Earth and Panicked.*"

"What about their pilgrims?" asked Bing.

"I don't know. They could have dropped them at any AI world. But . . . the crew all backed the captain's story. Maybe they all got a cut of the book. Maybe they're covering up a crime."

"Spacing the passengers?"

"Don't tell me you haven't been tempted."

"Not on this trip." The first mate laughed. "I'll have to tell you about some groundhogs we had on the *Jefferson Harbor*."

"What bothers me most is this was our proof it could be done. That it was possible to go to Earth and live. Now I'm looking at a story from twenty-two years ago as the most recent trip, and how do we know those guys told the truth?"

Journey Day 89. Vouvant System. Acceleration: 10 m/s^2

Captain Schwartzenberger slid down the last few rungs of the ladder. As soon as his feet hit the deck he drew his pistol. Mitchie and Alexi spread out behind him, hands on their guns, wishing they had permission to draw.

"Break it up! That's enough!" ordered Schwartzenberger. The outer ring of the brawl made way in front of the captain. The rest kept fighting until he swung his gun at their heads. They scrambled out of the way, revealing Billy holding the two instigators.

"Thanks for coming, Skipper." The deckhand's grin dripped blood from a split on one side. One eye was swollen up. The captain surveyed the rest of the damage. Broken finger, ripped pants, some sandwiches stomped flat between the combatants.

"Everyone get in your bunks," commanded the captain, pointing his pistol straight up. Most of the passengers fled. In a minute just Reed and the ones Billy held were left.

"Sir," said Reed. "I'm willing to handle disciplining these two. I'm sorry we dragged your crewman into it."

"Damned straight," said Schwartzenberger. "Mr. Lee, hand them over."

"Aye-aye." Billy flung them at Reed so hard they nearly fell. "You ought to make them eat those sandwiches they stepped on."

"Let's go," said the captain, waving his crew ahead of him. Billy went up letting his right leg drag. Schwartzenberger pulled a rag out of his cargo pocket and wiped the blood off his pistol before holstering it.

When everyone was in the galley the captain activated the intercom to bring Bing and Guo into the discussion. "Okay, Billy, what the hell happened there?"

"They did a normal meal line. About two-thirds of the way through a guy looked at the one behind him and accused him of going through a second time. Knocked the sandwich out of his hand. So I called in then grabbed them. But their friends mixed in so it went critical."

"Uh-huh." Billy shifted uneasily under the captain's stare. "Did it occur to you that they might have been trying to grab you as a hostage? Ransoming you for food?"

"Um . . . no," said the deckhand.

"Well, it's occurred to me. And now they've seen how easy it was to isolate you I'm sure it's occurred to some of them. So. New rules. We're not posting anyone in the hold any more. No one goes through the hold alone. Everyone stays armed while on duty. Twelve hour shifts. One on the bridge, two in the converter room, three off-duty."

"Skipper, there's not enough work here for two," said Guo over the intercom.

"There will be if the passengers figure out how to unlock your hatch." The mechanic had no answer. "First Mate, work out a watch rotation."

"Aye-aye."

***

Tonight's rotation had Billy and Alexi in the converter room. By the time they reached the bottom of the ladder the passengers were well clear of the path to the converter room hatch. A week of mutual suspicion had ended the previous casual contact between the groups.

The corridor was quiet. When they opened the hatch to the converter room Guo was saying, "—then she asked how it felt. I told her just like being secured for high-acceleration maneuvers. So she untied me, threw me out, and never talked to me again." Mitchie held her sides, helpless with laughter. Guo looked at the hatch. "What are you two doing here?"

"Shift change," said Alexi.

"Already?" Guo looked at the chronometer. "Huh. Okay, we're relieved. No anomalies. Readings in the green. Fuel needs to be restocked at 2030."

"Got it," said Alexi.

"Chow time! Y'all have a good shift," said Mitchie as she led Guo out.

Alexi waved good-bye. Once the hatch closed he said, "Those two didn't mind being cooped up together."

"Yeah, they get along," said Billy.

"They're getting more than that."

"Nah, Mitchie doesn't flirt with crew. She thinks it always goes bad."

"Maybe she didn't before. But that sure looked like something was happening."

"They were just talking."

"That's how everything starts."

Journey Day 102. Vouvant System. Acceleration: 0 m/s²

"Skipper, could you come by the bridge after changeover? I think we may have a problem." Mitchie's request had the captain up as soon as he was done with his shift in the converter room. Bing was already there for the night shift.

"What's the problem?" said Schwartzenberger as he flew through the hatch. Mitchie pointed at the telescope, clamped to a bracket on the dome frame. The captain kicked off the dome, steadied himself next to the telescope, and looked through it. "Okay, what *is* that?"

"I don't know, but radar says it's in our way," said Mitchie.

"Never seen anything like it myself," added Bing.

He stared some more. "Looks like a spider web with some flies buzzing around it." They nodded. "Okay, we need to stay clear. Can we just get between it and the gate?"

Mitchie pulled out her scratchpad. "There's not much room. I took a cut at it. Wouldn't be fun."

Schwartzenberger took the pad. "Dogleg to line up is easy." He flipped to the second page. "A fifty-five grav skew turn . . . gives us six minutes to take two sights and make corrections. Exciting."

"We can make the turn easier, but that means going slower on our closest approach to the whatever-it-is."

"Also exciting, and more mysterious."

"Can we skip it?" asked Bing. "Take another gate? There's at least two other systems connecting through to Old Earth we can get to from here."

"Good thought," said the captain. "Let's check. Mitchie, you've got the best eyes."

After a few minutes with the system almanac Mitchie began looking for the nearest gates. The first was right on the predicted angles. Shifting her view sunward . . . "Yep. There's another one of those things." She shifted to starboard to search for the next gate. It was off-position enough that she found the web first. "Damn. How much do you bet there's one on every gate, including the one toward home?"

"I'd put my share of Alexi's treasure on it," said Schwartzenberger. The trio floated silently for long minutes.

"I wish we had one of those damn Terraforming Service tables," said Bing. "Then we could go through at an angle and not worry about lining up our approach on the normal."

"Yep," said the captain. "But angling in without that would make a spectacular explosion."

Mitchie brightened up. "The drones!"

"What about them?" asked Schwartzenberger. A few more had been expended to distract AI ships but there were over a dozen left.

"If we fire one into the gate we can see if it has a good transition or not."

"And if it does we follow its vector in. I like it," said the captain.

"And if it doesn't?" asked Bing.

"We fire off a bunch of them," said the pilot. "If none of them make through then we boost to go past the gate and try again later."

"Work out vectors for ten of them. I'll break the news to Guo. Nobody tell the passengers."

"Good. I'll start my shift," said Bing.

***

The passengers had obediently gone to their bunks for the maneuvers to put *Fives Full* on a direct path to the gate. Orders to strap in six hours before gate transition did provoke some questions from Reed. Schwartzenberger answered, "We'll have to do some extra maneuvering this time. It's a bit too complicated to explain. Also, we have to do some work in the hold. Don't be worried if you hear some thumps."

The ship was already ballistic after braking to transition speed. Guo programmed cards while Billy and Alexi rigged cables and pulleys. "We're ahead of schedule," said Guo. "Get latrine breaks then suit up." He spent the break briefing Mitchie on the status, which drifted into jokes about how pretty exploding drones would look.

With all three of them suited it was time to pump the hold down to vacuum. Guo pressed his helmet against the second dorm. It had been weeks since he'd had a chance to inspect the seals he'd put in on the roughly cut doors. Calm conversation among the pilgrims, no whistles—they still held.

"Pressure zero," reported Billy.

"Open the main hatch," said Guo. The massive doors moved open in short jerks.

"Y'know, we're supposed to relube those things after two months in vacuum," said Alexi.

"It's top of my list when we land someplace with an atmosphere," said Guo. "Start hooking up the drones. And get yourself hooked up too." Alexi cursed and attached his safety line.

"Drone's in the sling," said Billy.

Guo switched channels. "Bridge, we're ready to launch the first one."

"Clear to launch," answered Mitchie.

All three men hauled on the cables, giving the drone enough momentum to sail out the open hatch. Once it was completely outside Guo reported, "It's out, good to pivot."

"Hang on," said the pilot unnecessarily. All three had gotten good grips as soon as they'd released the drone. Thrusters fired to spin the ship. The drone went out of sight as the hatch turned away.

White light reflected off the edge of the hatch. "Damn that's bright." Guo checked the chronometer in the corner of his faceplate. The drone had fired right on time. Thrusters fired again to take the rotation off the ship.

Guo switched back to local. "Next one."

***

The drones were equipped with tracking lights for ease of recovery. Mitchie appreciated the feature as she followed the first one with the telescope. All crew were in their acceleration couches with the intercom on. She'd promised a running narration of what happened to the drones.

"First one should be in the transition volume now," said Mitchie. The narrow shape was clearly visible. "Front half got clipped off. At an angle. Rear is spinning. And gone."

The drones were spaced five minutes apart. "Number two going in. Whoa—starburst. Just blew into fragments. Pretty. Huh, the frags are transitioning right to left." Guo and Alexi traded some speculation as to whether a steep gradient was a normal gate feature or a product of it being left untuned.

"Let's see if third's the charm. No. Clipped. Clipped again. And— okay, went through in four pieces. I wonder how far apart they wound up on the other side?" No one wanted to speculate.

"Number four in the zone. Damn. It's gone. Perfect transition."

"Get us on that track," said Captain Schwartzenberger.

Mitchie pivoted the ship and laid in thirty gravs. The captain held a timer, calling "Cut and reverse." She stopped thrust, flipped the ship end for end, and resumed accelerating. She cut thrust again just as he called time.

"Good. Let's get a sight in." The gate buoys and the net were close enough to provide precise position references. They'd never get enough accuracy for this if they had to sight off the sun and planets.

A second sighting five minutes out showed them on the proper trajectory. Mitchie tried not to think about Alexi's question when he heard the plan: "How do we know a hole big enough for a drone will be big enough for the ship?"

The bridge was quiet enough for Mitchie to hear the captain's whispered prayer. She decided to join him as best she could. *God, if you're listening, we'll take all the help we can get.*

She almost missed transition. The new system's sun didn't appear in the center of the bridge dome. It was halfway to the edge. "We made it."

"Yes, we did," said Schwartzenberger. "You get some rest. I'll find our position."

Journey Day 126. Solar System. Acceleration: 10 m/s²

The Solar System. Ancestral home of the human race. The goal of their quest. Burton Reed was thrilled. Well, he wanted to be thrilled, but it felt the same as everywhere else they'd been. All he could see was the inside of the cargo hold. Unchanged from when they'd first boarded the ship. He stared at the hull, wishing he could see through it to the stars outside.

WHANG.

Now the hull did look different. There was a hole high up in the side of the compartment. Air rushed out with a bass roar. A few pilgrims screamed, barely audible over the air leak. The floor rose up and smashed Reed in the face as *Fives Full* took evasive action. Reed rose to his knees, blood streaming from his nose, and yelled "Into the dorms! Quick! Into the dorms!" He ran toward his own. He paused at the door to look at the crowd. They were all moving. Two men slammed into Reed's back, forcing him inside.

"In your bunks!" he yelled. "We need a headcount!" The pilgrims scrambled to their places. The stragglers panted in. Everyone gasped in the thinning air. "That's all!" someone shouted. The doors slammed shut. The recycler pumped in more air, easing the pain in his ears.

"Burton, how long are we going to be stuck in here?" asked a pilgrim.

"Until they fix it."

***

"What's our status?" demanded Schwartzenberger over the intercom.

It was Alexi's turn on bridge watch. "Not sure, sir," he replied. "Lost pressure in the hold. No further impacts. Nothing nearby on radar. No visual contacts."

"Maybe just a rock, then. Put us back on course, then we'll go to free fall to do repairs."

***

Alexi had been bumped off the bridge to help Billy with the welding. "I only see the one hole," reported the deckhand. "Debris hit some of the containers and the landing barge. Don't see any penetrations."

"Did we lose any passengers?" asked the captain.

"I see two," said Alexi. "A couple of the white-robes."

Billy shone his light on the frozen figures. They still held onto the handle of the dorm door. "Yep, they're crystallized now."

"Shut up and get a patch on that hole," said Schwartzenberger.

While they welded the patch on Guo examined the debris from the impact. "It all looks like hull material and raw metal," he reported. "I'd say we ran into a boring piece of nickel-iron."

"An accident?" asked the captain. "In the center of the Betrayal?"

"I'm feeling paranoid too," said the mechanic. He poked at a few more bits of twisted metal. "But we've been buying a lot of tickets for this lottery."

***

Schwartzenberger waived the no-contact-with-passengers rule for the funeral. It didn't seem likely that any of them would throw a fit about food this close to Earth anyway. The bodies had been wrapped in tarps. Billy and Alexi were in pressure suits. Being a pallbearer for a burial in space was simple. Carry the body into the airlock, cycle, shove it out the other side. The torch plume would give it a partial cremation, best they could do out here.

The captain held his prayer book. The crowd should have been settling down but the pilgrims still jockeyed for position around the bier. Schwartzenberger bit his tongue. A dressing-down on proper protocol wasn't the right way to set the mood.

The white-robes had elbowed everyone else out to surround the bier. The captain briefly hoped he could start the ceremony. Then Crystal One raised his hands. "Before we can say farewell to our sisters we must consider the question of justice."

Reed demanded, "What are you talking about?" before Schwartzenberger could come up with a diplomatic way to ask it.

"Eight and Eleven did not die from the hull breach. They were alive, mobile, active, able to reach safety. They did reach safety." He walked over to the dorm door. "They found the door closed in their face." His fingers traced over dents in the thin metal. "They knocked. Knocked hard. I heard it at the other end of the dorm, but didn't know what it meant. This door can be opened from either side. Someone held it closed on them. Someone murdered them. Someone held this handle as they died. I want to know who murdered them. I want justice done."

"Him!" shouted a white-robe, pointing. A young man had gone pale during One's speech. At the accusation he gasped and stepped back.

"There! You see the guilt on his face," bellowed Crystal One. "Seize him and put him out the airlock! Let him die like they died. Let justice be done."

The Crystalline Order devotees surged forward. The other members of their target's transhumanist cult blocked them. Captain Schwartzenberger forced his way between them. "Settle down! There'll be no lynching on my ship, or Jesus help me," he pointed at the floor to ceiling cargo hatch, "we'll open the big door and every God-damned one of you can suck vacuum."

The pilgrims backed away from the captain, splitting themselves into pro- and anti-lynching groups, and a larger mass behind Reed. "We need a trial," said the pilgrim leader.

"You're getting one," said the captain. Crystal One opened his mouth and was told, "You shut up, you've said too much already." Schwartzenberger turned back to the accused. "Come here, son. I've got some questions for you. *And no one's going to interrupt you.*"

He identified himself as John Wang. His one visit to the captain's table had left no impression on Schwartzenberger's memory. "Mr. Wang, were you the one holding the door closed?"

"Yes, sir."

"Tell me what happened."

"Well, we heard the meteor and everyone was yelling to get in the dorms," said Wang. "I was one of the last ones in. I looked and didn't see anyone coming." Schwartzenberger snarled at the lynchers and they hushed. Wang continued, "I looked, I swear I did. No one was there so I shut it and shoved the lever for a full seal. Then, uh, then a couple of minutes later the lever started moving and there was banging. Everyone shouted at me to keep it closed or we'd die, so I pulled tight and kept it closed. A minute later it was quiet again. They told me to keep it closed." Some grim-faced nods marked the 'they.'

"All right, that's what I thought happened. Go on back, son. Now let me make a couple of things clear. One, no one is ever required to open a door to death pressure. You can't be sure you can close it again. Two, it looks like our late friends were in the hygiene when the strike happened. That exact scenario is why there's a dozen survival bubbles clipped to the ceiling of the hygiene. If those two had remembered their safety briefings they'd still be alive."

Crystal One broke his silence. "Are you saying they died from their own stupidity?"

"No. Saying that would be rude." *Crap. I said that out loud.* "Justice has already been served. Mr. Wang took the correct action. Now we have a funeral to do."

As a ritual the funeral was a disaster. The congregation was itching to riot. Schwartzenberger read out the prayers while wishing he hadn't left his gun behind. The deckhands handled the bodies with the brisk efficiency of trash disposal.

When they were back in the galley Bing served Schwartzenberger coffee with a shot of whiskey in it. "Damn it," he burst out, "one of the perks of being a captain is doing weddings. I've never married anyone on my ship. I just do funerals."

"Don't give up hope," said Bing. "When we get back let's grab a load of emigrants for the Disconnect. They're always getting married."

Journey Day 139. Solar System. Acceleration: 0 m/s^2

Using a keyboard was always jarring for Mitchie after a long time on an analog ship. This cruise had been the longest she'd ever gone without using a computer. Fortunately the landing barge's control system was designed for inexpert users. The guidance system had spun up error-free. Typing in the vectors for *Fives Full* and Old Earth had been tedious, especially the third time.

Mitchie was nervous about the planetary vector. Getting angles on Earth had been hard. A ring had grown out around the world, obscuring the planet's limb. She'd taken readings off the ring. Assuming it was centered on the geostationary belt, and really it had to be, her calculations should get the pilgrims safely to the ground.

Finding their sacred-compromise landing spot was a problem for the barge. She'd never gotten a clear enough look through ring and clouds to estimate a longitude.

Time to the let the passengers have their craft back. Mitchie unbuckled and pushed off toward the barge's hatch. Reed hung off its handle. His other hand nervously tapped on the rim. "Sir, your vehicle is ready for landing operations," said the pilot. "You may board when ready."

"Thank you," said the pilgrim leader. She kicked off to perch next to Alexi, who'd found a handhold with clear lines of fire to all the hatches. They watched the captain inspect the cables rigged to fling the barge overboard. The noise from the pilgrims reached a peak as Reed gave up enforcing the bidding order for boarding. They reformed in their ship-board cliques and lined up quietly.

The captain had finished with the cables and gone to talk to Reed when the argument broke out. One of the religious groups was at the end of the line. Now they shouted at each other as the line moved on without them. "No! I won't go! You can't make me!"

"Who's that?" asked Alexi.

"Abdul, the imam's kid," said Mitchie. His father poured out abuse on him, about half of it in English. Schwartzenberger and Reed drifted over to investigate. The volume dropped as Abdul appealed to the captain for permission to stay and Majead demanded Reed enforce the pilgrim agreement. Malak hung back and kept her eyes averted. The rest of the pilgrims filed into the landing barge.

"Wait, he wants to stay?" said Alexi. "We can't let him stay."

"Why not? I'm surprised he's the only one having an attack of common sense."

"We can't let him find out the secret." Alexi hopped to a container closer to the argument.

Mitchie followed. She remembered the fistfight at dinner, and the boy putting his body between his mother and the brawlers. "He's a good kid. He'll be okay."

"If we can't trust him he might have to go out the airlock."

"If he goes out the airlock he won't go alone." Free-fall was wonderful. She could get in someone's face and he'd back off instead of giggling.

Alexi tried a different tack. "We're low on food. How many kilos do you want to lose to bring a coward along?"

"There's plenty of algae crackers to go around." She even said it without gagging. "Doesn't matter what we think, anyway. Captain's made up his mind."

Schwartzenberger's comment that Abdul hadn't bought a return ticket extracted a passionate promise to work hard for his passage. The captain accepted it.

Majead cried, "Apostate! You'll burn in Jahannam for refusing the Hajj!" He turned to his wife. "Can't you talk some sense into him?"

Malak came forward, gave Abdul a hug and a kiss, and whispered in his ear. Then she pushed off him and floated to the hatch to wait. Majead let out a string of non-English words and went into the barge.

"Well, that's settled," said Reed. "Good luck, Abdul." The boy nodded. "Captain. Thank you for getting us here. I hope you have a safe trip home." They shook hands.

"I hope you find what you're looking for," said Schwartzenberger. "Flash the running lights when you're ready to go." Reed disappeared into the barge. Billy had taken his helmet off to listen to the commotion. The captain waved him over. "Meet your new apprentice. Abdul, this is

Billy. He's the one who'll decide when you've worked enough to have another meal."

The new recruit gave the deckhand an apprehensive smile.

"How much of my work can I give him?"

"All of it, if he can do it competently." That put a real grin on Billy's face. "But for now you're on the crane." The captain turned to Mitchie and Alexi. "You two get Abdul strapped down for the separation maneuvers."

Mitchie took charge of the ex-pilgrim. He looked like he could use some privacy for a good cry so she put him in an unused stateroom. The bunk was covered with empty food boxes but it only took a few minutes to secure them elsewhere. She strapped in Abdul and said, "You just relax. It'll be a few hours until we're back on steady acceleration. Then Billy will put you to work."

"Thanks."

She headed up to the bridge. The captain asked, "He okay?"

"I think so," Mitchie answered.

Bing gave her the pilot couch and switched to the commo seat. Billy was on the intercom from the hold. "We're pumped down. Their hatch isn't leaking."

"Roger," said the captain. "Opening cargo hatch."

"I love that view. Ready on the crane."

"Clear to move cargo."

"Moving." The crane on the hold's ceiling began winding up the cable. On the bridge they could feel the ship shift in reaction. "Cargo clear of the hatch," reported Billy.

"Closing hatch." In a few minutes the landing barge was visible from the bridge. With his mike off, Schwartzenberger asked, "Did you get that delay programmed in?"

"Yes," answered Mitchie. "We've got plenty of time to get away before they can plume us."

"Good. Get us headed for Eden Gate."

"I wonder what'll happen to them when they land," said Bing.

"Likely nothing good," said Mitchie.

"Not our problem," said Schwartzenberger.

Journey Day 140. Solar System. Acceleration: 10 m/s²

The captain kept Abdul for a private chat in the galley after breakfast. "Think you can handle life as a spacer?"

"Yes, sir."

"Good. You probably noticed this was a dangerous journey."

"We were afraid we'd die a few times."

"Which is why we charged so much to take the pilgrims," said Schwartzenberger.

"My father complained about that. Called you extortionists."

"Now. How are you at keeping secrets?"

"I decided to stay on the ship two months ago and didn't tell anyone," said Abdul.

"That's good. Good. How are you at keeping other people's secrets?"

"I don't think I've ever had one. Secrets are rare in the Fusion."

"You're going to hear a secret now. Those millions of keys weren't enough to make us take this trip. We have word of some valuable materials to be found in another system. Very valuable. That's why we took the risk to come here."

"I won't tell anyone about it."

"Good. Once we've sold some of it you will receive two hundred and fifty thousand keys."

Abdul's face went slack. He'd been expecting to live on the stipend.

"Understood?"

"Yes, sir!"

"Good. Now go get started on that manual Billy gave you." The boy scampered off. The captain refilled his coffee cup. "Michigan, you should spend some time reading manuals. Then you'd know the intercom panels all have indicator lights to show when a circuit is open." The 'bridge' light on the panel went out. He took a sip.

Journey Day 149. Solar System. Acceleration: 0 m/s²

Guo flashed a grin as Mitchie floated into the converter room. "What brings you downbelow?"

"Just checking if you'd let this place go totally to hell since you got to have it to yourself again." She could see it was back to its normal rigid order now that the deckhands weren't here half the time. "Actually we have an experiment."

"Oh?"

"Billy's making Abdul go through the hydroponics manuals. They found an alternate recipe for algae crackers. With some flavorings it's supposed to taste sweet."

"Algae cookies?" Guo was clearly dubious.

"In theory." She took out two napkins wrapped around a half-dozen cookies each. "I figured if I took yours down I'd get out of trying them with the kid watching."

"Don't have the heart to throw up in front of him?"

"Nope. He's like a puppy. A skinny puppy always afraid you're going to step on him or toss him out the door."

"Poor guy. Is Billy drunk with power yet?"

"Ha. He's pulling sixteen-hour days between doing his work and teaching the kid. Trying to get to where he can just snooze the rest of the trip."

Guo smirked. "Yeah, the Skipper knows how to push his buttons." He took his cookies. "Guess we should give them a try."

They each bit into a cookie, watching each other's expressions. They chewed, swallowed, and simultaneously popped the remainder into their mouths. Regular algae crackers were like wood shingles, or ceramic tile if they were left in the oven a little too long. These were as chewy as stiff cardboard. With sugar on top.

"It's better than the crackers," said Guo.

"Yeah. I don't think I'd call them cookies though. Soft crackers?"

"That works." Guo bit into another.

Mitchie studied hers for a moment. "It's better than military emergency rations." She bit.

"When did you eat milrats?"

"Shuttle service had picked up a bunch of them surplus. I had to sit out a blizzard in a mountain pass for a couple of days."

"It'd take a couple of days to make me eat one," said Guo.

"I was still growing. Took about twelve hours to finish the first one."

He swallowed his third cookie. "Worst I've eaten besides crackers was this fish-egg stuff."

"Were you stranded on an island?"

"Heh. No, I was being polite. A friend on Lapis was serving it as this special delicacy."

"Good friend, huh?" Mitchie smirked at him.

"You could say that."

Mitchie described some other terrible food she'd eaten. Akiak cooking focused on not wasting edible parts instead of great taste. Guo had more stories of his own. Finally they ran out of cookies and conversation together.

They shared a handhold, fingers comfortably overlapping. Guo let go of it and pulled on her wrist. His other hand grabbed her shoulder to stop her as her lips touched his.

The kiss started gently. When her hands pulled on his back he pressed more forcefully. Their lips parted. The sensation flooded them with fire. Mitchie gave up her foothold and wrapped both her legs around his. Only his left foot kept them from drifting into the room.

Mitchie could only think about the feel of his lips. *Remember, stay focused*, said the voice in the back of her brain. Guo pulled on her hip, pressing her belly against his. *Remember what you're looking for.* She ran her hands along his back, exploring the muscles she'd just seen hints of through his jumpsuit.

I don't understand, Mitchie thought. Her breast tingled as he brushed the side of it.

What is your mission objective? said the voice. Guo shifted her whole body in the air and began kisses down the side of her neck.

There isn't one. Guo's hand stroked her breast.

Why are you doing this? His teeth closed firmly on her earlobe.

I don't know! Mitchie put both hands on his chest and pushed away. She caught onto the converter assembly and hung there shaking.

"Sorry, was that too hard?" Guo's goofy grin drained away as he saw her expression. "Mitchie, are you okay?"

"I'm—it's not—fine."

He turned his palms toward her and flexed his ankle to tilt his whole body away from her. "Hey, I don't want to rush you. We can take things slow."

"No, I—it's that—I don't—I never—"

"Mitchie, there's no shame in being a virgin."

The confusion in her face flashed to anger. "I'm not a virgin, you idiot." She grabbed a wrench from its bracket and flung it at him.

It hit the bulkhead between a pressure gauge and a thin bleed line. Guo caught it in two more bounces. No damage other than chipped paint.

Mitchie had already disappeared through the hatch. Guo decided he should figure out what he did wrong before going after her. Which might take a while. He was too dazzled from those wonderful kisses to think straight.

***

Mitchie arrowed from the cargo hold hatch to her stateroom. The group in the galley saw her fly by.

"I guess they didn't want more cookies," said Abdul.

Billy laughed. "I bet Guo loves the taste of *her* cookies."

Schwartzenberger snapped, "Lock that shit up or you're going to have consequences." Suddenly it was time for Abdul to learn how to inspect container tie-downs.

When they were alone in the galley Bing said, "Those two are developing a relationship. It could be a morale issue."

"So?" replied Schwartzenberger. "I can't keep that pair from running off and murdering people. How am I supposed to make them keep their zippers up?"

***

Mitchie locked and bolted her hatch. The "off" light on the intercom panel was enough to let her find her bunk. She slid under the cover and loosely closed the hip belt. A teddy bear was secured at each corner. She pulled the largest out of its elastic sack and curled around it.

Sex isn't just for getting restricted data out of guys. She tried to find an example of when she'd had sex for a different reason. Soon she remembered Derry.

Strong, happy Derry. He planned one hitch in the Navy so they could afford to start married life on a homestead of their own. She'd wanted to give him a good sendoff but he was stubborn. "The Chief calls it Opsec. I'm not allowed to tell anyone when the ship will arrive."

So she'd wormed it out of him in the afterglow of their first time. Derry had almost panicked when the Chief crashed the going away party, but he'd just drunk and joked with the uncles. Great time.

After the party the Chief canceled Derry's security clearance. "No boring electronics bench for me," Derry had written. "I'll get to work on the hull and see the stars." Then a Fusion ship plumed BDS *Brave* and Derry came home in an urn.

Tears wouldn't drip in free-fall. Mitchie pressed her face into the teddy bear and let them soak its fur.

Journey Day 150. Solar System. Acceleration: 10 m/s²

Captain Schwartzenberger leaned on the bulkhead next to the hydroponics room hatch. As Mitchie came abreast he held a finger to his lips. She stopped and listened to the voices in the compartment.

Abdul hadn't done well at cleaning the growth medium filters. "It's just a speck," said the apprentice.

"That speck could start rot in the next batch of algae," said Billy. "You have no idea how bad a ship can smell when there's rot in the hydroponics."

"Is this another of those 'small detail, big effect' things?"

"Yes, dammit. You have to pay attention to all the little details. Details matter. Every single thing between your lungs and vacuum is a detail." Mitchie cocked her head as he went on. On Shishi it was pronounced "dee-tail" but Billy said "deh-tail" which was—she looked at the captain—a Bonaventure accent. He had to be reciting that speech from memory. "So check all the details. Your life is one of the ones you'll save."

Schwartzenberger wore the biggest smile she'd ever seen on him. She shook her head and moved on.

Interlude Three

Akiak, gravity 10.3 m/s^2

Pete's new friends stated emphatically that unlike the Fusion, Akiak's government didn't break into people's homes in the middle of the night. So the masked men hauling him out of his bed had to be crooks. By the time he was awake enough to realize what happened they'd taped his mouth shut and bound his hands behind his back.

They'd shouted something coming into his apartment. The word "police" had been in it. Maybe "Don't call the police?" The men were totally silent as they carried him out. Their truck was black. He didn't glimpse any markings on it in the two meters between his front door and its cargo compartment.

Two masked men rode with him. They had strapped Pete face down on a bench along the side. They sat on the opposite bench, staring at him. Or they slept bolt upright. He couldn't tell through the masks.

The truck was wheeled. It stayed on good roads. The trip went on for hours. Pete's original theory was a labor theft gang. Frontier conditions were harsh enough some owners tried slave labor. It was the top priority of the planetary police. The most popular vid on Akiak was a fictionalized version of anti-slavery detectives.

Pete knew the slavers on the show were exaggerated but these silent men were just too competent to be slavers. Bounty hunters? He didn't think his grey-area experiments were serious enough to make the Lapis government try to retrieve him. If someone wanted to make an example of illegal research maybe these men did mean to take him back to the Fusion.

When the truck stopped the pair quickly hauled him into a windowless building. Once inside they took the tape off his mouth (no pain) and recuffed his hands in front of him. "Thank you," said Pete. One nodded in reply. They took him into an office.

An elderly woman sat behind a desk. "Mr. Smith. Since you may be in protective custody for an extended period, your personal belongings have been placed in storage. Please sign this receipt." She slid an oversized datasheet toward him.

Pete read the legalese at the top, then looked at the first line of the inventory. "Socks, clean, 8; socks, dirty, 4."

He put the datasheet back down. "So . . . you people really are the government?"

The clerk's face filled with disdain. Pete quickly thumbprinted the corner of the datasheet. The guards took him down the hall to another office. This time they sent him into the room alone and closed the door.

A young man in a suit sat behind a desk. "Please sit down, Mr. Smith. I'm George Alverstoke, your case officer."

Pete sat in the chair. It was padded. He was beside the desk, nothing between him and Alverstoke.

"I apologize for the rough treatment in bringing you here," said the case officer. "We needed to get you into protective custody as quickly as possible. And keep anyone from knowing you're in our custody. Ideally as far as anyone knows you'll have just vanished." He touched the handcuffs. They retracted into a ball which he dropped into a desk drawer.

Pete rubbed his wrists. "Who are you protecting me from?" Alverstoke handed him a cup of water. He drained it.

"Um. How long has it been since you've seen a news report?"

Pete had to think. "Noon yesterday? I worked a night shift and then went straight to bed."

"I see." Alverstoke took a deep breath. He decided to rip the bandage off. "A Fusion warship dropped an atomic weapon on the town of Noisy Water five hours ago. They intended to destroy the AI technology conference. We're securing every known researcher into topics forbidden by the Fusion."

Alverstoke kept talking. Pete stopped listening. A chill clung to his skin. Connie, the Binary Club boys, all the real friends he had on Akiak, they all went to the conference. His brain believed it. That's the kind of situation it would take for Pete to be a government kidnap target. His heart . . . refused to accept it. They had to be alive. Words couldn't change that.

"Are there any survivors?" he interrupted.

"I'm sorry, the valley was completely devastated. Everyone there was in the total destruction radius."

"Have you checked for basements? People could have sheltered there."

The desktop was one big datasheet. Alverstoke made a few strokes to make it display a realtime image of Noisy Water. Pete recognized it from the bare stone hills running to either side. They'd framed the promotional video for the conference. The resort and village were gone, along with the spectacular waterfall. A crater slowly filled with water. The trees on the slopes still burned. The meadows along the brook were cold ash now.

"The Space Guard dropped a team in hardsuits to search. They didn't find anyone. It was just before local dawn. I'm very sorry."

Pete moaned. A few tears fell on the desk. "Why?" he demanded.

"We don't know, not for sure. The Fusion's always been paranoid. Why now, why here, we don't know. It might just be that there was such a big target."

Pete moaned again.

"So you see you're in danger. We need to keep you safe, out of sight. There are Fusion agents on Akiak we've lost track of. You could be attacked any time you're in public."

"Why do you care about me? I'm nobody important. I haven't done any research here."

"Your friends disagree. They've mentioned your assistance several times in their discussions. Brainstorming with you is—was quite productive for them."

Pete sniffed.

"Then there's your academic profile. Lapis sent your full records with their extradition request. Very impressive."

"They tried to extradite me?"

"For illegal research, yes."

"Why didn't you send me back?"

"Deploying uncontrolled software is a crime here. Researching it is not."

"Oh." Pete tried to put the shock aside. "Who are you people? Who do you work for?"

"I'm part of the Security Department. Which includes the Space Guard, Ground Guard, some secure research facilities, the usual sneaky types, and the clerks to keep them all paid and supplied. Which is where I fit."

Pete held out the empty cup. Alverstoke poured some more water into it. Pete drank then asked, "So now I'm just locked away somewhere?"

"We were hoping—well, there's no tactful way to put this. Our research division has a great many openings right now. We would deeply appreciate it if you would help us rebuild our team."

Pete stared at him, too bemused to answer.

"And if you take the job the Fusion will feel pain."

Pete wiped the tears off his cheeks. "Then yes."

Fives Full Cargo Hold

Part Four: Treasure of the SMX

Journey Day 155. Solar System. Acceleration: 10 m/s^2

Mitchie leaned against her couch as Bing went down the shift change checklist. ". . . as logged. You have the con."

"I have the con," said Mitchie. "On course and speed for gate passage in five hours." She smiled. "See you at dinner."

"Dinner in Eden," agreed Bing. She climbed down the ladder, leaving Mitchie alone on the bridge.

Mitchie laid down in the acceleration couch with the logbook. All the sightings put them right in the groove. She tucked the book under her console.

That's when she noticed the tightly folded note tucked into the thrust control lever slot. "MICHIGAN" was printed neatly on it. Her life would be much simpler if she shoved it into the trash bucket.

She unfolded the note. The page was filled with an ink drawing of a rose blossom, petals almost at full bloom. She traced the edges of the petals around and became lost in the spiral. She'd last seen roses in a garden on Bonaventure, none as perfectly shaped as this. She remembered their scent tickling her nose.

On the bottom edge next to the thorns was written, "I love you—Guo." *I give up.* Mitchie took a minute to adjust some switches on the communications console. Three hours of studying the intercom manual hadn't given her what she wanted, but she had found how to make sure no one else could listen in on an intercom link.

Mitchie pressed the Converter Room button. "Hi."

"Good morning," answered Guo.

"Thank you. It's beautiful."

"You're welcome. I just wanted to apologize for upsetting you."

"It's an amazing apology. I never expected to get flowers on board."

"I got as close as I could." He sounded smug.

"Well, technically a cup of algae would be closer to the traditional flowers."

"But that's not very romantic."

"No, it's not." He was silent, probably still gloating over how his plan had worked. "Did you really think I was a virgin? Doesn't anyone gossip on this ship?"

"Um, well," not a topic Guo wanted to deal with. "Billy's the only one who gossips."

"That should be plenty."

"He gossips, but he also jumps to conclusions and doesn't pay attention to details. So when you got all flustered . . ."

"You leapt to conclusions."

"Yeah."

Time to be nice again. "I've never kissed a fellow crew member before. *Elephant's Tail* was strict about that."

"Billy shared that story. If it helps I promise to never drop you out an airlock."

Mitchie laughed. "That helps a little. It's more that I'm conditioned not to do anything with crew."

"I'll just have to . . . *desensitize* you." The lilt in his voice made her lips tingle.

"I'd like that." She barely forced the words out through the tightness in her throat. "I need to get to work. I have to take my first set of sights. See you at dinner?"

"Absolutely. Hey, you should have some downtime before your last set of sights for thrust cut-off. Comm me then?"

Dammit, I need to set some limits. "Sure."

Journey Day 155. Eden System. Acceleration: 10 m/s²

Bing celebrated their arrival in Eden's system with a fancy dinner. Mitchie's mouth watered as she saw it. Four months ago she would have been offended, but right now some actual meat slices and a little jam to spread on the algae crackers looked delicious.

The first mate said a short grace. The crew all grabbed the meat off their plates first. Mitchie tried to savor hers but couldn't keep from gobbling it down. With the edge off she spread a tiny bit of jam on the cracker. She popped the whole thing in her mouth and sucked on it before trying to chew.

The rest were down to their crackers as well. "Why can't we get more of those cookie things?" complained Alexi.

"Nutrients," said Abdul. "The long, cool baking time ruins the proteins so you're just getting fat and cellulose." Billy nodded.

"It's pretty bad when these are the healthy option," said Guo. He held up a cracker while he mustered up the motivation to eat it.

"We need the protein," said Billy. "There isn't enough stored food to get us home. We're not producing enough carbon dioxide to support more algae."

"So if we burn stuff we can eat better?" quipped Mitchie.

Abdul paled. He didn't recognize the joke. Billy did, but he was too cranky to appreciate it. "Yeah, until we suffocate because the algae's all smoke poisoned."

Guo decided they needed a safer topic. "I bet the captain is really missing all those fancy meals he had as a senator."

Bing laughed. "No. He hated that stuff. Being polite to idiots always ruined his appetite." She spread jam on another cracker. "Which was a shame. He missed out on some great food."

Guo looked a little puzzled. "Did you get to go to one?"

"More than one. Turned out the old senator was eager to resign because it was almost time for the Spacers' annual shindig to celebrate the anniversary of the first launch from Bonaventure. So Al—Senator Schwartzenberger had to find a venue and caterers and everything while learning the job too. I helped him out. Wound up being hostess for the party."

"That must have been fun."

"It was by the end of the night."

"People must have been calling you Mrs. Senator by mistake," joked Alexi.

"Oh, it wasn't a mistake." Bing blushed slightly under their astonished stares. "We'd gotten married shortly before then. It didn't last. Nothing horrible, we just didn't fit."

"Then why are you here?" blurted Mitchie.

"I'd been on the *Jefferson Harbor* for five years, ending as second mate. When he swung the deal for this ship he asked me to be first."

"Why'd you say yes?" asked Billy.

"He's a terrible husband, but a good captain." She finished wiping jam streaks off her plate and cleared her place. Then Bing picked up the captain's plate and took it to the bridge.

Mitchie turned to Guo. "You didn't know?"

"No! I mean, I knew they were close. They'd both been on *Jefferson Harbor* together before I came on board."

"It's against regulations," said Alexi. "Fraternization is bad for efficiency and morale."

Billy snapped, "Stuff your regulations. This ain't a Fusion ship. The captain can have any rules he wants and there's no fraternization rule on this ship." Which was true. Mitchie wasn't sure if she was glad or sorry.

"I see how successful it's made this ship," shot back Alexi. He put his plate in the sink and left.

Billy turned to Abdul. Mitchie braced for a fraternization joke but instead he told his apprentice to go take a nap since they had some work scheduled for mid-shift.

"What's your plan for the evening?" she asked Guo.

"Back to the converter room. I figure I can read and babysit the system at the same time."

"Reading what?"

"*Romance of the Three Kingdoms.* I'm trying to improve my mastery of Classical. I've just been reading Modern and the texts lose in the simplification."

"You're reading a romance?"

"It's *Classical.* Romance meant story then. It's about a big war, with wizards. There's fights, treachery, tricks, all sorts of great stuff."

She smiled at his enthusiasm. "You'll have to find me an English translation when we get back to civilization."

"I could read it to you. Translating it is a good test of how well I'm understanding it."

"I'd . . . really like that. But it's my turn to do dishes."

"I'll help."

Journey Day 159. Eden System. Acceleration: 0 m/s²

Alexi's coordinates found them a comet. It was a half-million klicks out of position. Not pluming it meant waiting a day while *Fives Full* drifted up to it slowly enough that the attitude jets could stop them.

Everyone was tense. Bing had brought out some more real food to get the crew to eat. The dinner table was quiet. Alexi spun the bag of fish sticks in the air. They were highest protein food Bing could bake in free fall. The rest worked on their algae crackers. "Anybody want the rest of mine?"

"Hell, yes," said Billy. He caught Bing's glare. "If nobody else wants it."

"I'd be happy to split it with someone," said Abdul. The ex-pilgrim's neck still had tendons standing out. He'd been losing weight on passenger rations even before they were halved in Samnia.

"You need it most," said Bing. At her nod Alexi tossed the bag to the boy.

"I'm going to sack out early," said Alexi. He unhooked his feet from his chair legs and kicked off down the corridor to his cabin.

Once the hatch closed Billy said, "He needs to relax."

"Won't happen until we find the containers," said Guo. "If we don't find them we might have to put him on suicide watch."

"C'mon," scoffed Billy. "Worst thing that happens is we go back, have stories to tell, and spend the cash we got from the pilgrims. I saw what the skipper got for them. Better pay then we get most years. We'll be back to normal."

"You'll be back to normal. His normal is finding a way to get that treasure. If it's not there he's got nothing. He has to build a brand new life. And he's getting old for that."

Bing snorted. "The captain was older than Alexi when he had to start over. Just had a pile of debt, two amputations, and a cloud of debris that used to be a freightliner. If Alexi can't come up with something it's his own damn fault."

Guo answered, "He knew exactly where he wanted to get back to. Alexi's going to have to figure out what he wants to be when he grows up. That's tough."

"We can block all the airlocks," said Mitchie. "We'll get him home."

"He's safe enough now, people. Let's get to bed early. Tomorrow's going to be a busy day." Bing gathered up the bag with the captain's share of dinner and took it up the bridge. Billy headed for his cabin.

"Want to hear the next chapter of *Three Kingdoms?*" asked Guo.

"All right," said Mitchie. She felt her face heating up. "Just one chapter. We do have a lot of work tomorrow." They floated to his cabin together.

***

Captain Schwartzenberger had called the whole crew to the bridge for the final approach. "There it is, people. Comet SMX." It didn't look like much—another dirty snowball, just like the last one they'd topped the tanks off at. "We'll start by getting the mass processor hooked up. If we're shoveling snow we can get some water out of it. Then we'll just spread out and see what we can find. I want two people on safety watch at all times." Bing raised a hand. "Right, officers will take first shift for safety. Abdul."

"Yessir!" The bridge was so crowded the teenager had stayed in the hatch.

"Are you comfortable operating the communications console?" He nodded. "Fine. You're radio watch. Don't touch anything else in this room. Strap yourself in. Everybody else, suit up."

Mitchie kept the controls until the ship was gently touching the comet. The captain let her lead the way to the suit locker. Abdul formally took the con as Schwartzenberger went through the hatch.

It only took a few minutes for the captain to give up on making Alexi focus on the processor. The Edenite headed across the ice, staking down his safety line every couple dozen meters. "Now that he's out of our hair let's get this thing working. Then we can all start looking." It took Billy brute-forcing the box into position but they finally had it set up.

Schwartzenberger and Bing took up their watch positions on the hull as the younger crew scattered like puppies let out of the pen. Alexi was already coming back along his safety line, recoiling it and hooking stakes onto his belt. The captain yanked on his tether and landed in front of Alexi. "What's that on your leg?"

"Nothing."

"You have some vacctape on your leg. It wasn't there when we suited up."

"I scraped against a crystal. It didn't penetrate, just scratched the material. So I taped it to be safe."

"Uh-huh." The safety lecture he'd done while suiting had included sending inside anyone with suit damage. "Well, let's be a little safer." He took out his sealant tube and applied a neat bead along the edge of the tape. "Now you be careful. We can take our time looking for this."

"Yes, captain." Alexi bounded off again, his red safety line stretching in a different direction from the other crews' tethers.

The captain kicked off the comet and grabbed a handhold on the ship's hull to have a wide view of the comet. His crew had scattered, most close to going over the horizon. Bing landed next to him and touched helmets. "Relax. Even if he rips himself open we can get him inside in plenty of time."

"I'm not worried about a rip. I'm worried about a little hiss and him ignoring it because he's so close to finding the loot."

"How about this. You keep overwatch. I'll bounce around and talk to them. If they're too hypoxic to have a conversation we yank them."

"All right." As safety watcher Bing had their sole maneuvering pack. The propellant was too limited to use for routine maneuvering. She kicked hard toward Mitchie's position. She landed a bit short but pulled herself along the pilot's safety line.

"What's up?" asked Mitchie. She'd felt the tugs on the line and turned around to see Bing approach.

"Oxygen check. How's your level?"

Mitchie glanced toward the mirror pointed at the gauge on her earlobe. "Fine. A little high actually."

"Good. Keep at it." Mitchie expected Bing to go back along the safety line, not having her own attached to anything, but the mate surprised her. Bing uncoiled a few loops and clipped a spikey device to the end.

"What the heck is that?"

"Ice hook. Watch." Bing swung the three-tined hook around on a half meter of line until it blurred, then let go of it mostly up. The coils vanished from her arm until all the slack was gone. Then she yanked on the line as it went taut. The hook pivoted straight down and stuck into the surface. A few tugs proved it was firmly set. "See you later." Bing kicked off hard. Her line stayed taut, pulling her in a semicircle around the hook. She landed a hundred meters away, startling the hell out of Guo.

"Where did you come from? How did you do that?" complained the mechanic.

"Ice hook," said Bing with a chuckle. She started shaking the line back and forth, setting up a standing wave to vibrate the hook out of its hold.

"That thing can't be safe."

"Well, no, but it's cheap, it's fast, and it doesn't use any fuel. It's a trick I picked up in my mining days."

"Did you need something from me?"

"Yep, but you already answered it." She wound up the line as the hook drifted toward her, not wanting to hurry it.

"BINGO!" Billy's voice rang out on the all-hands frequency. "I found it! Follow the orange line."

Alexi arrived first. "I don't see the pointer. There's supposed to be a Y-shape pointing at the containers."

"Nope, I don't see it either. But look. There's a mound here that could hold a couple of containers, and trenches to either side. It looks like they dug out material and then piled it on top of them." Billy bounced from one side to the other, pointing out the trenches.

"That could be anything," said Alexi.

"It might be the boxes," said Captain Schwartzenberger. "Let's dig into this end a bit and see if we find anything."

After a few minutes of flailing and everyone being hit with shovelfuls of ice this became "Billy and Alexi dig in." The rest of the crew stood back from the backswings as the hole became deeper. "Metal!" yelled Billy.

Alexi shone his light into the hole. "Yep, I see rivets. This is it!"

"Good!" said the captain. "Everyone spread out over the mound. We'll have to clear it all off before we try to take it on board." After an hour it was clear they'd take days to get all the material off this way.

Guo suggested an alternate approach. "We've got a crust over a lot of crumbly ice. If we break the crust in a loop we could dig in under it, try to lever out most of this as one piece."

"What lever?" asked Alexi, still digging.

"The crane," said Billy. "We've got to bring the ship over here for loading anyway."

"We'll try it," said Schwartzenberger. "Pilot and mate, please reposition the ship." He switched from trying to deepen his hole to connecting it to Guo's.

They had to stop digging well before the ship "landed." Bing wanted plenty of safety margin. The base plate was cold from the day of drifting but still warm enough to blast some of the ice into steam as the attitude thrusters pressed it against the comet.

Billy wedged the crane hook into the most solid-looking chunk of ice by the ship. Retracting it at the lowest torque broke off a five-meter chunk, revealing the ends of two containers. The next three tries just dug scratches in the face of the ice. Alexi started shoveling ice away from the containers again.

"Well, that saved us some time," said the captain. "Any other ideas, or is it back to the shovels?"

"What we need is a bigger shovel," said Guo. "Billy, come give me a hand with the welding rig." The two disappeared into the ship.

"Captain?" said Mitchie.

"Yes?"

"Sir, I'm picking up a ship on radar, coming from Eden. Don't have a good speed on it yet. Looks like it'll be here in twenty or thirty hours."

"Lovely. Let me know when you've got a solid ETA."

The Pilgrims had used sturdy containers for their supplies. Guo and Billy sliced a side off one and cut a small hole in one end. They jabbed the thirteen meter long panel into the ice mound. Warming it with a welding torch helped it slide in a bit farther. Once they had it well stuck in they hooked the crane up to the end. Soon another chunk of ice sailed off. The captain assigned Abdul to tracking them in case one managed to do a full loop of the comet.

Mitchie reported the stranger would arrive in nineteen hours. Then she put her suit back on to help wrestle the shovel while Bing kept the bridge watch.

"Push with your feet, not your hands," instructed Guo. "The boots are insulated."

In three hours the top of the mound had been cleared off. Schwartzenberger had vetoed using the welding torch to clear ice directly—too much danger of a bursting crystal sending fragments through someone's suit. They dug around the containers with the big shovel in the hope they could be pulled up as one block.

The crew brushed off Alexi's demand that they dig under the containers to take them out gently until he stood in the way as Billy tried to attach the hook to the underside of one container. "Get out of the way, dammit!" snarled the deckhand.

"I didn't come all this way to see my inheritance scattered all over this snowball by you ripping the container in half. We need to dig under it."

"We've got a time limit, you idiot."

Guo tried a gentler approach. "The containers are top-quality. They're strong. We can pull at low torque and cut the crane the moment we see any flexing or cracking. We won't lose anything."

"They've been frozen for decades. They're probably brittle as hell by now. And so are the contents. We could ruin everything inside with rough handling."

"Everybody calm down." The captain pulled himself along the top of the container to get between Alexi and Billy. He waved Billy away with a thumb pointed at the other container. "Alexi, we all want to succeed at this. But if that ship arrives while we're still working we're going to lose it all. Maybe get killed into the deal. We've taken a lot of risks to get to this point, this is just one more."

"It won't take that long," said Alexi. "If we all dig we can separate them from the comet in a few hours."

"We don't have a few hours. We need to get them on ship and then get out of here before that AI ship arrives. I want a head start running away from it too."

"Hauling slack!" said Billy. He'd secured the hook on the base of the other container. The cable reeled in slowly.

Schwartzenberger blocked Alexi. The two bounced off each other as the Edenite tried to get past. "Enough, Alexi! We're doing it. Now settle down." The captain moved away to be clear of the cable.

Guo had stationed himself at the middle of the container. "No sign of trouble yet. Not moving."

Mitchie was at the pivot end, pressed against the ice. "I can hear crunching, the ice is feeling the pressure."

Billy pressed his helmet against the ice. "I can hear some too. More like snapping." He looked up at the stationary cable. "Still holding still. Whoa!" He hit the emergency stop button on the crane remote. Both containers had moved up together a couple of meters at the hook end.

The captain looked at the ice between the containers. "This looks pretty solid. I bet there was still some residual heat in the containers when they were laid down, so it melted the ice between them. It refroze hard. Give it another tug."

Billy pressed the "Low" button again. The containers shivered and moved up. Guo reported, "It's still straight. No cracks."

The two-container block was out of the hole for most of its length when the hook slipped off. Billy hit the stop again and the crew scattered to stay clear of the swinging cable. The deckhand looped a length of his safety line and caught the hook, stopping the wild pendulum. "Sir, I'm going to pay out some slack and loop it around the end, if you're okay with that?"

"Do it."

"That was a hell of a gamble you just got away with," said Alexi.

Schwartzenberger considered chasing Alexi down to make this reprimand private and decided he was too tired. "Mr. Frankovitch, we have all been gambling our lives repeatedly to get this far. We're gambling now that we can get this on board before that ship arrives. We're going to have some gambles between here and home. Stop pretending you're the only one with anything to lose here. Keep a civil tongue in your head. Is that clear?"

Alexi gave back a grudging "Yes, sir."

"Okay, ready to pull again," said Billy. "Stand clear of the base." The next pull got it almost upright. Guo and Mitchie connected their safety lines to put a loop around the base end of the block.

"Ready to belay," said Guo. Mitchie echoed him from the other side.

"Pulling," said Billy. The block came free of the comet. Loose bits of ice bounced all over. The crane boom projected eight meters out from the hull. It hauled up the block. Mitchie and Guo pulled on their lines to damp out dangerous swings.

When the cable was fully reeled in the containers hung parallel to the ship's hull. The outside crew hadn't noticed Bing firing the opposite thruster to keep the ship from toppling during the operation. Billy said, "Sir, I don't know how we're going to get it in. The end's too long for us to pivot it into the hold."

"Just retract the boom and haul it in," said Schwartzenberger.

"That's going to drag it along the lip of the cargo hatch. We'll probably ruin the door track!"

"Yes. And we can fix that when we get back to Demeter. Taking time to do it right will get us killed." Billy pressed the 'Retract' button. The captain went to help Mitchie with her line. Fortunately most of the force was handled by looping the line around a staple into the ice, or she would have already been yanked off the comet. Ice shards pelted them as the block scraped its way into the hold.

When it was clear of the hatch Alexi asked, "Do we want to look for another container?"

"If there's a third container here the Eden AI can have it with my blessing," said Schwartzenberger. "Everyone aboard and rig for acceleration."

"What about the mass processor?" asked Guo. It had been left at the original touchdown spot when the ship was shifted.

"The AI can have that too. Let's go."

"I can't wait to see what's inside them," said Mitchie as she bounced to the airlock.

"You'll have to," said Guo. "It'll probably be days before we can open them."

"I know. I just hate waiting."

Journey Day 160. Eden System. Acceleration: 30 m/s^2

"Drop us down to ten gravs. Let's take a look at our bogey." Captain Schwartzenberger took a deep breath as the two men lying on top of him got off.

Mitchie scribbled on a scratch pad as she integrated her sextant sights with radar readings. "It's still heading for the comet, Skipper," she said.

"Good." The captain pressed the PA button. "All hands, it's not chasing us. We're going to stay at ten gravs and work back to our planned course. Once we've completed maneuvers you can unsecure. Guo, Billy, Alexi, suit up and get the cargo hatch closed." A few "ayes" came back through the intercom.

***

"That's going to take some cutting," said Billy. The two sides of the cargo hatch almost met. The ledge they fit into had buckled under the ice block. Schwartzenberger had declared it "close enough" for lift-off.

Guo shone a light under an up-thrust panel. "Not as bad as it looks. The structure's fine. It's just the shell over it for the airtight that's busted."

"If we can't seal the hold it's pretty bad," groused Alexi.

"Relax. Once the doors close we can put a patch in. Heck, we could just seal it with vacctape. You two go get the welding rig while I take some measurements." They were still gone when he'd finished marking where to cut.

He studied the containers. The heat of the deck had already softened the ice. The rough block was pockmarked where methane and ammonia had melted first. Guo heard Billy on the intercom, sweet-talking Mitchie into dropping acceleration while they took the rig up the ladder. He walked around the ice slick surrounding it. It looked like chunks had fallen off, melted on the deck, and refrozen in the vacuum.

Some escaping ammonia had fractured one part of the block. Several pieces looked ready to fall off. Guo tugged on one.

"Trying to break in early?"

Guo whirled. Alexi had left Billy with the rig to confront him. "I'm not breaking in," said the mechanic. "I'm just seeing if I can take some ice off."

"Uh-huh. I think we need a rule about no one being alone in here," said Alexi.

"What the hell is your problem?"

"I've got the rig hooked up, guys," said Billy. "Let's get back to work."

It's pretty bad when Billy winds up as the peacemaker, thought Guo.

Making the cuts took less time than setting up the rig and safety gear. The doors stuttered the rest of the way closed. The latches locked smoothly. Guo tack-welded scrap over the obvious gaps then reported in. "Hatch closed. Probably still have some leaks. Ready to go to tenth-atmosphere for leak checks."

"Negative," said the captain. "I don't want any oxygen in there until all the nasty ice has cleared out. Can you tell if it's just down to water?"

There'd been the occasional pop while they worked. Methane and ammonia both boiled before water melted so gas pockets had formed and cracked the ice. "Not yet, sir. There's still some of the burnables in there."

"That's all right. We're not in a hurry. I want that stuff to warm up slow so we don't crack anything. Billy, you're on converter room duty. The rest of you are off shift."

Twelve hours later it seemed to be down to water ice. Billy cleaned up the scattered chunks and dumped them out the airlock. Alexi was supposed to help but spent the time staring at the containers.

When the ice had receded to halfway down the container door Schwartzenberger gave permission to repressurize the hold and remove the ice. Vacctape handled the leaks around the hatch. The shovels came out again as the younger members of the crew chopped at the ice. Bing didn't have to open her first aid kit. For all the sharp chunks flying around nobody got hurt worse than a bruise from slipping on the deck.

Finally all the ice was piled against the hatch and the crew gathered facing the container ends. "Alexi," said the captain, "Would you do the honors?"

The doors were unlocked. Alexi opened the nearest container, revealing two crates with illustrated labels. The left one showed a statue of a young man standing stiffly. Billy leaned in to read it. "Thera kouros, circa 580 BC. Packaged in SafeFliteFoam. Use dilute vinegar or other weak acid to remove."

"About three thousand years old," said Bing.

"That's got to be worth a lot," said Billy.

Mitchie said, "Maybe more than this ship. Every museum will want it."

"If it's intact," warned Guo.

"They'll buy it!" cried Alexi. "They'll buy it in pieces. They'll buy it if it's a jigsaw puzzle. They'll buy it if it's *sand!*"

Schwartzenberger tried to calm things. "A museum will give us a thousand key honorarium and a letter from the Ministry of Culture thanking us for preserving the common heritage of humanity. This is going to be *hard* to sell."

"It should be in a museum," said Guo. "This might be the oldest artifact in human hands. Not much came off Old Earth before the Betrayal."

"I've seen prehistoric artifacts in Fusion museums," said Bing.

"Replicas."

Alexi checked the other label—"Putto with dolphin, porphyry fountain, Florence, circa 1475"—and moved to the other container. The doors swung open on an array of small boxes. Alexi started scanning the labels.

Billy read one aloud. "Synthetic Vingium. Atomic number 148. 50 grams. Warning: unstable at temperatures above 450C."

"*That* we can sell," said Captain Schwartzenberger. He laughed. Stable synthetic elements were another Golden Age tech humans had never learned how to recreate. "We could be wearing masks in an alley and they'd buy it. Let's take a look at the other ends." He started walking around the containers. The crew got there ahead of him. Alexi left off reading labels and sprinted to catch up.

Billy opened a set of doors and found blank boxes. Pulling one partway out let him pry out a bundle of plastic slips. "Planetary Bank of Eden. Ten Thousand Rubles. What the heck?"

"Fancy coins, Billy," said the captain. "Worthless now."

"They're still valuable," said Alexi.

"As collectors' items, maybe. But this is enough to crash the market." Schwartzenberger waved Billy to the next one.

Those boxes were black. "Depleted uranium. Guaranteed 99.9% pure. 3kg," read Billy. He pulled one out. "Looks like another stack behind this one. Wow." Guo let out a low whistle.

"That'll be easy to sell," said Schwartzenberger. "And we can use it ourselves. Guo, how does the MC978 like U-238?"

"Loves it," said the mechanic. "One of the highest efficiency feed metals. That looks like enough to take us anywhere."

"Beautiful. That changes our course. We can run constant acceleration until we're safe in Demeter. We'll be there twice as fast as we expected."

Bing smiled. "I'll redo the rationing calcs. We might be able to have real meals again."

Schwartzenberger pulled a flask from his thigh pocket. "This is worth a toast. Ladies and Gentlemen, to success, and a safe trip home!" He drank deep and passed the whiskey to Bing. "Everybody take a good slug, don't be shy." The flask circulated slowly. "The mate and I will take tonight's shifts. The rest of you can celebrate."

***

Mitchie and Guo celebrated by sticking to their new routine, reading a chapter of *Romance of the Three Kingdoms* in his cabin. She was still impressed by his reading nook—an oversized easy chair with a lamp at the perfect angle. It was just big enough for them both if he wrapped his left arm around her.

I wonder how Cao Cao's going to get out of this mess? thought Mitchie as Guo turned the ancient poetry into a story for her. They'd started late after speculating about fencing the loot.

Guo stumbled over a phrase. "Argh. Hold this for me, please?" He put the book in her hands and walked over to his reference shelf. Mitchie held it carefully. He'd never admitted how much it cost, but the book had been calligraphed on hand-made paper. She studied the brushwork, picking out the ideograms she'd learned. Spaceport pidgin didn't have much overlap with Classical Chinese.

"Indebtedness doesn't make sense in context—unless I mangled the first half of the sentence. Argh." Guo closed the dictionary and put it back under the restraining cord. "I'll have to look up the passage in the modern version. I'm too drunk to figure it out now."

Mitchie giggled. Guo wasn't drunk, even if they were both warm from the captain's whiskey. He took out a bottle and poured into a pair of ceramic cups. "What's this?" she asked as he handed her one.

"Plum wine."

"You are *such* a traditionalist." Her first swallow was sweet but burned. It felt more like plum brandy.

"You were warned," he said.

She laughed and drank again. It took a moment for her to figure out the ideogram on her cup. "Happiness" never appeared in Port Control documentation. His cup said "Love." Guo took the book and put it back in its case.

She made room for him as he sat back down. He drained his cup, put it down, and wrapped both arms around her. She giggled as he pulled her into his lap. "Hey! Don't make me spill this."

"You'd better finish it then," he said as he nibbled her neck. Mitchie drank the last swallow and put her cup nested in his. She straddled him and pressed her lips to his.

This was when the voices in the back of her head normally started up. *Must be too drunk to bother me*, she thought. She'd been warm from the alcohol. Guo's touch had her on fire.

Unzipping her jump suit didn't bother her. His hands felt better on her skin than through the cloth. When he pulled it down to her waist she had a flash of panic. *No. It's all right. I can decide to do this, just for the fun of it.* "Guo. This is just for the trip, okay? It can't be anything serious."

"Okay," he said to her cleavage, "just for the trip." She squeaked and wrapped her legs around him as he stood up. He carried her four steps and laid her down on his bunk.

Journey Day 161. Eden System. Acceleration: 10 m/s²

The fast trip home wouldn't free them completely from algae crackers but they'd only be a once a week food. Bing had gone all out for dinner. Meatloaf, vegetables, bread, and a cake baking as they ate.

The only problem with the meal was the conversation. Bing had asked if anyone had thoughts about what they'd do with their share. Alexi had thoughts. He'd been planning what to do with the treasure for over a decade. When the cake came out of the oven to cool he was still describing his future palace on Pintoy. The crew was happy to focus on their food. Bing finally got fed up enough to say, "Thank you, Alexi, that's enough. Guo, what's your plan?"

The mechanic looked up from the bread he was buttering. "I don't have a real plan yet. I'll send some money home at first. One thing I would like to do—and this obviously depends on everyone agreeing—if we can't sell that Thera statue I'd like to take it as part of my share and donate it to a museum, after we've gotten to where we can tell the whole story."

"You'd have to buy it at full price," snarled Alexi.

"Of course. But its market value might be less than its historic value."

"I think it's a great idea," said Billy. "We could all bring our kids to come see it."

"You have kids?" asked Alexi.

"Um, well . . ."

"Billy?" asked a suddenly concerned Bing. "Is there something I should know about?"

"Well, I don't have any kids now. It's just, Yukio said she was planning on engineering her child, and she wanted me to be part of it."

Mitchie choked on her drink. He was a splendid example of hybrid vigor but she couldn't imagine Billy as part of the Terraforming Service's project to increase human intelligence.

"Something about my kinesthetic aptitude."

Okay, that makes sense, she thought. *The boy can dance.*

"What did she do?" asked Guo. "Take a skin sample before leaving the ship?"

"She, um," he actually looked abashed. "She said I'd already given her plenty of DNA."

"Should've asked for a receipt," said Mitchie.

"I don't know what to do. I mean, I know how to handle a kid showing up in the normal way. If she cooks one up in a vat I might never know. And if she sends me a picture or something am I a parent? It's not going to be half me and half her. If she takes one of my chromosomes, what does that make me, a great-grandfather?"

"Three and a half greats," said Guo.

"Cheer up, Billy," said Alexi. "When you get home rich you can have all the kids you want." Bing had cut him off before he could describe the harem quarters.

Journey Day 172. Tunxi System. Acceleration: 10 m/s^2

"Two pair," said Abdul, turning over his cards.

"Flush," answered Captain Schwartzenberger, revealing five spades. He pulled in the pot. It was the largest of the evening, over a million Eden rubles.

"You always have such good cards, sir," said the apprentice.

"No I don't. I fold my hand more often than you do. Poker isn't about winning individual hands. It's about making the most of it when you do have a good hand."

"I thought you didn't like this game," said Mitchie. She'd been surprised when the captain dealt himself into the impromptu lesson.

"I don't. It's a waste of time, and there's always someone better out there to take your money. But if you're going to waste your time you should do it right." He dumped his winnings in the basket and left. It was almost time for shift change on the bridge.

Guo finished shuffling and dealt. "Five card draw again." It had been his idea to start the game when Abdul had asked about the ship's name. "Ante up." He tossed a 10,000 ruble note in.

"Check," said Mitchie.

"Twenty thousand," said Abdul, putting more money in. The lovers matched him. Guo gave Mitchie three cards, Abdul one, and took none himself. The pilot and apprentice swiftly raised each other to a quarter million rubles. Guo quietly stayed in.

"Pair of kings," said Mitchie as she called.

Abdul blushed. "Ten high." He had four hearts.

"I knew you were bluffing," said Mitchie as she reached for the pot.

"Ahem." Guo turned over three sevens.

"Crap." She pushed the pot over to him.

"Bluffing doesn't work well with play money," he told Abdul. "Or against crazy people."

"Hey."

"I figured one in four odds weren't bad for pulling the card I needed."

"It's more like one in five. You already had a third of the hearts in your hand so there's fewer out there to draw."

"THIEVES!" Abdul was pulled out of his chair then flung to the deck. "How dare you steal my property! I should punish you all!" shouted Alexi.

"What the fuck are you doing!" yelled Guo. He came around the table to the injured boy. Abdul whimpered. The galley chairs were bolted to the deck. The metal back had cut hard into his ribs as Alexi dragged him across it.

"I'm protecting what's mine, you stinking betrayers." Alexi grabbed the cash off the table and stuffed it in the basket. Guo helped Abdul up and moved him back into the corner. Michigan held the carving knife she'd grabbed behind her as she slid around the table.

"I'm putting this back in the box," said Alexi as he grabbed the last of the cash. "And locking it." He turned and walked out.

"You okay, kid?" asked Guo.

"I think so." Abdul coughed. "Just bruises."

"We need to talk to the captain," said Mitchie.

***

The blow to her ear woke Mitchie from a sound sleep. She rolled out of the bed, landed on her feet, and looked for a clear escape route.

There was nothing between her and the hatch of Guo's cabin. She looked at the bed. Guo was in a nightmare, flailing his arms and muttering "no" and curses. Mitchie knelt on the bed and grabbed his hands. "Shhh, shhh, it's all right, wake up." He kept thrashing, pulling away from her. "Guo! Wake up!"

His eyes opened. "Oh, shit. Michigan—what are. Oh. I'm sorry. I thought I was past this."

"Don't apologize. It's all right. What is it?"

"Dreaming. About that night on Savannah. It's—I keep having bad dreams about it."

"That was a horrible night. But you saved me. I'm glad."

"I'm glad I saved you. That's not . . . it's, the dream . . . I murdered those two men."

"I think you were justified. I think a court would agree. From what they said I think they'd committed a lot of crimes before they attacked me. They had it coming."

"Yeah, probably. But I didn't fight fair, I didn't warn them, just snuck up and . . I can still feel that horrible crunch. I didn't care then, too scared you were already dead, too scared another guard would shoot me, too busy trying to get us out of there. Now you're safe, I'm not scared, and I keep remembering it. The feel of that *crunch* traveling up my arm. What kind of person am I, ending someone's life so easily?"

"You're a survivor," said Mitchie. She pressed her naked torso against his. "I want you to survive."

"Do I deserve to?"

"Yes. You do good things. You should stay alive and do more good things. They did bad things. They had to be stopped."

Guo started crying. She pulled his face into her breasts and let the tears flow across them. She stroked his hair and whispered nothings for a long while.

Finally he had his voice back. "Do you ever dream about it?"

"No, not dreams. Sometimes on long bridge watches when it's just me and the stars I think about it." *Mostly wondering is the Job turning me into a sociopath or was I always a sociopath and that's how I got the Job.*

"I still have that hammer. It's on its clip in the converter room. I haven't used it since then. I can't even touch it to throw it away."

"I'll buy you a new hammer. A solid gold hammer." She saw his expression change by the light of the intercom LED. "Ooh, mechanic face! Okay, it's too soft. How about a titanium hammer?"

"Too light."

"I know! We'll make it out of Vingium."

"Good grief. That'd cause riots." He tickled her neck to keep her from more suggestions. She went for his ribs. Then they were too busy to talk more.

Just before Guo fell asleep again he said, "Don't throw the hammer away. Might need it."

Damn you, Alexi, thought Mitchie. *You set him off. You better accept the captain's slap-down or I'll deal with you.*

Journey Day 173. Tunxi System. Acceleration: 10 m/s²

Leaving the converter room unattended for a few hours wasn't a problem. If all readings were in spec and the hopper had enough fuel it could stay empty for a full eight-hour shift. Guo just liked camping out there to keep his finger on the ship's pulse.

Now, well, it wasn't the ship's pulse he was most interested in. He'd intended to go downbelow when Mitchie went on her bridge shift. But she'd been running late and missed breakfast, so he'd taken a tray up to the bridge, and kept her company while she ate. Now he hurried across the cargo hold hoping that his fancy new converter hadn't developed any quirks since midnight.

The containers from comet SMX blocked the straight line to the lower deck hatch. Guo was nearly past them when he heard the metal creak. He'd seen Billy and Abdul working on the solid waste compactor before he came down. He stopped and looked at the top of the treasure container.

Alexi's head popped over the edge. "Keep moving, mechanic-boy. Don't touch my stuff."

"The captain ordered you confined to quarters!"

"So you could all go through it and hide the good stuff before we do the full inventory. Nice trick, but I'm not falling for it. Go belowdecks."

"You get back to your cabin or I'm calling in an all-hands, right now."

"I'm going nowhere." Alexi casually waved a pistol over his head.

Guo was too surprised to be scared. After all, he'd seen Alexi voluntarily give his gun to the captain yesterday—he couldn't be armed.

"Get away from what's mine or I'm making an example of you." Alexi slid forward, bracing his elbows on the edge of the container. When he brought his pistol into the cup of his left hand Guo's paralysis broke. He dashed behind an empty storage container.

Guo pulled out his handcomm. "All hands, all hands, our local lunatic has escaped, he's in the hold." A bullet came through the sheet metal over his shoulder and fragmented on the deck. *Idiot. Couldn't find a vacuum-rated container, had to hide behind a cheap one.* "And he's shooting at me." He shoved the comm in his pocket and crawled toward the lower deck hatch.

Some thumps and bongs said Alexi was moving too. Guo doubled back to thread through the dense cluster of containers around the recycler. He got almost to the hatch without any more shots fired at him but that last five meters was so exposed Alexi had to be watching. He backed up to where he couldn't be heard and pulled out his comm. "Can we get the hold PA out of the circuit?"

"Maybe," answered Mitchie from the bridge, "but I've locked it so only I'm hearing you for now. Are you hurt?"

"No, he missed. I can't get below without giving him another shot at me. Can you give me ten seconds of free-fall on my cue?"

"Yes." He could visualize her expression, tongue between her teeth, saving questions for later.

"Good. Stand by." He went back to the opening closest to the hatch. "Now." He squatted down, curling his legs as tight as he could.

"Free-fall in three, two, one," he was weightless.

Guo kicked the deck with his full strength. The turn was almost right, he pulled in his arms to make the 180 flip just as he reached a light bracket four meters off the deck. A hard kick off it sent him straight through the hatch. He heard two gunshots, presumably aimed at the straight path.

Once he was through the hatch Guo grabbed for the ladder. His hold on a rung held as he flipped around and smashed a kneecap on a pipe. His other hand found the ladder just as weight came back on. Two hands and his good leg were plenty to support him as he swore at the pain.

Once his head cleared he went up the ladder and pulled the hatch closed. Dogging and locking it wouldn't keep Alexi out for long. The toolbox by the lower airlock included a prybar. Wedging that into the locking wheel made him feel more secure. If this went on long enough he could weld it.

Guo limped into the converter room and called the bridge. "I'm okay. Hatch secure."

Mitchie's reply started with a long sigh. "Thank God. You scared me. Are you hurt?"

"No."

"Honestly."

"Just bruises. What's going on up there?"

"Billy went to the hatch and yelled down something like cut that out or it's the airlock. Alexi fired a shot, didn't hit the hatch. So we closed and secured it. Now we're trying to figure out what to do next."

"Let me know how that comes out. I have gauges to check." *And pain pills to take.*

***

"Let's just open the cargo hatch and dump him to vacuum."

"Michigan, I understand you feel very strongly about this," said Bing, "but we can't just kill him."

Mitchie's reply was fortunately cut off by Billy. "Can't. The door locks are mechanical. Can only open from inside the hold."

"So dump pressure some other way. We can splice the air lines to outside."

"Too slow. There's so much air in the hold he can find it and block it before he loses much."

"Dammit." As Mitchie pondered the problem Bing held her peace, hoping practicality would come out on the side of mercy. "What about the airlock? Override the interlock to open both doors."

Billy brightened. "That'd work. We've got the tools to do it from the outside." He frowned. "My suit's in the hold."

"Mine's by the upper airlock." Mitchie started to get up but froze when the captain cleared his throat.

Captain Schwartzenberger had put Abdul on bridge watch so the rest of the crew could brainstorm in the galley. Clearly it was time to broaden the solution space. "Pilot Long. Mr. Lee. There is one very big difference between killing someone and not killing someone. With not killing someone you can always change your mind later. So let's talk about ways to get Frankovitch out of the hold without killing him. Is that clear?"

"Yes, sir," said Billy.

The captain shifted his gaze to Mitchie. "Yes, sir," she said.

Schwartzenberger avoided meeting Bing's eyes.

"Well, I cut off the air feed to the hold," said Billy. "But I can't see him suffocating. He can get the pilgrims' recycler up with a shift's work."

"There's a lot else he can do," warned Mitchie. "He has access to all the piping and wiring trunks. Whatever we do has to be fast enough for him to not sabotage us in revenge."

That kicked off a couple of fruitless hours creating and discarding impractical plans. Finally Billy hit on their key advantage: acceleration couches. "He can't be in the pilgrim dorms if he's playing sentry. If we boost accel with no warning he'll have to take it lying on the deck. Headache, joint problems, bedsores and scalp cuts if we go long enough. When we go back to normal thrust he'd be easy to sneak up on."

Mitchie glared at him. "Sneak" had become a shorthand for "Michigan sneaks up on him with a hypodermic of sedative." She was tired of pointing out bullets were safer and cheaper.

"I like that," said Captain Schwartzenberger. "But we need a break. Everybody get a snack. Mitchie, once your personal needs are taken care of give Abdul a break on the bridge and take a position sight. I'll bring Guo up to speed."

***

Going down the ladder, Mitchie mentally cursed Guo for being a naïve idealist. He'd talked her into going with the hypodermic plan. Pointing out that risking her life to resolve his guilt issues was unfair hadn't stopped him. His clincher was a practical argument. "Sooner or later people are going to find out how we got this loot. Killing the guy who told us where to find it will look bad no matter what our excuse is." She'd promised him to use the needle first. The pistol on her belt was just-in-case.

Her bare toes found the deck instead of another ladder rung. Mitchie sighed—silently—and put her other foot down on the deck. She froze, listening to the sounds of the cargo hold. The dull roar of the torch, back at ten gravs acceleration instead of forty-five. The air circulation fans were silent. Water gurgled as it went to the nose of the ship to even the thermal load. A faint snoring.

She stepped toward the treasure containers, placing her feet flat. The hold lights were at the one-tenth dimness they'd been set to when they upped thrust. Alexi wasn't anywhere she could see from the ladder, so probably on their far side.

Alexi lay behind the second container. He was in his underwear. His pants and shirt were wadded into a pillow under his head. A little blood on the deck showed skin had split on heels and elbows. Twelve hours at high acceleration had hurt.

She pulled the hypodermic out, popped off the needle cap, and pocketed the cap. Alexi's pistol was on the deck by his right hand. She held her breath for the last two meters of the sneak. A quick stab in the thigh, thumb pushing the plunger.

"Gah!" Alexi sat up, reaching for his leg. She kicked his gun away then turned and ran. Once past the pilgrim dorm she stopped. Mitchie dropped into her favorite kneeling stance and held her pistol on the corner, ready for him to come after her.

Instead of seeing him she listened to low-voiced cursing. One high-pitched obscenity was probably the needle being yanked out. An exultant "Ha!" ended the babble. *He found his gun.* Footsteps came toward her. Alexi lurched around the corner of the dorm, waving his pistol. She lined her sights up on his chest. *As soon as he points it at me I fire.* The blurry figure beyond her front sight waved its gun left, right, up, and fell over. *Crap.*

Mitchie pulled out her handcomm. "He's out. You clean him up. I'm going belowdecks."

Journey Day 174. Tunxi System. Acceleration: 10 m/s²

Guo had welded a deadbolt on the outside of the eighth stateroom's hatch while Mitchie cleared it of everything she thought could be used as a weapon. This turned out to be everything not welded to a bulkhead except the mattress. They wouldn't let her strip Alexi before putting him in there.

"He's not going to kill anyone with his underwear," said Billy.

"I could kill you with your underwear," countered Mitchie.

"While I'm wearing them?"

"That just buys you two minutes."

"Enough, people," said the captain. Bing injected Alexi with the antagonist. They withdrew to the hatch. In a minute the prisoner woke up, looked around, and sat on the edge of the bed. He studied the three drawn pistols. "I gave you a second chance once," said Captain Schwartzenberger, "and it nearly got some of us killed. The plumbing in your foldaway is working. Bollix it up and we let you drown. This hatch will open once a day for you to get a meal delivered. Come near it and you'll be shot. Figure out any other way to make our lives more difficult and we'll just kill you."

The prisoner said nothing. Schwartzenberger waved his crew out then backed through the hatch. Guo slammed and bolted it as soon as he was clear.

The odd maneuvering to harass Alexi had put them well outsystem from their planned course. A few torchships had come out from Tunxi to investigate. Evading them was easy enough with unlimited fuel. It did stress the ship enough for Guo to demand a twelve hour coast with the cooling wings out before they made the run for the gate.

Crossing the Swakop system was even more boring. The crew started making plans for their arrival in Demeter in a week.

Journey Day 186. Swakop System. Acceleration: 10 m/s^2

Mitchie settled into the reading chair to await the next chapter. Guo was fiddling about with some stuff. "We finished the inventory today," he said.

"About time. Y'all must've been fondling every bit as you looked it over."

"The jewelry box was interesting. Some of the pieces had names on them. Might have historical value." He chuckled. "No diamond rings though."

Mitchie cocked her head. "I can't see you wearing a diamond. Maybe one in your ear."

Guo put down the cups he'd filled with plum wine and walked to the chair. "I'm not an earring guy." He knelt in front of the chair. Not the first time he'd been in that pose, but she was fully clothed, so she didn't see the point. "Michigan," he said as he took her hands. "These past few months, even with the danger and hunger and tension, have been the happiest time of my life. You make me happy. Happier than I've ever been. Where ever we go from here, however long our lives last, I want to be with you. Will you marry me?"

Mitchie realized the smile on her face had to be the goofiest one she'd ever had. She flung her arms around him. They toppled over and passionately kissed as they lay on the rug. A voice in the back of her head, silent for so many weeks, began calmly listing a number of practical points.

When she finally had to break the kiss for air he asked, "So that's a yes?" His grin was manic.

"It's—I wish—oh, God. It's complicated."

"I'm good at complicated."

He was, very. The back of her head considered this a very dangerous conversation, but she'd already rejected the advice to slap his face and run. "Marriage is complicated. It's not just we get to sleep together every night. Careers, kids, where to live, everything."

"You left out dying. My family has a good-sized plot back on Akiak. We'd be welcome in a joint grave even if we never move back. Mom told me that when I went to space."

"She was thinking that far ahead?"

"Arsenic Creek only keeps people who can plan many winters ahead. Don't change the subject."

"How do we even know we can keep working together a year or two from now? Being a spacer is pretty unstable."

He actually laughed. "You're worried about working for a living? We need to go roll around in all that loot we just finished counting."

"That's all fairy gold. One suspicious Fusion customs inspector and it all goes away. The art we can't prove is real without blowing the whole thing open. Legally it's all stolen goods."

"Legally it's Frankovitch family property and Alexi's the heir."

"Which means wills, and cousins, and taxes, and getting the psychotic git to cooperate."

"Okay, forget about being millionaire honeymooners." Guo rolled onto his back, propped up his feet, and wrapped his arms around her. Clearly ready for a long, serious talk. *Dammit.* "You're as good as a pilot gets outside fighters. I'm a damn good mechanic. That's a great combo for any captain with two slots to fill. We don't have to worry about finding work."

"You want to spend the rest of your life as a spaceship mechanic?"

"I want to spend the rest of my life with you. You never talk about the future. Where do you want to go? What would make you happy?"

Mitchie took a deep breath. *I can't tell you.* "I don't know. I'll have to think about it." She grabbed his zipper and pulled it down. "I can tell you what would make me happy right now."

It was obviously changing the subject, but he went along with it.

Interlude Four

Akiak, gravity 10.3 m/s^2

The military shuttle had no passenger windows. Pete sat up front where he could look over the pilot's shoulder. That just gave him a headache and a touch of snow blindness. The northern ice cap wasn't scenic. Finally he napped.

Alverstoke shook Pete awake. "We're here. The Secure Research Center. Your new home."

The shuttle hatch was already open. Pete grabbed his duffle and stepped out. More glare, this time the sun reflecting off a lake of meltwater around the landing pad. He followed Alverstoke to the doorway into the dome. An empty coldlock room led to another room lined with lockers.

"You can put your cold gear in there," said Alverstoke.

The next door led into the dome. Alverstoke led Pete through then turned around to enjoy the immigrant's reaction.

Pete stopped dead in the doorway. The dome was a greenhouse. Trees grew in the center. Topiary ringed the outside. The walls separating the unroofed offices supported ivy or flowerpots. "It's beautiful," said Pete. "I never expected something like this."

"Biophilia is a powerful force," said Alverstoke. "We want to keep all of you happy and sane."

"I'm amazed you can afford this."

"We can't. Bonaventure and the other DCC members provide most of the funds."

"I didn't think they did charity," said Pete.

"You'd be surprised. But this isn't. Akiak's contribution is accepting the risk of some of this research going bad."

Pete said nothing.

"We should find your office," said Alverstoke.

Pete's assigned desk sat just north of the oak tree. The dividing wall curved around it to offer some privacy. Pete dropped his duffle there. They searched for his boss next.

Dr. Tukhachev kept working for a full minute after Alverstoke greeted her. Then she turned around, politely welcomed them, and participated in a few minutes of small talk.

"Mr. Alverstoke, thank you for taking good care of Mr. Smith. Please feel free to return to your other duties," said Dr. Tukhachev when the formalities were done.

Pete felt a pang saying goodbye to Alverstoke. With all his friends turned to radioactive ash he'd latched onto the case officer as the only friendly face he had.

Once they were alone Dr. Tukhachev dropped her mask. "Listen, Fuzie. I don't care about your education in elaborate theories or your own fancy ideas. This is the Disconnect. We deal in practical solutions to real problems. We need results. So don't go off on your own wild schemes or I'll kick you out of the dome with a parka and a pair of snowshoes."

She leaned in as Pete shrank under her glare. "The only reason you're here, breathing the oxygen better men should be breathing, is that men like you killed them. Don't think you're good enough to replace them." She stared at Pete as if daring him to say something. "We need to build on their work and make sure it isn't lost. Your first task is to build an index of all the conference talks and related documents. Don't bother me until that's done."

Pete nodded and ran back to his desk. He fell into the soft chair and curled up, waiting for the shivers to stop. His loss hurt too much for him to stand up to that much hatred. It took half an hour for his breathing to steady.

When Pete felt he could try to work he wiped the tears off his cheeks and turned on the datasystem. He stared at the map of the Center's archives. After three minutes he decided to give himself a pep talk.

Look, he thought. *It's not about you. She's hurt too. She's angry. You're the first target she could lash out at. More people will join the team. It'll get better.* He took a deep breath and started looking for the conference papers.

"3rd Akiak Technology Conference" brought up a massive pile of text and video. The Center had mirrored the conference's entire datastream. Investigating how they'd stolen it revealed half the organizing committee worked for government agencies. Two did so openly.

Pete started skimming the presentations. The organizers had grouped the secondary tracks by topic, making his work easier. Speculation on the cause of the Betrayal had two tracks, serious and conspiracist. The main track slowed him down. These papers covered topics no one else had addressed or combined multiple fields. By the time Pete had read enough to categorize them he'd been sucked into reading the whole thing.

Pete flinched when Connie's paper came up. He'd helped her track down data for it but she'd refused to let him see the result. She'd teased him that going to the conference was his only chance to hear her paper. He considered marking it "history" and skipping past to avoid the pain. But he couldn't give up hearing her voice one last time. He started the video.

The Creation and Decay of Veto Culture

When near-AI technology went into use worrying about the danger of uncontrolled AI went from a fringe concern to a major political issue. Researchers were yanked out of their labs to testify on the effectiveness of proposed laws. Some were passed in a panic then repealed when the public whim demanded AI benefits.

Several laws were accepted by the AI development community. Hardware for hosting AIs was equipped with easily-accessible kill switches. Software also had to accept halt orders. Researchers were less enthusiastic about the requirement for AIs to halt processing every two hours until given a "resume" command by a human.

The AI restriction most popular with the general public was the personal veto option. Anyone wanting to avoid AIs could register their home location in a national database. All AIs were constrained to have no direct effect on any solid object within five hundred meters of the registered location (the developers rebelled at being forced to avoid moving vetoers). The first veto law was passed in the USA but was swiftly copied in other nations.

Establishing the Culture

Urban areas were solid veto zones. AIs were limited to virtual activity only. Some humans had full time jobs as the hands of AIs, carrying out instructions whispered in their ears. This was a happy compromise. The public received the benefit of AI innovation. The AIs operated freely within defined boundaries. Fear of runaway AI had been quelled.

More adventurous people could travel to remote areas to test their new concepts. A city named Burning Chrome sprang up in the Nevada desert populated by a hundred thousand techies and their packs of AIs. Less cutting-edge towns grew in other rural areas, a new kind of edge city. A Supreme Court decision enabled AI-friendly settlements by confirming a city's right to prevent vetoers from moving in.

Veto-free areas were still scarce. The strong push for new space access technology was driven by the need for unregulated sites for new AIs. When terraforming was developed it provided an alternative home for vetoers. Developers bribed Amish and Hutterite communities to move off Earth to Arcadia.

Decline of Veto Culture

The success of AI-run cities attracted many people to their lifestyle. Health, longevity, and happiness ratings all soared. AI errors were swiftly reverted by "clean up" AIs. Many people revoked their vetoes. Others bought out vetoers so their town could join the Golden Age. Direct bribes weren't always needed. The last vetoer in a neighborhood would increase his property value tenfold by revoking.

The Golden Age pulled people out of veto culture. Other factors pushed them away. Veto neighborhoods were depopulating. Maintenance was neglected. Services as basic as water and power would fail for days at a time. Twenty-first century technology no longer had the network of active supporting enterprises needed to keep it functioning.

Worse for the Vetoers, the medical profession had completely embraced the Golden Age. In 2150 only AIs diagnosed illnesses. Medicines were custom-made on the spot for patients, tailored for the genetic and behavioral profiles. Vetoers began dying of heart attacks, infections, and other conditions that had not killed anyone for fifty years.

By 2175 Vetoers began suffering from malnutrition. They'd isolated themselves from the global economy. No way to earn money, no way to spend what they had on food. Charity operations had been completely automated, excluding them from the veto zones. Once they were too weak to walk to an AI zone to get donations they had to wait for human volunteers to bring in supplies. Some volunteers did this from charity, more from curiosity, and a few for the rare opportunity to abuse a real person out of sight of ubiquitous surveillance.

By the end of the century only the most stubborn still held out. They suffered from paranoia and other mental illnesses, hiding from other humans or attacking intruders. Many died in total isolation.

The last Vetoer, Jordan Hammerstein, survived on the produce of the garden he tended in the ruins of downtown San Francisco. He chased visitors away by flinging chunks of concrete. Jordan had been one of the first Vetoers as well. As a young activist he held banners in demonstrations demanding passage of the Personal Exclusion Act.

The Betrayal destroyed too many records for us to know what happened to Jordan. It had been five months since anyone had tried to see him so he could have been dead for weeks or more by the Betrayal. He could have been one of the hundreds of millions killed on the first day. Or, since the Betrayers had little interest in off-network areas, he might have seen the disaster he feared pass him by. In that event he would have been perfectly justified to have his last words be "I told you so!"

Pete wiped his eyes. No wonder the attendees had bombarded Connie with questions. He had a dozen for her. Which he'd never get to ask. He marked the presentation "History, Earth, AI, Causes of Betrayal."

FIVES FULL
ENGINEERING DECK

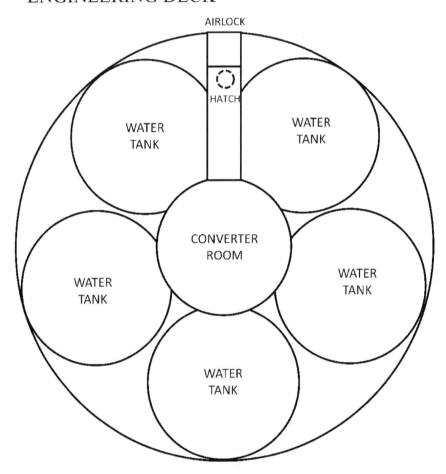

Fives Full Engineering Deck

Part Five: Hitchhikers

Journey Day 190. Swakop System. Acceleration: 0 m/s^2

Captain Schwartzenberger fiddled with the watch schedule to put both him and Mitchie on the bridge after a full shift's rest as they approached the Demeter gate. Having him on watch with her meant no chatting with Guo. She was more relieved than sorry. Guo had figured out that "I don't know" and "I need to think about it" boiled down to "no," but her method for avoiding talking about it encouraged him to keep bringing it up.

Mitchie finished the calculations from her latest sight. "In the groove, sir."

"Good. It'll be nice to be back in human space."

There was an outpost of humanity in the Swakop system. A Navy monitoring satellite sat near the gate. No messenger drone shot out from it. Apparently *Fives Full* wasn't big enough to trigger its simple circuits.

The jump was as quiet as ever. A warm feeling of safety washed over Mitchie. "Merchant Vessel *Fives Full* to Demeter Control. We are arrived from Sukhoi via Swakop per filed flight plan. Request clearance for landing." The captain was taking a turn with the sextant. "Sir, want me to start us for the planet?"

"No, they'll probably make us get inspected at some dreary base before we can go there. Might as well coast."

A minute later Mitchie repeated the call to Control without getting an answer. The captain got on the PA. "All hands, we've arrived safely in the Demeter system. We're waiting on instructions from traffic control. Out."

Mitchie's fourth repetition brought Control to life. "Swakop Gate Control to *Fives Full*. Acknowledge your arrival per flight plan. Proceed to Steelhome best time. You will receive further instructions there. Control out."

She turned toward Schwartzenberger. He looked as amazed as she felt. "That's it?" he said. "No lengthy interrogation to see if we're really human? No inspectors boarding us? Not even a threat to blow us up if we deviate from the assigned course? What the heck are they doing? AI security is their main mission. They sound like they're too busy to bother with us."

"You sound like an outraged taxpayer."

"I am. Tariffs are taxes. They didn't even complain about us being a month late from the flight plan." Mitchie had the Demeter almanac open to the minor planets section. "What is Steelhome, anyway?"

"Planetoid, surface accel 2.5, combination industrial town and naval base," she summarized. "Nearly 10k civilians. It's strange they'd send us there without checking us out."

"Very. Well, that base may include a lab that wants a look at us. Get us boosting in the general direction and then we'll work out our course."

After so many elaborate trajectories the course to Steelhome seemed too simple: boost two hours, flip, decelerate for about the same. Mitchie looked up from the plotting table. "My eyeball course was only off by five degrees."

"Nice guess. Put us on the real course."

"Aye-aye."

With such a pleasant reception the captain stood the crew down for a cracker-free lunch after turnover. No one could figure out why the Navy had ignored them, so conversation turned back to Alexi.

"If they're just going to wave us through," said Guo, "the Pintoy option looks a lot better. Drop him with a relative, someone we can tell the truth to."

"That means three more weeks of playing prison guard," replied Billy. "He's already going more nuts from being in solitary. The Navy can put him in a hospital and sort him out."

Mitchie buttered her bread. She couldn't believe the boys were running through this same argument again. She'd been tired of it the second time through.

"We can't do that," said Guo. "Whether they believe him or not we're in trouble. If they do believe him they come after us for the loot. If they don't, the therapists break down his mind until he believes it wasn't real."

Billy wasn't convinced. "When they turn him loose we come back, explain it to him, and give him his share."

"But first we hand him a pile of play money and say, 'Just kidding!'" interjected Mitchie. Abdul burst into laughter. *See, I'm not the only one who can hold a grudge.*

"Full therapy doesn't break that easily. The guy could be ruined for life," countered Guo.

"I'm okay with that," said Abdul. He rubbed his still-healing ribs.

"I'm not," said Captain Schwartzenberger. Everyone turned toward him. The captain had sat out the debate, saying a decision wasn't needed until they got to Demeter. "We'll tell Customs, or the Navy, or whoever else asks that he flipped and we're taking him back to his family. If they want to take him we give him up. We'll say we found a little stuff. If they don't take him we tell his family the truth." He glared at Mitchie and Abdul. "He's getting nasty treatment now. Maybe he deserves worse, but he also led us to where we are now. So let's have some gratitude for the man. It's not his fault the load was too merciless to bear." The table was silent. "Is that understood?" A stream of quiet 'yes, sir's came back. Mitchie just nodded.

Lunch broke up after that. Guo cornered Mitchie as she put her dishes in the sink. "Do you have to go right back to the bridge?"

"Yes, it's my turn to take a sight." She slipped around him and escaped.

Guo turned to the captain, waiting for his turn at the sink. Schwartzenberger shrugged.

***

After taking a position sight Mitchie spent some time with the radio frequency scanner. "More strangeness," she said. "There's a lot less traffic than usual. Hardly any analog signals. What I can pick up seems to be encrypted."

"Anything from Steelhome?" asked the captain.

"Not even data transmissions from there."

"Hopefully they'll talk to us when we arrive."

Unlike Gate Control, Steelhome answered immediately. *"Fives Full,* you are cleared for landing pad four. That's equatorial, east of your current position. Look for green circles. Out."

The green circles were rings of blinking lights. The "pad" was a pit in the surface of the airless rock. Mitchie brought the ship gently down the centerline.

Steelhome, Demeter System. Gravity 2.5 m/ s²

A short tunnel gave into a cavern. As they descended a hatch closed above them. Mitchie stopped the ship a meter above the pad and let the landing gear absorb the gentle drop. She looked at the atmosphere instruments under the port edge of the dome. "Pressure's coming up. Hospitable of them."

"Fine. Let's see if we can find someone who'll talk to us."

By the time they gathered in the hold and found the rope ladder there was breathable air outside. Billy opened both airlock doors and let in a waft of, if not fresh, different air. Mitchie took a deep breath. Steelhome smelled of dust and ozone, not lubricant and algae. Schwartzenberger kicked out the ladder and followed it down as it unrolled, not bothering with every rung. The rest followed.

Mitchie studied the scarring on the cavern walls. They'd mined iron here. Some of the infrastructure had been abandoned in place. Now it supported illumination banks. The pad was new, it must have been laid when they decided to open the cavern for ships. Tire scuffs led to a vehicle hatch which was just opening. A lone figure came through it on a blower.

"Finally," muttered the captain.

"Hey, they've got a water feed," said Guo. He'd opened an armored hatch to reveal a reel dispensing a thick hose.

"Go ahead, top us off," said Schwartzenberger. "Can't hurt anything." Abdul discovered this was another learning experience.

The stranger arrived, blower throwing dust on their pant legs. His uniform wasn't Navy. Probably local police. Mitchie thought he looked scared. *Did he hear rumors of us being contaminated?*

Captain Schwartzenberger stepped forward to introduce himself. The stranger spoke first. "What's your life support capacity?"

Crap. There's no good reason to ask that, thought Mitchie.

"Forty," answered the captain after a moment of poker-faced silence.

"That's long-term, right? You can hold more if it's just a few days?"

"Yes . . ."

"Chief, these guys can take them," said the cop into his comm.

"Take who?" demanded Schwartzenberger.

"You need to take the women and children, as many as you can lift."

The police uniform's concession to fashion was a long, flowing collar. The captain wrapped both fists in it and pulled. *"What is going on?"* Mitchie looked at Bing. By her expression it was very unusual for the captain to assault a police officer.

"You don't know?" gasped the cop.

"We just jumped into the system. Nobody's told us anything."

"Oh. Um. System's under attack. Big AI fleet jumped in from Ushuaia. Biggest in decades. Most going to Demeter. But there's a swarm coming here."

"Well." Schwartzenberger set him back on his feet. "Was that so hard?" The cop got back on his blower. "Go on, son, we've got work to do." He jetted off.

Captain Schwartzenberger turned to face his crew. "Let's get ready for passengers. Billy, is that spare recycler still hooked up?"

"Yessir."

"Get it turned on. Guo, don't just top off our tanks. That water should be near freezing—"

"It is."

"—so replace as much of the warm water with cold as you can. This run might get hot." Guo nodded and followed Billy up the ladder. "Mitchie, get everyone our pistols." Abdul was left controlling the water hose as it flopped around.

The captain and mate found some brackets to anchor the rope ladder to. "Why the guns, Alois?" Bing asked quietly.

"Shi, we're the only ticket off of a doomed world. This is a tough bunch of Fuzies—there's no stipend collectors here—but some will grab a ride if they see the chance. Stowaway, hijack, hostages, who knows."

"I don't think I can bring myself to shoot someone for just trying to escape."

"How about for stealing a little girl's chance?" She didn't answer. "Well, keep it holstered. I'll do the hard part."

Schwartzenberger kept Mitchie at the ladder with them when she came back. They discussed where to take their hitchhikers. A straight run for the Argo gate tempted them but too many passengers would foul the air before they could jump. If they had more than fifty or so they'd have to stop at another mining outpost on the way, probably a gas giant moon.

"Customers," interrupted Bing. Pedestrians trickled through the vehicle hatch, more crowding behind them.

"Skipper," said Mitchie. "That's more than fifty. More than a hundred." *Fives Full* could hold three hundred people if they carpeted the decks, but they'd suffocate in less than a day.

"Yep."

A middle-aged man had outdistanced the crowd. He had the skipping gait of a low-gee run down, keeping his balance even as he dragged along a child with each hand. A woman holding a baby followed him closely.

"Welcome to the *Fives Full*," bellowed Captain Schwartzenberger. "We will take women and children aboard only! Please form a single file for boarding!"

The leading man didn't slow.

Schwartzenberger addressed him directly. "Sir, men will not be allowed on board! Please let your children get in line."

"I'm not leaving my family!"

The captain drew his pistol. Mitchie followed suit. He aimed at the oncoming father. "Sir, stand aside!"

"You gonna shoot me in front of my kids? Really?"

Schwartzenberger lined his sights on the man's chest. *Those poor kids*, he thought. His finger took up the slack in the trigger.

"Hey! All right!" The man threw his hands up and bounced to a stop. His children tumbled as he released them.

"Go sit over there." The captain pointed his left hand at a random patch of pavement. Once the man sat he lowered the pistol. The mother had caught up. Her older children clutched her legs.

"Hi, I'm Bing, the first mate. Let's get you on board." She led the family up the rope ladder. The rest who'd been close enough to see the confrontation hung back.

Mitchie stepped forward. "You look like a little boy who wants to go on a spaceship." The family she'd picked moved up to the ladder. She urged a second and third forward. Then the line started flowing on its own.

Two men went to stand near the one Schwartzenberger had stopped. An elderly woman joined them, with civil nods for the two and a sniff for the sitter.

Schwartzenberger watched the refugees flow by. His mouth had lost its bone-dryness but he was content to let Mitchie do most of the talking. He pulled a teenage boy out of the line. "You. You're a maybe. Wait there." He pointed to the right.

"He's fifteen!" protested his mother.

"That's what makes him a maybe."

"Mom, I'll be fine. Take care of Cindy."

"Up the ladder or out of the way, dammit!" said the next mother in line. The flow restarted.

The "no" group now had over a dozen men and several grandmothers. One called to a contemporary in line. "Ludmilla! Where's Sharon?"

"She's manning the tracking radar for her turret. So I get to herd the kittens." Ludmilla had three children bouncing around her.

"You'll do fine."

"I'll keep an eye out for your Maria."

"Of course you will. Good luck."

The cop came back up on his blower. His collar was still rumpled. "Captain. I see you've got things under control. Do you need anything?"

"Yes. CO2 recyclers. Or absorbers if you can't find recyclers. The more you find the more people I can take." The "maybe" group was up to a dozen teenage boys and a couple of their girlfriends.

"I'll see what I can do." He dusted off.

Guo came down by climbing on the underside of the ladder. "I've got the water tanks cross-pumped, sir. We've been putting the cold water into empty tanks. I'm going to start dumping the warm tanks one at a time so we've always got an empty to fill."

"Good work."

Mitchie looked after Guo for a moment as he went around the ship, then went back to scanning the line for troublemakers. A few minutes later water began spreading out from under the ship. The landing pad was perfectly flat. The whole cavern wound up a finger deep. The line still hadn't ended.

"I think I figured it out," said Mitchie.

"Oh?"

"They do think we might be an AI trojan from Swakop. So they pointed us toward the nearest Ushuaia AI target and hoped we'd destroy each other. AIs always attack each other over humans."

"That . . . makes a scary amount of sense," said the captain. "I wonder if Steelhome has convinced System Control we're human yet?"

"Nah, they probably just think this is some incredibly devious ploy."

***

Alexi lay in his bunk. The ship had to be back in the Demeter system if they were actually in a gravity well. He didn't let it distract him from his project.

The fools had given him a fork and spoon with one meal. They hadn't noticed when he'd only returned the fork with the dishes. Now he'd found the roughest surface in the stateroom, one of the welds holding his bunk to the bulkhead, and was rubbing the handle of the spoon against it. Every day it grew a tiny bit more pointed. He was patient. He would take all the time needed to make his weapon.

Alexi paused in his scraping and held his breath to hear better. Voices. The babble of a crowd. Were the thieves giving tours of their booty? Or hiring more crew by promising shares of his inheritance to them?

He thought about it. New crew could be an opportunity for him. The Diskers were careless and lazy. Surely they'd put the new ones on feeding him. He could subvert them, win their loyalty, and become captain. He smiled at the mental image of Schwartzenberger being forced out of his own airlock.

The hard part would be starting the conversation. The new crew would have been told all sorts of lies about him. He'd have to intrigue them, soften them up before giving any orders.

Once he had his opening words figured out he said them out loud for practice. "How'd you like to know the real story of this ship?" That was terrible. Not talking to anyone for two weeks had his throat stiff. He'd have to practice that some.

But first he needed to get the handle of that spoon a little pointier.

***

The police blower returned, escorting a small truck. The line scattered as water sprayed over them. Schwartzenberger pulled out his handcomm. "Billy?"

"Busy, boss. Reseeding the hydroponics sheets with max-oxygen again."

"A truck showed up with air-processing gear. We'll need the crane."

"God be praised. I'm on it."

Mitchie raised her eyebrows. "Did Billy just pray?"

"Sounded like it," said the captain. "He must have run the life support numbers."

Opening the cargo hatch took Billy, Guo, and a sledgehammer. The welds had been mostly on the port side so they only opened the starboard hatch. Lowering a pallet didn't slow down the line. Several men from the "no" group helped load boxes onto the pallet. Unloading it was more complicated. Once the boxes were in the hold each one had several children sitting on top.

The line finally had an end. The trickle of new refugees had stopped. Some of the no group had already left. The maybes were getting nervous. Schwartzenberger called Billy to talk numbers.

"Now this is assuming we can believe the labels on those boxes, and get them running soon," cautioned the deckhand. "It works out to nine days."

"Not enough to get to Argo then. What if we add sixteen more, call them full adults?" Schwartzenberger could hear the sliderule swishing over his handcomm.

"Takes us down to seven days. We're on a steep part of the feedback curve."

"That'll get us most places in this system." There was no need to get the maybe group's attention, most of them were staring at him. He waved at them and pointed at the end of the line. They scrambled into place.

The captain walked halfway to the no group, far enough back to draw if someone lunged for him. "We're going to lift off as soon as we have everyone settled. Best y'all be on the other side of that hatch before we do. I thank you all for your cooperation."

They called back a jumbled mix of thanks, blessings, and hopes he'd watch after their children. Schwartzenberger gave them an embarrassed wave and went to tell Abdul and Guo to belay pumping. The apprentice actually reeled up the hose and secured its hatch. The captain didn't have the heart to interfere with his optimism.

He was the last one up the ladder after unhooking it. The hold was a madhouse. People lying everywhere, all talking, a few helping Billy set up the additional recyclers. He was glad they'd rearranged the containers to bury the loot under empties in case of a customs inspection. Last thing they needed was a refugee breaking into one in search of a comfortable spot.

Bing was conferring with a few volunteer organizers. He broke in to ask, "How are they getting settled?"

"Good! We've got all the second and third trimester ones in the dorms, at least they'll have beds for accel. Most brought blankets or something."

"How soon will you have them ready for lift?"

Bing chuckled. "Lift whenever you want, sir. This is as good as it's getting."

Schwartzenberger opened his mouth, closed it, nodded, and went to the bridge.

Mitchie greeted him with word that the last stragglers had cleared the cavern and Control had sealed it off. "When can we lift?"

"Now."

"*Fives Full* to Steelhome Control, request permission to lift."

"Granted. We're going to dump pressure. You are clear to lift when it's stable." The hatch over their heads opened to space. Air rushed out. The water on the pavement boiled until only a slick of ice was left.

Mitchie called "Up ship!" on the PA and gently boosted the ship up the tunnel. Schwartzenberger smiled grimly at the sight of another of his crew treating this landing pad as if it would ever be used again.

Demeter System. Acceleration 10 m/ s^2

"Good luck, *Fives Full*. Steelhome out."

"Good luck to you. *Fives Full* out," replied the captain.

Mitchie reported, "On course for Ossa." The gas giant had two inhabited moons and a space station to dump their hitchhikers on. Though if the Navy didn't get control of things they might have more trying to board.

"Good. Now let's see if that's where we really want to go," said Captain Schwartzenberger. The plotting table had been neglected in non-human space. Trajectories avoiding all known gravity sources were easy enough to do on paper.

Mitchie added the Argo gate and several outposts listed in the almanac to the table. "Having so much fuel takes the fun out of this game. The delta-V we can get out of a close fly-by isn't much when we're on continuous burn."

"That's not my worry," said Schwartzenberger. "I want to have alternates in case a swarm beats us to Ossa."

"Ah." Mitchie re-opened the almanac. Soon she had the plotting table as cluttered as they'd ever had it. The gas giant was still their target. Nothing else offered as many chances to re-air.

Four hours out of Steelhome she spotted an array of plumes moving in on them. Radar confirmed they were on a crossing course. A few more pings revealed they were accelerating at fifty gravs to match their vector. "Crap. No way we're evading them. I can try to plume them as they close then switch up."

"Do your best," said Captain Schwartzenberger.

Before plumes could be an issue the incoming ships opened into a loose circle and matched courses outside the danger zone.

The radio crackled. "*Fives Full*, this is House 17, commanding Fighter Squadron Sierra Five. Over."

"*Fives Full* here," answered Mitchie. "Thanks for introducing yourselves."

"We have been tasked as your escort. Please comply with all convoy instructions until released to independent running."

"Acknowledged. *Fives Full* is operating in convoy. It's nice to have you boys along, just in case."

"Thank you for your cooperation. Be advised that this is not a just in case escort. Part of the swarm headed for Steelhome has diverted in your direction." That voice sounded damn familiar but she couldn't place it. She hated the term 'swarm.' Why couldn't they just say 'more AI ships than we can count?'

"House 17, you are a bundle of joy. I'm surprised they could spare you from supporting Steelhome."

"That rock has more guns than two cruisers. They don't need our help. *Fives Full*, please maintain current acceleration and change vector to—" House 17 proceeded to read out a great many digits.

"Navy, please remember you don't allow us to carry the gear needed to reach that level of precision. This is an analog ship. Can I have that with five significant figures in each vector component?"

House 17 gave the simplified course with a minimum of sarcasm. Mitchie warned everyone to hang on then pivoted the ship.

"Damned if I can see anything on that line," said the captain from the plotting table.

"*Fives Full*, we see you within ten minutes of arc. Nicely done for prehistoric tech."

"Thank you, Navy," answered Mitchie with excessive sweetness. Suddenly she placed the voice. "Housefly 17, do you have a tattoo of a dragon biting your left nipple?"

The squadron commander was silent. His pilots filled the empty air. "Buss-sss-ted." "Oh, oh, you're in trouble." "Remember, Skipper, anything you say on an open channel may be used against—"

"Knock it off! *Fives Full*, who are you?"

"I told you I was a pilot."

"Michigan?"

The pilots erupted again. "He remembers her name! It must be true love." "Don't be a fool, girl, run!" "Skipper and Michigan, sitting in a tree—"

"Lock it up! Pilot Long. I'm very pleased to meet you again. I'd like to know how you wound up *here*."

"That, Housefly 17, will take a lot of beers."

"Did you really jump in from Swakop?"

"Yes. After looking at Old Earth through a telescope."

That silenced the fighter squadron for a minute. Housefly 17 finally said, "We'll all buy the beer for that story. Heck, Jimbo just put on senior grade, he still owes us a party. You can have his beers."

"Dammit, Skipper," said Jimbo, "I don't make you pay for my girlfriend's drinks."

"We all chipped in to pay for your girlfriend," quipped another pilot. Housefly 17 let the bickering go on.

A previously-silent voice broke in. "Skipper, report from Fleet. Our swarm just cut the corner. They're accelerating up our vector."

"Can you track them, Eyes?" asked Housefly 17.

One of the fighters pivoted and cut thrust. "Have them on Doppler, sir," said Eyes.

"*Fives Full*, how much acceleration can you give us?"

"Lots," answered Mitchie. "But we've got kids on bare decks and pregnant women in plain cots. Won't take much to hurt them."

"Shit. Give me another two gravs. Let's see how they react."

"Aye-aye." Mitchie opened the ship's throttle.

"They're matching," said Eyes.

"Put it back down," ordered Housefly 17. Mitchie complied.

"And they're back where they were," reported Eyes.

"Thanks for resource-constrained AIs," muttered the commander. "We'll let this run out for a bit then take our next action."

***

In the hold Bing made an announcement. "In case of sudden maneuvers we normally ask passengers to strap in. Since we're not set up for so many we're going to give you something to hold on to instead. The deckhands are spreading a net over the deck. Please help unroll it as it passes over your heads. We'll tie it down so it'll give you better support if we need to maneuver the ship."

Abdul helped Billy wrestle the cargo net out of its niche. "What is this thing for?"

"In case we get a pile of crates we need to strap down, or something big that doesn't have attachments. Last used it on a reactor shell." Billy showed him how to unhook a recessed handhold and lock it around one of the net lines. "We'll tie down the edges as it unrolls. Then go back through the middle and get as many spots as we can."

"Is this going to keep them from getting hurt?"

"It'll keep them from all sliding into a pile against the wall."

***

"Skipper, the swarm has hit the quarter-million klick mark." Mitchie thought for a moment and decided that had to be Eyes, the recon pilot.

Housefly 17 said, "*Fives Full*, we're going to leave you for a bit. Ensign Greer will stay as escort. Stay out of trouble."

"Good luck, Sierra Five," said Mitchie.

All but one of the fighters flipped around and tripled thrust. In an instant they were out of sight behind *Five Full's* torch plume.

Mitchie got out of her acceleration couch and stood by the plotting table. Captain Schwartzenberger had updated their position and velocity marker. "Looks like we're headed for nowhere," she said.

"Yep. If we didn't have those piles of DU I'd be worried about refueling."

"I wonder why the Navy wants us here."

"No idea. Could just be trying to scatter the AI forces as widely as they can."

After a bit more profitless brooding over the plotting table they returned to their couches and profitlessly brooded there.

The left-behind fighter mentioned that he was receiving comm traffic, did the ship want a relay? "Yes!" demanded Mitchie.

Housefly 17 was talking. "Prepare to execute charlie romeo on my mark. . . . Execute!"

"They're reforming," reported Eyes. "Disk normal to our vector."

"Then we'll punch through. Close-in on me, max thrust."

"Got one!" yelled Jimbo's tormentor.

"Stay in formation. Cover your sector," said the commander.

Eyes: "They're splitting. Looks like they're going for a globe."

"Vector plus-Z."

"Watch for smart gravel."

"Two more down."

"Disperse! Reform at mike zulu." Housefly 17 again.

"Lost Oscar."

"Bogey down."

"Back me up, Perks."

"Sphere is breaking up," warned Eyes.

"Lovey, help Perks."

"Lovey is gone."

"Mug, help—never mind. All to mike zulu."

"More evasive action, dammit. What are you saving your fuel for?" That was Jimbo.

"Ball on mike zulu. Take a sector and watch it," said Housefly 17.

"Mug, tighter in," ordered Jimbo.

"Here they come!" said someone not Eyes. She hadn't heard Eyes' voice lately.

"Focus minus X."

"Long bursts, dammit," said Jimbo. "Ammo in the hopper ain't doing you any good."

"Got one!"

"That's right, keep shooting, you might get lucky."

"Where's Mug?"

"Lost him and Jax."

"Full thrust, aim for the densest group, scatter them." Jimbo was giving the orders now.

"Watch plus Z."

"Got another."

"Damn all you mechanical bastards."

"Look left!"

When the channel had been silent a minute the newbie came on. "*Fives Full*, this is Ensign Greer, I mean Housefly 28. I am assuming command of the convoy."

"Acknowledged, Housefly 28. *Fives Full* is continuing on convoy vector as directed." Mitchie switched off her mike and turned to the captain. "Want to run to Ossa? I could plume this guy and then we'd be free to pick our own course."

"Attack a human ship? What the hell are you thinking?" snarled Schwartzenberger.

"It's the Demeter Fleet. Call it a down payment for nuking Noisy Water."

"He didn't do that."

"He would have if he'd been in that ship."

"Doesn't matter. We're not going to attack him. And we're not going to Ossa. We're going to stay on course and hope the Navy has a plan."

"Aye-aye, sir."

The frigid silence on the bridge was interrupted by the radio. "Okay, uh, Housefly 28 to *Fives Full*. Good news, the swarm is back in formation but it lost a lot of momentum in the engagement. So it's at least five hours from overtaking us. More if they want to match velocity."

"Thank you, Housefly 28," said Mitchie calmly to the man she'd offered to kill.

"Um, the bad news is another swarm is vectoring on us. A bigger one. It'll catch us about the same time."

"Ain't we popular," replied Mitchie. The ensign stayed silent.

Mitchie did a position sight. They were a tiny bit off the course they'd been given. Odd that the Navy hadn't demanded a correction. Well, if they were a diversion it didn't matter where they went.

The frequency scanner suddenly showed a spike. Captain Schwartzenberger tuned into the new signal. "Steelhome Control to all stations. Our turret array is heavily damaged. Landers are coming in. Disregard all future messages from this location. Make the Betrayers pay. Steelhome out."

Schwartzenberger cursed.

"Should we tell the refugees?" asked Mitchie.

"No. They've only got four hours left, why make them more miserable?"

***

The intercom crackled. "What's the latest reading?" asked Guo.

"They'll overtake us in two hours," answered Mitchie. "Assuming they don't slow to board."

"Damn. Anything from the Navy?"

"I've been watching that rendezvous point they ordered us to and don't see anything waiting for us."

A brief silence. "I'm glad we had this time together."

"Me, too. Any regrets?"

Guo answered immediately. "Not moving faster with you. Do you have any regrets?"

She thought a moment. "Not telling you yes."

"Seriously?"

"Yeah. The reasons don't matter now."

He laughed. "Michigan Long, will you marry me?"

"Over the *intercom*? Yes, I will."

"Great! Captain Schwartzenberger?"

The captain had been pretending to not overhear the conversation. Now he activated his mike. "Yes?"

"Sir, would you be willing to perform a wedding on board?"

"Yes, if everyone's consenting." He looked at Mitchie. She nodded, but her expression was slipping from cheerful to wary.

"Okay, sir, I'll get back to you when we're ready," said Guo. The intercom went dead. Schwartzenberger contemplated pulling the plug on his eager mechanic's scheme. They probably should stay at their posts in case something changed. But they'd spent the last hour just watching everything smoothly march toward inevitable disaster. Taking a short break likely wouldn't make any difference. He pulled the *Captain's Bible* out from its elastic restraints and started reading through the ceremony.

Abdul came up to the bridge. Bing had tagged him to cover bridge watch. Mitchie gave him a quick brief on how comm with the Navy worked.

It was fifteen minutes until the intercom squawked again, this time with Bing. "Okay, we're ready. Come on down to the hold."

"On our way," said Mitchie. She was down the ladder first but Schwartzenberger had no trouble catching up to her in the corridor.

"Hold up." He leaned down to look her in the eye. "Let's talk about this a moment."

"Sir?"

"Do you want to do this?"

"Sure. You heard me tell him."

"That's what I'm trying to make sure of. Do you love him?" asked the captain.

"Yes, very much," said Mitchie.

"Do you want to marry him?"

"Yes, sir."

"If he's holding anything over you, threat, bribe, whatever, to make you do this, you don't have to go through with it. Talk to me, or talk to Bing, and we can figure out a way to fix it."

"No, sir. It's nothing like that. Come on, they're waiting for us." She led the way down the cargo hold ladder.

Guo had press-ganged Billy into setting up an improvised altar for the wedding. The cargo was all stacked against the back of the hold. Bing had herded the refugees into staying clear. Now they all gathered in to see the bride who'd provoked this sudden ceremony. A middle-aged woman stepped out of the crowd to address her. "Miss Long?"

"Yes?"

"We thought a bride should have a bouquet." The refugee held out a bunch of colorful flowers.

Mitchie was almost too startled to take it—who grabbed flowers during an evacuation? As she held it she realized the flowers were fabric, folded and stitched into flower shapes. A blue one caught her eye. She looked to the woman's matching dress, then down to her hem where a ragged notch had been cut. "Oh, thank you. Thank you so much." She gave the refugee a one-armed hug as her eyes misted up.

Bing steered Mitchie to the improvised altar. Guo waited there, beaming. Billy stood behind him, nervously patting his pants pocket. The captain rested his bible on the altar and looked out at the crowd. The flower-makers and other romantics were up front, basking in this sign of hope. The confused and indifferent milled behind them. Leaning against the bulkheads and containers were the cynical. Their expressions made it clear they thought taking time out for personal business was proof the crew could do nothing to increase their odds of survival above zero. Not having any disagreement with them, Schwartzenberger opened the bible to his bookmark and began. "Dearly beloved . . . "

He kept the ritual to the bare bones. In a few minutes he asked, "Guo Kwan, will you take Michigan to be your wife, to live together in matrimony? Will you love her, comfort her, honor her, and keep her, in sickness and in health, for richer and for poorer, as long as you both shall live?" His throat tightened on the last phrase.

"I will," he said.

"Michigan Long, will you take Guo to be your husband, to live together in matrimony? Will you love him, comfort him, honor him, and keep him, in sickness and in health, for richer and for poorer, as long as you both shall live?"

"I will," she said.

The captain waved at Billy, who produced the ring and handed it to Guo. He slid it smoothly onto her finger. "How'd you get my size?" she whispered.

"I maintain your spacesuit."

The captain gave them a shhhh and launched into the closing prayers. "I now proclaim you husband and wife. You may kiss the bride!" The refugees cheered, even the bulkhead-proppers. Once they came up for air Schwartzenberger muttered, "You've had the honeymoon already. Back to work now, everyone."

A low chorus of "yes, sirs" answered him. Mitchie paused to toss the bouquet at a cluster of teenage girls. She went up the ladder without looking to see who caught it.

***

Fives Full fled blind through space. Looking back at her pursuers would give up precious seconds of her lead. But Housefly 28 regularly turned around to measure the distance so there was no need. As Mitchie listened to his latest report she thought she'd like less information. "About a quarter of the swarm has dropped behind. The way they're spread out I think they'll be the rear half of a globe. The leading edge will overtake us in forty-five minutes." So the same status as ten minutes ago.

She didn't mind someone nervously over-analyzing. It was inflicting it all on her that made her lose patience with the newbie. The captain was obsessively trying to pick up voice transmissions from around the system. He didn't bother her with his inferences from them.

Some were obvious. A civilian vessel pleading to be let through Demeter's orbital defenses and being directed to land on an arctic island meant the real battle hadn't started. "I have to wonder if this is it," said Mitchie. "Are the AIs going to start taking human worlds again?"

"I can't see it," replied Schwartzenberger. "They've always had the resources to do it. Could've happened a century ago. This is just a probe, collecting data or something. Bigger than usual."

"Or something? What else would they want?"

"Could just be a game to them. We don't know what they really want. Probably couldn't understand it if they told us."

"A *game?* All this is a game?"

"Look. Last time I was on Akiak, there was this defective—dunno what was wrong with him, bad gengineering maybe—who made his living sweeping out the spacer's hall. Some of the deckhands were having fun with him. Held out a couple of ten gram coins, silver and copper, and asked which one he wanted.

"Defective said, 'Ooh! Can I have the pretty gold one please?' The spacers laughed and gave him the copper.

"So I found him taking out the trash and told him, 'Hey, that coin is copper, not gold.' He bonked me on the head and said, 'Shhh! If they find out I know they stop playing the game.'" Schwartzenberger chuckled. "So the AIs can't take Demeter. They wouldn't be able to play the game anymore."

Mitchie contemplated her captain's view. "That makes us the copper piece?"

"Well . . ."

"Sir, please don't try to cheer me up any more." She looked at the strange new ring on her finger. At least *she'd* been able to make someone happy in his last hours.

Housefly 28 reported the swarm was thirty-three minutes away.

***

At fifteen minutes to doom Housefly 28's ever more frequent updates were drowned out by a wave of static. "Is somebody setting off nukes?" asked Captain Schwartzenberger.

"No, doesn't sound like it," said Mitchie. "Probably active jamming. Guess the swarm doesn't want our last words getting out." Schwartzenberger raised an eyebrow at her. Mitchie ignored it and fired up the radar.

Its display was strange. The screen was covered with snow while the space ahead of *Fives Full* was filled with fuzzy objects. Mitchie picked one of the larger fuzzies and focused the beam on it. The return was larger and fuzzier. Someone jammed their pings. She hastily shut down the radar.

"Sir, I think I figured out why the Navy wanted us here." She felt a surge of anger as she realized how they'd been used.

"Ambush," said Captain Schwartzenberger. "With over a hundred women and children as bait. Wouldn't let us run for cover, wouldn't let us go someplace defended, just dragged us out here in the most attention-getting way possible. May God pass true judgment on the Fusion Navy."

The jamming went silent. A new voice came on the radio. "Task Force Ajax to Merchant Vessel *Fives Full*. You are released from convoy and authorized for independent maneuver. Recommend evasive action and a hasty departure. Good luck. Ajax out."

"Acknowledged, Ajax." Mitchie turned off her mike before she could let any other words slip out. The jamming came back on. She lowered the volume.

The space in front of them began filling with plumes as dozens of warships lit off their torches.

The captain activated the PA. "Attention everyone. Hang on tight. Strap yourself in if you can. The Navy has arrived and we're going to have a bumpy ride." He switched it off and snarled, "Get us the hell out of here before the shooting starts."

Housefly 28 had already vanished. No debris so likely off to rendezvous with some squadron. Mitchie pivoted *Fives Full* ninety degrees, hoping to get out from between the clashing forces.

Pilot and captain now had their first view of the enemy. The near swarm was a simple disk, spreading slightly as the AI craft braked at full thrust. The larger swarm was huge. Subformations spread out, plumes aligned neatly, covering more of the sky every moment. It was shockingly beautiful. "Looks like a chrysanthemum," said Mitchie. Then she shook her head and turned the ship back toward the approaching warships.

"Don't plume them, dammit," said the captain.

"The Navy's safe from me for now. I won't plume anybody who can shoot back. Or has friends who'll shoot back." She started some gentle evasive action. Enough to make it necessary to use a seeker on them instead of ballistic shells.

Finding a gap to pass through would be tough. The Navy had a massive fleet here. Radar didn't help. Navy electronic counter-measures made the returns fuzzier than what she could eyeball. After three pings her whole screen went white with signal overload. Probably some Navy operator telling them to shut up before their pings gave the swarm some information.

The closest thing she could spot to a gap was a circle with one ship in the center. That one had a dim plume, as if it ran low thrust so only the outer fringes of the plume were visible past the hull.

Doing a sharp turn to aim for that would attract attention. Instead Mitchie varied the evasive action, always going longer on the legs toward her target.

Sometimes she'd make an evasive turn sharp enough for them to look back. The Navy's frigates and fighters had leapt ahead to scout out the AI swarms. The plumes swirled insanely as the skirmishers maneuvered for position. There were already casualties visible. Sometimes a ship exploded in a bright flash. More often a plume just went out. They couldn't tell which side they belonged to.

***

"I hate cutting this," said Billy. "It's a good rope."

"Can it," ordered Bing. "Gimme another five." The deckhand sighed and cut off some more one meter pieces. "You and Abdul take some, too. Hand them out to anyone you see rolling around."

"Aye-aye."

She left them to it and started picking her way to the center of the hold. There was plenty of room to put her feet as long as she didn't mind stepping over a head or leg. She'd managed to avoid hurting anyone when bracing herself against the evasive maneuvers though there'd been some rude belly pokes.

Bing caught a twelve year old as he tumbled by. Two knees on the deck and a hand on a cargo net line braced him enough to hold against a ninety degree pivot.

When the ship steadied he said, "Thanks," and tried to stand.

"Lie down, kid. You can't walk around now."

"I have to! I promised my mom I'd come right back after using the hygiene."

"This is a locked room. She knows you're safe in here. Hook your belt on to this rope so you don't roll away again. Just stay put. Don't go anywhere."

"But what if I have to go to the hygiene again?"

"Just hold it as long as you can. And then, well, we can wash your pants when it's all over. Stay strong, kid."

Bing started stepping over bodies again. A few more ropes got handed out. One refugee got a lecture on why looping a slack bit of net around her leg was dangerous. She got two ropes.

A tall woman moved to intercept Bing. It was Katie, one of the volunteers who'd helped settle everyone in. "We need towels," she said.

"Don't have any," answered Bing. She was tired of saying that.

"Can't the crew spare some?"

"I can't climb the ladder with this maneuvering. I don't think anyone can."

"We need something. Some of the little ones are throwing up from the rough ride. The puddles are sloshing around. When they hit someone they vomit too half the time."

"And I was only worried about them messing their pants." Bing heard the port thrusters fire. She bent her knees and put a hand on the deck as it tilted, bending her elbow to absorb her momentum without landing on the child next to her.

Katie had straight-armed it. She was sobbing in pain on top of a matron twice her age.

"Let me see that," ordered Bing. Katie held up her arm. "Sprained wrist. Let's get you tied to the net. And stay put."

"Shouldn't I have a bandage on it?"

"We're out of them." Once Katie was tied down with Bing's last rope the mate said, "I'll check on the pilgrim dorms. There might be some towels or blankets or something."

The pregnant women strapped down in the dorm bunks were pitifully grateful she'd come to check on them. Bing didn't burst their bubble. The pilgrims hadn't left any towels but Bing pulled a bunch of absorbent looking blankets from under the current occupants.

"Ma'am? Um, ma'am? Please?"

Bing tracked the plea to a middle bunk. "Yes, what is it?"

"Um . . . I think my water broke."

The bunk was wet and didn't smell like pee. Bing didn't have anything more to go on. Her medic training was purely in trauma. "I'll get you someone," she said.

She ditched the blankets by the doorway and stepped out into the hold. Deep breath, loosen the throat, from the diaphragm. "Listen up! Is there a midwife or doctor on board? I repeat, is there a midwife or doctor here?"

After a long quiet pause someone piped up, "I'm a nurse."

God be praised. "Over here, ma'am. Crawl, dammit. You're no good as a casualty." In a couple of minutes the nurse was with her patient.

Bing set to ripping up blankets with her utility blade. Billy came by to report the rope was all cut up. She tossed a square meter of soft cloth at him. "There's your next project. Figure out how to make an acceleration harness for a newborn."

"You're shitting me."

"Nope. Mother's started labor."

"Aw, c'mon," whined Billy. "That's impossible. I don't even know how to hold a baby."

Bing had no sympathy. "There's moms out there with babies in slings. Imitate one."

"If they complain about me staring at them I'm sending them to you."

"You do that. Now get." He got.

Bing picked up a pile of blanket squares and headed out to find moving puddles. *Please, God, let this end soon.*

***

Mitchie wished the radar was available. The ship she aimed for kept up with the rest of the second wave despite its dim plume. Which meant it was light, but what good was a hollow shell in a battle? Eyeballing her way past a ship behaving unpredictably was asking for trouble. Unfortunately at this point any other course might get them plumed.

At close approach she stopped evasive maneuvers. Best to look safe and predictable when in range of twitchy anti-missile gunners.

That damn ship was still annoying her. They were close enough to see its side, but it still looked like a nose-on circle. Even the Fusion Navy's heaviest cruisers had enough streamlining to land if they had to. This thing didn't match any ship she'd ever seen.

Well, they were going to pass each other at over ten klicks per second in a few minutes. Then she could forget about it and concentrate on finding their way through the third wave.

At close approach it was still a circle. As they flashed by Mitchie could see it was actually spherical. Huge. Covered in weapons. And thrusting at full power—the width of the sphere had hidden the core of the plume coming out of its narrow base.

"Take the con, sir." She pulled the logbook out from its straps under her console. The ship was already a dot again. She focused her mind on the one good look she'd gotten. Opening the book to a blank page she started sketching.

"Long? What's the problem?"

The sketch started as a circle with an equator drawn off-center. Latitude lines of alternating missile ports and gun turrets followed. Massive antenna arrays were drawn next.

"What the hell are you—screw it. I have the con." Schwartzenberger pivoted the ship to keep her clear of the sphere's expanding exhaust.

Mitchie kept sketching. That oversize opening at the zenith. A bridge dome at the opening's edge. A lot of maneuvering jet towers. Fighter bays at the equator. Cryptic notes on the side to help estimate the size of it later. She closed the logbook.

"Sorry, skipper. Never saw one like that before. Distracting. I'm ready to take her back."

"Your priorities are fucked up, girl."

"Sorry, sir. Back in the groove now."

His expression was a new one to her. *Is he actually biting his tongue?* The captain said only, "You have the con."

The third wave had a clumpier formation. Mitchie didn't foresee any trouble finding a place to pass through. Her new main worry was avoiding flights of missiles. Both sides sent volleys at each other's reserves.

Evasive maneuvering had gone from "throw off a theoretical targeting solution" to "stay out of the way of flocks of rockets accelerating at 200 gravs." They had a better view of the battle by being forced to look in all directions for new hazards.

Mitchie noticed a pattern. "Sir, some of the AI missiles are moving with us."

"Are they aiming at us?"

"No, I think they're using our plume as cover." She called Guo on the intercom. "I think we need to pull out those drones again."

"What's the problem?" asked the mechanic—and, oh God, her husband. When she explained he laughed. "I found a trick for that. In the troubleshooting portion of the drone user manual it describes a specific set of commands you should never do or it makes the drone blow up. That sound useful?"

"Sheesh. The things you pick for pleasure reading. Yes, very."

"I can time it between 45 seconds and two minutes."

She thought a moment. "Make it one minute. Get ready to drop it on my signal."

"Right. Might need you to cut thrust while we're setting up."

"Let me know when."

***

Billy met Guo at the lower deck hatch. "What do you want? We're going to break an arm moving around in this."

"We have to launch a drone. You get to help carry it."

"No way."

"She'll cut thrust, it won't take much muscle."

"Ain't the problem. Look at this deck. Can't carry anything without tripping over a baby or slipping on shit."

"Well, we have to launch a drone. You're the cargo handler."

"Fine. We use the crane." Billy had his feet spread wide and one hand holding a bracket on the bulkhead, so he barely budged as Mitchie pivoted the ship sixty degrees. "She'll just have to hold it steady until we get the drone in the lock."

"Do it. I have a card to program."

***

Three minutes of accelerating in a straight line made Mitchie tense up. When Guo commed, "In the airlock," she sighed.

"Pivoting starboard," she warned him. The new angle let her see the latest missile swarm. Twenty little plumes closing in on *Fives Full*. She waited for them to get close enough for this to work. "Now!"

"It's away," answered Guo.

"Pivot ventral." She turned the ship to keep their plume away from the ballistic drone as it fell behind them. Twenty seconds on this vector . . . another twenty pointed directly away . . . then work back to the line they were on. She could see the missiles turning to follow her exactly. She led them to where she wanted them to be.

The exploding drone wasn't that bright. But half the missile plumes went out. Two more started stuttering. The rest scattered.

Mitchie smiled in satisfaction. "Not using us for cover any more."

"I'm proud of you," said Captain Schwartzenberger.

"Just trying to keep us alive."

"No, this makes us a higher priority target for the AIs. We're being a player now. But it's giving the Navy a better chance to win the battle."

Mitchie chose her words carefully. "I didn't do it for them, sir. I did it so some Demeter asshole wouldn't blow us up to get a better firing solution."

"You really think they'd do that?"

"Yes. Oh, they'd feel bad about it. Just as bad as they felt about using us as bait for their ambush."

They covered their eyes as the ships ahead of them glowed with a FLASH-FLASH-FLASH-FLASH-FLASH outshining their drive plumes. Mitchie blinked, every ship an afterimage. She closed her eyes as it happened again. The flashes were bright enough to see through the lids.

"What the hell was that?" asked Schwartzenberger. "Not a nuke. Frequency scanner just shows the same jamming."

"It was a reflection. Too simultaneous to be something they did." Mitchie laughed. "I'm glad we didn't pick then for a look back."

"No. Let's evade a little more gently until we're clear."

It took over an hour for *Fives Full* to be past all the warships. They gave in to the temptation to look back. The battle receded, explosions dimmer in the distance.

"We're winning," said Schwartzenberger. He looked at Mitchie. "You do want them to win, don't you?"

"Yes, sir. I want them to win. Expensively."

***

Free at last, *Fives Full* set course for Ossa again. That lasted six hours until the fleet ordered them to Naval Station Telamon. Since the orders also directed them to offload the hitchhikers Schwartzenberger didn't complain.

Naval Station Telamon, Demeter System. Gravity 7 m/ s²

As soon as the thrust stopped and she heard the creak of the ship's weight settling on the landing gear Bing opened the inner airlock door. As she locked it behind her the handcomm crackled with Schwartzenberger's voice. "Air outside is good. Clear to open the doors."

"Aye-aye," she said. The outer door swung open. Sweet, sweet air poured over her. Bing closed her eyes and took deep breaths through her nose, savoring it. The best air she'd ever smelled. Well, it was military station air, disinfectant and floor polish dominating nastier chemicals. But there was no vomit, urine, feces, tears, or fear sweat in it.

"Hello the ship!"

Bing looked down. A dozen Navy types approached, one driving a portable ramp up to the cargo hatch. "Hi!"

"We show you have one hundred and sixty-two to off-load, is that right?"

"It's a hundred and sixty-three now."

"Wow. We thought you'd lose a few coming through that."

"No. A bunch of broken bones. And we'll want a gurney for the newborn and mom."

"We've got 'em. But we want to get the able-bodied out of the way first."

"However you want to do it." She raised her handcomm. "Billy, open the main cargo hatch."

"Aye-aye." It was a few minutes before the starboard side of the hatch opened. The deckhand had to cut through the layers of vacctape they'd applied on Steelhome. When they had enough room the pair of ratings at the top of the ramp flipped some panels over to cover the gap.

"If you can walk, please come down the ramp," called one. "We need to clear the way so we have room to help the injured. Please come down the ramp if you can walk. You will be guided to sickbay for an examination."

The crowd was slow to get moving. Everyone had bruises at least. This planetoid had three times the gravity of Steelhome. Families tried to find their misplaced members. Relatives insisted on staying with the injured. The line down the ramp was a trickle.

When a third of the refugees were off the ship the Navy brought up some gurneys. Triaging by who had the most hangers-on offended the corpsmen's sensibilities but gave them more room to work. The newest mother received a cheer from the ground crews as she came down the ramp.

After that it went quickly. When the last hitchhiker was gone Bing stood alone in the hold, looking at the mess. Billy and Abdul had already been sent to bed. A Chief Bosun's Mate came up the ramp and looked around the hold. Bing blushed as his nose wrinkled. "I'm sorry, Chief, the ship isn't normally like this, we're just not set up for so many passengers."

"No worries, ma'am. I'll have some spacers in to clean this up."

"Oh, you don't have to do that."

"I've been looking for a shit detail to put some rowdy one-stripers on. Scrubbing this deck to kitchen standards is just what they need." His smile was an evil one.

"Well . . . glad we can help, then."

***

Mitchie raised her hand to knock on the hatch, saw the gold ring, and opened it instead. Guo was brushing his teeth. "Uhuh?"

"I brought my toothbrush—'cause I'm moving in, right?"

He hastily wiped his mouth, revealing a delighted grin. He wrapped his arms around her. After a long kiss he said, "When I realized we'd survived my first thought was that I'd get to see you again." She pulled him down for another kiss. Her reaction had been *Oh, shit, I'm married*, but she'd managed to not say it aloud. Now she'd just have to juggle as hard as she could.

***

Once all the refugees were processed the Navy insisted on medical exams for the crew. This time Mitchie went first instead of avoiding it. After sitting her in the scanner for five minutes the doctor said, "You seem to be in good health. I'm going to give you a list of vitamins to take. Do you have any concerns?"

"I'm scared about radiation exposure from the battle. I was on the bridge." Her voice quivered a little. "We saw these huge bright flashes. Thought it had to be big nukes."

"No, you're showing no signs of radiation damage. The flashes were a new weapon, not bombs."

"It's not just my own health I'm worried about. Um, you see, it's—having children is very important in the Disconnect. So even if it's a low level of exposure . . ." She flushed and averted her eyes.

The doctor gave a sympathetic chuckle. "I understand. But the conversion beam is tightly focused. You're in no danger of additional exposure from it." He produced a printout. "If you think you might become pregnant here's a better nutrient supplement regime for you."

She took it with thanks. That had been *very* useful. The hard part was not laughing at the doctor for believing someone terrified of radiation exposure would become a spacer in the first place.

The check-up was followed by a mandatory chat with a security agent. He sat her down in a small room and lectured for fifteen minutes on the importance of not ever telling anyone what she'd seen in the battle, because AI spies could be everywhere. When he ran down she said, "So if I just told my buddy I'd seen a ball-shaped ship shooting out a beam of light, that could get back to the Betrayers?" His stiff face went totally rigid. *Hah! That ship* was *the one with the new weapon*, she thought.

"That is exactly the sort of thing we wouldn't want leaking out. Having the advantage of surprise was huge in this battle. We don't want AIs finding out what we have."

"No worries, Chief," she told the petty officer second class. "I didn't say it to anyone but you and I give you my word of honor never to tell anyone else."

"Thank you. That's exactly what this meeting is about. Now, if you'd be willing to sign these forms . . ." Mitchie applied her thumbprint to several documents threatening her with jail or worse if she spread "information of operational value" about.

***

"Now, please understand, he's not a *bad* man. It's just that he was never prepared for that kind of isolation." Mitchie was still irked that the rest of the crew had unanimously assigned her to explain Alexi to the Navy doctor. Just because she could outtalk the rest of them shouldn't make her Official Ship's Liar.

"Had he been in space before?" asked the doc.

"Oh, yes, he's very experienced. But it was all on Fusion ships. On an analog ship you have to learn to make your own distractions. Hard copy reading, art, games," *screwing crewmates*, "something. He was used to always having the Net available." Mitchie led him across the hanger to *Five Full's* landing pad.

"How did his problems manifest?"

"Didn't have any trouble with him until after we dropped off the pilgrims. Then he started going on about Golden Age tech and Old Earth artifacts and how rich we'd be if we brought some of that home. We thought we'd put an end to that by refusing to land on a Betrayer-controlled world. Then he started going on that some could be hidden on a comet."

The doctor barked a laugh. "I'm sorry, I should never mock a patient's delusions." His two orderlies traded amused glances.

"Well, he was starting to get us to think there might be something to it. But with ships chasing us and webs blocking gates and we never did find out what knocked that hole in the hull . . . anyway, we wanted to get home as soon as we could."

"And he disagreed?"

"He said he'd go along with us. But when he had a bridge watch he changed course to a comet he said had to have treasure. Captain relieved him and confined him to quarters. He got out and assaulted Abdul." She watched to make sure he didn't trip coming up the ramp into the ship.

"His ribs are mostly healed, by the way. I saw the scans."

"Oh, good. Thank you. Then Guo—the mechanic—found him in the hold, standing on top of an empty container and yelling about it being his inheritance. Fortunately he can't shoot worth a damn."

Now the orderlies paid attention. "How'd you get him back in his room?" asked the bigger one as he grunted up the ladder.

"Twenty hours of forty-five gravs lying on a bare deck. Made him take a nap. Then stuck him with a sedative."

"Nice work."

The doctor took over the conversation again, asking about Alexi's diet (one big meal a day), sleeping (don't know), and general health (no problems visible at three meters). That finished with them at Alexi's cabin.

"Well, let's have a look at him," said the doctor.

Mitchie knocked on the hatch, slid back the deadbolt, and pulled it open.

"Hello, Alexi! I'm Dr. Chang. May I come in and talk to you?"

"Not if you're believing the lies they're telling," said Alexi. His voice was rough from disuse. Mitchie couldn't see around the doctor. Alexi had the lights dim.

"I've listened to them. But I'm not believing anything yet. Want to come back to my office and tell me your story?"

"No! I'm not leaving this ship! They'll fly off and take my inheritance with them."

Dr. Chang took a couple more steps in. The orderlies slid in behind him, keeping Mitchie from seeing anything. "We can talk here. I'm fine with that. Do you mind if I sit down?"

"Sit, sure, just don't come any closer."

"All right." It sounded like Chang just sat on the deck. "You mentioned your inheritance. Who did you inherit it from?"

"I'm the heir of Maxim Frankovitch, the founder of the Eden Colony." Alexi proceeded on his well-practiced speech about his family and the treasure they'd hidden during the Betrayal. All true, but with his net connection cut off, Dr. Chang probably didn't believe a word. Mitchie remembered how Alexi always started waving his hands about as he got to the good parts—

"Weapon!" shouted an orderly. Mitchie sidestepped as Dr. Chang was flung out of the hatch. She peeked in. They had Alexi in a tight grip against the bulkhead. A piece of metal rang as it bounced off the deck. "Wanna dose him, sir?"

Mitchie helped Chang up. He gently applied an injector to Alexi's neck. The stream of curses stopped.

"I'm so sorry," she apologized. "I thought we'd disarmed him."

"You did," replied an orderly, "but he got a spoon." He pricked a finger with its handle and showed the blood drop to Mitchie. She gasped.

"Well, he certainly needs help," said Dr. Chang. "We're not set up for that kind of therapy but we can hold him until he can be transferred to Demeter."

"Do you have to? We're planning on taking him back to his family on Pintoy. Familiar faces and all that."

"That would be best. Can they afford full therapy?"

"Oh, he has plenty of money coming from the pilgrim run."

"Hazard pay?" joked an orderly.

Mitchie looked up at him. "How much money would it take for you to go to Old Earth in an unarmed ship?"

He thought a moment. "There ain't that much money."

Dr. Chang said, "Let me give him a physical and I'll prescribe some medications to keep him stable on the trip."

"Oh, thank you, doctor."

***

After a week on Telamon they had good meals again. Naval hydroponics produce wasn't what anyone would call great food, but it provided better ingredients than *Five Full's* own tanks. Billy had found who to sweet-talk for the best stuff. Bing and Guo made meals something to look forward to again. Mitchie was surprised when they started without the captain. It was unlike him to be late.

Schwartzenberger arrived halfway through dinner. "Mail call!" he cried.

"Mail? Here? Really?" blurted Billy.

"This is what's been getting held for us on Demeter for the past few months. I knew as soon as they lifted the siege of the planet the Navy would send a supply ship. I talked the captain into going by the spacer's hall for our mail. He just landed a little bit ago." He started passing out crystals and envelopes.

"What did you trade him for it?" asked Bing. She received a stack of crystals.

"We were never going to finish that bottle of MacNally." It had been the only alcohol to survive the trip to Earth and back.

"Because it's terrible! You actually pretended that was something of value?"

"Ah, but now it's whiskey from the Solar System, so it's a treasure." Everyone laughed except Bing, who'd tasted it.

Guo noticed Mitchie had more envelopes than the rest of the crew combined. "Don't your people hold with beaming messages?" he asked.

"My mom thinks the point of mail is for me to hold something she's held. Makes the connection stronger. Some of these have probably been chasing me around the Fusion for a year," answered Mitchie. She ignored them in favor of popping a crystal of news reports into her loaner datasheet.

***

Once the Demeter Fleet of the Fusion Navy, backed up by units from Argo and Coatlicue, recaptured the gate to Ushuaia they declared the emergency over. AI ships were still scattered around the system wherever they could find a hiding spot but they weren't attacking. With civilian travel allowed again *Fives Full* was free to go.

Captain Schwartzenberger wouldn't let the Navy's end of it be free. He returned to the ship with the grin of a successful trophy hunter and dropped a datasheet in front of Bing. "Charter fee for hauling the hitchhikers."

"Good God!" said the first mate. "Did you stick a gun in his face?"

"No, just pointed out the usual fees that applied."

Mitchie looked over Bing's shoulder. "Hazardous materials handling surcharge?"

"The babies pooped on our deck. That's untreated human waste, which is a biohazard. Biohazards make it toxic waste. Mixing in toxics makes the whole shipment hazmat."

"And we're charging them for being available for further shipments."

"They wanted us to stay here."

"Are we released now?"

"Yes. So we need to decide where we're going next. I think we're all due for a couple weeks of shore leave, paid." Smiles all around the table at that. "So we need to decide between a two day run to Demeter or spending a week to go to Argo, which gets us closer to Pintoy."

Alexi looked up from his soup at the name of his homeworld. The Navy-provided pacifier shots let him take care of himself, but eliminated talking as well as violence.

"Demeter," said Mitchie. Billy seconded it.

"How bad did it get hit?" asked Bing. "I don't want to vacation in a bombed out city."

"It's just the orbital defenses that are damaged," said Schwartzenberger. "No damage to the surface other than some debris landing."

"All the news says the worst impact to the civilians on Demeter is that the citizen stipend is being cut by a third until they're rebuilt," said Guo.

"Did the news say anything about Steelhome?"

Guo looked grim. "A marine unit landed but couldn't find any survivors, so they pulled out. The Navy used 'strategic weapons' to clear the AIs off." The galley was quiet for a moment.

"Anybody want to speak up for Argo?" asked the captain. "Demeter it is then."

***

Now for the hard part, thought Mitchie. She'd been nodding and smiling as Guo spewed out ideas for how to spend two weeks together on Demeter. Introducing her to his favorite museums, theaters, and concert halls was his top choice. He also liked the tropical beach resort and private cabin in the woods. Half a dozen other options went by. Finally he ran down. "You're being really quiet," he said. "When you spoke up for Demeter I thought you'd have some specific things in mind."

I did. "Mostly I wanted to see a real sky again as soon as I could."

"Sounds like you'd want the outdoor ones then." He had the options ranked on his datasheet. The cultural tour slid down to third.

"For a few days, sure."

"So—beach then city?" Guo was clearly ready to circle the planet if that's what would make her happy.

"Well, here's the thing. I have some personal errands to run so I can't just take the whole time as vacation."

That produced his I-see-how-to-fix-this face. "Okay. Let me know when and where you'll be doing stuff and I'll find things that fit around them. How long are they going to take?"

"I'm going to need a week solid, I'm afraid."

"A week! What kind of 'errand' takes a whole week?"

Finding combat vets on leave and pouring booze into them until they start talking too much. "It's—really, I've just been cooped up on this ship so long I want to be alone for a while."

He wasn't hiding his frustration any more. "Mitchie, if that's what you wanted, you would have said so before I got to the spelunking tour. What do you really want?"

This is the problem with falling in love with a smart guy. The voice in the back of her head offered a hearty I-told-you-so. She offered another rationale for separate honeymoons which Guo promptly shredded. *Dammit, I used to be good at making stuff up on the fly.*

It was all downhill from there.

***

Fives Full lifted off in the morning. By lunchtime the whole crew knew they were arguing. At dinner Mitchie and Guo didn't speak to each other. They left the table early, going opposite directions.

"My aunt had a marriage like that," said Billy. "One week and poof, like it never happened."

"She wasn't from Akiak," said Bing.

"They take marriage seriously there?"

"They take promises seriously there. Life's a lot closer to the edge. If word gets out you're a promise breaker you won't get the help you need to make it through winter. And if someone makes you break a promise you let everyone know what they did."

"I don't *want* to know what they're fighting about," protested Billy.

"Too bad."

Demeter System. Acceleration 10 m/ s²

The captain was sharing some coffee with his first mate in the galley when the argument spilled out into the corridor. A compartment hatch slammed open. Rapid bootsteps—Mitchie's, by the soft sound—headed toward them.

Guo yelled, "I knew you'd lie to me! I always knew you'd lie to me! But I thought you'd have enough respect for me to make them *good* lies!" He slammed his hatch closed. Mitchie reached her compartment and slammed the hatch behind her.

Schwartzenberger turned back to his cup. Bing stared at him. "I asked her," he said. He pointed to where the corridor passed under the bridge hatch. "I stood right there and asked her. I told her she didn't have to go through with it."

"We can't go on with them acting like this," she said.

"I know. I was hoping they'd sort it out one way or the other but it keeps going."

"Someone's going to have to help them work it out."

"That's a people problem," said the captain. That described the category of problems he generally left to the mate to handle.

"I tried. She won't talk to me."

He sighed. "Okay. I'll talk to her." Bing smiled. "In the morning. After she's calmed down some."

"All right." She topped off their cups.

***

Schwartzenberger sat on the bridge, listening to the very quiet ship. Everyone stayed in their rooms or below decks to avoid the former-lovebirds. He finally heard the sound he was waiting for, Mitchie's hatch opening. A minute later he heard one of the galley cabinets open and close. Then her compartment hatch closed. He gave her ten minutes for her breakfast before knocking on the hatch.

"Come in." He stepped in, blinking at the dim light. She was in her bunk, two meters above the deck, a pair of teddy bears at each end. "Oh, sorry, sir. Didn't realize it was you." She turned the light to full. "Um, have a seat."

The bulge of the crane extension shaft made a nice bench, especially with the cushions she'd put on it. He sat and leaned against the wall. "Pilot Long, why are you on this ship?"

Mitchie had dropped down and sat in a fold-out chair. "Sir? You hired me."

"That doesn't explain why you asked for the job or why you're staying."

"It was the only Disconnect ship hiring on Lapis."

"Look, we all have reasons for being on this bucket," said the captain. "It's an honest ship, but it's a dead end. No future in it. I'm here because I fucked up so badly no one ever thought I'd be able to repay the damage. Bing keeps following me around. Guo is a control freak who doesn't have the seniority to have his own converter room on a bigger ship. Billy—well, he actually deserves to be here. Why are you here?"

"It's a good job."

"With your skill you could be piloting a racing yacht, or a rescue ship, or co-pilot on a liner. You've even got a little fame to help you make the connections for it. Why the hell are you still here?"

Mitchie smiled. "I guess I'm like Billy. It's an easy job and I get to party a lot."

"No, you're not a party girl. You act it on leave, but I've worked with enough to see the pattern and you don't fit. You never show up to duty hungover. You never get arrested. And when party girls get married they give it a real hard try for three months or so before they fuck it up."

"You're going to fire me for being a lousy wife?"

"No. I'm considering firing you because you don't make sense. And things that don't make sense bother me. That's the sort of thing that might blow up and take out my whole ship."

"Fine, fire me for not making sense. There'll be another ship along that'll take me."

"I'd be firing you for a regular pattern of lying that makes you untrustworthy. And putting that report into the captains' net. You can go fly yachts but I don't want to inflict you on another working ship."

Mitchie sat very still. "Are you formally threatening to blacklist me?"

"Does it matter?"

"Yes, actually. I need to know: are you threatening to blacklist me?"

"Yes," said Captain Schwartzenberger.

Mitchie stood and went up the foothold Guo had welded onto the bulkhead when she first came on board. She took a teddy bear and sliced a multiply resewn seam open with a knife from under her pillow. A roll of plastic sheets came out. She handed the outer one to Schwartzenberger. "Sir, since you're threatening to break my cover I'm now authorized to reveal this information to you."

He recognized the header markings from his time on the Defense Force Budget Committee. "SECRET: Defense Coordinating Committee" with a holographic background. He tilted it to a few angles to bring out some of the details he remembered. The message began, "Shipmaster: Lieutenant Senior Grade Michigan Long of the Akiak Space Guard has been assigned to an intelligence mission of critical importance. You are required to render all possible assistance to support the successful completion of this mission." It went on to list the applicable law of each Disconnected World belonging to the DCC.

"So, I work for you now?" asked Captain Schwartzenberger.

"Well, you would, if I hadn't gotten some more mail. This was under the same need-to-know as my identity." She peeled off another sheet and handed it to him.

This had the same header, but began "Effective this date, ALOIS SCHWARTZENBERGER is appointed an officer in the Bonaventure Planetary Defense Force Reserve with the grade of Commander."

The captain skimmed down the densely-written page. "Been telling stories about me, Long?"

"Writing reports is my job, sir."

"Full Commander, huh. Must've been nice reports. Good Lord, they're paying me already. And you didn't tell me about it?"

She shrugged. "Can't collect until you're back on Bonaventure, sir. Didn't seem urgent."

"So, I'm guessing your arguments with your husband have something to do with your Naval duties."

She sighed. "I need to do things, he can't know why, and he's smart enough to see through the cover stories I tried."

"I'm not surprised." He went back to reading his commission. "What the fuck is a letter of marque? Never mind, that only applies if a war breaks out." He started reading the back side. "Aha! 'Authorized to appoint subordinate personnel to Naval rank, authority, and privileges as needed to support carrying out Naval missions.' That solves our problem."

"Sir?"

"I'm now appointing Guo as Chief Engineer's Mate Kwan and giving him full security clearances for all classified information on this ship."

Mitchie chuckled. "I'm glad the DCC isn't as hung up about fraternization as the Fusion Navy or I'd be in trouble right now."

"You're already in trouble, that's why we're having this conversation."

"I know. My . . . intelligence gathering methods aren't compatible with being married."

"So you need some advice on developing new ones. From Chief Kwan," said the captain.

"I can't tell him about this! He isn't cleared!"

"He is now. I cleared him."

"He doesn't have need-to-know!" protested Mitchie.

"I say he does. And this," he waved his commission, "says you have to follow my orders on it."

She stared at him as it sank in. "How much do I have to tell him?"

"Everything. Including all the details you haven't bothered me with."

"This can't be legal."

"It's an order," said Captain Schwartzenberger. "Want it in writing?"

"Yes. In case I have to explain to a court-martial why exactly I blabbed 'burn before reading' to my brand-new husband." She got a notepad and pen out and handed them to him. She was pretty sure there were some regulations she should consult, but she felt too relieved to argue it.

"There." He signed the order and handed it to her. It went back in the teddy bear with her mission letter. "I included the word 'today.'"

"Yes, sir. I'll do it. Just . . . let me wash and change first, okay?" He gave her a wave and left.

She wound up washing her face an extra time after overdoing her makeup. Honesty called for the minimum. Guo'd seen her without plenty of times, but she wanted a little polish to buck her up through it. When she was out of excuses to delay she went down the corridor and knocked on his hatch.

"Yes?"

She pulled it open. "Can I come in?"

"Why?"

"To talk," said Mitchie. He sat on the edge of the double bed he'd installed after Comet SMX. At a grudging wave she slipped in and closed the hatch. She sat on the floor with her back against it. "I want to tell you the truth." She felt it boiling up inside her, waiting to all flood out.

"Good."

"Okay." She sat silently for another minute. "I'm not very good at telling the truth." His lips quirked, and that was enough of a smile for her to start pouring it out. "To begin with, I'm not twenty-five, I'm twenty-nine."

Mitchie braced for an explosion. Guo nearly let out something— she'd expected at least a "What!"—but he kept his jaw clamped shut and nodded at her to go on.

"Everything I said up to age nineteen was true. When Derry died I was angry. I started poking around to find out what happened. When I found out the Fusion did it I tried to enlist, but they threw me out of the recruiting station. Too short to be a pilot, they said." *I sound angry. Guess I'm carrying more of a grudge about that than I thought.*

Mitchie continued, "I kept poking around, trying to find enough that I could publicize the incident, get people angry enough to get some revenge. That got me arrested for security violations, and then a job offer. So I went from flying shuttles to the Planetary Guard Academy.

After a couple of years they commissioned me and sent me on exchange to Bonaventure's Intelligence & Security School. Did some counter-intel fieldwork there. Then I started this undercover assignment as a spacer."

She paused for breath. Guo asked, "If it's undercover, why are you telling me?"

"I've been ordered to." She explained Schwartzenberger's sudden promotion, Guo's rank, and her orders.

He collapsed on his bunk, shouting with laughter. "Now we're all in the Guard! That's fantastic." Mitchie waited for him to catch his breath. Patiently. "Hey, don't I get a say in this? Conscription's against the constitution."

"No, it's not," said Mitchie, who'd gotten a B+ in Military Law at the Academy. "It just takes the legislature passing a law with your name in it."

"Which the captain hasn't done. Wait, this is a Bonaventure ship, so Akiak law doesn't apply."

"Um . . . I think Bonaventure bans it completely. Not sure. The skipper accepted it when I gave him the commission."

"Nobody minds being conscripted into the top of the hierarchy," said Guo.

"You're close to the top, Chief Kwan."

"Not on this ship. Chief's only worth something if there's some ratings to kick around. Can't conscript Abdul, he's a Fusion citizen."

Mitchie contemplated their shared vision of Billy in uniform. "Billy'd jump ship."

"Without waiting for us to land it."

"Yeah, he's a good argument against conscription," she said. Sharing a laugh over Billy with him eased the pain that had been gripping her heart for days. She sat on the bed and leaned in to her husband.

"Oh! That's what you were doing," exclaimed Guo.

"What?"

"Billy always came back from shore leave with stories of how you'd grabbed some guy at random and dragged him off. Which did not sound like the fussy control freak I knew. They were intelligence sources."

"Yes. Um . . . Billy wasn't all wrong about what I was doing."

"It gets guys to talk?" asked Guo.

"Usually guys. And yes." They were lying on the bed now, arms around each other. "That's not very compatible with marriage."

"I've seen a lot of different marriages," said Guo. "Mostly dyads. Some with more. Open and closed. There's actually a six-group in Arsenic Creek." He paused. She waited. "But . . . fucking total strangers you don't even like is outside even the most open marriage arrangement I've ever heard of."

"I said it was complicated."

"Yes, you did. And I shouldn't have asked you to marry me when there was a gun to your head, even if I wasn't the one holding it. Do . . . do you want me to let you out of your promise?"

"No, I don't want that." Mitchie hugged him tight.

"Then what do you want?"

***

Captain Schwartzenberger climbed up the ladder into the bridge. "Wasn't Mitchie supposed to relieve you three hours ago?" he asked Bing.

"Yes. But she didn't, and she's not answering her cabin intercom."

"Did you try Guo's?"

"No. They've reconciled or murdered each other. Either way I'm enjoying the quiet."

Hanrahan's Pub, Demeter, Gravity 7.5 m/s^2

Guo threaded the tray back to their table, not spilling any of the drinks despite the boisterous crowd. He passed out the mugs. The ones with whiskey depth charges went to the three Navy men. Mitchie's old mug was still half-full. He put it on the tray with the empties to make it less obvious.

The middle Navy man was still talking. "So then there's this huge noise and we're looking at the stars. Which is an ugly sight when you're as deep in the hull as the engine room. Half a meter of diamond matrix, ripped away like paper. Hey, I was going to get this round."

"When we were running away from the swarm we passed your ships going the other way," said Guo. "We can buy some beers."

"Well, if you put it that way . . ." They drank.

"I'm amazed you weren't hurt," said Mitchie.

"Ha!" The talker—Rodriguez—slapped his thigh with a metallic ring. "Took the leg off above the knee. I'm wearing a temp. The organ growth tanks are so overloaded I won't get my new leg for months."

Mitchie looked appropriately horrified.

"Oh, it wasn't so bad," said Rodriguez. "Rags got my leg tied off and injected so fast it hardly hurt." Rodriguez took a deep drink. "Really, Rags should tell the rest of this. I only saw chunks of it."

"Don't make me talk when I'm drinking," said the two-striper.

"So Rags got my leg tied off and Chief Wang into a bubble." Rodriguez jerked a thumb at the third Navy man, who hadn't said much. From the way his voice rasped he'd need a few more weeks to recover from having a lungful of vacuum. "Then he got to work. See, the busbars for the alternate power run were designed for a five minute ramp-up. Kill the drive, trickle some power, increase it gradually. But the officers want it at full instantly. Which means thermal expansion, magnetic torqueing, and bars popping out of their brackets. This time two popped out. Rags grabbed Wang's magic hammer—and Chief, you are a genius, stop denying."

"Nothing genius about a non-conducting sledgehammer," rasped Wang.

"No, the hammer's not genius. Getting the captain to pay for it, that was genius."

"Hmph."

"Anyway, back to Rags, here," said Rodriguez. "He's got his feet braced and hammering the bars into place. I'm floating there, tied down, watching him 'cause he's the only show. Then four boarding robots came in the hole. Spider-like things. Flat disk with long legs all around. Two meters across. They see Rags and go for him." He took a sip on this cliffhanger, enjoying Mitchie and Guo's fascination.

"He turns and lets them have it with the hammer. Smash! Captain's on the PA screaming, 'Where's my power? I need beam power now!' and

Rags just smashes, doesn't say a word, legs flying everywhere. Then he smushes the last one and cool as you please gets on the comm," his voice went flat, "Engine Room to Bridge. Alt Power ETR two minutes." Rodriguez broke out laughing as Rags hid his blush behind his beer.

"Minute and a half of hammering and beam power was on. Whole damn ship rings like a bell when they fire that thing. He never said anything about it until we asked where all the legs came from." Rodriguez slapped Rags on the back. "And that's why Engineer Apprentice Ragout is the next recipient of the Comet of Valor."

Rags' mug dropped back to the table. "You didn't."

"Why do you think I was the last one on the leave shuttle? The Exec wanted to go over my witness statement." Rodriguez beamed.

"That's bullshit. That's not what happened."

"I was stoned on pain meds, but there was a security camera still running and there's debris from the boarding bots. You did good, son."

"That's not—you want to know why I didn't say anything about the boarders?" demanded Ragout.

"Don't see that it matters, but tell if you want to."

Guo bribed a passing waitress to give him someone else's pitcher. He topped off the Navy men's mugs.

Ragout blushed furiously. He burst out, "I thought they were hallucinations! I mean, what's more likely, robots shaped like my worst nightmare with no guns, or that I had a suit leak and was going hypoxic? I didn't think they were real until the hull was patched and we were out of our suits cleaning up."

"Don't matter," rasped Chief Wang. "You did the jobs of five men and a squad of Marines. I don't care what you thought."

Mitchie raised her mug. "To Engineer Ragout. He gets the job done."

"Hear, hear." Four mugs clinked as the honoree stared at the table.

"Curfew, gentlemen." A master at arms stood over the table.

"They're enforcing that?" asked Rodriguez.

"Sure are, EM. Something about the barkeeps wanting you all out before the beer runs out and the riot starts." More MAs were clearing the bar of everyone in uniform.

The trio stood, expressed slurred thanks to the diskers for their drinks, and went off. Mitchie and Guo let the MA inspect their passes and sipped until the bar quieted.

"I told you this would be fun," she said.

"Fun and educational," Guo agreed. He now knew far more about the *Kydoimos*-class battleships than he'd expected to, given that their existence was still classified.

Mitchie had her datasheet out. "There's a Marine bar three blocks East of here. Let's see if they get to stay up late."

He sighed.

"Don't you want to show our appreciation to those brave men?" asked Mitchie.

No, and neither do you, thought Guo. "All right."

They walked to the next bar hand in hand.

About the Author

Karl Gallagher has earned engineering degrees from MIT and USC, controlled weather satellites for the Air Force, designed weather satellites for TRW, designed a rocketship for a start-up, and done systems engineering for a fighter plane. He is husband to Laura and father to Maggie, James, and dearly missed Alanna.

Karl has written white papers, engineering proposals, blog posts, fanfic, trade studies, rants, graduate school papers, RPG adventures, operations orders, forum flames, conference papers, short stories, after action reports, wargame rules, satires, and a sestina. This is his first novel.

About Kelt Haven Press

Kelt Haven Press is releasing print, ebook, and audiobooks by Karl K. Gallagher. *Torchship Pilot* will be released in late spring 2016. For updates see:

www.kelthavenpress.com

Subscribe to the monthly newsletter for updates on new releases, art previews, and snippets of the next book.

If you enjoyed *Torchship* please leave a review on Amazon.com.

Made in the USA
Lexington, KY
20 February 2016